BEST "THINKING MACHINE" DETECTIVE STORIES

JACQUES FUTRELLE

Edited by
E. F. BLEILER

DOVER PUBLICATIONS, INC.
NEW YORK

Best "Thinking Machine" Detective Stories, first
published by Dover Publications, Inc., in 1973, is
a new selection of stories by Jacques Futrelle. The
selection was made by E. F. Bleiler, who also
wrote the Introduction. The texts of all the stories
are complete and unabridged, but for the sake of
consistency a slight plot change has been made in
the story "Kidnapped Baby Blake, Millionaire."

International Standard Book Number: 0-486-20537-1
Library of Congress Catalog Card Number: 73-85054

Manufactured in the United States of America
Dover Publications, Inc.
180 Varick Street
New York, N. Y. 10014

INTRODUCTION

Just as there are poets who are known by a single poem, there are prose writers who are remembered only for a single story. Sometimes this is proper and suitable, but on other occasions both the author and the public are being poorly served. Jacques Futrelle, for instance, is familiar to almost everyone who reads detective stories as the author of "The Problem of Cell 13," which is surely one of the dozen most famous detective stories ever written. Yet it is not generally known that Futrelle wrote almost fifty other stories that continue the marvelous deductions of The Thinking Machine in his perpetual contest with the Impossible.

This situation is not entirely fair, for Futrelle at his best was an ingenious author who had many good, original ideas, a flair for contemporary dialogue, and (for us in the 1970's) a period flavor that evokes the dazzling, rootless world of the Edwardians.

Jacques Futrelle was born in Georgia in 1875, of French Huguenot stock. He did newspaper work in Richmond, Virginia; acted as a theatrical manager for a short time; and then settled in the Boston area. At the time that he created The Thinking Machine he was a member of the editorial staff of the *Boston American,* the local Hearst newspaper. Futrelle and his wife May, herself a writer, were on the *Titanic* on the fateful night of April 14–15, 1912. Futrelle pushed his wife into a lifeboat, but refused to get in himself, and went down with the ship.

At the time of his death Futrelle had achieved an international reputation as a skilled writer who could please the popular taste for light, sentimental fiction, yet could also write more solid work. Over the past 60 years or so, however, his writing chaff has blown away, and he is now remembered as the creator of that remarkable, irritating, fascinating monster-genius, The Thinking Machine.

Professor Augustus S. F. X. Van Dusen (with more honorary

degrees after his name than it is convenient to list), also known as The Thinking Machine, first saw the black of printer's ink in the *Boston American* on October 30, 1905. This was on a Monday. On this day he uttered his challenge—that he could escape from the strongest prison available—but his readers did not have the chance to follow his elusive actions, as we can today, when we read the story through. Instead, purchasers of the *American* had to wait a week, for "The Problem of Cell 13" was serialized as a contest, in six parts. $100 in prize money was offered to readers who submitted the best resolution to the Professor's predicament. The final episode, the solution, was printed on Sunday rather than Saturday. This was presumably to give the editors time to grade the entries, possibly also to boost sales on the more expensive Sunday paper with its comics and special sections.

The final episode of "The Problem of Cell 13" was printed on Sunday, November 5, 1905, and Van Dusen escaped from the old Charlestown (Chisholm) Prison in a manner that would have done credit to Houdini. On November 6 a rival to Professor Van Dusen was revealed: Mr. P. C. Hosmer of 10 Milk Street (presumably a broker or lawyer from the address), who had equalled the Professor's feat and had won the $50 first prize in the contest. Mr. Hosmer now drops out of sight, but The Thinking Machine goes on, to occupy an important position in the history of the detective story.

In several ways Futrelle anticipated later developments in the evolution of the mystery and detective form. Although to us, having lived through the hardboiled and the sexual schools, the Gibson-Girl types that appear in the earlier stories about The Thinking Machine may seem to be a concession to local fashion, there are other areas where Futrelle anticipated realism. The police in his stories are real detectives, such as Futrelle may have known from his newspaper work. They are neither strawmen nor idiots. Where they have limitations, these are such as might have been expected of a harness bull of the turn of the century. The crime reporter Hutchinson Hatch, too, knows exactly what he is doing when he gathers information for The Thinking Machine.

Futrelle, like R. A. Freeman in England a couple of years later, made an effort to be factually accurate, and the mechanisms that he invokes for crime are usually more solid than those of most of his contemporaries. (*Kidnapped Baby Blake,* of course, must be excepted from this statement and what follows!) It is here that Futrelle differs most markedly from the prevailing detective form of his day, the so-called school of Doyle. The essence of a typical British story of the period was a murder committed by outlandish means. Indian snakes that slide down bell cords, hallucinatory drugs (imaginary, of course), giant sea anemones, Oriental images with secret springs, obscure poisons (usually unreliably described) come immediately to mind. For Futrelle, on the other hand, mystery may surround the crime densely, but the means by which the crime has been committed are realistic. To put both approaches into a larger context: Futrelle's contemporaries usually applied the Romantic mode of exoticizing the rational; Futrelle used the Gothic mode of rationalizing the exotic. Futrelle's approach, of course, turned out to be the detective story of the following years.

Futrelle was writing detective stories of idea at a time when most of his colleagues were writing stories of incident or situation. Futrelle was not greatly concerned with action, nor with personalities (beyond the well-drawn Thinking Machine). He was greatly concerned, however, with evoking a plausible story out of a germ idea that involved special knowledge. Here, too, Futrelle was something of a pioneer, for while similar stories had appeared occasionally in the past, Futrelle was the first to create them consistently and systematically, and (at his best) to present them clearly and without encumbrance. About ten years earlier, it is true, M. D. Post had started his series of stories about Randolph Mason, where the point was quirks in the law that permitted a criminal to escape punishment; but it wasn't until later that Post achieved the capsulation that Futrelle demonstrated earlier.

The basic concept of the best of the stories about The Thinking Machine is the insoluble problem, the situation that is "impossible" —to use the word that so infuriates Professor Van Dusen. A murder committed in a sealed room, an escape from an inescapable receptacle, a true vision in a crystal ball, a flawless charge of murder against a perfect alibi—these are typical. In each instance the Professor solves the problem by logical means, reducing the mystery into situations that yield to rationality.

The background out of which Futrelle built his stories is varied. He obviously was aware of British developments in the detective story, and he obviously knew Poe's work. It seems equally clear that he was immersed in the dime-novel phenomenon that was coming to a close around the first decade of the twentieth century. While his concept of a case is reminiscent of Great Britain, his use of dialogue parallels the dime novel at its best. He also seems to have borrowed one peculiar technique from the dime novel. The multimillion worders who wrote Nick Carter and Old King Brady, for example, simply sloughed off loose ends and inconsistencies by saying frankly, at the end of each story, that they did not know. Futrelle often uses the same technique, although with him it creates an impression of verisimilitude. It may also be significant that Nick Carter uses the expression, "Two and two makes four," the catchword of The Thinking Machine, but I would not push this parallelism too far.

It cannot be claimed that all of Futrelle's stories are on the same level of quality. Some are weak, perhaps because of haste, perhaps because of their destination in newspapers. His earlier stories, on the whole, where the situation of impossibility is sustained, are superior to the later, which sometimes are routine detective mysteries. But his better stories have a strange buoyant enthusiasm that carries them through. His narrative is fast, and The Thinking Machine is always wrapped in excitement. Historically, of course, Professor Van Dusen is an immensely important individual, for (with the exception of a few Sherlock Holmes stories) there is no other story from the earlier period of the detective story that has been reprinted and enjoyed more than "The Problem of Cell 13." It is also quite possible that the Professor did much to establish for science fiction the image of the *savant manqué*.

About half of the stories involving Professor Van Dusen appear in *The Thinking Machine* (1906) and *The Thinking Machine on the Case* (1907). The other stories are scattered about in newspapers and periodicals. It is possible that some still remain to be rediscovered. It has been said that six unpublished tales went down on the *Titanic* with Futrelle. There is also a novel in which The Thinking Machine appears: *The Chase of the Golden Plate* (1906). This novel has a certain socio-historical interest, but as a tale it is inferior to the short stories. Mrs. May Futrelle, followed by the standard reference works, has stated that *The Chase of the Golden Plate* was the first story written about Van Dusen. If this is correct, the novel must have waited long for publication, since it appeared serially in the *Saturday Evening Post* about a year later than the Professor's appearance in the *Boston American*.

In addition to the stories about The Thinking Machine Futrelle wrote a fair amount of other fiction. His books include *The Simple Case of Susan* (1908), a sentimental romance about confused identities; *The Diamond Master* (1909), a mystery novel with an element of science fiction; *Elusive Isobel* (1909), crime and impersonation in an embassy setting; *The High Hand* (1911), a political novel; and two posthumous books, *My Lady's Garter* (1912), burglary, impersonation and detection, and *Blind Man's Buff* (1916, which was printed earlier in periodical form) sentimental adventure in Paris, to a crime background. Of all these books, none is now worth reading except *The Diamond Master*, which displays craftsmanship and ingenuity and is in some ways his best work. Futrelle also wrote short stories featuring the detectives Fred Boyd, Dr. Spence, Garron and Louis Harding. Since most of his work first appeared in newspapers and magazines, it is almost certain that this listing is not complete.

The first ten stories that follow have been selected as the best adventures of The Thinking Machine. In their flair and gusto, they remain among the most vital detective stories of their period, members of the scant group that can still be read with enjoyment some seventy years after their composition. The last two stories are members of the original 1905-6 series that first appeared in newspaper form and have never been reprinted. They seem to have been completely forgotten. Since they exist (apart from this book) only in a single, decomposing file of old newspapers, it has seemed worthwhile to preserve them as lesser but inimitable adventures of the curious Professor.

E. F. BLEILER

CONTENTS

	page
The Problem of Cell 13	1
The Crystal Gazer	34
The Scarlet Thread	48
The Flaming Phantom	77
The Problem of the Stolen Rubens	106
The Missing Necklace	116
The Phantom Motor	130
The Brown Coat	144
His Perfect Alibi	159
The Lost Radium	173
Kidnapped Baby Blake, Millionaire	190
The Fatal Cipher	216
Postscript	243

THE PROBLEM OF CELL 13

I

Practically all those letters remaining in the alphabet after Augustus S. F. X. Van Dusen was named were afterward acquired by that gentleman in the course of a brilliant scientific career, and, being honorably acquired, were tacked on to the other end. His name, therefore, taken with all that belonged to it, was a wonderfully imposing structure. He was a Ph.D., an LL.D., an F.R.S., an M.D., and an M.D.S. He was also some other things—just what he himself couldn't say—through recognition of his ability by various foreign educational and scientific institutions.

In appearance he was no less striking than in nomenclature. He was slender with the droop of the student in his thin shoulders and the pallor of a close, sedentary life on his clean-shaven face. His eyes wore a perpetual, forbidding squint—the squint of a man who studies little things—and when they could be seen at all through his thick spectacles, were mere slits of watery blue. But above his eyes was his most striking feature. This was a tall, broad brow, almost abnormal in height and width, crowned by a heavy shock of bushy, yellow hair. All these things conspired to give him a peculiar, almost grotesque, personality.

Professor Van Dusen was remotely German. For generations his ancestors had been noted in the sciences; he was the logical result, the master mind. First and above all he was a logician. At least thirty-five years of the half-century or so of his existence had been devoted exclusively to proving that two and two always equal four, except in unusual cases, where they equal three or five, as the case may be. He stood broadly on the general proposition that all things that start must go somewhere, and was able to bring the concentrated mental force of his forefathers to bear on a given problem. Incidentally it may be remarked that Professor Van Dusen wore a No. 8 hat.

The world at large had heard vaguely of Professor Van Dusen as The Thinking Machine. It was a newspaper catch-phrase applied to him at the time of a remarkable exhibition at chess; he had demonstrated then that a stranger to the game might, by the force of inevitable logic, defeat a champion who had devoted a lifetime to its study. The Thinking Machine! Perhaps that more nearly described him than all his honorary initials, for he spent week after week, month after month, in the seclusion of his small laboratory from which had gone forth thoughts that staggered scientific associates and deeply stirred the world at large.

It was only occasionally that The Thinking Machine had visitors, and these were usually men who, themselves high in the sciences, dropped in to argue a point and perhaps convince themselves. Two of these men, Dr. Charles Ransome and Alfred Fielding, called one evening to discuss some theory which is not of consequence here.

"Such a thing is impossible," declared Dr. Ransome emphatically, in the course of the conversation.

"Nothing is impossible," declared The Thinking Machine with equal emphasis. He always spoke petulantly. "The mind is master of all things. When science fully recognizes that fact a great advance will have been made."

"How about the airship?" asked Dr. Ransome.

"That's not impossible at all," asserted The Thinking Machine. "It will be invented some time. I'd do it myself, but I'm busy."

Dr. Ransome laughed tolerantly.

"I've heard you say such things before," he said. "But they mean nothing. Mind may be master of matter, but it hasn't yet found a way to apply itself. There are some things that can't be *thought* out of existence, or rather which would not yield to any amount of thinking."

"What, for instance?" demanded The Thinking Machine.

Dr. Ransome was thoughtful for a moment as he smoked.

"Well, say prison walls," he replied. "No man can *think* himself out of a cell. If he could, there would be no prisoners."

"A man can so apply his brain and ingenuity that he can leave a cell, which is the same thing," snapped The Thinking Machine.

Dr. Ransome was slightly amused.

"Let's suppose a case," he said, after a moment. "Take a cell where prisoners under sentence of death are confined—men who are desperate and, maddened by fear, would take any chance to escape—suppose you were locked in such a cell. Could you escape?"

"Certainly," declared The Thinking Machine.

"Of course," said Mr. Fielding, who entered the conversation for the first time, "you might wreck the cell with an explosive—but inside, a prisoner, you couldn't have that."

"There would be nothing of that kind," said The Thinking Machine. "You might treat me precisely as you treated prisoners under sentence of death, and I would leave the cell."

"Not unless you entered it with tools prepared to get out," said Dr. Ransome.

The Thinking Machine was visibly annoyed and his blue eyes snapped.

"Lock me in any cell in any prison anywhere at any time, wearing only what is necessary, and I'll escape in a week," he declared, sharply.

Dr. Ransome sat up straight in the chair, interested. Mr. Fielding lighted a new cigar.

"You mean you could actually *think* yourself out?" asked Dr. Ransome.

"I would get out," was the response.

"Are you serious?"

"Certainly I am serious."

Dr. Ransome and Mr. Fielding were silent for a long time.

"Would you be willing to try it?" asked Mr. Fielding, finally.

"Certainly," said Professor Van Dusen, and there was a trace of irony in his voice. "I have done more asinine things than that to convince other men of less important truths."

The tone was offensive and there was an undercurrent strongly resembling anger on both sides. Of course it was an absurd thing, but Professor Van Dusen reiterated his willingness to undertake the escape and it was decided upon.

"To begin now," added Dr. Ransome.

"I'd prefer that it begin to-morrow," said The Thinking Machine, "because——"

"No, now," said Mr. Fielding, flatly. "You are arrested, figuratively, of course, without any warning locked in a cell with no chance to communicate with friends, and left there with identically the same care and attention that would be given to a man under sentence of death. Are you willing?"

"All right, now, then," said the Thinking Machine, and he arose.

"Say, the death-cell in Chisholm Prison."

"The death-cell in Chisholm Prison."

"And what will you wear?"

"As little as possible," said The Thinking Machine. "Shoes, stockings, trousers and a shirt."

"You will permit yourself to be searched, of course?"

"I am to be treated precisely as all prisoners are treated," said The Thinking Machine. "No more attention and no less."

There were some preliminaries to be arranged in the matter of obtaining permission for the test, but all three were influential men and everything was done satisfactorily by telephone, albeit the prison commissioners, to whom the experiment was explained on purely scientific grounds, were sadly bewildered. Professor Van Dusen would be the most distinguished prisoner they had ever entertained.

When The Thinking Machine had donned those things which he was to wear during his incarceration he called the little old woman who was his housekeeper, cook and maid servant all in one.

"Martha," he said, "it is now twenty-seven minutes past nine o'clock. I am going away. One week from to-night, at half-past nine, these gentlemen and one, possibly two, others will take supper with me here. Remember Dr. Ransome is very fond of artichokes."

The three men were driven to Chisholm Prison, where the Warden was awaiting them, having been informed of the matter by telephone. He understood merely that the eminent Professor Van Dusen was to be his prisoner, if he could keep him, for one week; that he had committed no crime, but that he was to be treated as all other prisoners were treated.

"Search him," instructed Dr. Ransome.

The Thinking Machine was searched. Nothing was found on him; the pockets of the trousers were empty; the white, stiff-bosomed shirt had no pocket. The shoes and stockings were removed, examined, then replaced. As he watched all these preliminaries—the rigid search and noted the pitiful, childlike physical weakness of the man, the colorless face, and the thin, white hands—Dr. Ransome almost regretted his part in the affair.

"Are you sure you want to do this?" he asked.

"Would you be convinced if I did not?" inquired The Thinking Machine in turn.

"No."

"All right. I'll do it."

What sympathy Dr. Ransome had was dissipated by the tone. It nettled him, and he resolved to see the experiment to the end; it would be a stinging reproof to egotism.

"It will be impossible for him to communicate with anyone outside?" he asked.

"Absolutely impossible," replied the warden. "He will not be permitted writing materials of any sort."

"And your jailers, would they deliver a message from him?"

"Not one word, directly or indirectly," said the warden. "You may rest assured of that. They will report anything he might say or turn over to me anything he might give them."

"That seems entirely satisfactory," said Mr. Fielding, who was frankly interested in the problem.

"Of course, in the event he fails," said Dr. Ransome, "and asks for his liberty, you understand you are to set him free?"

"I understand," replied the warden.

The Thinking Machine stood listening, but had nothing to say until this was all ended, then:

"I should like to make three small requests. You may grant them or not, as you wish."

"No special favors, now," warned Mr. Fielding.

"I am asking none," was the stiff response. "I would like to have some tooth powder—buy it yourself to see that it is tooth powder— and I should like to have one five-dollar and two ten-dollar bills."

Dr. Ransome, Mr. Fielding and the warden exchanged astonished glances. They were not surprised at the request for tooth powder, but were at the request for money.

"Is there any man with whom our friend would come in contact that he could bribe with twenty-five dollars?" asked Dr. Ransome of the warden.

"Not for twenty-five hundred dollars," was the positive reply.

"Well, let him have them," said Mr. Fielding. "I think they are harmless enough."

"And what is the third request?" asked Dr. Ransome.

"I should like to have my shoes polished."

Again the astonished glances were exchanged. This last request was the height of absurdity, so they agreed to it. These things all being attended to, The Thinking Machine was led back into the prison from which he had undertaken to escape.

"Here is Cell 13," said the warden, stopping three doors down the steel corridor. "This is where we keep condemned murderers. No one can leave it without my permission; and no one in it can communicate with the outside. I'll stake my reputation on that. It's only three doors back of my office and I can readily hear any unusual noise."

"Will this cell do, gentlemen?" asked The Thinking Machine. There was a touch of irony in his voice.

"Admirably," was the reply.

The heavy steel door was thrown open, there was a great scurrying and scampering of tiny feet, and The Thinking Machine passed into the gloom of the cell. Then the door was closed and double locked by the warden.

"What is that noise in there?" asked Dr. Ransome, through the bars.

"Rats—dozens of them," replied The Thinking Machine, tersely.

The three men, with final good-nights, were turning away when The Thinking Machine called:

"What time is it exactly, warden?"

"Eleven seventeen," replied the warden.

"Thanks. I will join you gentlemen in your office at half-past eight o'clock one week from to-night," said The Thinking Machine.

"And if you do not?"

"There is no 'if' about it."

II

Chisholm Prison was a great, spreading structure of granite, four stories in all, which stood in the center of acres of open space. It was surrounded by a wall of solid masonry eighteen feet high, and so smoothly finished inside and out as to offer no foothold to a climber, no matter how expert. Atop of this fence, as a further precaution, was a five-foot fence of steel rods, each terminating in a keen point. This fence in itself marked an absolute deadline between freedom and imprisonment, for, even if a man escaped from his cell, it would seem impossible for him to pass the wall.

The yard, which on all sides of the prison building was twenty-five feet wide, that being the distance from the building to the wall, was by day an exercise ground for those prisoners to whom was granted the boon of occasional semi-liberty. But that was not for those in

Cell 13. At all times of the day there were armed guards in the yard, four of them, one patrolling each side of the prison building.

By night the yard was almost as brilliantly lighted as by day. On each of the four sides was a great arc light which rose above the prison wall and gave to the guards a clear sight. The lights, too, brightly illuminated the spiked top of the wall. The wires which fed the arc lights ran up the side of the prison building on insulators and from the top story led out to the poles supporting the arc lights.

All these things were seen and comprehended by The Thinking Machine, who was only enabled to see out his closely barred cell window by standing on his bed. This was on the morning following his incarceration. He gathered, too, that the river lay over there beyond the wall somewhere, because he heard faintly the pulsation of a motor boat and high up in the air saw a river bird. From that same direction came the shouts of boys at play and the occasional crack of a batted ball. He knew then that between the prison wall and the river was an open space, a playground.

Chisholm Prison was regarded as absolutely safe. No man had ever escaped from it. The Thinking Machine, from his perch on the bed, seeing what he saw, could readily understand why. The walls of the cell, though built he judged twenty years before, were perfectly solid, and the window bars of new iron had not a shadow of rust on them. The window itself, even with the bars out, would be a difficult mode of egress because it was small.

Yet, seeing these things, The Thinking Machine was not discouraged. Instead, he thoughtfully squinted at the great arc light— there was bright sunlight now—and traced with his eyes the wire which led from it to the building. That electric wire, he reasoned, must come down the side of the building not a great distance from his cell. That might be worth knowing.

Cell 13 was on the same floor with the offices of the prison—that is, not in the basement, nor yet upstairs. There were only four steps up to the office floor, therefore the level of the floor must be only three or four feet above the ground. He couldn't see the ground directly beneath his window, but he could see it further out toward the wall. It would be an easy drop from the window. Well and good.

Then The Thinking Machine fell to remembering how he had come to the cell. First, there was the outside guard's booth, a part of the wall. There were two heavily barred gates there, both of steel. At this gate was one man always on guard. He admitted persons to the prison after much clanking of keys and locks, and let them out when ordered to do so. The warden's office was in the prison building, and in order to reach that official from the prison yard one had to pass a gate of solid steel with only a peep-hole in it. Then coming from that inner office to Cell 13, where he was now, one must pass a heavy wooden door and two steel doors into the corridors of the prison; and always there was the double-locked door of Cell 13 to reckon with.

There were then, The Thinking Machine recalled, seven doors to be overcome before one could pass from Cell 13 into the outer world, a free man. But against this was the fact that he was rarely interrupted. A jailer appeared at his cell door at six in the morning with a breakfast of prison fare; he would come again at noon, and again at six in the afternoon. At nine o'clock at night would come the inspection tour. That would be all.

"It's admirably arranged, this prison system," was the mental tribute paid by The Thinking Machine. "I'll have to study it a little when I get out. I had no idea there was such great care exercised in the prisons."

There was nothing, positively nothing, in his cell, except his iron bed, so firmly put together that no man could tear it to pieces save with sledges or a file. He had neither of these. There was not even a chair, or a small table, or a bit of tin or crockery. Nothing! The jailer stood by when he ate, then took away the wooden spoon and bowl which he had used.

One by one these things sank into the brain of The Thinking Machine. When the last possibility had been considered he began an examination of his cell. From the roof, down the walls on all sides, he examined the stones and the cement between them. He stamped over the floor carefully time after time, but it was cement, perfectly solid. After the examination he sat on the edge of the iron bed and was lost in thought for a long time. For Professor Augustus S. F. X. Van Dusen, The Thinking Machine, had something to think about.

He was disturbed by a rat, which ran across his foot, then scampered away into a dark corner of the cell, frightened at its own daring. After awhile The Thinking Machine, squinting steadily into the darkness of the corner where the rat had gone, was able to make out in the gloom many little beady eyes staring at him. He counted six pair, and there were perhaps others; he didn't see very well.

Then The Thinking Machine, from his seat on the bed, noticed for the first time the bottom of his cell door. There was an opening there of two inches between the steel bar and the floor. Still looking steadily at this opening, The Thinking Machine backed suddenly into the corner where he had seen the beady eyes. There was a great scampering of tiny feet, several squeaks of frightened rodents, and then silence.

None of the rats had gone out the door, yet there were none in the cell. Therefore there must be another way out of the cell, however small. The Thinking Machine, on hands and knees, started a search for this spot, feeling in the darkness with his long, slender fingers.

At last his search was rewarded. He came upon a small opening in the floor, level with the cement. It was perfectly round and somewhat larger than a silver dollar. This was the way the rats had gone. He put his fingers deep into the opening; it seemed to be a disused drainage pipe and was dry and dusty.

Having satisfied himself on this point, he sat on the bed again for an hour, then made another inspection of his surroundings through the small cell window. One of the outside guards stood directly opposite, beside the wall, and happened to be looking at the window of Cell 13 when the head of The Thinking Machine appeared. But the scientist didn't notice the guard.

Noon came and the jailer appeared with the prison dinner of repulsively plain food. At home The Thinking Machine merely ate to live; here he took what was offered without comment. Occasionally he spoke to the jailer who stood outside the door watching him.

"Any improvements made here in the last few years?" he asked.

"Nothing particularly," replied the jailer. "New wall was built four years ago."

"Anything done to the prison proper?"

"Painted the woodwork outside, and I believe about seven years ago a new system of plumbing was put in."

"Ah!" said the prisoner. "How far is the river over there?"

"About three hundred feet. The boys have a baseball ground between the wall and the river."

The Thinking Machine had nothing further to say just then, but when the jailer was ready to go he asked for some water.

"I get very thirsty here," he explained. "Would it be possible for you to leave a little water in a bowl for me?"

"I'll ask the warden," replied the jailer, and he went away. Half an hour later he returned with water in a small earthen bowl.

"The warden says you may keep this bowl," he informed the prisoner. "But you must show it to me when I ask for it. If it is broken, it will be the last."

"Thank you," said The Thinking Machine. "I shan't break it."

The jailer went on about his duties. For just the fraction of a second it seemed that The Thinking Machine wanted to ask a question, but he didn't.

Two hours later this same jailer, in passing the door of Cell No. 13, heard a noise inside and stopped. The Thinking Machine was down on his hands and knees in a corner of the cell, and from that same corner came several frightened squeaks. The jailer looked on interestedly.

"Ah, I've got you," he heard the prisoner say.

"Got what?" he asked, sharply.

"One of these rats," was the reply. "See?" And between the scientist's long fingers the jailer saw a small gray rat struggling. The prisoner brought it over to the light and looked at it closely. "It's a water rat," he said.

"Ain't you got anything better to do than to catch rats?" asked the jailer.

"It's disgraceful that they should be here at all," was the irritated reply. "Take this one away and kill it. There are dozens more where it came from."

The jailer took the wriggling, squirmy rodent and flung it down on the floor violently. It gave one squeak and lay still. Later he reported the incident to the warden, who only smiled.

Still later that afternoon the outside armed guard on Cell 13 side of the prison looked up again at the window and saw the prisoner looking out. He saw a hand raised to the barred window and then something white fluttered to the ground, directly under the window of Cell 13. It was a little roll of linen, evidently of white shirting material, and tied around it was a five-dollar bill. The guard looked up at the window again, but the face had disappeared.

With a grim smile he took the little linen roll and the five-dollar bill to the warden's office. There together they deciphered something which was written on it with a queer sort of ink, frequently blurred. On the outside was this:

"Finder of this please deliver to Dr. Charles Ransome."

"Ah," said the warden, with a chuckle. "Plan of escape number one has gone wrong." Then, as an afterthought: "But why did he address it to Dr. Ransome?"

"And where did he get the pen and ink to write with?" asked the guard.

The warden looked at the guard and the guard looked at the warden. There was no apparent solution of that mystery. The warden studied the writing carefully, then shook his head.

"Well, let's see what he was going to say to Dr. Ransome," he said at length, still puzzled, and he unrolled the inner piece of linen.

"Well, if that—what—what do you think of that?" he asked, dazed.

The guard took the bit of linen and read this:

"Epa cseot d'net niiy awe htto n'si sih.　　"T."

III

The warden spent an hour wondering what sort of a cipher it was, and half an hour wondering why his prisoner should attempt to communicate with Dr. Ransome, who was the cause of him being there. After this the warden devoted some thought to the question of where the prisoner got writing materials, and what sort of writing materials he had. With the idea of illuminating this point, he examined the linen again. It was a torn part of a white shirt and had ragged edges.

Now it was possible to account for the linen, but what the prisoner had used to write with was another matter. The warden knew it would have been impossible for him to have either pen or pencil, and, besides, neither pen nor pencil had been used in this writing. What, then? The warden decided to personally investigate. The Thinking Machine was his prisoner; he had orders to hold his prisoners; if this one sought to escape by sending cipher messages to persons outside, he would stop it, as he would have stopped it in the case of any other prisoner.

The warden went back to Cell 13 and found The Thinking Machine on his hands and knees on the floor, engaged in nothing more alarming than catching rats. The prisoner heard the warden's step and turned to him quickly.

"It's disgraceful," he snapped, "these rats. There are scores of them."

"Other men have been able to stand them," said the warden. "Here is another shirt for you—let me have the one you have on."

"Why?" demanded The Thinking Machine, quickly. His tone was hardly natural, his manner suggested actual perturbation.

"You have attempted to communicate with Dr. Ransome," said the warden severely. "As my prisoner, it is my duty to put a stop to it."

The Thinking Machine was silent for a moment.

"All right," he said, finally. "Do your duty."

The warden smiled grimly. The prisoner arose from the floor and removed the white shirt, putting on instead a striped convict shirt the warden had brought. The warden took the white shirt eagerly, and then there compared the pieces of linen on which was written the cipher with certain torn places in the shirt. The Thinking Machine looked on curiously.

"The guard brought *you* those, then?" he asked.

"He certainly did," replied the warden triumphantly. "And that ends your first attempt to escape."

The Thinking Machine watched the warden as he, by comparison, established to his own satisfaction that only two pieces of linen had been torn from the white shirt.

"What did you write this with?" demanded the warden.

"I should think it a part of your duty to find out," said The Thinking Machine, irritably.

The warden started to say some harsh things, then restrained himself and made a minute search of the cell and of the prisoner instead. He found absolutely nothing; not even a match or toothpick which might have been used for a pen. The same mystery surrounded the fluid with which the cipher had been written. Although the warden left Cell 13 visibly annoyed, he took the torn shirt in triumph.

"Well, writing notes on a shirt won't get him out, that's certain," he told himself with some complacency. He put the linen scraps into his desk to await developments. "If that man escapes from that cell I'll—hang it—I'll resign."

On the third day of his incarceration The Thinking Machine openly attempted to bribe his way out. The jailer had brought his dinner and was leaning against the barred door, waiting, when The Thinking Machine began the conversation.

"The drainage pipes of the prison lead to the river, don't they?" he asked.

"Yes," said the jailer.

"I suppose they are very small?"

"Too small to crawl through, if that's what you're thinking about," was the grinning response.

There was silence until The Thinking Machine finished his meal. Then:

"You know I'm not a criminal, don't you?"

"Yes."

"And that I've a perfect right to be freed if I demand it?"

"Yes."

"Well, I came here believing that I could make my escape," said the prisoner, and his squint eyes studied the face of the jailer.

"Would you consider a financial reward for aiding me to escape?"

The jailer, who happened to be an honest man, looked at the slender, weak figure of the prisoner, at the large head with its mass of yellow hair, and was almost sorry.

"I guess prisons like these were not built for the likes of you to get out of," he said, at last.

"But would you consider a proposition to help me get out?" the prisoner insisted, almost beseechingly.

"No," said the jailer, shortly.

"Five hundred dollars," urged The Thinking Machine. "I am not a criminal."

"No," said the jailer.

"A thousand?"

"No," again said the jailer, and he started away hurriedly to escape further temptation. Then he turned back. "If you should give me ten thousand dollars I couldn't get you out. You'd have to pass through seven doors, and I only have the keys to two."

Then he told the warden all about it.

"Plan number two fails," said the warden, smiling grimly. "First a cipher, then bribery."

When the jailer was on his way to Cell 13 at six o'clock, again bearing food to The Thinking Machine, he paused, startled by the unmistakable scrape, scrape of steel against steel. It stopped at the sound of his steps, then craftily the jailer, who was beyond the prisoner's range of vision, resumed his tramping, the sound being apparently that of a man going away from Cell 13. As a matter of fact he was in the same spot.

After a moment there came again the steady scrape, scrape, and the jailer crept cautiously on tiptoes to the door and peered between the bars. The Thinking Machine was standing on the iron bed working at the bars of the little window. He was using a file, judging from the backward and forward swing of his arms.

Cautiously the jailer crept back to the office, summoned the warden in person, and they returned to Cell 13 on tiptoes. The steady scrape was still audible. The warden listened to satisfy himself and then suddenly appeared at the door.

"Well?" he demanded, and there was a smile on his face.

The Thinking Machine glanced back from his perch on the bed and leaped suddenly to the floor, making frantic efforts to hide something. The warden went in, with hand extended.

"Give it up," he said.

"No," said the prisoner, sharply.

"Come, give it up," urged the warden. "I don't want to have to search you again."

"No," repeated the prisoner.

"What was it, a file?" asked the warden.

The Thinking Machine was silent and stood squinting at the warden with something very nearly approaching disappointment on his face—nearly, but not quite. The warden was almost sympathetic.

"Plan number three fails, eh?" he asked, goodnaturedly. "Too bad, isn't it?"

The prisoner didn't say.

"Search him," instructed the warden.

The jailer searched the prisoner carefully. At last, artfully concealed in the waist band of the trousers, he found a piece of steel about two inches long, with one side curved like a half moon.

"Ah," said the warden, as he received it from the jailer. "From your shoe heel," and he smiled pleasantly.

The jailer continued his search and on the other side of the trousers waist band found another piece of steel identical with the first. The edges showed where they had been worn against the bars of the window.

"You couldn't saw a way through those bars with these," said the warden.

"I could have," said The Thinking Machine firmly.

"In six months, perhaps," said the warden, goodnaturedly.

The warden shook his head slowly as he gazed into the slightly flushed face of his prisoner.

"Ready to give it up?" he asked.

"I haven't started yet," was the prompt reply.

Then came another exhaustive search of the cell. Carefully the two men went over it, finally turning out the bed and searching that. Nothing. The warden in person climbed upon the bed and examined the bars of the window where the prisoner had been sawing. When he looked he was amused.

"Just made it a little bright by hard rubbing," he said to the prisoner, who stood looking on with a somewhat crestfallen air. The warden grasped the iron bars in his strong hands and tried to shake them. They were immovable, set firmly in the solid granite. He examined each in turn and found them all satisfactory. Finally he climbed down from the bed.

"ᵗGive it up, professor," he advised.

The Thinking Machine shook his head and the warden and jailer passed on again. As they disappeared down the corridor The Thinking Machine sat on the edge of the bed with his head in his hands.

"He's crazy to try to get out of that cell," commented the jailer.

"Of course he can't get out," said the warden. "But he's clever. I would like to know what he wrote that cipher with."

It was four o'clock next morning when an awful, heart-racking shriek of terror resounded through the great prison. It came from a cell, somewhere about the center, and its tone told a tale of horror, agony, terrible fear. The warden heard and with three of his men rushed into the long corridor leading to Cell 13.

IV

As they ran there came again that awful cry. It died away in a sort of wail. The white faces of prisoners appeared at cell doors upstairs and down, staring out wonderingly, frightened.

"It's that fool in Cell 13," grumbled the warden.

He stopped and stared in as one of the jailers flashed a lantern. "That fool in Cell 13" lay comfortably on his cot, flat on his back with his mouth open, snoring. Even as they looked there came again the piercing cry, from somewhere above. The warden's face blanched a little as he started up the stairs. There on the top floor he found a man in Cell 43, directly above Cell 13, but two floors higher, cowering in a corner of his cell.

"What's the matter?" demanded the warden.

"Thank God you've come," exclaimed the prisoner, and he cast himself against the bars of his cell.

"What is it?" demanded the warden again.

He threw open the door and went in. The prisoner dropped on his knees and clasped the warden about the body. His face was white with terror, his eyes were widely distended, and he was shuddering. His hands, icy cold, clutched at the warden's.

"Take me out of this cell, please take me out," he pleaded.

"What's the matter with you, anyhow?" insisted the warden, impatiently.

"I heard something—something," said the prisoner, and his eyes roved nervously around the cell.

"What did you hear?"

"I—I can't tell you," stammered the prisoner. Then, in a sudden burst of terror: "Take me out of this cell—put me anywhere—but take me out of here."

The warden and the three jailers exchanged glances.

"Who is this fellow? What's he accused of?" asked the warden.

"Joseph Ballard," said one of the jailers. "He's accused of throwing acid in a woman's face. She died from it."

"But they can't prove it," gasped the prisoner. "They can't prove it. Please put me in some other cell."

He was still clinging to the warden, and that official threw his arms off roughly. Then for a time he stood looking at the cowering wretch, who seemed possessed of all the wild, unreasoning terror of a child.

"Look here, Ballard," said the warden, finally, "if you heard anything, I want to know what it was. Now tell me."

"I can't, I can't," was the reply. He was sobbing.

"Where did it come from?"

"I don't know. Everywhere—nowhere. I just heard it."

"What was it—a voice?"

"Please don't make me answer," pleaded the prisoner.

"You must answer," said the warden, sharply.

"It was a voice—but—but it wasn't human," was the sobbing reply.

"Voice, but not human?" repeated the warden, puzzled.

"It sounded muffled and—and far away—and ghostly," explained the man.

"Did it come from inside or outside the prison?"

"It didn't seem to come from anywhere—it was just here, here, everywhere. I heard it. I heard it."

For an hour the warden tried to get the story, but Ballard had become suddenly obstinate and would say nothing—only pleaded to be placed in another cell, or to have one of the jailers remain near him until daylight. These requests were gruffly refused.

"And see here," said the warden, in conclusion, "if there's any more of this screaming, I'll put you in the padded cell."

Then the warden went his way, a sadly puzzled man. Ballard sat at his cell door until daylight, his face, drawn and white with terror, pressed against the bars, and looked out into the prison with wide, staring eyes.

That day, the fourth since the incarceration of The Thinking Machine, was enlivened considerably by the volunteer prisoner, who spent most of his time at the little window of his cell. He began proceedings by throwing another piece of linen down to the guard, who picked it up dutifully and took it to the warden. On it was written:

"Only three days more."

The warden was in no way surprised at what he read; he understood that The Thinking Machine meant only three days more of his imprisonment, and he regarded the note as a boast. But how was the thing written? Where had The Thinking Machine found this new piece of linen? Where? How? He carefully examined the linen. It was white, of fine texture, shirting material. He took the shirt which he had taken and carefully fitted the two original pieces of the linen to the torn places. This third piece was entirely superfluous; it didn't fit anywhere, and yet it was unmistakably the same goods.

"And where—where does he get anything to write with?" demanded the warden of the world at large.

Still later on the fourth day The Thinking Machine, through the window of his cell, spoke to the armed guard outside.

"What day of the month is it?" he asked.

"The fifteenth," was the answer.

The Thinking Machine made a mental astronomical calculation and satisfied himself that the moon would not rise until after nine o'clock that night. Then he asked another question:

"Who attends to those arc lights?"

"Man from the company."

"You have no electricians in the building?"

"No."

"I should think you could save money if you had your own man."

"None of my business," replied the guard.

The guard noticed The Thinking Machine at the cell window frequently during that day, but always the face seemed listless and there was a certain wistfulness in the squint eyes behind the glasses. After a while he accepted the presence of the leonine head as a matter of course. He had seen other prisoners do the same thing; it was the longing for the outside world.

That afternoon, just before the day guard was relieved, the head appeared at the window again, and The Thinking Machine's hand held something out between the bars. It fluttered to the ground and the guard picked it up. It was a five-dollar bill.

"That's for you," called the prisoner.

As usual, the guard, took it to the warden. That gentleman looked at it suspiciously; he looked at everything that came from Cell 13 with suspicion.

"He said it was for me," explained the guard.

"It's a sort of a tip, I suppose," said the warden. "I see no particular reason why you shouldn't accept——"

Suddenly he stopped. He had remembered that The Thinking Machine had gone into Cell 13 with one five-dollar bill and two ten-dollar bills; twenty-five dollars in all. Now a five-dollar bill had been tied around the first pieces of linen that came from the cell. The warden still had it, and to convince himself he took it out and looked at it. It was five dollars; yet here was another five dollars, and The Thinking Machine had only had ten-dollar bills.

"Perhaps somebody changed one of the bills for him," he thought at last, with a sigh of relief.

But then and there he made up his mind. He would search Cell 13 as a cell was never before searched in this world. When a man could write at will, and change money, and do other wholly inexplicable things, there was something radically wrong with his prison. He planned to enter the cell at night—three o'clock would be an excellent time. The Thinking Machine must do all the weird things he did sometime. Night seemed the most reasonable.

Thus it happened that the warden stealthily descended upon Cell

13 that night at three o'clock. He paused at the door and listened. There was no sound save the steady, regular breathing of the prisoner. The keys unfastened the double locks with scarcely a clank, and the warden entered, locking the door behind him. Suddenly he flashed his dark-lantern in the face of the recumbent figure.

If the warden had planned to startle The Thinking Machine he was mistaken, for that individual merely opened his eyes quietly, reached for his glasses and inquired, in a most matter-of-fact tone:

"Who is it?"

It would be useless to describe the search that the warden made. It was minute. Not one inch of the cell or the bed was overlooked. He found the round hole in the floor, and with a flash of inspiration thrust his thick fingers into it. After a moment of fumbling there he drew up something and looked at it in the light of his lantern.

"Ugh!" he exclaimed.

The thing he had taken out was a rat—a dead rat. His inspiration fled as a mist before the sun. But he continued the search. The Thinking Machine, without a word, arose and kicked the rat out of the cell into the corridor.

The warden climbed on the bed and tried the steel bars in the tiny window. They were perfectly rigid; every bar of the door was the same.

Then the warden searched the prisoner's clothing, beginning at the shoes. Nothing hidden in them! Then the trousers waist band. Still nothing! Then the pockets of the trousers. From one side he drew out some paper money and examined it.

"Five one-dollar bills," he gasped.

"That's right," said the prisoner.

"But the—you had two tens and a five—what the—how do you do it?"

"That's my business," said the Thinking Machine.

"Did any of my men change this money for you—on your word of honor?"

The Thinking Machine paused just a fraction of a second.

"No," he said.

"Well, do you make it?" asked the warden. He was prepared to believe anything.

"That's my business," again said the prisoner.

The warden glared at the eminent scientist fiercely. He felt—he knew—that this man was making a fool of him, yet he didn't know how. If he were a real prisoner he would get the truth—but, then, perhaps, those inexplicable things which had happened would not have been brought before him so sharply. Neither of the men spoke for a long time, then suddenly the warden turned fiercely and left the cell, slamming the door behind him. He didn't dare to speak, then.

He glanced at the clock. It was ten minutes to four. He had hardly settled himself in bed when again came that heart-breaking shriek through the prison. With a few muttered words, which, while not elegant, were highly expressive, he relighted his lantern and rushed through the prison again to the cell on the upper floor.

Again Ballard was crushing himself against the steel door, shrieking, shrieking at the top of his voice. He stopped only when the warden flashed his lamp in the cell.

"Take me out, take me out," he screamed. "I did it, I did it, I killed her. Take it away."

"Take what away?" asked the warden.

"I threw the acid in her face—I did it—I confess. Take me out of here."

Ballard's condition was pitiable; it was only an act of mercy to let him out into the corridor. There he crouched in a corner, like an animal at bay, and clasped his hands to his ears. It took half an hour to calm him sufficiently for him to speak. Then he told incoherently what had happened. On the night before at four o'clock he had heard a voice—a sepulchral voice, muffled and wailing in tone.

"What did it say?" asked the warden, curiously.

"Acid—acid—acid!" gasped the prisoner. "It accused me. Acid! I threw the acid, and the woman died. Oh!" It was a long, shuddering wail of terror.

"Acid?" echoed the warden, puzzled. The case was beyond him.

"Acid. That's all I heard—that one word, repeated several times. There were other things, too, but I didn't hear them."

"That was last night, eh?" asked the warden. "What happened to-night—what frightened you just now?"

"It was the same thing," gasped the prisoner. "Acid—acid—acid!" He covered his face with his hands and sat shivering. "It was acid I used on her, but I didn't mean to kill her. I just heard the words. It was something accusing me—accusing me." He mumbled, and was silent.

"Did you hear anything else?"

"Yes—but I couldn't understand—only a little bit—just a word or two."

"Well, what was it?"

"I heard 'acid' three times, then I heard a long, moaning sound, then—then—I heard 'No. 8 hat.' I heard that twice."

"No. 8 hat," repeated the warden. "What the devil—No. 8 hat? Accusing voices of conscience have never talked about No. 8 hats, so far as I ever heard."

"He's insane," said one of the jailers, with an air of finality.

"I believe you," said the warden. "He must be. He probably heard something and got frightened. He's trembling now. No. 8 hat! What the——"

V

When the fifth day of The Thinking Machine's imprisonment rolled around the warden was wearing a hunted look. He was anxious for the end of the thing. He could not help but feel that his distinguished prisoner had been amusing himself. And if this were so, The Thinking Machine had lost none of his sense of humor. For on this fifth day he flung down another linen note to the outside guard, bearing the words: "Only two days more." Also he flung down half a dollar.

Now the warden knew—he *knew*—that the man in Cell 13 didn't have any half dollars—he *couldn't* have any half dollars, no more than he could have pen and ink and linen, and yet he did have them. It was a condition, not a theory; that is one reason why the warden was wearing a hunted look.

That ghastly, uncanny thing, too, about "Acid" and "No. 8 hat" clung to him tenaciously. They didn't mean anything, of course, merely the ravings of an insane murderer who had been driven by fear to confess his crime, still there were so many things that "didn't mean anything" happening in the prison now since The Thinking Machine was there.

On the sixth day the warden received a postal stating that Dr. Ransome and Mr. Fielding would be at Chisholm Prison on the following evening, Thursday, and in the event Professor Van Dusen had not yet escaped—and they presumed he had not because they had not heard from him—they would meet him there.

"In the event he had not yet escaped!" The warden smiled grimly. Escaped!

The Thinking Machine enlivened this day for the warden with three notes. They were on the usual linen and bore generally on the appointment at half-past eight o'clock Thursday night, which appointment the scientist had made at the time of his imprisonment.

On the afternoon of the seventh day the warden passed Cell 13 and glanced in. The Thinking Machine was lying on the iron bed, apparently sleeping lightly. The cell appeared precisely as it always did to a casual glance. The warden would swear that no man was going to leave it between that hour—it was then four o'clock— and half-past eight o'clock that evening.

On his way back past the cell the warden heard the steady breathing again, and coming close to the door looked in. He wouldn't have done so if The Thinking Machine had been looking, but now— well, it was different.

A ray of light came through the high window and fell on the face of the sleeping man. It occurred to the warden for the first time that his prisoner appeared haggard and weary. Just then The Thinking Machine stirred slightly and the warden hurried on up the corridor guiltily. That evening after six o'clock he saw the jailer.

"Everything all right in Cell 13?" he asked.

"Yes, sir," replied the jailer. "He didn't eat much, though."

It was with a feeling of having done his duty that the warden received Dr. Ransome and Mr. Fielding shortly after seven o'clock. He intended to show them the linen notes and lay before them the full story of his woes, which was a long one. But before this came to pass, the guard from the river side of the prison yard entered the office.

"The arc light in my side of the yard won't light," he informed the warden.

"Confound it, that man's a hoodoo," thundered the official. "Everything has happened since he's been here."

The guard went back to his post in the darkness, and the warden 'phoned to the electric light company.

"This is Chisholm Prison," he said through the 'phone. "Send three or four men down here quick, to fix an arc light."

The reply was evidently satisfactory, for the warden hung up the receiver and passed out into the yard. While Dr. Ransome and Mr. Fielding sat waiting the guard at the outer gate came in with a special delivery letter. Dr. Ransome happened to notice the address, and, when the guard went out, looked at the letter more closely.

"By George!" he exclaimed.

"What is it?" asked Mr. Fielding.

Silently the doctor offered the letter. Mr. Fielding examined it closely.

"Coincidence," he said. "It must be."

It was nearly eight o'clock when the warden returned to his office. The electricians had arrived in a wagon, and were now at work. The warden pressed the buzz-button communicating with the man at the outer gate in the wall.

"How many electricians came in?" he asked, over the short 'phone. "Four? Three workmen in jumpers and overalls and the manager? Frock coat and silk hat? All right. Be certain that only four go out. That's all."

He turned to Dr. Ransome and Mr. Fielding. "We have to be careful here—particularly," and there was broad sarcasm in his tone, "since we have scientists locked up."

The warden picked up the special delivery letter carelessly, and then began to open it.

"When I read this I want to tell you gentlemen something about how——Great Caesar!" he ended, suddenly, as he glanced at the letter. He sat with mouth open, motionless, from astonishment.

"What is it?" asked Mr. Fielding.

"A special delivery from Cell 13," gasped the warden. "An invitation to supper."

"What?" and the two others arose, unanimously.

The warden sat dazed, staring at the letter for a moment, then called sharply to a guard outside in the corridor.

"Run down to Cell 13 and see if that man's in there."

The guard went as directed, while Dr. Ransome and Mr. Fielding examined the letter.

"It's Van Dusen's handwriting; there's no question of that," said Dr. Ransome. "I've seen too much of it."

Just then the buzz on the telephone from the outer gate sounded, and the warden, in a semi-trance, picked up the receiver.

"Hello! Two reporters, eh? Let 'em come in." He turned suddenly to the doctor and Mr. Fielding. "Why, the man *can't* be out. He must be in his cell."

Just at that moment the guard returned.

"He's still in his cell, sir," he reported. "I saw him. He's lying down."

"There, I told you so," said the warden, and he breathed freely again. "But how did he mail that letter?"

There was a rap on the steel door which led from the jail yard into the warden's office.

"It's the reporters," said the warden. "Let them in," he instructed the guard; then to the two other gentlemen: "Don't say anything about this before them, because I'd never hear the last of it."

The door opened, and the two men from the front gate entered.

"Good-evening, gentlemen," said one. That was Hutchinson Hatch; the warden knew him well.

"Well?" demanded the other, irritably. "I'm here."

That was The Thinking Machine.

He squinted belligerently at the warden, who sat with mouth agape. For the moment that official had nothing to say. Dr. Ransome and Mr. Fielding were amazed, but they didn't know what the warden knew. They were only amazed; he was paralyzed. Hutchinson Hatch, the reporter, took in the scene with greedy eyes.

"How—how—how did you do it?" gasped the warden, finally.

"Come back to the cell," said The Thinking Machine, in the irritated voice which his scientific associates knew so well.

The warden, still in a condition bordering on trance, led the way.

"Flash your light in there," directed The Thinking Machine.

The warden did so. There was nothing unusual in the appearance of the cell, and there—there on the bed lay the figure of The Thinking Machine. Certainly! There was the yellow hair! Again the warden looked at the man beside him and wondered at the strangeness of his own dreams.

With trembling hands he unlocked the cell door and The Thinking Machine passed inside.

"See here," he said.

He kicked at the steel bars in the bottom of the cell door and three of them were pushed out of place. A fourth broke off and rolled away in the corridor.

"And here, too," directed the erstwhile prisoner as he stood on the bed to reach the small window. He swept his hand across the opening and every bar came out.

"What's this in the bed?" demanded the warden, who was slowly recovering.

"A wig," was the reply. "Turn down the cover."

The warden did so. Beneath it lay a large coil of strong rope, thirty feet or more, a dagger, three files, ten feet of electric wire, a thin, powerful pair of steel pliers, a small tack hammer with its handle, and—and a Derringer pistol.

"How did you do it?" demanded the warden.

"You gentlemen have an engagement to supper with me at half-past nine o'clock," said The Thinking Machine. "Come on, or we shall be late."

"But how did you do it?" insisted the warden.

"Don't ever think you can hold any man who can use his brain," said The Thinking Machine. "Come on; we shall be late."

VI

It was an impatient supper party in the rooms of Professor Van Dusen and a somewhat silent one. The guests were Dr. Ransome, Albert Fielding, the warden, and Hutchinson Hatch, reporter. The meal was served to the minute, in accordance with Professor Van Dusen's instructions of one week before; Dr. Ransome found the artichokes delicious. At last the supper was finished and The Thinking Machine turned full on Dr. Ransome and squinted at him fiercely.

"Do you believe it now?" he demanded.

"I do," replied Dr. Ransome.

"Do you admit that it was a fair test?"

"I do."

With the others, particularly the warden, he was waiting anxiously for the explanation.

"Suppose you tell us how——" began Mr. Fielding.

"Yes, tell us how," said the warden.

The Thinking Machine readjusted his glasses, took a couple of preparatory squints at his audience, and began the story. He told it from the beginning logically; and no man ever talked to more interested listeners.

"My agreement was," he began, "to go into a cell, carrying nothing except what was necessary to wear, and to leave that cell within a week. I had never seen Chisholm Prison. When I went into the cell I asked for tooth powder, two ten and one five-dollar bills, and also to have my shoes blacked. Even if these requests had been refused it would not have mattered seriously. But you agreed to them."

"I knew there would be nothing in the cell which you thought I might use to advantage. So when the warden locked the door on me I was apparently helpless, unless I could turn three seemingly innocent things to use. They were things which would have been permitted any prisoner under sentence of death, were they not, warden?"

"Tooth powder and polished shoes, yes, but not money," replied the warden.

"Anything is dangerous in the hands of a man who knows how to use it," went on The Thinking Machine. "I did nothing that first night but sleep and chase rats." He glared at the warden. "When the matter was broached I knew I could do nothing that night, so suggested next day. You gentlemen thought I wanted time to arrange an escape with outside assistance, but this was not true. I knew I could communicate with whom I pleased, when I pleased."

The warden stared at him a moment, then went on smoking solemnly.

"I was aroused next morning at six o'clock by the jailer with my breakfast," continued the scientist. "He told me dinner was at twelve and supper at six. Between these times, I gathered, I would be pretty much to myself. So immediately after breakfast I examined my outside surroundings from my cell window. One look told me it would be useless to try to scale the wall, even should I decide to leave my cell by the window, for my purpose was to leave not only the cell, but the prison. Of course, I could have gone over the wall, but it would have taken me longer to lay my plans that way. Therefore, for the moment, I dismissed all idea of that.

"From this first observation I knew the river was on that side of the prison, and that there was also a playground there. Subsequently these surmises were verified by a keeper. I knew then one important thing—that anyone might approach the prison wall from that side if necessary without attracting any particular attention. That was well to remember. I remembered it.

"But the outside thing which most attracted my attention was the feed wire to the arc light which ran within a few feet—probably three or four—of my cell window. I knew that would be valuable in the event I found it necessary to cut off that arc light."

"Oh, you shut it off to-night, then?" asked the warden.

"Having learned all I could from that window," resumed The Thinking Machine, without heeding the interruption, "I considered the idea of escaping through the prison proper. I recalled just how I had come into the cell, which I knew would be the only way. Seven doors lay between me and the outside. So, also for the time being, I gave up the idea of escaping that way. And I couldn't go through the solid granite walls of the cell."

The Thinking Machine paused for a moment and Dr. Ransome lighted a new cigar. For several minutes there was silence, then the scientific jail-breaker went on:

"While I was thinking about these things a rat ran across my foot. It suggested a new line of thought. There were at least half a dozen rats in the cell—I could see their beady eyes. Yet I had noticed none come under the cell door. I frightened them purposely and watched the cell door to see if they went out that way. They did not, but they were gone. Obviously they went another way. Another way meant another opening.

"I searched for this opening and found it. It was an old drain pipe, long unused and partly choked with dirt and dust. But this was the way the rats had come. They came from somewhere. Where? Drain pipes usually lead outside prison grounds. This one probably led to the river, or near it. The rats must therefore come from that direction. If they came a part of the way, I reasoned that they came all the way, because it was extremely unlikely that a solid iron or lead pipe would have any hole in it except at the exit.

"When the jailer came with my luncheon he told me two important things, although he didn't know it. One was that a new system of plumbing had been put in the prison seven years before; another that the river was only three hundred feet away. Then I knew positively that the pipe was a part of an old system; I knew, too, that it slanted generally toward the river. But did the pipe end in the water or on land?

"This was the next question to be decided. I decided it by catching several of the rats in the cell. My jailer was surprised to see me engaged in this work. I examined at least a dozen of them. They were perfectly dry; they had come through the pipe, and, most important of all, they were *not house rats, but field rats.* The other end of the pipe was on land, then, outside the prison walls. So far, so good.

"Then, I knew that if I worked freely from this point I must attract the warden's attention in another direction. You see, by telling the warden that I had come there to escape you made the test more severe, because I had to trick him by false scents."

The warden looked up with a sad expression in his eyes.

"The first thing was to make him think I was trying to communicate with you, Dr. Ransome. So I wrote a note on a piece of linen I tore from my shirt, addressed it to Dr. Ransome, tied a five-dollar bill around it and threw it out of the window. I knew the guard would take it to the warden, but I rather hoped the warden would send it as addressed. Have you that first linen note, warden?"

The warden produced the cipher.

"What the deuce does it mean, anyhow?" he asked.

"Read it backward, beginning with the 'T' signature and disregard the division into words," instructed The Thinking Machine.

The warden did so.

"T-h-i-s, this," he spelled, studied it a moment, then read it off, grinning:

"This is not the way I intend to escape."

"Well, now what do you think o' that?" he demanded, still grinning.

"I knew that would attract your attention, just as it did," said The Thinking Machine, "and if you really found out what it was, it would be a sort of gentle rebuke."

"What did you write it with?" asked Dr. Ransome, after he had examined the linen and passed it to Mr. Fielding.

"This," said the erstwhile prisoner, and he extended his foot. On it was the shoe he had worn in prison, though the polish was gone—scraped off clean. "The shoe blacking, moistened with water, was my ink; the metal tip of the shoe lace made a fairly good pen."

The warden looked up and suddenly burst into a laugh, half of relief, half of amusement.

"You're a wonder," he said, admiringly. "Go on."

"That precipitated a search of my cell by the warden, as I had intended," continued The Thinking Machine. "I was anxious to get the warden into the habit of searching my cell, so that finally, constantly finding nothing, he would get disgusted and quit. This at last happened, practically."

The warden blushed.

"He then took my white shirt away and gave me a prison shirt. He was satisfied that those two pieces of the shirt were all that was missing. But while he was searching my cell I had another piece of that same shirt, about nine inches square, rolled into a small ball in my mouth."

"Nine inches off that shirt?" demanded the warden. "Where did it come from?"

"The bosoms of all stiff white shirts are of triple thickness," was the explanation. "I tore out the inside thickness, leaving the bosom only two thicknesses. I knew you wouldn't see it. So much for that."

There was a little pause, and the warden looked from one to another of the men with a sheepish grin.

"Having disposed of the warden for the time being by giving him something else to think about, I took my first serious step toward freedom," said Professor Van Dusen. "I knew, within reason, that the pipe led somewhere to the playground outside; I knew a great many boys played there; I knew that rats came into my cell from out there. Could I communicate with some one outside with these things at hand?

"First was necessary, I saw, a long and fairly reliable thread, so— but here," he pulled up his trousers legs and showed that the tops of both stockings, of fine, strong lisle, were gone. "I unraveled those —after I got them started it wasn't difficult—and I had easily a quarter of a mile of thread that I could depend on.

"Then on half of my remaining linen I wrote, laboriously enough I assure you, a letter explaining my situation to this gentleman here," and he indicated Hutchinson Hatch. "I knew he would assist me— for the value of the newspaper story. I tied firmly to this linen letter a ten-dollar bill—there is no surer way of attracting the eye of any-one—and wrote on the linen: 'Finder of this deliver to Hutchinson Hatch, *Daily American,* who will give another ten dollars for the information.'

"The next thing was to get this note outside on that playground where a boy might find it. There were two ways, but I chose the best. I took one of the rats—I became adept in catching them—tied the linen and money firmly to one leg, fastened my lisle thread to another, and turned him loose in the drain pipe. I reasoned that the natural fright of the rodent would make him run until he was outside the pipe and then out on earth he would probably stop to gnaw off the linen and money.

"From the moment the rat disappeared into that dusty pipe I became anxious. I was taking so many chances. The rat might gnaw the string, of which I held one end; other rats might gnaw it; the rat might run out of the pipe and leave the linen and money where they would never be found; a thousand other things might have happened. So began some nervous hours, but the fact that the rat ran on until only a few feet of the string remained in my cell made me think he was outside the pipe. I had carefully instructed Mr. Hatch what to do in case the note reached him. The question was: Would it reach him?

"This done, I could only wait and make other plans in case this one failed. I openly attempted to bribe my jailer, and learned from him that he held the keys to only two of seven doors between me and freedom. Then I did something else to make the warden nervous. I took the steel supports out of the heels of my shoes and made a pretense of sawing the bars of my cell window. The warden raised a pretty row about that. He developed, too, the habit of shaking the bars of my cell window to see if they were solid. They were—then."

Again the warden grinned. He had ceased being astonished.

"With this one plan I had done all I could and could only wait to see what happened," the scientist went on. "I couldn't know whether my note had been delivered or even found, or whether the rat had gnawed it up. And I didn't dare to draw back through the pipe that one slender thread which connected me with the outside.

"When I went to bed that night I didn't sleep, for fear there would come the slight signal twitch at the thread which was to tell me that Mr. Hatch had received the note. At half-past three o'clock, I judge, I felt this twitch, and no prisoner actually under sentence of death ever welcomed a thing more heartily."

The Thinking Machine stopped and turned to the reporter.

"You'd better explain just what you did," he said.

"The linen note was brought to me by a small boy who had been playing baseball," said Mr. Hatch. "I immediately saw a big story in it, so I gave the boy another ten dollars, and got several spools of silk, some twine, and a roll of light, pliable wire. The professor's note suggested that I have the finder of the note show me just where it was picked up, and told me to make my search from there, beginning at two o'clock in the morning. If I found the other end of the thread I was to twitch it gently three times, then a fourth.

"I began the search with a small bulb electric light. It was an hour and twenty minutes before I found the end of the drain pipe, half hidden in weeds. The pipe was very large there, say twelve inches across. Then I found the end of the lisle thread, twitched it as directed and immediately I got an answering twitch.

"Then I fastened the silk to this and Professor Van Dusen began to pull it into his cell. I nearly had heart disease for fear the string would break. To the end of the silk I fastened the twine, and when that had been pulled in, I tied on the wire. Then that was drawn into the pipe and we had a substantial line, which rats couldn't gnaw, from the mouth of the drain into the cell."

The Thinking Machine raised his hand and Hatch stopped.

"All this was done in absolute silence," said the scientist. "But when the wire reached my hand I could have shouted. Then we tried another experiment, which Mr. Hatch was prepared for. I tested the pipe as a speaking tube. Neither of us could hear very clearly, but I dared not speak loud for fear of attracting attention in the prison. At last I made him understand what I wanted immediately. He seemed to have great difficulty in understanding when I asked for nitric acid, and I repeated the word 'acid' several times.

"Then I heard a shriek from a cell above me. I knew instantly that some one had overheard, and when I heard you coming, Mr. Warden, I feigned sleep. If you had entered my cell at that moment that whole plan of escape would have ended there. But you passed on. That was the nearest I ever came to being caught.

"Having established this improvised trolley it is easy to see how I got things in the cell and made them disappear at will. I merely dropped them back into the pipe. You, Mr. Warden, could not have reached the connecting wire with your fingers; they are too large. My fingers, you see, are longer and more slender. In addition I guarded the top of that pipe with a rat—you remember how."

"I remember," said the warden, with a grimace.

"I thought that if any one were tempted to investigate that hole the rat would dampen his ardor. Mr. Hatch could not send me anything useful through the pipe until next night, although he did send me change for ten dollars as a test, so I proceeded with other parts of my plan. Then I evolved the method of escape, which I finally employed.

"In order to carry this out successfully it was necessary for the guard in the yard to get accustomed to seeing me at the cell window. I arranged this by dropping linen notes to him, boastful in tone, to make the warden believe, if possible, one of his assistants was communicating with the outside for me. I would stand at my window for hours gazing out, so the guard could see, and occasionally I spoke to him. In that way I learned that the prison had no electricians of its own, but was dependent upon the lighting company if anything should go wrong.

"That cleared the way to freedom perfectly. Early in the evening of the last day of my imprisonment, when it was dark, I planned to cut the feed wire which was only a few feet from my window, reaching it with an acid-tipped wire I had. That would make that side of the prison perfectly dark while the electricians were searching for the break. That would also bring Mr. Hatch into the prison yard.

"There was only one more thing to do before I actually began the work of setting myself free. This was to arrange final details with Mr. Hatch through our speaking tube. I did this within half an hour after the warden left my cell on the fourth night of my imprisonment. Mr. Hatch again had serious difficulty in understanding me, and I repeated the word 'acid' to him several times, and later the words: 'Number eight hat'—that's my size—and these were the things which made a prisoner upstairs confess to murder, so one of the jailers told me next day. This prisoner heard our voices, confused of course, through the pipe, which also went to his cell. The cell directly over me was not occupied, hence no one else heard.

"Of course the actual work of cutting the steel bars out of the window and door was comparatively easy with nitric acid, which I got through the pipe in thin bottles, but it took time. Hour after hour on the fifth and sixth and seven days the guard below was looking at me as I worked on the bars of the window with the acid on a piece of wire. I used the tooth powder to prevent the acid spreading. I looked away abstractedly as I worked and each minute the acid cut deeper into the metal. I noticed that the jailers always tried the door by shaking the upper part, never the lower bars, therefore I cut the lower bars, leaving them hanging in place by thin strips of metal. But that was a bit of dare-deviltry. I could not have gone that way so easily."

The Thinking Machine sat silent for several minutes.

"I think that makes everything clear," he went on. "Whatever points I have not explained were merely to confuse the warden and jailers. These things in my bed I brought in to please Mr. Hatch, who wanted to improve the story. Of course, the wig was necessary in my plan. The special delivery letter I wrote and directed in my cell with Mr. Hatch's fountain pen, then sent it out to him and he mailed it. That's all, I think."

"But your actually leaving the prison grounds and then coming in through the outer gate to my office?" asked the warden.

"Perfectly simple," said the scientist. "I cut the electric light wire with acid, as I said, when the current was off. Therefore when the current was turned on, the arc light didn't light. I knew it would take some time to find out what was the matter and make repairs. When the guard went to report to you the yard was dark. I crept out the window—it was a tight fit, too—replaced the bars by standing on a narrow ledge and remained in a shadow until the force of electricians arrived. Mr. Hatch was one of them.

"When I saw him I spoke and he handed me a cap, a jumper and overalls, which I put on within ten feet of you, Mr. Warden, while you were in the yard. Later Mr. Hatch called me, presumably as a workman, and together we went out the gate to get something out of the wagon. The gate guard let us pass out readily as two work-men who had just passed in. We changed our clothing and re-appeared, asking to see you. We saw you. That's all."

There was silence for several minutes. Dr. Ransome was first to speak.

"Wonderful!" he exclaimed. "Perfectly amazing."

"How did Mr. Hatch happen to come with the electricians?" asked Mr. Fielding.

"His father is manager of the company," replied The Thinking Machine.

"But what if there had been no Mr. Hatch outside to help?"

"Every prisoner has one friend outside who would help him escape if he could."

"Suppose—just suppose—there had been no old plumbing system there?" asked the warden, curiously.

"There were two other ways out," said The Thinking Machine, enigmatically.

Ten minutes later the telephone bell rang. It was a request for the warden.

"Light all right, eh?" the warden asked, through the 'phone. "Good. Wire cut beside Cell 13? Yes, I know. One electrician too many? What's that? Two came out?"

The warden turned to the others with a puzzled expression.

"He only let in four electricians, he has let out two and says there are three left."

"I was the odd one," said The Thinking Machine.

"Oh," said the warden. "I see." Then through the 'phone: "Let the fifth man go. He's all right."

THE CRYSTAL GAZER

I

With hideous, goggling eyes the great god Budd sat cross-legged on a pedestal and stared stolidly into the semi-darkness. He saw, by the wavering light of a peacock lamp which swooped down from the ceiling with wings outstretched, what might have been a nook in a palace of East India. Draperies hung here, there, everywhere; richly embroidered divans sprawled about; fierce tiger rugs glared up from the floor; grotesque idols grinned mirthlessly in unexpected corners; strange arms were grouped on the walls. Outside, the trolley cars clanged blatantly.

The single human figure was a distinct contradition of all else. It was that of a man in evening dress, smoking. He was fifty, perhaps sixty, years old with the ruddy color of one who has lived a great deal out of doors. There was only a touch of gray in his abundant hair and mustache. His eyes were steady and clear, and indolent.

For a long time he sat, then the draperies to his right parted and a girl entered. She was a part of the picture of which the man was a contradiction. Her lustrous black hair flowed about her shoulders; lambent mysteries lay in her eyes. Her dress was the dress of the East. For a moment she stood looking at the man and then entered with light tread.

"Varick Sahib," she said, timidly, as if it were a greeting. "Do I intrude?" Her voice was softly guttural with the accent of her native tongue.

"Oh no, Jadeh. Come in," said the man.

She smiled frankly and sat down on a hassock near him.

"My brother?" she asked.

"He is in the cabinet."

Varick had merely glanced at her and then continued his thoughtful gaze into vacancy. From time to time she looked up at him shyly, with a touch of eagerness, but there was no answering interest in his manner. His thoughts were far away.

"May I ask what brings you this time, Sahib?" she inquired at last.

"A little deal in the market," responded Varick, carelessly. "It seems to have puzzled Adhem as much as it did me. He has been in the cabinet for half an hour."

He stared on musingly as he smoked, then dropped his eyes to the slender, graceful figure of Jadeh. With knees clasped in her hands she leaned back on the hassock deeply thoughtful. Her head was tilted upward and the flickering light fell full on her face. It crossed Varick's mind that she was pretty, and he was about to say so as he would have said it to any other woman, when the curtains behind them were thrown apart and they both glanced around.

Another man—an East Indian—entered. This man was Adhem Singh, the crystal gazer, in the ostentatious robes of a seer. He, too, was a part of the picture. There was an expression of apprehension, mingled with some other impalpable quality on his strong face.

"Well, Adhem?" inquired Varick.

"I have seen strange things, Sahib," replied the seer, solemnly. "The crystal tells me of danger."

"Danger?" repeated Varick with a slight lifting of his brows. "Oh well, in that case I shall keep out of it."

"Not danger to your business, Sahib," the crystal gazer went on with troubled face, "but danger in another way."

The girl, Jadeh, looked at him with quick, startled eyes and asked some question in her native tongue. He answered in the same language, and she rose suddenly with terror stricken face to fling herself at Varick's feet, weeping. Varick seemed to understand too, and looked at the seer in apprehension.

"Death?" he exclaimed. "What do you mean?"

Adhem was silent for a moment and bowed his head respectfully before the steady, inquiring gaze of the white man.

"Pardon, Sahib," he said at last. "I did not remember that you understood my language."

"What is it?" insisted Varick, abruptly. "Tell me."

"I can not, Sahib."

"You must," declared the other. He had arisen commandingly. "You must."

The crystal gazer crossed to him and stood for an instant with his hand on the white man's shoulder, and his eyes studying the fear he found in the white man's face.

"The crystal, Sahib," he began. "It tells me that—that——"

"No, no, brother," pleaded the girl.

"Go on," Varick commanded.

"It grieves me to say that which will pain one whom I love as I do you, Sahib," said the seer, slowly. "Perhaps you had rather see for yourself?"

"Well, let me see then," said Varick. "Is it in the crystal?"

"Yes, by the grace of the gods."

"But I can't see anything there." Varick remembered. "I've tried scores of times."

"I believe this will be different, Sahib," said Adhem, quietly. "Can you stand a shock?"

Varick shook himself a little impatiently.

"Of course," he replied. "Yes, yes."

"A very serious shock?"

Again there was an impatient twist of Varick's shoulders.

"Yes, I can stand anything," he exclaimed shortly. "What is it? Let me see."

He strode toward that point in the draperies where Adhem had entered while the girl on her knees, sought with entreating hands to stop him.

"No, no, no," she pleaded. "No."

"Don't do that," Varick expostulated in annoyance, but gently he stooped and lifted her to her feet. "I am not a child—or a fool."

He threw aside the curtains. As they fell softly behind him he heard a pitiful little cry of grief from Jadeh and set his teeth together hard.

He stood in the crystal cabinet. It was somewhat larger than an ordinary closet and had been made impenetrable to the light by hangings of black velvet. For awhile he stood still so that his eyes might become accustomed to the utter blackness, and gradually the sinister fascinating crystal ball appeared, faintly visible by its own mystic luminosity. It rested on a pedestal of black velvet.

Varick was accustomed to his surroundings—he had been in the cabinet many times. Now he dropped down on a stool in front of the table whereon the crystal lay and leaning forward on his arms stared into its limpid depths. Unblinkingly for one, two, three minutes he sat there with his thoughts in a chaos.

After awhile there came a change in the ball. It seemed to glow with a growing light other than its own. Suddenly it darkened completely, and out of this utter darkness grew shadowy, vague forms to which he could give no name. Finally a veil seemed lifted for the globe grew brighter and he leaned forward, eagerly, fearfully. Another veil melted away and a still brighter light illumined the ball.

Now Varick was able to make out objects. Here was a table littered with books and papers, there a chair, yonder a shadowy mantel. Gradually the light grew until his tensely fixed eyes pained him, but he stared steadily on. Another quick brightness came and the objects all became clear. He studied them incredulously for a few seconds, and then he recognized what he saw. It was a room—his study—miles away in his apartments.

A sudden numb chilliness seized him but he closed his teeth hard and gazed on. The outlines of the crystal were disappearing, now they were gone and he saw more. A door opened and a man entered the room into which he was looking. Varick gave a little gasp as he recognized the man. It was—himself. He watched the man—himself—as he moved about the study aimlessly for a time as if deeply troubled, then as he dropped into a chair at the desk. Varick read clearly on the vision-face those emotions which he was suffering in person. As he looked the man made some hopeless gesture with his hands—*his* hands—and leaned forward on the desk with his head on his arms. Varick shuddered.

For a long time, it seemed, the man sat motionless, then Varick became conscious of another figure—a man—in the room. This figure had come into the vision from his own view point. His face was averted—Varick did not recognize the figure, but he saw something else and started in terror. A knife was in the hand of the unknown, and he was creeping stealthily toward the unconscious figure in the chair—himself—with the weapon raised.

An inarticulate cry burst from Varick's colorless lips—a cry of warning—as he saw the unknown creep on, on, on toward—himself. He saw the figure that was himself move a little and the unknown leaped. The upraised knife swept down and was buried to the handle. Again a cry, an unintelligible shriek, burst from Varick's lips; his heart fluttered and perspiration poured from his face. With incoherent mutterings he sank forward helplessly.

How long he remained there he didn't know, but at last he

compelled himself to look again. The crystal glittered coldly on its pedestal of velvet but that hideous thing which had been there was gone. The thought came to him to bring it back, to see more, but repulsive fear, terror seized upon him. He rose and staggered out of the cabinet. His face was pallid and his hands clasped and unclasped nervously.

Jadeh was lying on a divan sobbing. She leaped to her feet when he entered, and looking into his face she knew. Again she buried her face in her hands and wept afresh. Adhem stood with moody eyes fixed on the great god Budd.

"I saw—I understand," said Varick between his teeth, "but—I don't believe it."

"The crystal never lies, Sahib," said the seer, sorrowfully.

"But it can't be—that," Varick declared protestingly.

"Be careful, Sahib, oh, be careful," urged the girl.

"Of course I shall be careful," said Varick, shortly. Suddenly he turned to the crystal gazer and there was a menace in his tone. "Did such a thing ever appear to you before?"

"Only once, Sahib."

"And did it come true?"

Adhem inclined his head, slowly.

"I may see you tomorrow," exclaimed Varick suddenly. "This room is stifling. I must go out."

With twitching hands he drew on a light coat over his evening dress, picked up his hat and rushed out into the world of realities. The crystal gazer stood for a moment while Jadeh clung to his arm, tremblingly.

"It is as the gods will," he said sadly, at last.

Professor Augustus S. F. X. Van Dusen—The Thinking Machine—received Howard Varick in the small reception room and invited him to a seat. Varick's face was ashen; there were dark lines under his eyes and in them there was the glitter of an ungovernable terror. Every move showed the nervousness which gripped him. The Thinking Machine squinted at him curiously, then dropped back into his big chair.

For several minutes Varick said nothing; he seemed to be struggling to control himself. Suddenly he burst out:

"I'm going to die some day next week. Is there any way to prevent it?"

The Thinking Machine turned his great yellow head and looked at him in a manner which nearly indicated surprise.

"Of course if you've made up your mind to do it," he said irritably, "I don't see what can be done." There was a trace of irony in his voice, a coldness which brought Varick around a little. "Just how is it going to happen?"

"I shall be murdered—stabbed in the back—by a man whom I don't know," Varick rushed on desperately.

"Dear me, dear me, how unfortunate," commented the scientist. "Tell me something about it. But here." He arose and went into his laboratory. After a moment he returned and handed a glass of some effervescent liquid to Varick, who gulped it down. "Take a minute to pull yourself together," instructed the scientist.

He resumed his seat and sat silent with his long, slender fingers pressed tip to tip. Gradually Varick recovered. It was a fierce fight for the mastery of emotion.

"Now," directed The Thinking Machine at last, "tell me about it."

Varick told just what happened lucidly enough, and The Thinking Machine listened with polite interest. Once or twice he turned and looked at his visitor.

"Do you believe in any psychic force?" Varick asked once.

"I don't disbelieve in anything until I have proven that it cannot be," was the answer. "The God who hung a sun up there has done other things which we will never understand." There was a little pause, then: "How did you meet this man, Adhem Singh?"

"I have been interested for years in the psychic, the occult, the things we don't understand," Varick replied. "I have a comfortable fortune, no occupation, no dependents and made this a sort of hobby. I have studied it superficially all over the world. I met Adhem Singh in India ten years ago, afterwards in England where he went through Oxford with some financial assistance from me, and later here. Two years ago he convinced me that there was something in crystal gazing—call it telepathy, self hypnotism, sub-conscious mental action—what you will. Since then the science, I can call it nothing else, has guided me in every important act of my life."

"Through Adhem Singh?"

"Yes."

"And under a pledge of secrecy, I imagine—that is secrecy as to the nature of his revelations?"

"Yes."

"Any taint of insanity in your family?"

Varick wondered whether the question was in the nature of insolent reproof, or was a request for information. He construed it as the latter.

"No," he answered. "Never a touch of it."

"How often have you consulted Mr. Singh?"

"Many times. There have been occasions when he would tell me nothing because, he explained, the crystal told him nothing. There have been other times when he advised me correctly. He has never given me bad advice even in intricate stock operations, therefore I have been compelled to believe him in all things."

"You were never able to see anything yourself in the crystal until this vision of death, last Tuesday night you say?"

"That was the first."

"How do you know the murder is to take place at any given time—that is next week, as you say?"

"That is the information Adhem Singh gave me," was the reply. "He can read the visions—they mean more to him than——"

"In other words he makes it a profession?" interrupted the scientist.

"Yes."

"Go on."

"The horror of the thing impressed me so—both of us—that he has at my request twice invoked the vision since that night. He, like you, wanted to know when it would happen. There is a calendar by weeks in my study; that is, only one week is shown on it at a time. The last time the vision appeared he noted this calendar. The week was that beginning next Sunday, the 21st of this month. The only conclusion we could reach was that it would happen during that week."

The Thinking Machine arose and paced back and forth across the room deeply thoughtful. At last he stopped before the visitor.

"It's perfectly amazing," he commented emphatically. "It approaches nearer to the unbelievable than anything I have ever heard of."

Varick's response was a look that was almost grateful.

"You don't believe it impossible then?" he asked, eagerly.

"Nothing is impossible," declared the other aggressively. "Now, Mr. Varick, you are firmly convinced that what you saw was prophetic? That you will die in that manner, in that place?"

"I can't believe anything else—I can't," was the response.

"And you have no idea of the identity of the murderer-to-be, If I may use that phrase?"

"Not the slightest. The figure was wholly unfamiliar to me."

"And you know—*you know*—that the room you saw in the crystal was yours?"

"I know that absolutely. Rugs, furniture, mantel, books, everything was mine."

The Thinking Machine was again silent for a time.

"In that event," he said at last, "the affair is perfectly simple. Will you place yourself in my hands and obey my directions implicitly?"

"Yes." There was an eager, hopeful note in Varick's voice now.

"I am going to try to disarrange the affairs of Fate a little bit," explained the scientist gravely. "I don't know what will happen but it will be interesting to try to throw the inevitable, the pre-ordained I might say, out of gear, won't it?"

With a quizzical, grim expression about his thin lips The Thinking Machine went to the telephone in an adjoining room and called some one. Varick heard neither the name nor what was said, merely the mumble of the irritable voice. He glanced up as the scientist returned.

"Have you any servants—a valet for instance?" asked the scientist.

"Yes, I have an aged servant, a valet, but he is now in France, I gave him a little vacation. I really don't need one now as I live in an apartment house—almost a hotel."

"I don't suppose you happen to have three or four thousand dollars in your pocket?"

"No, not so much as that," was the puzzled reply. "If it's your fee——"

"I never accept fees," interrupted the scientist. "I interest myself in affairs like these because I like them. They are good mental exercise. Please draw a check for, say four thousand dollars, to Hutchinson Hatch."

"Who is he?" asked Varick. There was no reply. The check was drawn and handed over without further comment.

It was fifteen or twenty minutes later that a cab pulled up in front of the house. Hutchinson Hatch, reporter, and another man whom he introduced as Philip Byrne were ushered in. As Hatch shook hands with Varick The Thinking Machine compared them mentally. They were relatively of the same size and he bobbed his head as if satisfied.

"Now, Mr. Hatch," he instructed, "take this check and get it cashed immediately, then return here. Not a word to anybody."

Hatch went out and Byrne discussed politics with Varick until he returned with the money. The Thinking Machine thrust the bills into Byrne's hand and he counted it, afterward stowing it away in a pocket.

"Now, Mr. Varick, the keys to your apartment, please," asked the scientist.

They were handed over and he placed them in his pocket. Then he turned to Varick.

"From this time on," he said, "your name is John Smith. You are going on a trip, beginning immediately, with Mr. Byrne here. You are not to send a letter, a postal, a telegram or a package to anyone; you are to buy nothing, you are to write no checks, you are not to speak to or recognize anyone, you are not to telephone or attempt in any manner to communicate with anyone, not even me. You are to obey Mr. Byrne in everything he says."

Varick's eyes had grown wider and wider as he listened.

"But my affairs—my business?" he protested.

"It is a matter of your life or death," said The Thinking Machine shortly.

For a moment Varick wavered a little. He felt that he was being treated like a child.

"As you say," he said finally.

"Now, Mr. Byrne," continued the scientist, "you heard those instructions. It is your duty to enforce them. You must lose this man and yourself. Take him away somewhere to another place. There is enough money there for ordinary purposes. When you learn that there has been an arrest in connection with a certain threat against Mr. Varick, come back to Boston—to me—and bring him. That's all."

Mr. Byrne arose with a business like air.

"Come on, Mr. Smith," he commanded.

Varick followed him out of the room.

II

Here was a table littered with books and papers, there a chair, yonder a shadowy mantel * * * * A door opened and a man entered the room * * * * moved about the study aimlessly for a

time as if deeply troubled, then dropped into a chair at the desk
* * * * made some hopeless gesture with his hands and leaned
forward on the desk with his head on his arms * * * * another
figure in the room * * * * knife in his hand * * * * creeping
stealthily toward the unconscious figure in the chair with the knife
raised * * * * the unknown crept on, on, on * * * *

There was a blinding flash, a gush of flame and smoke, a sharp
click and through the fog came the unexcited voice of Hutchinson
Hatch, reporter.

"Stay right where you are, please."

"That ought to be a good picture," said The Thinking Machine.

The smoke cleared and he saw Adhem Singh standing watching
with deep concern a revolver in the hand of Hatch, who had suddenly
arisen from the desk in Varick's room. The Thinking Machine
rubbed his hands briskly.

"Ah, I thought it was you," he said to the crystal gazer. "Put
down the knife, please. That's right. It seems a little bold to have
interfered with what was to be like this, but you wanted too much
detail Mr. Singh. You might have murdered your friend if you
hadn't gone into so much trivial theatrics."

"I suppose I am a prisoner?" asked the crystal gazer.

"You are," The Thinking Machine assured him cheerfully. "You
are charged with the attempted murder of Mr. Varick. Your wife
will be a prisoner in another half hour with all those who were with
you in the conspiracy."

He turned to Hatch, who was smiling broadly. The reporter was
thinking of that wonderful flash-light photograph in the camera
that The Thinking Machine held,—the only photograph in the world,
so far as he knew, of a man in the act of attempting an assassination.

"Now, Mr. Hatch," the scientist went on, "I will 'phone to
Detective Mallory to come here and get this gentleman, and also
to send men and arrest every person to be found in Mr. Singh's
home. If this man tries to run—shoot."

The scientist went out and Hatch devoted his attention to his
sullen prisoner. He asked half a dozen questions and receiving no
answers he gave it up as hopeless. After awhile Detective Mallory
appeared in his usual state of restrained astonishment and the crystal
gazer was led away.

Then Hatch and The Thinking Machine went to the Adhem Singh
house. The police had preceded them and gone away with four

prisoners, among them the girl Jadeh. They obtained an entrance through the courtesy of a policeman left in charge and sought out the crystal cabinet. Together they bowed over the glittering globe as Hatch held a match.

"But I still don't see how it was done," said the reporter after they had looked at the crystal.

The Thinking Machine lifted the ball and replaced it on its pedestal half a dozen times apparently trying to locate a slight click. Then he fumbled all around the table, above and below. At his suggestion Hatch lifted the ball very slowly, while the scientist slid his slender fingers beneath it.

"Ah," he exclaimed at last. "I thought so. It's clever, Mr. Hatch, clever. Just stand here a few minutes in the dark and I'll see if I can operate it for you."

He disappeared and Hatch stood staring at the crystal until he was developing a severe case of the creeps himself. Just then a light flashed in the crystal, which had been only dimly visible, and he found himself looking into—the room in Howard Varick's apartments, miles away. As he looked, startled, he saw The Thinking Machine appear in the crystal and wave his arms. The creepiness passed instantly in the face of this obvious attempt to attract his attention.

It was later that afternoon that The Thinking Machine turned the light of his analytical genius on the problem for the benefit of Hatch and Detective Mallory.

"Charlatanism is a luxury which costs the peoples of the world incredible sums," he began. "It had its beginning, of course, in the dark ages when man's mind grasped at some tangible evidence of an Infinite Power, and through its very eagerness was easily satisfied. Then quacks began to prey upon man, and do to this day under many guises and under many names. This condition will continue until enlightenment has become so general that man will realize the absurdity of such a thing as Nature, or the other world's forces, going out of its way to tell him whether a certain stock will go up or down. A sense of humor ought to convince him that disembodied spirits do not come back and rap on tables in answer to asinine questions. These things are merely prostitutions of the Divine Revelations."

Hatch smiled a little at the lecture platform tone, and Detective Mallory chewed his cigar uncomfortably. He was there to find out something about crime; this thing was over his head.

"This is merely preliminary," The Thinking Machine went on after a moment. "Now as to this crystal gazing affair—a little reason, a little logic. When Mr. Varick came to me I saw he was an intelligent man whc had devoted years to a study of the so-called occult. Being intelligent he was not easily hoodwinked, yet he had been hood-winked for years, therefore I could see that the man who did it must be far beyond the blundering fool usually found in these affairs.

"Now Mr. Varick, personally, had never seen *anything in any* crystal—remember that—until this 'vision' of death. When I knew this I knew that 'vision' was stamped as quackery; the mere fact of him seeing it proved that, but the quackery was so circumstantial that he was convinced. Thus we have quackery. Why? For a fee? I can imagine successful guesses on the stock market bringing fees to Adhem Singh, but the 'vision' of a man's death is not the way to his pocket-book. If not for a fee—then what?

"A deeper motive was instantly apparent. Mr. Varick was wealthy, he had known Singh and had been friendly with him for years, had supplied him with funds to go through Oxford, and he had no family or dependents. Therefore it seemed probable that a will, or perhaps in another way, Singh would benefit by Mr. Varick's death. There was a motive for the 'vision', which might have been at first an effort to scare him to death, because he had a bad heart. I saw all these things when Mr. Varick talked to me first, several days after he saw the 'vision' but did not suggest them to him. Had I done so he would not have believed so sordid a thing, for he believed in Singh, and would probably have gone his way to be murdered or to die of fright as Singh intended.

"Knowing these things there was only the labor of trapping a clever man. Now the Hindu mind works in strange channels. It loves the mystic, the theatric, and I imagined that having gone so far Singh would attempt to bring the 'vision' to a reality. He presumed, of course, that Mr. Varick would keep the matter to himself.

"The question of saving Varick's life was trifling. If he was to die at a given time in a given room the thing to do was to place him beyond possible reach of that room at that time. I 'phoned to you, Mr. Hatch, and asked you to bring me a private detective who would obey orders, and you brought Mr. Byrne. You heard my instructions to him. It was necessary to hide Mr. Varick's identity and my elabor-ate directions were to prevent anyone getting the slightest clue as to him having gone, or as to where he was. I don't know where he is now.

"Immediately Mr. Varick was off my hands, I had Martha, my housekeeper, write a note to Singh explaining that Mr. Varick was ill, and confined to his room, and for the present was unable to see anyone. In this note a date was specified when he would call on Singh. Martha wrote, of course, as a trained nurse who was in attendance merely in *day time*. All these points were made perfectly clear to Singh.

"That done it was only a matter of patience. Mr. Hatch and I went to Mr. Varick's apartments each night—I had Martha there in day time to answer questions—and waited, in hiding. Mr. Hatch is about Varick's size and a wig helped us along. What happened then you know. I may add that when Mr. Varick told me the story I commented on it as being almost unbelievable. He understood, as I meant he should, that I referred to the 'vision.' I really meant that the elaborate scheme which Singh had evolved was unbelievable. He might have killed him just as well with a drop of poison or something equally pleasant."

The Thinking Machine stopped as if that were all.

"But the crystal?" asked Hatch. "How did that work? How was it I saw you?"

"That was a little ingenious and rather expensive," said The Thinking Machine, "so expensive that Singh must have expected to get a large sum from success. I can best describe the manufacture of the 'vision' as a variation of the principle of the camera obscura. It was done with lenses of various sorts and a multitude of mirrors, and required the assistance of two other men—those who were taken from Singh's house with Jadeh.

"First, the room in Mr. Varick's apartments was duplicated in the basement of Singh's house, even to rugs, books and wall decorations. There two men rehearsed the murder scene that Mr. Varick saw. They were disguised of course. You have looked through the wrong end of a telescope of course? Well, the original reduction of the murder scene to a size where all of it would appear in a small mirror was accomplished that way. From this small mirror there ran pipes with a series of mirrors and lenses, through the house, carrying the reflection of what was happening below, so vaguely though that features were barely distinguishable. This pipe ran up inside one of the legs of the table on which the crystal rested, and then, by reflection to the pedestal.

"You, Mr. Hatch, saw me lift that crystal several times and each time you might have noticed the click. I was trying to find then, how the reflection reached it. When you lifted it slowly and I put my fingers under it I knew. There was a small trap in the pedestal, covered with velvet. This closed automatically and presented a solid surface when the crystal was lifted, and opened when the crystal was replaced. Thus the reflection reached the crystal which reversed it the last time and made it appear right side up to the watcher. The apparent growth of the light in the crystal was caused below. Some one simply removed several sheets of gauze, one at a time, from in front of the first lens."

"Well!" exclaimed Detective Mallory. "That's the most elaborate affair I ever heard of."

"Quite right," commented the scientist, "but we don't know how many victims Singh had. Of course any 'vision' was possible with a change of scene in the basement. I imagine it was a profitable investment because there are many fools in this world."

"What did the girl have to do with it?" asked Hatch.

"That I don't know," replied the scientist. "She was pretty. Perhaps she was used as a sort of bait to attract a certain class of men. She was really Singh's wife I imagine, not his sister. She was a prominent figure in the mummery with Varick of course. With her aid Singh was able to lend great effectiveness to the general scheme."

A couple of days later Howard Varick returned to the city in tow of Philip Byrne. The Thinking Machine asked Mr. Varick only one question of consequence.

"How much money did you intend to leave Singh?"

"About two hundred and fifty thousand dollars," was the reply. "It was to be used under his direction in furthering an investigation into the psychic. He and I had planned just how it was to be spent."

Personally Mr. Varick is no longer interested in the occult.

THE SCARLET THREAD

I

The Thinking Machine—Professor Augustus S. F. X. Van Dusen, Ph.D., LL.D., F.R.S., M.D., etc., scientist and logician—listened intently and without comment to a weird, seemingly inexplicable story. Hutchinson Hatch, reporter, was telling it. The bowed figure of the savant lay at ease in a large chair. The enormous head with its bushy yellow hair was thrown back, the thin, white fingers were pressed tip to tip and the blue eyes, narrowed to mere slits, squinted aggressively upward. The scientist was in a receptive mood.

"From the beginning, every fact you know," he had requested.

"It's all out in the Back Bay," the reporter explained. "There is a big apartment house there, a fashionable establishment, in a side street, just off Commonwealth Avenue. It is five stories in all, and is cut up into small suites, of two and three rooms with bath. These suites are handsomely, even luxuriously furnished, and are occupied by people who can afford to pay big rents. Generally these are young unmarried men, although in several cases they are husband and wife. It is a house of every modern improvement, elevator service, hall boys, liveried door men, spacious corridors and all that. It has both the gas and electric systems of lighting. Tenants are at liberty to use either or both.

"A young broker, Weldon Henley, occupies one of the handsomest of these suites, being on the second floor, in front. He has met with considerable success in the Street. He is a bachelor and lives there alone. There is no personal servant. He dabbles in photography as a hobby, and is said to be remarkably expert.

"Recently there was a report that he was to be married this Winter to a beautiful Virginia girl who has been visiting Boston from time to time, a Miss Lipscomb—Charlotte Lipscomb, of Richmond. Henley has never denied or affirmed this rumor, although he has been asked about it often. Miss Lipscomb is impossible of access even when she visits Boston. Now she is in Virginia, I understand, but will return to Boston later in the season."

The reporter paused, lighted a cigarette and leaned forward in his chair, gazing steadily into the inscrutable eyes of the scientist.

"When Henley took the suite he requested that all the electric lighting apparatus be removed from his apartments," he went on. "He had taken a long lease of the place, and this was done. Therefore he uses only gas for lighting purposes, and he usually keeps one of his gas jets burning low all night."

"Bad, bad for his health," commented the scientist.

"Now comes the mystery of the affair," the reporter went on. "It was five weeks or so ago Henley retired as usual—about midnight. He locked his door on the inside—he is positive of that— and awoke about four o'clock in the morning nearly asphyxiated by gas. He was barely able to get up and open the window to let in the fresh air. The gas jet he had left burning was out, and the suite was full of gas."

"Accident, possibly," said The Thinking Machine. "A draught through the apartments; a slight diminution of gas pressure; a hundred possibilities."

"So it was presumed," said the reporter. "Of course it would have been impossible for——"

"Nothing is impossible," said the other, tartly. "Don't say that. It annoys me exceedingly."

"Well, then, it seems highly improbable that the door had been opened or that anyone came into the room and did this deliberately," the newspaper man went on, with a slight smile. "So Henley said nothing about this; attributed it to accident. The next night he lighted his gas as usual, but he left it burning a little brighter. The same thing happened again."

"Ah," and The Thinking Machine changed his position a little. "The second time."

"And again he awoke just in time to save himself," said Hatch. "Still he attributed the affair to accident, and determined to avoid a recurrence of the affair by doing away with the gas at night. Then he got a small night lamp and used this for a week or more."

"Why does he have a light at all?" asked the scientist, testily.

"I can hardly answer that," replied Hatch. "I may say, however, that he is of a very nervous temperament, and gets up frequently during the night. He reads occasionally when he can't sleep. In addition to that he has slept with a light going all his life; it's a habit."

"Go on."

"One night he looked for the night lamp, but it had disappeared—at least he couldn't find it—so he lighted the gas again. The fact of the gas having twice before gone out had been dismissed as a serious possibility. Next morning at five o'clock a bell boy, passing through the hall, smelled gas and made a quick investigation. He decided it came from Henley's place, and rapped on the door. There was no answer. It ultimately developed that it was necessary to smash in the door. There on the bed they found Henley unconscious with the gas pouring into the room from the jet which he had left lighted. He was revived in the air, but for several hours was deathly sick."

"Why was the door smashed in?" asked The Thinking Machine. "Why not unlocked?"

"It was done because Henley had firmly barred it," Hatch explained. "He had become suspicious, I suppose, and after the second time he always barred his door and fastened every window before he went to sleep. There may have been a fear that some one used a key to enter."

"Well?" asked the scientist. "After that?"

"Three weeks or so elapsed, bringing the affair down to this morning," Hatch went on. "Then the same thing happened a little differently. For instance, after the third time the gas went out Henley decided to find out for himself what caused it, and so expressed himself to a few friends who knew of the mystery. Then, night after night, he lighted the gas as usual and kept watch. It was never disturbed during all that time, burning steadily all night. What sleep he got was in daytime.

"Last night Henley lay awake for a time; then, exhausted and tired, fell asleep. This morning early he awoke; the room was filled with gas again. In some way my city editor heard of it and asked me to look into the mystery."

That was all. The two men were silent for a long time, and finally The Thinking Machine turned to the reporter.

"Does anyone else in the house keep gas going all night?" he asked.

"I don't know," was the reply. "Most of them, I know, use electricity."

"Nobody else has been overcome as he has been?"

"No. Plumbers have minutely examined the lighting system all over the house and found nothing wrong."

"Does the gas in the house all come through the same meter?"

"Yes, so the manager told me. This meter, a big one, is just off the engine room. I supposed it possible that some one shut it off there on these nights long enough to extinguish the lights all over the house, and then turned it on again. That is, presuming that it was done purposely. Do you think it was an attempt to kill Henley?"

"It might be," was the reply. "Find out for me just who in the house uses gas; also if anyone else leaves a light burning all night; also what opportunity anyone would have to get at the meter, and then something about Henley's love affair with Miss Lipscomb. Is there anyone else? If so, who? Where does he live? When you find out these things come back here."

That afternoon at one o'clock Hatch returned to the apartments of The Thinking Machine, with excitement plainly apparent on his face.

"Well?" asked the scientist.

"A French girl, Louise Regnier, employed as a maid by Mrs. Standing in the house, was found dead in her room on the third floor to-day at noon," Hatch explained quickly. "It looks like suicide."

"How?" asked The Thinking Machine.

"The people who employed her—husband and wife—have been away for a couple of days," Hatch rushed on. "She was in the suite alone. This noon she had not appeared, there was an odor of gas and the door was broken in. Then she was found dead."

"With the gas turned on?"

"With the gas turned on. She was asphyxiated."

"Dear me, dear me," exclaimed the scientist. He arose and took up his hat. "Let's go see what this is all about."

II

When Professor Van Dusen and Hatch arrived at the apartment house they had been preceded by the Medical Examiner and the police. Detective Mallory, whom both knew, was moving about in the apartment where the girl had been found dead. The body had been removed and a telegram sent to her employers in New York.

"Too late," said Mallory, as they entered.

"What was it, Mr. Mallory?" asked the scientist.

"Suicide," was the reply. "No question of it. It happened in this room," and he led the way into the third room of the suite. "The maid, Miss Regnier, occupied this, and was here alone last night. Mr. and Mrs. Standing, her employers, have gone to New York for a few days. She was left alone, and killed herself."

Without further questioning The Thinking Machine went over to the bed, from which the girl's body had been taken, and, stooping beside it, picked up a book. It was a novel by "The Duchess." He examined this critically, then, standing on a chair, he examined the gas jet. This done, he stepped down and went to the window of the little room. Finally The Thinking Machine turned to the detective.

"Just how much was the gas turned on?" he asked.

"Turned on full," was the reply.

"Were both the doors of the room closed?"

"Both, yes."

"Any cotton, or cloth, or anything of the sort stuffed in the cracks of the window?"

"No. It's a tight-fitting window, anyway. Are you trying to make a mystery out of this?"

"Cracks in the doors stuffed?" The Thinking Machine went on.

"No." There was a smile about the detective's lips.

The Thinking Machine, on his knees, examined the bottom of one of the doors, that which led into the hall. The lock of this door had been broken when employees burst into the room. Having satisfied himself here and at the bottom of the other door, which connected with the bedroom adjoining, The Thinking Machine again climbed on a chair and examined the doors at the top.

"Both transoms closed, I suppose?" he asked.

"Yes," was the reply. "You can't make anything but suicide out of it," explained the detective. "The Medical Examiner has given that as his opinion—and everything I find indicates it."

"All right," broke in The Thinking Machine abruptly. "Don't let us keep you."

After awhile Detective Mallory went away. Hatch and the scientist went down to the office floor, where they saw the manager. He seemed to be greatly distressed, but was willing to do anything he could in the matter.

"Is your night engineer perfectly trustworthy?" asked The Thinking Machine.

"Perfectly," was the reply. "One of the best and most reliable men I ever met. Alert and wide-awake."

"Can I see him a moment? The night man, I mean?"

"Certainly," was the reply. "He's downstairs. He sleeps there. He's probably up by this time. He sleeps usually till one o'clock in the daytime, being up all night."

"Do you supply gas for your tenants?"

"Both gas and electricity are included in the rent of the suites. Tenants may use one or both."

"And the gas all comes through one meter?"

"Yes, one meter. It's just off the engine room."

"I suppose there's no way of telling just who in the house uses gas?"

"No. Some do and some don't. I don't know."

This was what Hatch had told the scientist. Now together they went to the basement, and there met the night engineer, Charles Burlingame, a tall, powerful, clean-cut man, of alert manner and positive speech. He gazed with a little amusement at the slender, almost childish figure of The Thinking Machine and the grotesquely large head.

"You are in the engine room or near it all night every night?" began The Thinking Machine.

"I haven't missed a night in four years," was the reply.

"Anybody ever come here to see you at night?"

"Never. It's against the rules."

"The manager or a hall boy?"

"Never."

"In the last two months?" The Thinking Machine persisted.

"Not in the last two years," was the positive reply. "I go on duty every night at seven o'clock, and I am on duty until seven in the morning. I don't believe I've seen anybody in the basement here with me between those hours for a year at least."

The Thinking Machine was squinting steadily into the eyes of the engineer, and for a time both were silent. Hatch moved about the scrupulously clean engine room and nodded to the day engineer, who sat leaning back against the wall. Directly in front of him was the steam gauge.

"Have you a fireman?" was The Thinking Machine's next question.

"No. I fire myself," said the night man. "Here's the coal," and he indicated a bin within half a dozen feet of the mouth of the boiler.

"I don't suppose you ever had occasion to handle the gas meter?" insisted The Thinking Machine.

"Never touched it in my life," said the other. "I don't know anything about meters, anyway."

"And you never drop off to sleep at night for a few minutes when you get lonely? Doze, I mean?"

The engineer grinned good-naturedly.

"Never had any desire to, and besides I wouldn't have the chance," he explained. "There's a time check here,"—and he indicated it. "I have to punch that every half hour all night to prove that I have been awake."

"Dear me, dear me," exclaimed The Thinking Machine, irritably. He went over and examined the time check—a revolving paper disk with hours marked on it, made to move by the action of a clock, the face of which showed in the middle.

"Besides there's the steam gauge to watch," went on the engineer. "No engineer would dare go to sleep. There might be an explosion."

"Do you know Mr. Weldon Henley?" suddenly asked The Thinking Machine.

"Who?" asked Burlingame.

"Weldon Henley?"

"No-o," was the slow response. "Never heard of him. Who is he?"

"One of the tenants, on the second floor, I think."

"Lord, I don't know any of the tenants. What about him?"

"When does the inspector come here to read the meter?"

"I never saw him. I presume in daytime, eh Bill?" and he turned to the day engineer.

"Always in daytime—usually about noon," said Bill from his corner.

"Any other entrance to the basement except this way—and you could see anyone coming here this way I suppose?"

"Sure I could see 'em. There's no other entrance to the cellar except the coal hole in the sidewalk in front."

"Two big electric lights in front of the building, aren't there?"

"Yes. They go all night."

A slightly puzzled expression crept into the eyes of The Thinking Machine. Hatch knew from the persistency of the questions that he was not satisfied; yet he was not able to fathom or to understand all the queries. In some way they had to do with the possibility of some one having access to the meter.

"Where do you usually sit at night here?" was the next question.

"Over there where Bill's sitting. I always sit there."

The Thinking Machine crossed the room to Bill, a typical, grimy-handed man of his class.

"May I sit there a moment?" he asked.

Bill arose lazily, and The Thinking Machine sank down into the chair. From this point he could see plainly through the opening into the basement proper—there was no door—the gas meter of enormous proportions through which all the gas in the house passed. An electric light in the door made it bright as daylight. The Thinking Machine noted these things, arose, nodded his thanks to the two men and, still with the puzzled expression on his face, led the way upstairs. There the manager was still in his office.

"I presume you examine and know that the time check in the engineer's room is properly punched every half-hour during the night?" he asked.

"Yes. I examine the dial every day—have them here, in fact, each with the date on it."

"May I see them?"

Now the manager was puzzled. He produced the cards, one for each day, and for half an hour The Thinking Machine studied them minutely. At the end of that time, when he arose and Hatch looked at him inquiringly, he saw still the perplexed expression.

After urgent solicitation, the manager admitted them to the apartments of Weldon Henley. Mr. Henley himself had gone to his office in State Street. Here The Thinking Machine did several things which aroused the curiosity of the manager, one of which was to minutely study the gas jets. Then The Thinking Machine opened one of the front windows and glanced out into the street. Below fifteen feet was the sidewalk; above was the solid front of the building, broken only by a flagpole which, properly roped, extended from the hall window of the next floor above out over the sidewalk a distance of twelve feet or so.

"Ever use that flagpole?" he asked the manager.

"Rarely," said the manager. "On holidays sometimes—Fourth of July and such times. We have a big flag for it."

From the apartments The Thinking Machine led the way to the

hall, up the stairs and to the flagpole. Leaning out of this window, he looked down toward the window of the apartments he had just left. Then he inspected the rope of the flagpole, drawing it through his slender hands slowly and carefully. At last he picked off a slender thread of scarlet and examined it.

"Ah," he exclaimed. Then to Hatch: "Let's go, Mr. Hatch. Thank you," this last to the manager, who had been a puzzled witness.

Once on the street, side by side with The Thinking Machine, Hatch was bursting with questions, but he didn't ask them. He knew it would be useless. At last The Thinking Machine broke the silence.

"That girl, Miss Regnier, *was murdered,*" he said suddenly, positively. "There have been four attempts to murder Henley."

"How?" asked Hatch, startled.

"By a scheme so simple that neither you nor I nor the police have ever heard of it being employed." was the astonishing reply. *"It is perfectly horrible in its simplicity."*

"What was it?" Hatch insisted, eagerly.

"It would be futile to discuss that now," was the rejoinder. "There has been murder. We know how. Now the question is— who? What person would have a motive to kill Henley?"

III

There was a pause as they walked on.

"Where are we going?" asked Hatch finally.

"Come up to my place and let's consider this matter a bit further," replied The Thinking Machine.

Not another word was spoken by either until half an hour later, in the small laboratory. For a long time the scientist was thoughtful— deeply thoughtful. Once he took down a volume from a shelf and Hatch glanced at the title. It was *Gases: Their Properties.* After awhile he returned this to the shelf and took down another, on which the reporter caught the title, *Anatomy.*

"Now, Mr. Hatch," said The Thinking Machine in his perpetually crabbed voice, "we have a most remarkable riddle. It gains this remarkable aspect from its very simplicity. It is not, however, necessary to go into that now. I will make it clear to you when we know the motives.

"As a general rule, the greatest crimes never come to light because the greatest criminals, their perpetrators, are too clever to be caught. Here we have what I might call a great crime committed with a subtle simplicity that is wholly disarming, and a greater crime even than this was planned. This was to murder Weldon Henley. The first thing for you to do is to see Mr. Henley and warn him of his danger. Asphyxiation will not be attempted again, but there is a possibility of poison, a pistol shot, a knife, anything almost. As a matter of fact, he is in great peril.

"Superficially, the death of Miss Regnier, the maid, looks to be suicide. Instead it is the fruition of a plan which has been tried time and again against Henley. There is a possibility that Miss Regnier was not an intentional victim of the plot, but the fact remains that she was murdered. Why? Find the motive for the plot to murder Mr. Henley and you will know why."

The Thinking Machine reached over to the shelf, took a book, looked at it a moment, then went on:

"The first question to determine positively is: Who hated Weldon Henley sufficiently to desire his death? You say he is a successful man in the Street. Therefore there is a possibility that some enemy there is at the bottom of the affair, yet it seems hardly probable. If by his operations Mr. Henley ever happened to wreck another man's fortune, find this man and find out all about him. He may be the man. There will be innumerable questions arising from this line of inquiry to a man of your resources. Leave none of them unanswered.

"On the other hand there is Henley's love affair. Had he a rival who might desire his death? Had he any rival? If so, find out all about him. He may be the man who planned all this. Here, too, there will be questions arising which demand answers. Answer them —all of them—fully and clearly before you see me again.

"Was Henley ever a party to a liaison of any kind? Find that out, too. A vengeful woman or a discarded sweetheart of a vengeful woman, you know, will go to any extreme. The rumor of his engagement to Miss—Miss——"

"Miss Lipscomb," Hatch supplied.

"The rumor of his engagement to Miss Lipscomb might have caused a woman whom he had once been interested in or who was once interested in him to attempt his life. The subtler murders— that is, the ones which are most attractive as problems—are nearly always the work of a cunning woman. I know nothing about women myself," he hastened to explain; "but Lombroso has taken that attitude. Therefore, see if there is a woman."

Most of these points Hatch had previously seen—seen with the unerring eye of a clever newspaper reporter—yet there were several which had not occurred to him. He nodded his understanding.

"Now the center of the affair, of course," The Thinking Machine continued, "is the apartment house where Henley lives. The person who attempted his life either lives there or has ready access to the place, and frequently spends the night there. This is a vital question for you to answer. I am leaving all this to you because you know better how to do these things than I do. That's all, I think. When these things are all learned come back to me."

The Thinking Machine arose as if the interview were at an end, and Hatch also arose, reluctantly. An idea was beginning to dawn in his mind.

"Does it occur to you that there is any connection whatever between Henley and Miss Regnier?" he asked.

"It is possible," was the reply. "I had thought of that. If there is a connection it is not apparent yet."

"Then how—how was it she—she was killed, or killed herself, whichever may be true, and——"

"The attempt to kill Henley killed her. That's all I can say now."

"That all?" asked Hatch, after a pause.

"No. Warn Mr. Henley immediately that he is in grave danger. Remember the person who has planned this will probably go to any extreme. I don't know Mr. Henley, of course, but from the fact that he always had a light at night I gather that he is a timid sort of man—not necessarily a coward, but a man lacking in stamina—therefore, one who might better disappear for a week or so until the mystery is cleared up. Above all, impress upon him the import-ance of the warning."

The Thinking Machine opened his pocketbook and took from it the scarlet thread which he had picked from the rope of the flagpole.

"Here, I believe, is the real clew to the problem," he explained to Hatch. "What does it seem to be?"

Hatch examined it closely.

"I should say a strand from a Turkish bath robe," was his final judgment.

"Possibly. Ask some cloth expert what he makes of it, then if it sounds promising look into it. Find out if by any possibility it can be any part of any garment worn by any person in the apartment house."

"But it's so slight——" Hatch began.

"I know," the other interrupted, tartly. "It's slight, but I believe it is a part of the wearing apparel of the person, man or woman, who has four times attempted to kill Mr. Henley and who did kill the girl. Therefore, it is important."

Hatch looked at him quickly.

"Well, how—in what manner—did it come where you found it?"

"Simple enough," said the scientist. "It is a wonder that there were not more pieces of it—that's all."

Perplexed by his instructions, but confident of results, Hatch left The Thinking Machine. What possible connection could this tiny bit of scarlet thread, found on a flagpole, have with some one shutting off the gas in Henley's rooms? How did any one go into Henley's rooms to shut off the gas? How was it Miss Regnier was dead? What was the manner of her death?

A cloth expert in a great department store turned his knowledge on the tiny bit of scarlet for the illumination of Hatch, but he could go no further than to say that it seemed to be part of a Turkish bath robe.

"Man or woman's?" asked Hatch.

"The material from which bath robes are made is the same for both men and women," was the reply. "I can say nothing else. Of course there's not enough of it to even guess at the pattern of the robe."

Then Hatch went to the financial district and was ushered into the office of Weldon Henley, a slender, handsome man of thirty-two or three years, pallid of face and nervous in manner. He still showed the effect of the gas poisoning, and there was even a trace of a furtive fear—fear of something, he himself didn't know what—in his actions.

Henley talked freely to the newspaper man of certain things, but of other things was resentfully reticent. He admitted his engagement to Miss Lipscomb, and finally even admitted that Miss Lipscomb's hand had been sought by another man, Regnault Cabell, formerly of Virginia.

"Could you give me his address?" asked Hatch.

"He lives in the same apartment house with me—two floors above," was the reply.

Hatch was startled; startled more than he would have cared to admit.

"Are you on friendly terms with him?" he asked.

"Certainly," said Henley. "I won't say anything further about this matter. It would be unwise for obvious reasons."

"I suppose you consider that this turning on of the gas was an attempt on your life?"

"I can't suppose anything else."

Hatch studied the pallid face closely as he asked the next question. "Do you know Miss Regnier was found dead to-day?"

"Dead?" exclaimed the other, and he arose. "Who—what—who is she?"

It seemed a distinct effort for him to regain control of himself.

The reporter detailed then the circumstances of the finding of the girl's body, and the broker listened without comment. From that time forward all the reporter's questions were either parried or else met with a flat refusal to answer. Finally Hatch repeated to him the warning which he had from The Thinking Machine, and feeling that he had accomplished little, went away.

At eight o'clock that night—a night of complete darkness— Henley was found unconscious, lying in a little used walk in the Common. There was a bullet hole through his left shoulder, and he was bleeding profusely. He was removed to the hospital, where he regained consciousness for just a moment.

"Who shot you?" he was asked.

"None of your business," he replied, and lapsed into unconsciousness.

IV

Entirely unaware of this latest attempt on the life of the broker, Hutchinson Hatch steadily pursued his investigations. They finally led him to an intimate friend of Regnault Cabell. The young Southerner had apartments on the fourth floor of the big house off Commonwealth Avenue, directly over those Henley occupied, but two flights higher up. This friend was a figure in the social set of the Back Bay. He talked to Hatch freely of Cabell.

"He's a good fellow," he explained, "one of the best I ever met, and comes of one of the best families Virginia ever had—a true

F. F. V. He's pretty quick tempered and all that, but an excellent chap, and everywhere he has gone here he has made friends."

"He used to be in love with Miss Lipscomb of Virginia, didn't he?" asked Hatch, casually.

"Used to be?" the other repeated with a laugh. "He *is* in love with her. But recently he understood that she was engaged to Weldon Henley, a broker—you may have heard of him?—and that, I suppose, has dampened his ardor considerably. As a matter of fact, Cabell took the thing to heart. He used to know Miss Lipscomb in Virginia—she comes from another famous family there—and he seemed to think he had a prior claim on her."

Hatch heard all these things as any man might listen to gossip, but each additional fact was sinking into his mind, and each additional fact led his suspicions on deeper into the channel they had chosen.

"Cabell is pretty well to do," his informant went on, "not rich as we count riches in the North, but pretty well to do, and I believe he came to Boston because Miss Lipscomb spent so much of her time here. She is a beautiful young woman of twenty-two and extremely popular in the social world everywhere, particularly in Boston. Then there was the additional fact that Henley was here."

"No chance at all for Cabell?" Hatch suggested.

"Not the slightest," was the reply. "Yet despite the heartbreak he had, he was the first to congratulate Henley on winning her love. And he meant it, too."

"What's his attitude toward Henley now?" asked Hatch. His voice was calm, but there was an underlying tense note imperceptible to the other.

"They meet and speak and move in the same set. There's no love lost on either side, I don't suppose, but there is no trace of any ill feeling."

"Cabell doesn't happen to be a vindictive sort of man?"

"Vindictive?" and the other laughed. "No. He's like a big boy, forgiving, and all that; hot-tempered, though. I could imagine him in a fit of anger making a personal matter of it with Henley, but I don't think he ever did."

The mind of the newspaper man was rapidly focusing on one point; the rush of thoughts, questions and doubts silenced him for a moment. Then:

"How long has Cabell been in Boston?"

"Seven or eight months—that is, he has had apartments here for that long—but he has made several visits South. I suppose it's South. He has a trick of dropping out of sight occasionally. I understand that he intends to go South for good very soon. If I'm not mistaken, he is trying now to rent his suite."

Hatch looked suddenly at his informant; an idea of seeing Cabell and having a legitimate excuse for talking to him had occurred to him.

"I'm looking for a suite," he volunteered at last. "I wonder if you would give me a card of introduction to him? We might get together on it."

Thus it happened that half an hour later, about ten minutes past nine o'clock, Hatch was on his way to the big apartment house. In the office he saw the manager.

"Heard the news?" asked the manager.

"No," Hatch replied. "What is it?"

"Somebody's shot Mr. Henley as he was passing through the Common early to-night."

Hatch whistled his amazement.

"Is he dead?"

"No, but he is unconscious. The hospital doctors say it is a nasty wound, but not necessarily dangerous."

"Who shot him? Do they know?"

"He knows, but he won't say."

Amazed and alarmed by this latest development, an accurate fulfillment of The Thinking Machine's prophecy, Hatch stood thoughtful for a moment, then recovering his composure a little asked for Cabell.

"I don't think there's much chance of seeing him," said the manager. "He's going away on the midnight train—going South, to Virginia."

"Going away to-night?" Hatch gasped.

"Yes; it seems to have been rather a sudden determination. He was talking to me here half an hour or so ago, and said something about going away. While he was here the telephone boy told me that Henley had been shot; they had 'phoned from the hospital to inform us. Then Cabell seemed greatly agitated. He said he was going away to-night, if he could catch the midnight train, and now he's packing."

"I suppose the shooting of Henley upset him considerably?" the reporter suggested.

"Yes, I guess it did," was the reply. "They moved in the same set and belonged to the same clubs."

The manager sent Hatch's card of introduction to Cabell's apartments. Hatch went up and was ushered into a suite identical with that of Henley's in every respect save in minor details of furnishings. Cabell stood in the middle of the floor, with his personal belongings scattered about the room; his valet, evidently a Frenchman, was busily engaged in packing.

Cabell's greeting was perfunctorily cordial; he seemed agitated. His face was flushed and from time to time he ran his fingers through his long, brown hair. He stared at Hatch in a preoccupied fashion, then they fell into conversation about the rent of the apartments.

"I'll take almost anything reasonable," Cabell said hurriedly. "You see, I am going away to-night, rather more suddenly than I had intended, and I am anxious to get the lease off my hands. I pay two hundred dollars a month for these just as they are."

"May I look them over?" asked Hatch.

He passed from the front room into the next. Here, on a bed, was piled a huge lot of clothing, and the valet, with deft fingers, was brushing and folding, preparatory to packing. Cabell was directly behind him.

"Quite comfortable, you see," he explained. "There's room enough if you are alone. Are you?"

"Oh, yes," Hatch replied.

"This other room here," Cabell explained, "is not in very tidy shape now. I have been out of the city for several weeks, and—— What's the matter?" he demanded suddenly.

Hatch had turned quickly at the words and stared at him, then recovered himself with a start.

"I beg your pardon," he stammered. "I rather thought I saw you in town here a week or so ago—of course I didn't know you—and I was wondering if I could have been mistaken."

"Must have been," said the other easily. "During the time I was away a Miss ——, a friend of my sister's, occupied the suite. I'm afraid some of her things are here. She hasn't sent for them as yet. She occupied this room, I think; when I came back a few days ago she took another place and all her things haven't been removed."

"I see," remarked Hatch, casually. "I don't suppose there's any chance of her returning here unexpectedly if I should happen to take her apartments?"

"Not the slightest. She knows I am back, and thinks I am to remain. She was to send for these things."

Hatch gazed about the room ostentatiously. Across a trunk lay a Turkish bath robe with a scarlet stripe in it. He was anxious to get hold of it, to examine it closely. But he didn't dare to, then. Together they returned to the front room.

"I rather like the place," he said, after a pause, "but the price is——"

"Just a moment," Cabell interrupted. "Jean, before you finish packing that suit case be sure to put my bath robe in it. It's in the far room."

Then one question was settled for Hatch. After a moment the valet returned with the bath robe, which had been in the far room. It was Cabell's bath robe. As Jean passed the reporter an end of the robe caught on a corner of the trunk, and, stopping, the reporter unfastened it. A tiny strand of thread clung to the metal; Hatch detached it and stood idly twirling it in his fingers.

"As I was saying," he resumed. "I rather like the place, but the price is too much. Suppose you leave it in the hands of the manager of the house——"

"I had intended doing that," the Southerner interrupted.

"Well, I'll see him about it later," Hatch added.

With a cordial, albeit pre-occupied, handshake, Cabell ushered him out. Hatch went down in the elevator with a feeling of elation; a feeling that he had accomplished something. The manager was waiting to get into the lift.

"Do you happen to remember the name of the young lady who occupied Mr. Cabell's suite while he was away?" he asked.

"Miss Austin," said the manager, "but she's not young. She was about forty-five years old, I should judge."

"Did Mr. Cabell have his servant Jean with him?"

"Oh, no," said the manager. "The valet gave up the suite to Miss Austin entirely, and until Mr. Cabell returned occupied a room in the quarters we have for our own employees."

"Was Miss Austin ailing any way?" asked Hatch. "I saw a large number of medicine bottles upstairs."

"I don't know what was the matter with her," replied the manager, with a little puzzled frown. "She certainly was not a woman of sound mental balance—that is, she was eccentric, and all that. I think rather it was an act of charity for Mr. Cabell to let her have the suite in his absence. Certainly we didn't want her."

Hatch passed out and burst in eagerly upon The Thinking Machine in his laboratory.

"Here," he said, and triumphantly he extended the tiny scarlet strand which he had received from The Thinking Machine, and the other of the identical color which came from Cabell's bath robe. "Is that the same?"

The Thinking Machine placed them under the microscope and examined them immediately. Later he submitted them to a chemical test.

"*It is the same,*" he said, finally.

"Then the mystery is solved," said Hatch, conclusively.

V

The Thinking Machine stared steadily into the eager, exultant eyes of the newspaper man until Hatch at last began to fear that he had been precipitate. After awhile, under close scrutiny, the reporter began to feel convinced that he had made a mistake—he didn't quite see where, but it must be there, and the exultant manner passed. The voice of The Thinking Machine was like a cold shower.

"Remember, Mr. Hatch," he said, critically, "that unless every possible question has been considered one cannot boast of a solution. Is there any possible question lingering yet in your mind?"

The reporter silently considered that for a moment, then:

"Well, I have the main facts, anyway. There may be one or two minor questions left, but the principal ones are answered."

"Then tell me, to the minutest detail, what you have learned, what has happened."

Professor Van Dusen sank back in his old, familiar pose in the large arm chair and Hatch related what he had learned and what he surmised. He related, too, the peculiar circumstances surrounding the wounding of Henley, and right on down to the beginning and end of the interview with Cabell in the latter's apartments. The Thinking Machine was silent for a time, then there came a host of questions.

"Do you know where the woman—Miss Austin—is now?" was the first.

"No," Hatch had to admit.

"Or her precise mental condition?"

"No."

"Or her exact relationship to Cabell?"

"No."

"Do you know, then, what the valet, Jean, knows of the affair?"

"No, not that," said the reporter, and his face flushed under the close questioning. "He was out of the suite every night."

"Therefore might have been the very one who turned on the gas," the other put in testily.

"So far as I can learn, nobody could have gone into that room and turned on the gas," said the reporter, somewhat aggressively. "Henley barred the doors and windows and kept watch, night after night."

"Yet the moment he was exhausted and fell asleep the gas was turned on to kill him," said The Thinking Machine; "thus we see that *he was watched more closely than he watched.*"

"I see what you mean now," said Hatch, after a long pause.

"I should like to know what Henley and Cabell and the valet knew of the girl who was found dead," The Thinking Machine suggested. "Further, I should like to know if there was a good-sized mirror—not one set in a bureau or dresser—either in Henley's room or the apartments where the girl was found. Find out this for me and—never mind. I'll go with you."

The scientist left the room. When he returned he wore his coat and hat. Hatch arose mechanically to follow. For a block or more they walked along, neither speaking. The Thinking Machine was the first to break the silence:

"You believe Cabell is the man who attempted to kill Henley?"

"Frankly, yes," replied the newspaper man.

"Why?"

"Because he had the motive—disappointed love."

"How?"

"I don't know," Hatch confessed. "The doors of the Henley suite were closed. I don't see how anybody passed them."

"And the girl? Who killed her? How? Why?"

Disconsolately Hatch shook his head as he walked on. The Thinking Machine interpreted his silence aright.

"Don't jump at conclusions," he advised sharply. "You are confident Cabell was to blame for this—and he might have been, I don't know yet—but you can suggest nothing to show how he did it. I have told you before that imagination is half of logic."

At last the lights of the big apartment house where Henley lived came in sight. Hatch shrugged his shoulders. He had grave doubts— based on what he knew—whether The Thinking Machine would be able to see Cabell. It was nearly eleven o'clock and Cabell was to leave for the South at midnight.

"Is Mr. Cabell here?" asked the scientist of the elevator boy.

"Yes, just about to go, though. He won't see anyone."

"Hand him this note," instructed The Thinking Machine, and he scribbled something on a piece of paper. "He'll see us."

The boy took the paper and the elevator shot up to the fourth floor. After awhile he returned.

"He'll see you," he said.

"Is he unpacking?"

"After he read your note twice he told his valet to unpack," the boy replied.

"Ah, I thought so," said The Thinking Machine.

With Hatch, mystified and puzzled, following, The Thinking Machine entered the elevator to step out a second or so later on the fourth floor. As they left the car they saw the door of Cabell's apartment standing open; Cabell was in the door. Hatch traced a glimmer of anxiety in the eyes of the young man.

"Professor Van Dusen?" Cabell inquired.

"Yes," said the scientist. "It was of the utmost importance that I should see you, otherwise I should not have come at this time of night."

With a wave of his hand Cabell passed that detail.

"I was anxious to get away at midnight," he explained, "but, of course, now I shan't go, in view of your note. I have ordered my valet to unpack my things, at least until to-morrow."

The reporter and the scientist passed into the luxuriously furnished apartments. Jean, the valet, was bending over a suit case as they entered, removing some things he had been carefully placing there. He didn't look back or pay the least attention to the visitors.

"This is your valet?" asked The Thinking Machine.

"Yes," said the young man.

"French, isn't he?"

"Yes."

"Speak English at all?"

"Very badly," said Cabell. "I use French when I talk to him."

"Does he know that you are accused of murder?" asked The Thinking Machine, in a quiet, conversational tone.

The effect of the remark on Cabell was startling. He staggered back a step or so as if he had been struck in the face, and a crimson flush overspread his brow. Jean, the valet, straightened up suddenly and looked around. There was a queer expression, too, in his eyes; an expression which Hatch could not fathom.

"Murder?" gasped Cabell, at last.

"Yes, he speaks English all right," remarked The Thinking Machine. "Now Mr. Cabell, will you please tell me just who Miss Austin is, and where she is, and her mental condition? Believe me, it may save you a great deal of trouble. What I said in the note is not exaggerated."

The young man turned suddenly and began to pace back and forth across the room. After a few minutes he paused before The Thinking Machine, who stood impatiently waiting for an answer.

"I'll tell you, yes," said Cabell, firmly. "Miss Austin is a middle-aged woman whom my sister befriended several times—was, in fact, my sister's governess when she was a child. Of late years she has not been wholly right mentally, and has suffered a great deal of privation. I had about concluded arrangements to put her in a private sanitarium. I permitted her to remain in these rooms in my absence, South. I did not take Jean—he lived in the quarters of the other employees of the place, and gave the apartment entirely to Miss Austin. It was simply an act of charity."

"What was the cause of your sudden determination to go South to-night?" asked the scientist.

"I won't answer that question," was the sullen reply.

There was a long, tense silence. Jean, the valet, came and went several times.

"How long has Miss Austin known Mr. Henley?"

"Presumably since she has been in these apartments," was the reply.

"Are you sure *you* are not Miss Austin?" demanded the scientist.

The question was almost staggering, not only to Cabell, but to Hatch. Suddenly, with flaming face, the young Southerner leaped forward as if to strike down The Thinking Machine.

"That won't do any good," said the scientist, coldly. "Are you sure you are not Miss Austin?" he repeated.

"Certainly I am not Miss Austin," responded Cabell, fiercely.

"Have you a mirror in these apartments about twelve inches by twelve inches?" asked The Thinking Machine, irrelevantly.

"I—I don't know," stammered the young man. "I —have we, Jean?"

"Oui," replied the valet.

"Yes," snapped The Thinking Machine. "Talk English, please. May I see it?"

The valet, without a word but with a sullen glance at the questioner, turned and left the room. He returned after a moment with the mirror. The Thinking Machine carefully examined the frame, top and bottom and on both sides. At last he looked up; again the valet was bending over a suit case.

"Do you use gas in these apartments?" the scientist asked suddenly.

"No," was the bewildered response. "What is all this, anyway?"

Without answering, The Thinking Machine drew a chair up under the chandelier where the gas and electric fixtures were and began to finger the gas tips. After awhile he climbed down and passed into the next room, with Hatch and Cabell, both hopelessly mystified, following. There the scientist went through the same process of fingering the gas jets. Finally, one of the gas tips came out in his hand.

"Ah," he exclaimed, suddenly, and Hatch knew the note of triumph in it. The jet from which the tip came was just on a level with his shoulder, set between a dressing table and a window. He leaned over and squinted at the gas pipe closely. Then he returned to the room where the valet was.

"Now, Jean," he began, in an even, calm voice, "please tell me *if you did or did not kill Miss Regnier purposely?"*

"I don't know what you mean," said the servant sullenly, angrily, as he turned on the scientist.

"You speak very good English now," was The Thinking Machine's terse comment. "Mr. Hatch, lock the door and use this 'phone to call the police."

Hatch turned to do as he was bid and saw a flash of steel in young Cabell's hand, which was drawn suddenly from a hip pocket. It was a revolver. The weapon glittered in the light, and Hatch flung himself forward. There was a sharp report, and a bullet was buried in the floor.

VI

Then came a fierce, hard fight for possession of the revolver. It ended with the weapon in Hatch's hand, and both he and Cabell blowing from the effort they had expended. Jean, the valet, had turned at the sound of the shot and started toward the door leading into the hall. The Thinking Machine had stepped in front of him, and now stood there with his back to the door. Physically he would have been a child in the hands of the valet, yet there was a look in his eyes which stopped him.

"Now, Mr. Hatch," said the scientist quietly, a touch of irony in his voice. "hand me the revolver, then 'phone for Detective Mallory to come here immediately. Tell him we have a murderer—and if he can't come at once get some other detective whom you know."

"Murderer!" gasped Cabell.

Uncontrollable rage was blazing in the eyes of the valet, and he made as if to throw The Thinking Machine aside, despite the revolver, when Hatch was at the telephone. As Jean started forward, however, Cabell stopped him with a quick, stern gesture. Suddenly the young Southerner turned on The Thinking Machine; but it was with a question.

"What does it all mean?" he asked, bewildered.

"It means that that man there," and The Thinking Machine indicated the valet by a nod of his head, "is a murderer—that he killed Louise Regnier; that he shot Weldon Henley on Boston Common, and that, with the aid of Miss Regnier, he had four times previously attempted to kill Mr. Henley. Is he coming, Mr. Hatch?"

"Yes," was the reply. "He says he'll be here directly."

"Do you deny it?" demanded The Thinking Machine of the valet.

"I've done nothing," said the valet sullenly. "I'm going out of here."

Like an infuriated animal he rushed forward. Hatch and Cabell seized him and bore him to the floor. There, after a frantic struggle, he was bound and the other three men sat down to wait for Detective Mallory. Cabell sank back in his chair with a perplexed frown on his face. From time to time he glanced at Jean. The flush of anger which had been on the valet's face was gone now; instead there was the pallor of fear.

"Won't you tell us?" pleaded Cabell impatiently.

"When Detective Mallory comes and takes his prisoner," said The Thinking Machine.

Ten minutes later they heard a quick step in the hall outside and Hatch opened the door. Detective Mallory entered and looked from one to another inquiringly.

"That's your prisoner, Mr. Mallory," said the scientist, coldly. "I charge him with the murder of Miss Regnier, whom you were so confident committed suicide; I charge him with five attempts on the life of Weldon Henley, four times by gas poisoning, in which Miss Regnier was his accomplice, and once by shooting. He is the man who shot Mr. Henley."

The Thinking Machine arose and walked over to the prostrate man, handing the revolver to Hatch. He glared down at Jean fiercely.

"Will you tell how you did it or shall I?" he demanded.

His answer was a sullen, defiant glare. He turned and picked up the square mirror which the valet had produced previously.

"That's where the screw was, isn't it?" he asked, as he indicated a small hole in the frame of the mirror. Jean stared at it and his head sank forward hopelessly. "And this is the bath robe you wore, isn't it?" he demanded again, and from the suit case he pulled out the garment with the scarlet stripe.

"I guess you got me all right," was the sullen reply.

"It might be better for you if you told the story then?" suggested The Thinking Machine.

"You know so much about it, tell it yourself."

"Very well," was the calm rejoinder. "I will. If I make any mistake you will correct me."

For a long time no one spoke. The Thinking Machine had dropped back into a chair and was staring through his thick glasses at the ceiling; his finger tips were pressed tightly together. At last he began:

"There are certain trivial gaps which only the imagination can supply until the matter is gone into more fully. I should have supplied these myself, but the arrest of this man, Jean, was precipitated by the attempted hurried departure of Mr. Cabell for the South to-night, and I did not have time to go into the case to the fullest extent.

"Thus, we begin with the fact that there were several clever attempts made to murder Mr. Henley. This was by putting out the gas which he habitually left burning in his room. It happened four times in all; thus proving that it was an attempt to kill him. If it had been only once it might have been accident, even twice it might have been accident, but the same accident does not happen four times at the same time of night.

"Mr. Henley finally grew to regard the strange extinguishing of the gas as an effort to kill him, and carefully locked and barred his door and windows each night. He believed that some one came into his apartments and put out the light, leaving the gas flow. This, of course, was not true. Yet the gas was put out. How? My first idea, a natural one, was that it was turned off for an instant at the meter, when the light would go out, then turned on again. This, I convinced myself, was not true. Therefore still the question—how?

"It is a fact—I don't know how widely known it is—but it is a fact that every gas light in this house might be extinguished at the same time from this room without leaving it. How? Simply by removing the gas jet tip and blowing into the gas pipe. It would not leave a jet in the building burning. It is due to the fact that the lung power is greater than the pressure of the gas in the pipes, and forces it out.

"Thus we have the method employed to extinguish the light in Mr. Henley's rooms, and all the barred and locked doors and windows would not stop it. At the same time it threatened the life of every other person in the house—that is, every other person who used gas. It was probably for this reason that the attempt was always made late at night, I should say three or four o'clock. That's when it was done, isn't it?" he asked suddenly of the valet.

Staring at The Thinking Machine in open-mouthed astonishment the valet nodded his aquiescence before he was fully aware of it.

"Yes, that's right," The Thinking Machine resumed complacently. "This was easily found out—comparatively. The next question was how was a watch kept on Mr. Henley? It would have done no good to extinguish the gas before he was asleep, or to have turned it on when he was not in his rooms. It might have led to a speedy discovery of just how the thing was done.

"There's a spring lock on the door of Mr. Henley's apartment. Therefore it would have been impossible for anyone to peep through the keyhole. There are no cracks through which one might see. How was this watch kept? How was the plotter to satisfy himself positively of the time when Mr. Henley was asleep? How was it the gas was put out at no time of the score or more nights Mr. Henley himself kept watch? Obviously he was watched through a window.

"No one could climb out on the window ledge and look into Mr.

Henley's apartments. No one could see into that apartment from the street—that is, could see whether Mr. Henley was asleep or even in bed. They could see the light. Watch was kept with the aid offered by a flagpole, supplemented with a mirror—this mirror. A screw was driven into the frame—it has been removed now—it was swung on the flagpole rope and pulled out to the end of the pole, facing the building. To a man standing in the hall window of the third floor it offered precisely the angle necessary to reflect the interior of Mr. Henley's suite, possibly even showed him in bed through a narrow opening in the curtain. There is no shade on the windows of that suite; heavy curtains instead. Is that right?"

Again the prisoner was surprised into a mute acquiescence.

"I saw the possibility of these things, and I saw, too, that at three or four o'clock in the morning it would be perfectly possible for a person to move about the upper halls of this house without being seen. If he wore a heavy bath robe, with a hood, say, no one would recognize him even if he were seen, and besides the garb would not cause suspicion. This bath robe has a hood.

"Now, in working the mirror back and forth on the flagpole at night a tiny scarlet thread was pulled out of the robe and clung to the rope. I found this thread; later Mr. Hatch found an identical thread in these apartments. Both came from that bath robe. Plain logic shows that the person who blew down the gas pipes worked the mirror trick; the person who worked the mirror trick left the thread; the thread comes back to the bath robe—that bath robe there," he pointed dramatically. "Thus the person who desired Henley's death was in these apartments, or had easy access to them."

He paused a moment and there was a tense silence. A great light was coming to Hatch, slowly but surely. The brain that had followed all this was unlimited in possibilities.

"Even before we traced the origin of the crime to this room," went on the scientist, quietly now, "attention had been attracted here, particularly to you, Mr. Cabell. It was through the love affair, of which Miss Lipscomb was the center. Mr. Hatch learned that you and Henley had been rivals for her hand. It was that, even before this scarlet thread was found, which indicated that you might have some knowledge of the affair, directly or indirectly.

"You are not a malicious or revengeful man, Mr. Cabell. But you are hot-tempered—extremely so. You demonstrated that just now, when, angry and not understanding, but feeling that your honor was at stake, you shot a hole in the floor."

"What?" asked Detective Mallory.

"A little accident," explained The Thinking Machine quickly. "Not being a malicious or revengeful man, you are not the man to deliberately go ahead and make elaborate plans for the murder of Henley. In a moment of passion you might have killed him—but never deliberately as the result of premeditation. Besides you were out of town. Who was then in these apartments? Who had access to these apartments? Who might have used your bath robe? Your valet, possibly Miss Austin. Which? Now, let's see how we reached this conclusion which led to the valet.

"Miss Regnier was found dead. It was not suicide. How did I know? Because she had been reading with the gas light at its full. If she had been reading by the gas light, how was it then that it went out and suffocated her before she could arise and shut it off? Obviously she must have fallen asleep over her book and left the light burning.

"If she was in this plot to kill Henley, why did she light the jet in her room? There might have been some slight defect in the electric bulb in her room which she had just discovered. Therefore she lighted the gas, intending to extinguish it—turn it off entirely—later. But she fell asleep. Therefore when the valet here blew into the pipe, intending to kill Mr. Henley, he unwittingly killed the woman he loved—Miss Regnier. It was perfectly possible, meanwhile, that she did not know of the attempt to be made that particular night, although she had participated in the others, knowing that Henley had night after night sat up to watch the light in his rooms.

"The facts, as I knew them, showed no connection between Miss Regnier and this man at that time—nor any connection between Miss Regnier and Henley. It might have been that the person who blew the gas out of the pipe from these rooms knew nothing whatever of Miss Regnier, just as he didn't know who else he might have killed in the building.

"But I had her death and the manner of it. I had eliminated you, Mr. Cabell. Therefore there remained Miss Austin and the valet. Miss Austin was eccentric—insane, if you will. Would she have any motive for killing Henley? I could imagine none. Love? Probably not. Money? They had nothing in common on that ground. What? Nothing that I could see. Therefore, for the moment, I passed Miss Austin by, after asking you, Mr. Cabell, if you were Miss Austin.

"What remained? The valet. Motive? Several possible ones, one or two probable. He is French, or says he is. Miss Regnier is French. Therefore I had arrived at the conclusion that they knew each other as people of the same nationality will in a house of this sort. And remember, I had passed by Mr. Cabell and Miss Austin, so the valet was the only one left; he could use the bath robe.

"Well, the motive. Frankly that was the only difficult point in the entire problem—difficult because there were so many possibilities. And each possibility that suggested itself suggested also a woman. Jealousy? There must be a woman. Hate? Probably a woman. Attempted extortion? With the aid of a woman. No other motive which would lead to so elaborate a plot of murder would come forward. Who was the woman? Miss Regnier.

"Did Miss Regnier know Henley? Mr. Hatch had reason to believe he knew her because of his actions when informed of her death. Knew her how? People of such relatively different planes of life can know each other—or do know each other—only on one plane. Henley is a typical young man, fast, I dare say, and liberal. Perhaps, then, there had been a liaison. When I saw this possibility I had my motives—all of them—jealousy, hate and possibly attempted extortion as well.

"What was more possible than Mr. Henley and Miss Regnier had been acquainted? All liaisons are secret ones. Suppose she had been cast off because of the engagement to a young woman of Henley's own level? Suppose she had confided in the valet here? Do you see? Motives enough for any crime, however diabolical. The attempts on Henley's life possibly followed an attempted extortion of money. The shot which wounded Henley was fired by this man, Jean. Why? Because the woman who had cause to hate Henley was dead. Then the man? He was alive and vindictive. Henley knew who shot him, and knew why, but he'll never say it publicly. He can't afford to. It would ruin him. I think probably that's all. Do you want to add anything?" he asked of the valet.

"No," was the fierce reply. "I'm sorry I didn't kill him, that's all. It was all about as you said, though God knows how you found it out," he added, desperately.

"Are you a Frenchman?"

"I was born in New York, but lived in France for eleven years. I first knew Louise there."

Silence fell upon the little group. Then Hatch asked a question:

"You told me, Professor, that there would be no other attempt to kill Henley by extinguishing the gas. How did you know that?"

"Because one person—the wrong person—had been killed that way," was the reply. "For this reason it was hardly likely that another attempt of that sort would be made. You had no intention of killing Louise Regnier, had you, Jean?"

"No, God help me, no."

"It was all done in these apartments," The Thinking Machine added, turning to Cabell, "at the gas jet from which I took the tip. It has been only loosely replaced and the metal was tarnished where the lips had dampened it."

"It must take great lung power to do a thing like that," remarked Detective Mallory.

"You would be amazed to know how easily it is done," said the scientist. "Try it some time."

The Thinking Machine arose and picked up his hat; Hatch did the same. Then the reporter turned to Cabell.

"Would you mind telling me why you were so anxious to get away to-night?" he asked.

"Well, no," Cabell explained, and there was a rush of red to his face. "It's because I received a telegram from Virginia—Miss Lipscomb, in fact. Some of Henley's past had come to her knowledge and the telegram told me that the engagement was broken. On top of this came the information that Henley had been shot and—I was considerably agitated."

The Thinking Machine and Hatch were walking along the street.

"What did you write in the note you sent to Cabell that made him start to unpack?" asked the reporter, curiously.

"There are some things that it wouldn't be well for everyone to know," was the enigmatic response. "Perhaps it would be just as well for you to overlook this little omission."

"Of course, of course," replied the reporter, wonderingly.

THE FLAMING PHANTOM

I

Hutchinson Hatch, reporter, stood beside the City Editor's desk, smoking and waiting patiently for that energetic gentleman to dispose of several matters in hand. City Editors always have several matters in hand, for the profession of keeping count of the pulse-beat of the world is a busy one. Finally this City Editor emerged from a mass of other things and picked up a sheet of paper on which he had scribbled some strange hieroglyphics, these representing his interpretation of the art of writing.

"Afraid of ghosts?" he asked.

"Don't know," Hatch replied, smiling a little. "I never happened to meet one."

"Well, this looks like a good story," the City Editor explained. "It's a haunted house. Nobody can live in it; all sorts of strange happenings, demoniacal laughter, groans and things. House is owned by Ernest Weston, a broker. Better jump down and take a look at it. If it is promising, you might spend a night in it for a Sunday story. Not afraid, are you?"

"I never heard of a ghost hurting anyone," Hatch replied, still smiling a little. "If this one hurts me it will make the story better."

Thus attention was attracted to the latest creepy mystery of a small town by the sea which in the past had not been wholly lacking in creepy mysteries.

Within two hours Hatch was there. He readily found the old Weston house, as it was known, a two-story, solidly built frame structure, which had stood for sixty or seventy years high upon a cliff overlooking the sea, in the center of a land plot of ten or twelve acres. From a distance it was imposing, but close inspection showed that, outwardly, at least, it was a ramshackle affair.

Without having questioned anyone in the village, Hatch climbed the steep cliff road to the old house, expecting to find some one who might grant him permission to inspect it. But no one appeared; a settled melancholy and gloom seemed to overspread it; all the shutters were closed forbiddingly.

There was no answer to his vigorous knock on the front door, and he shook the shutters on a window without result. Then he passed around the house to the back. Here he found a door and dutifully hammered on it. Still no answer. He tried it, and passed in. He stood in the kitchen, damp, chilly and darkened by the closed shutters.

One glance about this room and he went on through a back hall to the dining-room, now deserted, but at one time a comfortable and handsomely furnished place. Its hardwood floor was covered with dust; the chill of disuse was all-pervading. There was no furniture, only the litter which accumulates of its own accord.

From this point, just inside the dining-room door, Hatch began a sort of study of the inside architecture of the place. To his left was a door, the butler's pantry. There was a passage through, down three steps into the kitchen he had just left.

Straight before him, set in the wall, between two windows, was a large mirror, seven, possibly eight, feet tall and proportionately wide. A mirror of the same size was set in the wall at the end of the room to his left. From the dining-room he passed through a wide archway into the next room. This archway made the two rooms almost as one. This second, he presumed, had been a sort of living-room, but here, too, was nothing save accumulated litter, an old-fashioned fireplace and two long mirrors. As he entered, the fireplace was to his immediate left, one of the large mirrors was straight ahead of him and the other was to his right.

Next to the mirror in the end was a passageway of a little more than usual size which had once been closed with a sliding door. Hatch went through this into the reception-hall of the old house. Here, to his right, was the main hall, connected with the reception-hall by an archway, and through this archway he could see a wide, old-fashioned stairway leading up. To his left was a door, of ordinary size, closed. He tried it and it opened. He peered into a big room beyond. This room had been the library. It smelled of books and damp wood. There was nothing here—not even mirrors.

Beyond the main hall lay only two rooms, one a drawing-room of the generous proportions our old folks loved, with its gilt all tarnished and its fancy decorations covered with dust. Behind this, toward the back of the house, was a small parlor. There was nothing here to attract his attention, and he went upstairs. As he went he could see through the archway into the reception-hall as far as the library door, which he had left closed.

Upstairs were four or five roomy suites. Here, too, in small rooms designed for dressing, he saw the owner's passion for mirrors again. As he passed through room after room he fixed the general arrangement of it all in his mind, and later on paper, to study it, so that, if necessary, he could leave any part of the house in the dark. He didn't know but what this might be necessary, hence his care—the same care he had evidenced downstairs.

After another casual examination of the lower floor, Hatch went out the back way to the barn. This stood a couple of hundred feet back of the house and was of more recent construction. Above, reached by outside stairs, were apartments intended for the servants. Hatch looked over these rooms, but they, too, had the appearance of not having been occupied for several years. The lower part of the barn, he found, was arranged to house half a dozen horses and three or four traps.

"Nothing here to frighten anybody," was his mental comment as he left the old place and started back toward the village. It was three o'clock in the afternoon. His purpose was to learn then all he could of the "ghost," and return that night for developments.

He sought out the usual village bureau of information, the town constable, a grizzled old chap of sixty years, who realized his importance as the whole police department, and who had the gossip and information, more or less distorted, of several generations at his tongue's end.

The old man talked for two hours—he was glad to talk—seemed to have been longing for just such a glorious opportunity as the reporter offered. Hatch sifted out what he wanted, those things which might be valuable in his story.

It seemed, according to the constable, that the Weston house had not been occupied for five years, since the death of the father of Ernest Weston, present owner. Two weeks before the reporter's appearance there Ernest Weston had come down with a contractor and looked over the old place.

"We understand here," said the constable, judicially, "that Mr. Weston is going to be married soon, and we kind of thought he was having the house made ready for his Summer home again."

"Whom do you understand he is to marry?" asked Hatch, for this was news.

"Miss Katherine Everard, daughter of Curtis Everard, a banker up in Boston," was the reply. "I know he used to go around with her before the old man died, and they say since she came out in Newport he has spent a lot of time with her."

"Oh, I see," said Hatch. "They were to marry and come here?"

"That's right," said the constable. "But I don't know when, since this ghost story has come up."

"Oh, yes, the ghost," remarked Hatch. "Well, hasn't the work of repairing begun?"

"No, not inside," was the reply. "There's been some work done on the grounds—in the daytime—but not much of that, and I kind of think it will be a long time before it's all done."

"What is the spook story, anyway?"

"Well," and the old constable rubbed his chin thoughtfully. "It seems sort of funny. A few days after Mr. Weston was down here a gang of laborers, mostly Italians, came down to work and decided to sleep in the house—sort of camp out—until they could repair a leak in the barn and move in there. They got here late in the afternoon and didn't do much that day but move into the house, all upstairs, and sort of settle down for the night. About one o'clock they heard some sort of noise downstairs, and finally all sorts of a racket and groans and yells, and they just naturally came down to see what it was.

"Then they saw the ghost. It was in the reception-hall, some of 'em said, others said it was in the library, but anyhow it was there, and the whole gang left just as fast as they knew how. They slept on the ground that night. Next day they took out their things and went back to Boston. Since then nobody here has heard from 'em."

"What sort of a ghost was it?"

"Oh, it was a man ghost, about nine feet high, and he was blazing from head to foot as if he was burning up," said the constable. "He had a long knife in his hand and waved it at 'em. They didn't stop to argue. They ran, and as they ran they heard the ghost a-laughing at them."

"I should think he would have been amused," was Hatch's somewhat sarcastic comment. "Has anybody who lives in the village seen the ghost?"

"No; we're willing to take their word for it, I suppose," was the grinning reply, "because there never was a ghost there before. I go up and look over the place every afternoon, but everything seems to be all right, and I haven't gone there at night. It's quite a way off my beat," he hastened to explain.

"A man ghost with a long knife," mused Hatch. "Blazing, seems to be burning up, eh? That sounds exciting. Now, a ghost who knows his business never appears except where there has been a murder. Was there ever a murder in that house?"

"When I was a little chap I heard there was a murder or something there, but I suppose if I don't remember it nobody else here does," was the old man's reply. "It happened one winter when the Westons weren't there. There was something, too, about jewelry and diamonds, but I don't remember just what it was."

"Indeed?" asked the reporter.

"Yes, something about somebody trying to steal a lot of jewelry— a hundred thousand dollars' worth. I know nobody ever paid much attention to it. I just heard about it when I was a boy, and that was at least fifty years ago."

"I see," said the reporter.

That night at nine o'clock, under cover of perfect blackness, Hatch climbed the cliff toward the Weston house. At one o'clock he came racing down the hill, with frequent glances over his shoulder. His face was pallid with a fear which he had never known before and his lips were ashen. Once in his room in the village hotel Hutchinson Hatch, the nerveless young man, lighted a lamp with trembling hands and sat with wide, staring eyes until the dawn broke through the east.

He had seen the flaming phantom.

II

It was ten o'clock that morning when Hutchinson Hatch called on Professor Augustus S. F. X. Van Dusen—The Thinking Machine. The reporter's face was still white, showing that he had slept little, if at all. The Thinking Machine squinted at him a moment through his thick glasses, then dropped into a chair.

"Well?" he queried.

"I'm almost ashamed to come to you, Professor," Hatch confessed, after a minute, and there was a little embarrassed hesitation in his speech. "It's another mystery."

"Sit down and tell me about it."

Hatch took a seat opposite the scientist.

"I've been frightened," he said at last, with a sheepish grin; "horribly, awfully frightened. I came to you to know what frightened me."

"Dear me! Dear me!" exclaimed The Thinking Machine. "What is it?"

Then Hatch told him from the beginning the story of the haunted house as he knew it; how he had examined the house by daylight, just what he had found, the story of the old murder and the jewels, the fact that Ernest Weston was to be married. The scientist listened attentively.

"It was nine o'clock that night when I went to the house the second time." said Hatch. "I went prepared for something, but not for what I saw."

"Well, go on," said the other, irritably.

"I went in while it was perfectly dark. I took a position on the stairs because I had been told the—the THING—had been seen from the stairs, and I thought that where it had been seen once it would be seen again. I had presumed it was some trick of a shadow, or moonlight, or something of the kind. So I sat waiting calmly. I am not a nervous man—that is, I never have been until now.

"I took no light of any kind with me. It seemed an interminable time that I waited, staring into the reception-room in the general direction of the library. At last, as I gazed into the darkness, I heard a noise. It startled me a bit, but it didn't frighten me, for I put it down to a rat running across the floor.

"But after awhile I heard the most awful cry a human being ever listened to. It was neither a moan nor a shriek—merely a—a cry. Then, as I steadied my nerves a little, a figure—a blazing, burning white figure—grew out of nothingness before my very eyes, in the reception room. It actually grew and assembled as I looked at it."

He paused, and The Thinking Machine changed his position slightly.

"The figure was that of a man, apparently, I should say, eight feet high. Don't think I'm a fool—I'm not exaggerating. It was all in white and seemed to radiate a light, a ghostly, unearthly light, which, as I looked, grew brighter. I saw no face to the THING, but it had a head. Then I saw an arm raised and in the hand was a dagger, blazing as was the figure.

"By this time I was a coward, a cringing, frightened coward—frightened not at what I saw, but at the weirdness of it. And then, still as I looked, the—the THING—raised the other hand, and there, in the air before my eyes, wrote with his own finger—*on the very face of the air,* mind you—one word: 'Beware!' "

"Was it a man's or woman's writing?" asked The Thinking Machine.

The matter-of-fact tone recalled Hatch, who was again being carried away by fear, and he laughed vacantly.

"I don't know," he said. "I don't know."

"Go on."

"I have never considered myself a coward, and certainly I am not a child to be frightened at a thing which my reason tells me is not possible, and, despite my fright, I compelled myself to action. If the THING were a man I was not afraid of it, dagger and all; if it were not, it could do me no injury.

"I leaped down the three steps to the bottom of the stairs, and while the THING stood there with upraised dagger, with one hand pointing at me, I rushed for it. I think I must have shouted, because I have a dim idea that I heard my own voice. But whether or not I did I——"

Again he paused. It was a distinct effort to pull himself together. He felt like a child; the cold, squint eyes of The Thinking Machine were turned on him disapprovingly.

"Then—the THING disappeared just as it seemed I had my hands on it. I was expecting a dagger thrust. Before my eyes, while I was staring at it, I suddenly saw *only half of it.* Again I heard the cry, and the other half disappeared—my hands grasped empty air.

"Where the THING had been there was nothing. The impetus of my rush was such that I went right on past the spot where the THING had been, and found myself groping in the dark in a room which I didn't place for an instant. Now I know it was the library.

"By this time I was mad with terror. I smashed one of the windows and went through it. Then from there, until I reached my room, I didn't stop running. I couldn't. I wouldn't have gone back to the reception-room for all the millions in the world."

The Thinking Machine twiddled his fingers idly; Hatch sat gazing at him with anxious, eager inquiry in his eyes.

"So when you ran and the—the THING moved away or disappeared you found yourself in the library?" The Thinking Machine asked at last.

"Yes."

"Therefore you must have run from the reception-room through the door into the library?"

"Yes."

"You left that door closed that day?"

"Yes."

Again there was a pause.

"Smell anything?" asked The Thinking Machine.

"No."

"You figure that the THING, as you call it, must have been just about in the door?"

"Yes."

"Too bad you didn't notice the handwriting—that is, whether it seemed to be a man's or a woman's."

"I think, under the circumstances, I would be excused for omitting that," was the reply.

"You said you heard something that you thought must be a rat," went on The Thinking Machine. "What was this?"

"I don't know."

"Any squeak about it?"

"No, not that I noticed."

"Five years since the house was occupied," mused the scientist. "How far away is the water?"

"The place overlooks the water, but it's a steep climb of three hundred yards from the water to the house."

That seemed to satisfy The Thinking Machine as to what actually happened.

"When you went over the house in daylight, did you notice if any of the mirrors were dusty?" he asked.

"I should presume that all were," was the reply. "There's no reason why they should have been otherwise."

"But you didn't notice particularly that some were not dusty?" the scientist insisted.

"No. I merely noticed that they were there."

The Thinking Machine sat for a long time squinting at the ceiling, then asked, abruptly:

"Have you seen Mr. Weston, the owner?"

"No."

"See him and find out what he has to say about the place, the murder, the jewels, and all that. It would be rather a queer state of affairs if, say, a fortune in jewels should be concealed somewhere about the place, wouldn't it?"

"It would," said Hatch. "It would."

"Who is Miss Katherine Everard?"

"Daughter of a banker here, Curtis Everard. Was a reigning belle at Newport for two seasons. She is now in Europe, I think, buying a trousseau, possibly."

"Find out all about her, and what Weston has to say, then come back here," said The Thinking Machine, as if in conclusion. "Oh, by the way," he added, "look up something of the family history of the Westons. How many heirs were there? Who are they? How much did each one get? All those things. That's all."

Hatch went out, far more composed and quiet than when he entered, and began the work of finding out those things The Thinking Machine had asked for, confident now that there would be a solution of the mystery.

That night the flaming phantom played new pranks. The town constable, backed by half a dozen villagers, descended upon the place at midnight, to be met in the yard by the apparition in person. Again the dagger was seen; again the ghostly laughter and the awful cry were heard.

"Surrender or I'll shoot," shouted the constable, nervously.

A laugh was the answer, and the constable felt something warm spatter in his face. Others in the party felt it, too, and wiped their faces and hands. By the light of the feeble lanterns they carried they examined their handkerchiefs and hands. Then the party fled in awful disorder.

The warmth they had felt was the warmth of blood—red blood, freshly drawn.

III

Hatch found Ernest Weston at luncheon with another gentleman at one o'clock that day. This other gentleman was introduced to Hatch as George Weston, a cousin. Hatch instantly remembered George Weston for certain eccentric exploits at Newport a season or so before; and also as one of the heirs of the original Weston estate.

Hatch thought he remembered, too, that at the time Miss Everard had been so prominent socially at Newport George Weston had been her most ardent suitor. It was rumored that there would have been an engagement between them, but her father objected. Hatch looked at him curiously; his face was clearly a dissipated one, yet there was about him the unmistakable polish and gentility of the well-bred man of society.

Hatch knew Ernest Weston as Weston knew Hatch; they had met frequently in the ten years Hatch had been a newspaper reporter, and Weston had been courteous to him always. The reporter was in doubt as to whether to bring up the subject on which he had sought out Ernest Weston, but the broker brought it up himself, smilingly.

"Well, what is it this time?" he asked, genially. "The ghost down on the South Shore, or my forthcoming marriage?"

"Both," replied Hatch.

Weston talked freely of his engagement to Miss Everard, which he said was to have been announced in another week, at which time she was due to return to America from Europe. The marriage was to be three or four months later, the exact date had not been set.

"And I suppose the country place was being put in order as a Summer residence?" the reporter asked.

"Yes. I had intended to make some repairs and changes there, and furnish it, but now I understand that a ghost has taken a hand in the matter and has delayed it. Have you heard much about this ghost story?" he asked, and there was a slight smile on his face.

"I have seen the ghost," Hatch answered.

"You have?" demanded the broker.

George Weston echoed the words and leaned forward, with a new interest in his eyes, to listen. Hatch told them what had happened in the haunted house—all of it. They listened with the keenest interest, one as eager as the other.

"By George!" exclaimed the broker, when Hatch had finished. "How do you account for it?"

"I don't," said Hatch, flatly. "I can offer no possible solution. I am not a child to be tricked by the ordinary illusion, nor am I of the temperament which imagines things, but I can offer no explanation of this."

"It must be a trick of some sort," said George Weston.

"I was positive of that," said Hatch, "but if it is a trick, it is the cleverest I ever saw."

The conversation drifted on to the old story of missing jewels and a tragedy in the house fifty years before. Now Hatch was asking questions by direction of The Thinking Machine; he himself hardly saw their purport, but he asked them.

"Well, the full story of that affair, the tragedy there, would open up an old chapter in our family which is nothing to be ashamed of, of course," said the broker, frankly; "still it is something we have not paid much attention to for many years. Perhaps George here knows it better than I do. His mother, then a bride, heard the recital of the story from my grandmother."

Ernest Weston and Hatch looked inquiringly at George Weston, who lighted a fresh cigarette and leaned over the table toward them. He was an excellent talker.

"I've heard my mother tell of it, but it was a long time ago," he began. "It seems, though, as I remember it, that my great-grandfather, who built the house, was a wealthy man, as fortunes went in those days, worth probably a million dollars.

"A part of this fortune, say about one hundred thousand dollars, was in jewels, which had come with the family from England. Many of those pieces would be of far greater value now than they were then, because of their antiquity. It was only on state occasions, I might say, when these were worn, say, once a year.

"Between times the problem of keeping them safely was a difficult one, it appeared. This was before the time of safety deposit vaults. My grandfather conceived the idea of hiding the jewels in the old place down on the South Shore, instead of keeping them in the house he had in Boston. He took them there accordingly.

"At this time one was compelled to travel down the South Shore, below Cohasset anyway, by stagecoach. My grandfather's family was then in the city, as it was Winter, so he made the trip alone. He planned to reach there at night, so as not to attract attention to himself, to hide the jewels about the house, and leave that same night for Boston again by a relay of horses he had arranged for. Just what happened after he left the stagecoach, below Cohasset, no one ever knew except by surmise."

The speaker paused a moment and relighted his cigarette.

"Next morning my great-grandfather was found unconscious and badly injured on the veranda of the house. His skull had been fractured. In the house a man was found dead. No one knew who he was; no one within a radius of many miles of the place had ever seen him.

"This led to all sorts of surmises, the most reasonable of which, and the one which the family has always accepted, being that my grandfather had gone to the house in the dark, had there met some one who was stopping there that night as a shelter from the intense cold, that this man learned of the jewels, that he had tried robbery and there was a fight.

"In this fight the stranger was killed inside the house, and my great-grandfather, injured, had tried to leave the house for aid. He collapsed on the veranda where he was found and died without having regained consciousness. That's all we know or can surmise reasonably about the matter."

"Were the jewels ever found?" asked the reporter.

"No. They were not on the dead man, nor were they in the possession of my grandfather."

"It is reasonable to suppose, then, that there was a third man and that he got away with the jewels?" asked Ernest Weston.

"It seemed so, and for a long time this theory was accepted. I suppose it is now, but some doubt was cast on it by the fact that only two trails of footsteps led to the house and none out. There was a heavy snow on the ground. If none led out, it was obviously impossible that anyone came out."

Again there was silence. Ernest Weston sipped his coffee slowly.

"It would seem from that," said Ernest Weston, at last, "that the jewels were hidden before the tragedy, and have never been found."

George Weston smiled.

"Off and on for twenty years the place was searched, according to my mother's story," he said. "Every inch of the cellar was dug up; every possible nook and corner was searched. Finally the entire matter passed out of the minds of those who knew of it, and I doubt if it has ever been referred to again until now."

"A search even now would be almost worth while, wouldn't it?" asked the broker.

George Weston laughed aloud.

"It might be," he said, "but I have some doubt. A thing that was searched for for twenty years would not be easily found."

So it seemed to strike the others after awhile and the matter was dropped.

"But this ghost thing," said the broker, at last.

"I'm interested in that. Suppose we make up a ghost party and go down to-night. My contractor declares he can't get men to work there."

"I would be glad to go," said George Weston, "but I'm running over to the Vandergrift ball in Providence to-night."

"How about you, Hatch?" asked the broker.

"I'll go, yes," said Hatch, "as one of several," he added with a smile.

"Well, then, suppose we say the constable and you and I?" asked the broker; "to-night?"

"All right."

After making arrangements to meet the broker later that afternoon he rushed away—away to The Thinking Machine. The scientist listened, then resumed some chemical test he was making.

"Can't you go down with us to-night?" Hatch asked.

"No," said the other. "I'm going to read a paper before a scientific society and prove that a chemist in Chicago is a fool. That will take me all evening."

"To-morrow night?" Hatch insisted.

"No—the next night."

This would be on Friday night—just in time for the feature which had been planned for Sunday. Hatch was compelled to rest content with this, but he foresaw that he would have it all, with a solution. It never occurred to him that this problem, or, indeed, that any problem, was beyond the mental capacity of Professor Van Dusen.

Hatch and Ernest Weston took a night train that evening, and on their arrival in the village stirred up the town constable.

"Will you go with us?" was the question.

"Both of you going?" was the counter-question.

"Yes."

"I'll go," said the constable promptly. "Ghost!" and he laughed scornfully. "I'll have him in the lockup by morning."

"No shooting, now," warned Weston. "There must be somebody back of this somewhere; we understand that, but there is no crime that we know of. The worst is possibly trespassing."

"I'll get him all right," responded the constable, who still remembered the experience where blood—warm blood—had been thrown in his face. "And I'm not so sure there isn't a crime."

That night about ten the three men went into the dark, forbidding house and took a station on the stairs where Hatch had sat when he saw the THING—whatever it was. There they waited. The constable moved nervously from time to time, but neither of the others paid any attention to him.

At last the—the THING appeared. There had been a preliminary sound as of something running across the floor, then suddenly a flaming figure of white seemed to grow into being in the reception-room. It was exactly as Hatch had described it to The Thinking Machine.

Dazed, stupefied, the three men looked, looked as the figure raised a hand, pointing toward them, and wrote a word in the air—positively in the air. The finger merely waved, and there, floating before them, were letters, flaming letters, in the utter darkness. This time the word was: "Death."

Faintly, Hatch, fighting with a fear which again seized him, remembered that The Thinking Machine had asked him if the hand-writing was that of a man or woman; now he tried to see. It was as if drawn on a blackboard, and there was a queer twist to the loop at the bottom. He sniffed to see if there was an odor of any sort. There was not.

Suddenly he felt some quick, vigorous action from the constable behind him. There was a roar and a flash in his ear; he knew the constable had fired at the THING. Then came the cry and laugh—almost a laugh of derision—he had heard them before. For one instant the figure lingered and then, before their eyes, faded again into utter blackness. Where it had been was nothing—nothing.

The constable's shot had had no effect.

IV

Three deeply mystified men passed down the hill to the village from the old house. Ernest Weston, the owner, had not spoken since before the—the THING appeared there in the reception room, or was it in the library? He was not certain—he couldn't have told. Suddenly he turned to the constable.

"I told you not to shoot."

"That's all right," said the constable. "I was there in my official capacity, and I shoot when I want to."

"But the shot did no harm," Hatch put in.

"I would swear it went right through it, too," said the constable, boastfully. "I can shoot."

Weston was arguing with himself. He was a cold-blooded man of business; his mind was not one to play him tricks. Yet now he felt benumbed; he could conceive no explanation of what he had seen. Again in his room in the little hotel, where they spent the remainder of the night, he stared blankly at the reporter.

"Can you imagine any way it could be done?"

Hatch shook his head.

"It isn't a spook, of course," the broker went on, with a nervous smile; "but—but I'm sorry I went. I don't think probably I shall have the work done here as I thought."

They slept only fitfully and took an early train back to Boston. As they were about to separate at the South Station, the broker had a last word.

"I'm going to solve that thing," he declared, determinedly. "I know one man at least who isn't afraid of it—or of anything else. I'm going to send him down to keep a lookout and take care of the place. His name is O'Heagan, and he's a fighting Irishman. If he and that—that—THING ever get mixed up together——"

Like a schoolboy with a hopeless problem, Hatch went straight to The Thinking Machine with the latest developments. The scientist paused just long enough in his work to hear it.

"Did you notice the handwriting?" he demanded.

"Yes," was the reply; "so far as I *could* notice the style of a handwriting that floated in air."

"Man's or woman's?"

Hatch was puzzled.

"I couldn't judge," he said. "It seemed to be a bold style, whatever it was. I remember the capital D clearly."

"Was it anything like the handwriting of the broker—what's-his-name?—Ernest Weston?

"I never saw his handwriting."

"Look at some of it, then, particularly the capital D's," instructed The Thinking Machine. Then, after a pause: "You say the figure is white and seems to be flaming?"

"Yes."

"Does it give out any light? That is, does it light up a room, for instance?"

"I don't quite know what you mean."

"When you go into a room with a lamp," explained The Thinking Machine, "it lights the room. Does this thing do it? Can you see the floor or walls or anything by the light of the figure itself?"

"No," replied Hatch, positively.

"I'll go down with you to-morrow night," said the scientist, as if that were all.

"Thanks," replied Hatch, and he went away.

Next day about noon he called at Ernest Weston's office. The broker was in.

"Did you send down your man O'Heagan?" he asked.

"Yes," said the broker, and he was almost smiling.

"What happened?"

"He's outside. I'll let him tell you."

The broker went to the door and spoke to some one and O'Heagan entered. He was a big, blue-eyed Irishman, frankly freckled and red-headed—one of those men who look trouble in the face and are glad of it if the trouble can be reduced to a fighting basis. An ever-lasting smile was about his lips, only now it was a bit faded.

"Tell Mr. Hatch what happened last night," requested the broker.

O'Heagan told it. He, too, had sought to get hold of the flaming figure. As he ran for it, it disappeared, was obliterated, wiped out, gone, and he found himself groping in the darkness of the room beyond, the library. Like Hatch, he took the nearest way out, which happened to be through a window already smashed.

"Outside," he went on. "I began to think about it, and I saw there was nothing to be afraid of, but you couldn't have convinced me of that when I was inside. I took a lantern in one hand and a revolver in the other and went all over that house. There was nothing; if there had been we would have had it out right there. But there was nothing. So I started out to the barn, where I had put a cot in a room.

"I went upstairs to this room—it was then about two o'clock—and went to sleep. It seemed to be an hour or so later when I awoke suddenly—I knew something was happening. And the Lord forgive me if I'm a liar, but there was a cat—a ghost cat in my room, racing around like mad. I just naturally got up to see what was the matter and rushed for the door. The cat beat me to it, and cut a flaming streak through the night.

"The cat looked just like the thing inside the house—that is, it was a sort of shadowy, waving white light like it might be afire. I went back to bed in disgust, to sleep it off. You see, sir," he apologized to Weston, "that there hadn't been anything yet I could put my hands on."

"Was that all?" asked Hatch, smilingly.

"Just the beginning. Next morning when I awoke I was bound to my cot, hard and fast. My hands were tied and my feet were tied, and all I could do was lie there and yell. After awhile, it seemed years, I heard some one outside and shouted louder than ever. Then the constable come up and let me loose. I told him all about it—and then I came to Boston. And with your permission, Mr. Weston, I resign right now. I'm not afraid of anything I can fight, but when I can't get hold of it—well——"

Later Hatch joined The Thinking Machine. They caught a train for the little village by the sea. On the way The Thinking Machine asked a few questions, but most of the time he was silent, squinting out the window. Hatch respected his silence, and only answered questions.

"Did you see Ernest Weston's handwriting?" was the first of these.

"Yes."

"The capital D's?"

"They are not unlike the one the—the THING wrote, but they are not wholly like it," was the reply.

"Do you know anyone in Providence who can get some information for you?" was the next query.

"Yes."

"Get him by long-distance 'phone when we get to this place and let me talk to him a moment."

Half an hour later The Thinking Machine was talking over the long-distance 'phone to the Providence correspondent of Hatch's paper. What he said or what he learned there was not revealed to the wondering reporter, but he came out after several minutes, only to re-enter the booth and remain for another half an hour.

"Now," he said.

Together they went to the haunted house. At the entrance to the grounds something else occurred to The Thinking Machine.

"Run over to the 'phone and call Weston," he directed. "Ask him if he has a motor-boat or if his cousin has one. We might need one. Also find out what kind of a boat it is—electric or gasoline."

Hatch returned to the village and left the scientist alone, sitting on the veranda gazing out over the sea. When Hatch returned he was still in the same position.

"Well?" he asked.

"Ernest Weston has no motor-boat," the reporter informed him.

"George Weston has an electric, but we can't get it because it is away. Maybe I can get one somewhere else if you particularly want it."

"Never mind," said The Thinking Machine. He spoke as if he had entirely lost interest in the matter.

Together they started around the house to the kitchen door.

"What's the next move?" asked Hatch.

"I'm going to find the jewels," was the startling reply.

"Find them?" Hatch repeated.

"Certainly."

They entered the house through the kitchen and the scientist squinted this way and that, through the reception-room, the library, and finally the back hall-way. Here a closed door in the flooring led to a cellar.

In the cellar they found heaps of litter. It was damp and chilly and dark. The Thinking Machine stood in the center, or as near the center as he could stand, because the base of the chimney occupied this precise spot, and apparently did some mental calculation.

From that point he started around the walls, solidly built of stone, stooping and running his fingers along the stones as he walked. He made the entire circuit as Hatch looked on. Then he made it again, but this time with his hands raised above his head, feeling the walls carefully as he went. He repeated this at the chimney, going carefully around the masonry, high and low.

"Dear me, dear me!" he exclaimed, petulantly. "You are taller than I am, Mr. Hatch. Please feel carefully around the top of this chimney base and see if the rocks are all solidly set."

Hatch then began a tour. At last one of the great stones which made this base trembled under his hand.

"It's loose," he said.

"Take it out."

It came out after a deal of tugging.

"Put your hand in there and pull out what you find," was the next order. Hatch obeyed. He found a wooden box, about eight inches square, and handed it to The Thinking Machine.

"Ah!" exclaimed that gentleman.

A quick wrench caused the decaying wood to crumble. Tumbling out of the box were the jewels which had been lost for fifty years.

V

Excitement, long restrained, burst from Hatch in a laugh—almost hysterical. He stooped and gathered up the fallen jewelry and handed it to The Thinking Machine, who stared at him in mild surprise.

"What's the matter?" inquired the scientist.

"Nothing," Hatch assured him, but again he laughed.

The heavy stone which had been pulled out of place was lifted up and forced back into position, and together they returned to the village, with the long-lost jewelry loose in their pockets.

"How did you do it?" asked Hatch.

"Two and two always make four," was the enigmatic reply. "It was merely a sum in addition." There was a pause as they walked on, then: "Don't say anything about finding this, or even hint at it in any way, until you have my permission to do so."

Hatch had no intention of doing so. In his mind's eye he saw a story, a great, vivid, startling story spread all over his newspaper about flaming phantoms and treasure trove—$100,000 in jewels. It staggered him. Of course he would say nothing about it—even hint at it, yet. But when he did say something about it——!

In the village The Thinking Machine found the constable.

"I understand some blood was thrown on you at the Weston place the other night?"

"Yes. Blood—warm blood."

"You wiped it off with your handkerchief?"

"Yes."

"Have you the handkerchief?"

"I suppose I might get it," was the doubtful reply. "It might have gone into the wash."

"Astute person," remarked The Thinking Machine. "There might have been a crime and you throw away the one thing which would indicate it—the blood stains."

The constable suddenly took notice.

"By ginger!" he said. "Wait here and I'll go see if I can find it."

He disappeared and returned shortly with the handkerchief. There were half a dozen blood stains on it, now dark brown.

The Thinking Machine dropped into the village drug store and had a short conversation with the owner, after which he disappeared into the compounding room at the back and remained for an hour or more—until darkness set in. Then he came out and joined Hatch, who, with the constable, had been waiting.

The reporter did not ask any questions, and The Thinking Machine volunteered no information.

"Is it too late for anyone to get down from Boston to-night?" he asked the constable.

"No. He could take the eight o'clock train and be here about half-past nine."

"Mr. Hatch, will you wire to Mr. Weston—Ernest Weston—and ask him to come to-night, sure. Impress on him the fact that it is a matter of the greatest importance."

Instead of telegraphing, Hatch went to the telephone and spoke to Weston at his club. The trip would interfere with some other plans, the broker explained, but he would come. The Thinking Machine had meanwhile been conversing with the constable and had given some sort of instructions which evidently amazed that official exceedingly, for he kept repeating "By ginger!" with considerable fervor.

"And not one word or hint of it to anyone," said The Thinking Machine. "Least of all to the members of your family."

"By ginger!" was the response, and the constable went to supper.

The Thinking Machine and Hatch had their supper thoughtfully that evening in the little village "hotel." Only once did Hatch break this silence.

"You told me to see Weston's handwriting," he said. "Of course you knew he was with the constable and myself when we saw the THING, therefore it would have been impossible——"

"Nothing is impossible," broke in The Thinking Machine. "Don't say that, please."

"I mean that, as he was with us——"

"We'll end the ghost story to-night," interrupted the scientist.

Ernest Weston arrived on the nine-thirty train and had a long, earnest conversation with The Thinking Machine, while Hatch was permitted to cool his toes in solitude. As last they joined the reporter.

"Take a revolver by all means," instructed The Thinking Machine.

"Do you think that necessary?" asked Weston.

"It is—absolutely," was the emphatic response.

Weston left them after awhile. Hatch wondered where he had gone, but no information was forthcoming. In a general sort of way he knew that The Thinking Machine was to go to the haunted house, but he didn't know when; he didn't even know if he was to accompany him.

At last they started, The Thinking Machine swinging a hammer he had borrowed from his landlord. The night was perfectly black, even the road at their feet was invisible. They stumbled frequently as they walked on up the cliff toward the house, dimly standing out against the sky. They entered by way of the kitchen, passed through to the stairs in the main hall, and there Hatch indicated in the darkness the spot from which he had twice seen the flaming phantom.

"You go in the drawing-room behind here," The Thinking Machine instructed. "Don't make any noise whatever."

For hours they waited, neither seeing the other. Hatch heard his heart thumping heavily; if only he could see the other man; with an effort he recovered from a rapidly growing nervousness and waited, waited. The Thinking Machine sat perfectly rigid on the stair, the hammer in his right hand, squinting steadily through the darkness.

At last he heard a noise, a slight nothing; it might almost have been his imagination. It was as if something had glided across the floor, and he was more alert than ever. Then came the dread misty light in the reception-hall, or was it in the library? He could not say. But he looked, looked, with every sense alert.

Gradually the light grew and spread, a misty whiteness which was unmistakably light, but which did not illuminate anything around it. The Thinking Machine saw it without the tremor of a nerve; saw the mistiness grow more marked in certain places, saw these lines gradually grow into the figure of a person, a person who was the center of a white light.

Then the mistiness fell away and The Thinking Machine saw the outline in bold relief. It was that of a tall figure, clothed in a robe, with head covered by a sort of hood, also luminous. As The Thinking Machine looked he saw an arm raised, and in the hand he saw a dagger. The attitude of the figure was distinctly a threat. And yet The Thinking Machine had not begun to grow nervous; he was only interested.

As he looked, the other hand of the apparition was raised and seemed to point directly at him. It moved through the air in bold sweeps, and The Thinking Machine saw the word "Death," written in air luminously, swimming before his eyes. Then he blinked incredulously. There came a wild, demoniacal shriek of laughter from somewhere. Slowly, slowly the scientist crept down the steps in his stocking feet, silent as the apparition itself, with the hammer still in his hand. He crept on, on toward the figure. Hatch, not knowing the movements of The Thinking Machine, stood waiting for something, he didn't know what. Then the thing he had been waiting for happened. There was a sudden loud clatter as of broken glass, the phantom and writing faded, crumbled up, disappeared, and somewhere in the old house there was the hurried sound of steps. At last the reporter heard his name called quietly. It was The Thinking Machine.

"Mr. Hatch, come here."

The reporter started, blundering through the darkness toward the point whence the voice had come. Some irresistible thing swept down upon him; a crashing blow descended on his head, vivid lights flashed before his eyes; he fell. After awhile, from a great distance, it seemed, he heard faintly a pistol shot.

VI

When Hatch fully recovered consciousness it was with the flickering light of a match in his eyes—a match in the hand of The Thinking Machine, who squinted anxiously at him as he grasped his left wrist. Hatch, instantly himself again, sat up suddenly.

"What's the matter?" he demanded.

"How's your head?" came the answering question.

"Oh," and Hatch suddenly recalled those incidents which had immediately preceded the crash on his head. "Oh, it's all right, my head, I mean. What happened?"

"Get up and come along," requested The Thinking Machine, tartly. "There's a man shot down here."

Hatch arose and followed the slight figure of the scientist through the front door, and toward the water. A light glimmered down near the water and was dimly reflected; above, the clouds had cleared somewhat and the moon was struggling through.

"What hit me, anyhow?" Hatch demanded, as they went. He rubbed his head ruefully.

"The ghost," said the scientist. "I think probably he has a bullet in him now—the ghost."

Then the figure of the town constable separated itself from the night and approached.

"Who's that?"

"Professor Van Dusen and Mr. Hatch."

"Mr. Weston got him all right," said the constable, and there was satisfaction in his tone. "He tried to come out the back way, but I had that fastened, as you told me, and he came through the front way. Mr. Weston tried to stop him, and he raised the knife to stick him; then Mr. Weston shot. It broke his arm, I think. Mr. Weston is down there with him now."

The Thinking Machine turned to the reporter.

"Wait here for me, with the constable," he directed. "If the man is hurt he needs attention. I happen to be a doctor; I can aid him. Don't come unless I call."

For a long while the constable and the reporter waited. The constable talked, talked with all the bottled-up vigor of days. Hatch listened impatiently; he was eager to go down there where The Thinking Machine and Weston and the phantom were.

After half an hour the light disappeared, then he heard the swift, quick churning of waters, a sound as of a powerful motor-boat maneuvering, and a long body shot out on the waters.

"All right down there?" Hatch called.

"All right," came the response.

There was again silence, then Ernest Weston and The Thinking Machine came up.

"Where is the other man?" asked Hatch.

"The ghost—where is he?" echoed the constable.

"He escaped in the motor-boat," replied Mr. Weston, easily.

"Escaped?" exclaimed Hatch and the constable together.

"Yes, escaped," repeated The Thinking Machine, irritably. "Mr. Hatch, let's go to the hotel."

Struggling with a sense of keen disappointment, Hatch followed the other two men silently. The constable walked beside him, also silent. At last they reached the hotel and bade the constable, a sadly puzzled, bewildered and crestfallen man, goodnight.

"By ginger!" he remarked, as he walked away into the dark.

Upstairs the three men sat, Hatch impatiently waiting to hear the story. Weston lighted a cigarette and lounged back; The Thinking Machine sat with finger tips pressed together, studying the ceiling.

"Mr. Weston, you understand, of course, that I came into this thing to aid Mr. Hatch?" he asked.

"Certainly," was the response. "I will only ask a favor of him when you conclude."

The Thinking Machine changed his position slightly, readjusted his thick glasses for a long, comfortable squint, and told the story, from the beginning, as he always told a story. Here it is:

"Mr. Hatch came to me in a state of abject, cringing fear and told me of the mystery. It would be needless to go over his examination of the house, and all that. It is enough to say that he noted and told me of four large mirrors in the dining-room and living-room of the house; that he heard and brought to me the stories in detail of a tragedy in the old house and missing jewels, valued at a hundred thousand dollars, or more.

"He told me of his trip to the house that night, and of actually seeing the phantom. I have found in the past that Mr. Hatch is a cool, level-headed young man, not given to imagining things which are not there, and controls himself well. Therefore I knew that anything of charlatanism must be clever, exceedingly clever, to bring about such a condition of mind in him.

"Mr. Hatch saw, as others had seen, the figure of a phantom in the reception-room near the door of the library, or in the library near the door of the reception-room, he couldn't tell exactly. He knew it was near the door. Preceding the appearance of the figure he heard a slight noise which he attributed to a rat running across the floor. Yet the house had not been occupied for five years. Rodents rarely remain in a house—I may say never—for that long if it is uninhabited. Therefore what was this noise? A noise made by the apparition itself? How?

"Now, there is only one white light of the kind Mr. Hatch described known to science. It seems almost superfluous to name it. It is phosphorus, compounded with Fuller's earth and glycerine and one or two other chemicals, so it will not instantly flame as it does in the pure state when exposed to air. Phosphorus has a very pronounced odor if one is within, say, twenty feet of it. Did Mr. Hatch smell anything? No.

"Now, here we have several facts, these being that the apparition in appearing made a slight noise; that phosphorus was the luminous quality; that Mr. Hatch did not smell phosphorus even when he ran through the spot where the phantom had appeared. Two and two make four; Mr. Hatch saw phosphorus, passed through the spot where he had seen it, but did not smell it, therefore it was not there.

It was a reflection he saw—a reflection of phosphorus. So far, so good.

"Mr. Hatch saw a finger lifted and write a luminous word in the air. Again he did not actually see this; he saw a reflection of it. This first impression of mine was substantiated by the fact that when he rushed for the phantom *a part of it* disappeared, first half of it, he said—then the other half. So his extended hands grasped only air.

"Obviously those reflections had been made on something, probably a mirror as the most perfect ordinary reflecting surface. Yet he actually passed through the spot where he had seen the apparition and had not struck a mirror. He found himself in another room, the library, having gone through a door which, that afternoon, he had himself closed. He did not open it then.

"Instantly a sliding mirror suggested itself to me to fit all these conditions. He saw the apparition in the door, then saw only half of it, then all of it disappeared. He passed through the spot where it had been. All of this would have happened easily if a large mirror, working as a sliding door, and hidden in the wall, were there. Is it clear?"

"Perfectly," said Mr. Weston.

"Yes," said Hatch, eagerly. "Go on."

"This sliding mirror, too, might have made the noise which Mr. Hatch imagined was a rat. Mr. Hatch had previously told me of four large mirrors in the living- and dining-rooms. With these, from the position in which he said they were, I readily saw how the reflection could have been made.

"In a general sort of way, in my own mind, I had accounted for the phantom. Why was it there? This seemed a more difficult problem. It was possible that it had been put there for amusement, but I did not wholly accept this. Why? Partly because no one had ever heard of it until the Italian workmen went there. Why did it appear just at the moment they went to begin the work Mr. Weston had ordered? Was it the purpose to keep the workmen away?

"These questions arose in my mind in order. Then, as Mr. Hatch had told me of a tragedy in the house and hidden jewels, I asked him to learn more of these. I called his attention to the fact that it would be a queer circumstance if these jewels were still somewhere in the old house. Suppose some one who knew of their existence were searching for them, believed he could find them, and wanted something which would effectually drive away any inquiring persons, tramps or villagers, who might appear there at night. A ghost? Perhaps.

"Suppose some one wanted to give the old house such a reputation that Mr. Weston would not care to undertake the work of repair and refurnishing. A ghost? Again perhaps. In a shallow mind this ghost might have been interpreted even as an effort to prevent the marriage of Miss Everard and Mr. Weston. Therefore Mr. Hatch was instructed to get all the facts possible about you, Mr. Weston, and members of your family. I reasoned that members of your own family would be more likely to know of the lost jewels than anyone else after a lapse of fifty years.

"Well, what Mr. Hatch learned from you and your cousin, George Weston, instantly, in my mind, established a motive for the ghost. It was, as I had supposed possible, an effort to drive workmen away, perhaps only for a time, while a search was made for the jewels. The old tragedy in the house was a good pretext to hang a ghost on. A clever mind conceived it and a clever mind put it into operation.

"Now, what one person knew most about the jewels? Your cousin George, Mr. Weston. Had he recently acquired any new information as to these jewels? I didn't know. I thought it possible. Why? On his own statement that his mother, then a bride, got the story of the entire affair direct from his grandmother, who remembered more of it than anybody else—who might even have heard his grandfather say where he intended hiding the jewels."

The Thinking Machine paused for a little while, shifted his position, then went on:

"George Weston refused to go with you, Mr. Weston, and Mr. Hatch, to the ghost party, as you called it, because he said he was going to a ball in Providence that night. He did not go to Providence; I learned that from your correspondent there, Mr. Hatch; so George Weston might, possibly, have gone to the ghost party after all.

"After I looked over the situation down there it occurred to me that the most feasible way for a person, who wished to avoid being seen in the village, as the perpetrator of the ghost did, was to go to and from the place at night in a motor-boat. He could easily run in the dark and land at the foot of the cliff, and no soul in the village would be any the wiser. Did George Weston have a motor-boat? Yes, an electric, which runs almost silently.

"From this point the entire matter was comparatively simple. I *knew*—the pure logic of it told me—how the ghost was made to appear and disappear; one look at the house inside convinced me beyond all doubt. I knew the motive for the ghost—a search for the jewels. I knew, or thought I knew, the name of the man who was seeking the jewels; the man who had fullest knowledge and fullest opportunity, the man whose brain was clever enough to devise the scheme. Then, the next step to prove what I knew. The first thing to do was to find the jewels."

"Find the jewels?" Weston repeated, with a slight smile.

"Here they are," said The Thinking Machine, quietly.

And there, before the astonished eyes of the broker, he drew out the gems which had been lost for fifty years. Mr. Weston was not amazed; he was petrified with astonishment and sat staring at the glittering heap in silence. Finally he recovered his voice.

"How did you do it?" he demanded. "Where?"

"I used my brain, that's all," was the reply. "I went into the old house seeking them where the owner, under all conditions, would have been most likely to hide them, and there I found them."

"But—but——" stammered the broker.

"The man who hid these jewels hid them only temporarily, or at least that was his purpose," said The Thinking Machine, irritably. "Naturally he would not hide them in the woodwork of the house, because that might burn; he did not bury them in the cellar, because that has been carefully searched. Now, in that house there is nothing except woodwork and chimneys above the cellar. Yet he hid them in the house, proven by the fact that the man he killed was killed in the house, and that the outside ground, covered with snow, showed two sets of tracks into the house and none out. Therefore he did hide them in the cellar. Where? In the stonework. There was no other place.

"Naturally he would not hide them on a level with the eye, because the spot where he took out and replaced a stone would be apparent if a close search were made. He would, therefore, place them either above or below eye level. He placed them above. A large loose stone in the chimney was taken out and there was the box with these things."

Mr. Weston stared at The Thinking Machine with a new wonder and admiration in his eyes.

"With the jewels found and disposed of, there remained only to prove the ghost theory by an actual test. I sent for you, Mr. Weston, because I thought possibly, as no actual crime had been committed, it would be better to leave the guilty man to you. When you came

I went into the haunted house with a hammer—an ordinary hammer
—and waited on the steps.

"At last the ghost laughed and appeared. I crept down the steps
where I was sitting in my stocking feet. I knew what it was. Just
when I reached the luminous phantom I disposed of it for all time
by smashing it with a hammer. It shattered a large sliding mirror
which ran in the door inside the frame, as I had thought. The crash
startled the man who operated the ghost from the top of a box,
giving it the appearance of extreme height, and he started out through
the kitchen, as he had entered. The constable had barred that door
after the man entered; therefore the ghost turned and came toward
the front door of the house. There he ran into and struck down Mr.
Hatch, and ran out through the front door, which I afterwards
found was not securely fastened. You know the rest of it; how you
found the motor-boat and waited there for him; how he came there,
and——"

"Tried to stab me," Weston supplied. "I had to shoot to save
myself."

"Well, the wound is trivial," said The Thinking Machine. "His
arm will heal up in a little while. I think then, perhaps, a little trip
of four or five years in Europe, at your expense, in return for the
jewels, might restore him to health."

"I was thinking of that myself," said the broker, quietly. "Of
course, I couldn't prosecute."

"The ghost, then, was——?" Hatch began.

"George Weston, my cousin," said the broker. "There are some
things in this story which I hope you may see fit to leave unsaid, if
you can do so with justice to yourself."

Hatch considered it.

"I think there are," he said, finally, and he turned to The Thinking Machine. "Just where was the man who operated the phantom?"

"In the dining-room, beside the butler's pantry," was the reply.
"With that pantry door closed he put on the robe already covered
with phosphorus, and merely stepped out. The figure was reflected
in the tall mirror directly in front, as you enter the dining-room
from the back, from there reflected to the mirror on the opposite
wall in the living-room, and thence reflected to the sliding mirror
in the door which led from the reception-hall to the library. This
is the one I smashed."

"And how was the writing done?"

"Oh, that? Of course that was done by reversed writing on a piece of clear glass held before the apparition as be posed. This made it read straight to anyone who might see the last reflection in the reception-hall."

"And the blood thrown on the constable and the others when the ghost was in the yard?" Hatch went on.

"Was from a dog. A test I made in the drug store showed that. It was a desperate effort to drive the villagers away and keep them away. The ghost cat and the tying of the watchman to his bed were easily done."

All sat silent for a time. At length Mr. Weston arose, thanked the scientist for the recovery of the jewels, bade them all good-night and was about to go out. Mechanically Hatch was following. At the door he turned back for the last question.

"How was it that the shot the constable fired didn't break the mirror?"

"Because he was nervous and the bullet struck the door beside the mirror," was the reply. "I dug it out with a knife. Good night."

THE PROBLEM OF THE STOLEN RUBENS

Matthew Kale made fifty million dollars out of axle grease, after which he began to patronize the high arts. It was simple enough: he had the money, and Europe had the old masters. His method of buying was simplicity itself. There were five thousand square yards, more or less, in the huge gallery of his marble mansion which were to be covered, so he bought five thousand yards, more or less, of art. Some of it was good, some of it fair, and much of it bad. The chief picture of the collection was a Rubens, which he had picked up in Rome for fifty thousand dollars.

Soon after acquiring his collection, Kale decided to make certain alterations in the vast room where the pictures hung. They were all taken down and stored in the ball room, equally vast, with their faces toward the wall. Meanwhile Kale and his family took refuge in a nearby hotel.

It was at this hotel that Kale met Jules de Lesseps. De Lesseps was distinctly French, the sort of Frenchman whose conversation resembles callisthenics. He was nervous, quick, and agile, and he told Kale in confidence that he was not only a painter himself, he was a connoisseur in the high arts. Pompous in the pride of possession, Kale went to a good deal of trouble to exhibit his private collection for de Lesseps's delectation. It happened in the ball room, and the true artist's delight shone in the Frenchman's eyes as he handled the pieces which were good. Some of the others made him smile, but it was an inoffensive sort of smile.

With his own hands Kale lifted the precious Rubens and held it before the Frenchman's eyes. It was a Madonna and Child, one of those wonderful creations which have endured through the years with all the sparkle and color beauty of their pristine days. Kale seemed disappointed because de Lesseps was not particularly enthusiastic about the picture.

"Why, it's a Rubens!" he exclaimed.

"Yes, I see," replied de Lesseps.

"It cost me fifty thousand dollars."

"It is perhaps worth more than that," and the Frenchman shrugged his shoulders as he turned away.

Kale looked at him in chagrin. Could it be that de Lesseps did not understand that it was a Rubens, and that Rubens was a painter? Or was it that he had failed to hear him say that it cost him fifty thousand dollars? Kale was accustomed to seeing people bob their heads and open their eyes when he said fifty thousand dollars; therefore, "Don't you like it?" he asked.

"Very much indeed," replied de Lesseps; "but I have seen it before. I saw it in Rome just a week or so before you purchased it."

"They rummaged on through the pictures, and at last a Whistler turned up for their inspection. It was one of the famous Thames series, a water color. De Lesseps' face radiated excitement, and several times he glanced from the water color to the Rubens, as if mentally comparing the exquisitely penciled and colored modern work with the bold, masterly technic of the old.

Kale misunderstood the silence. "I don't think much of this one, myself," he explained apologetically. "It's a Whistler, and all that, and it cost me five thousand dollars, and I sort of had to have it, but still it isn't just the kind of thing that I like. What do you think of it?"

"I think it is perfectly wonderful," replied the Frenchman enthusiastically. "It is the essence, the superlative of modern work. I wonder if it would be possible," and he turned to face Kale, "for me to make a copy of that? I have some slight skill in painting myself, and dare say I could make a fairly creditable copy of it."

Kale was flattered. He was more and more impressed each moment with the picture. "Why, certainly," he replied. "I will have it sent up to the hotel, and you can——"

"No, no, no!" interrupted de Lesseps quickly. "I wouldn't care to accept the responsibility of having the picture in my charge. There is always the danger of fire. But if you would give me permission to come here—this room is large and airy and light, and besides it is quiet——"

"Just as you like," said Kale magnanimously. "I merely thought the other way would be most convenient for you."

De Lesseps drew near, and laid one hand on the millionaire's arm. "My dear friend," he said earnestly, "if these pictures were my pictures, I shouldn't try to accommodate anybody where they were concerned. I dare say the collection as it stands cost you——"

"Six hundred and eighty-seven thousand dollars," volunteered Kale proudly.

"And surely they must be well protected here in your house during your absence?"

"There are about twenty servants in the house while the workmen are making the alterations," said Kale, "and three of them don't do anything but watch this room. No one can go in or out except by the door we entered—the others are locked and barred—and then only with my permission, or a written order from me. No, sir, nobody can get away with anything in this room."

"Excellent—excellent!" said de Lesseps admiringly. He smiled a little bit. "I am afraid I did not give you credit for being the far-sighted business man that you are." He turned and glanced over the collection of pictures abstractedly. "A clever thief, though," he ventured, "might cut a valuable painting, for instance the Rubens, out of the frame, roll it up, conceal it under his coat and escape."

Kale laughed pleasantly and shook his head.

It was a couple of days later at the hotel that de Lesseps brought up the subject of copying the Whistler. He was profuse in his thanks when Kale volunteered to accompany him to the mansion and witness the preliminary stages of the work. They paused at the ballroom door.

"Jennings," said Kale to the liveried servant there, "this is Mr. de Lesseps. He is to come and go as he likes. He is going to do some work in the ballroom here. See that he isn't disturbed."

De Lesseps noticed the Rubens leaning carelessly against some other pictures, with the holy face of the Madonna toward them. "Really, Mr. Kale," he protested, "that picture is too valuable to be left about like that. If you will let your servants bring me some canvas, I shall wrap it and place it up on the table here off the floor. Suppose there were mice here?"

Kale thanked him. The necessary orders were given, and finally the picture was carefully wrapped and placed beyond harm's reach, whereupon de Lesseps adjusted himself, paper, easel, stool and all, and began his work of copying. There Kale left him.

Three days later Kale just happened to drop in, and found the artist still at his labor.

"I just dropped by," he explained, "to see how the work in the gallery was coming along. It will be finished in another week. I hope I am not disturbing you."

"Not at all," said de Lesseps. "I have nearly finished. See how I am getting along?" He turned the easel toward Kale.

The millionaire gazed from that toward the original which stood on a chair near by, and frank admiration for the artist's efforts was in his eyes. "Why, it's fine!" he exclaimed. "It's just as good as the other one, and I bet you don't want any five thousand dollars for it, eh?"

That was all that was said about it at the time. Kale wandered about the house for an hour or so, then dropped into the ballroom where the artist was just getting his paraphernalia together, and they walked back to the hotel. The artist carried under one arm his copy of the Whistler, loosely rolled up.

Another week passed and the workman who had been engaged in refinishing and decorating the gallery had gone. De Lesseps volunteered to assist in the work of rehanging the pictures, and Kale gladly turned the matter over to him. It was in the afternoon of the day this work began that de Lesseps, chatting pleasantly with Kale, ripped loose the canvas which enshrouded the precious Rubens. Then he paused with an exclamation of dismay. The picture was gone; the frame which had held it was empty. A thin strip of canvas around the inside edge showed that a sharp penknife had been used to cut out the painting.

All of these facts came to the attention of Professor Augustus S. F. X. Van Dusen—The Thinking Machine. This was a day or so after Kale had rushed into Detective Mallory's office at police headquarters, with the statement that his Rubens had been stolen. He banged his fist down on the detective's desk and roared at him.

"It cost me fifty thousand dollars!" he declared violently. "Why don't you do something? What are you sitting there staring at me for?"

"Don't excite yourself, Mr. Kale," the detective advised. "I will put my men at work right now to recover the—the—— What is a Rubens, anyway?"

"It's a picture!" bellowed Mr. Kale. "A piece of canvas with some paint on it, and it cost me fifty thousand dollars—don't you forget that!"

So the police machinery was set in motion to recover the painting.

And in time the matter fell under the watchful eye of Hutchinson Hatch, reporter. He learned the facts preceding the disappearance of the picture, and then called on de Lesseps. He found the artist in a state of excitement bordering on hysteria; an intimation from the reporter of the object of his visit caused de Lesseps to burst into words.

"*Mon dieu!* It is outrageous!" he exclaimed. "What can I do? I was the only one in the room for several days. I was the one who took such pains to protect the picture. And now it is gone! The loss is irreparable. What can I do?"

Hatch didn't have any very definite idea as to just what he could do, so he let him go on. "As I understand it, Mr. de Lesseps," he interrupted at last, "no one else was in the room, except you and Mr. Kale, all the time you were there?"

"No one else."

"And I think Mr. Kale said that you were making a copy of some famous water color, weren't you?"

"Yes, a Thames scene. By Whistler," was the reply. "That is it, hanging over the mantel."

Hatch glanced at the picture admiringly. It was an exquisite copy, and showed the deft touch of a man who was himself an artist of great ability.

De Lesseps read the admiration in his face. "It is not bad," he said modestly. "I studied with Carolus Duran."

With all else that was known, and this little additional information, which seemed of no particular value to the reporter, the entire matter was laid before The Thinking Machine. That distinguished man listened from beginning to end without comment.

"Who had access to the room?" he asked finally.

"That is what the police are working on now," was the reply. "There are a couple of dozen servants in the house, and I suppose in spite of Kale's rigid orders there was a certain laxity in their enforcement."

"Of course that makes it more difficult," said The Thinking Machine in the perpetually irritated voice which was so distinctly a part of himself. "Perhaps it would be best for us to go to Mr. Kale's home and personally investigate."

Kale received them with the reserve which all rich men show in the presence of representatives of the press. He stared frankly and somewhat curiously at the diminutive figure of the scientist, who explained the object of their visit.

"I guess you fellows can't do anything with them," the millionaire assured them. "I've got some regular detectives on it."

"Is Mr. Mallory here now?" asked The Thinking Machine curtly.

"Yes, he is upstairs in the servants quarters."

"May we see the room from which the picture was taken?" inquired the scientist with a suave intonation which Hatch knew well.

Kale granted the permission with a wave of his hand and ushered them into the ballroom, where the pictures had been stored. From the relative center of the room The Thinking Machine surveyed it all. The windows were high. Half a dozen doors leading out into the hallways, to the conservatory, and quiet nooks of the mansion offered innumerable possibilities of access. After this one long comprehensive squint, The Thinking Machine went over and picked up the frame from which the Rubens had been cut. For a long time he examined it. Kale's impatience was painfully evident. Finally the scientist turned to him.

"How well do you know Mr. de Lesseps?" he asked.

"I've known him only for a month or so. Why?"

"Did he bring you letters of introduction, or did you meet him casually?"

Kale regarded him with evident displeasure. "My own personal affairs have nothing whatever to do with this matter," he said pointedly. "Mr. de Lesseps is a gentleman of integrity and certainly he is the last whom I would suspect of any connection with the disappearance of the picture."

"That is usually the case," remarked The Thinking Machine tartly. He turned to Hatch. "Just how good a copy was that he made of the Whistler picture?" he asked.

"I have never seen the original," Hatch replied, "but the workmanship was superb. Perhaps Mr. Kale wouldn't object to our seeing——"

"Oh, of course not," said Kale resignedly. "Come in. It's in the gallery."

Hatch submitted the picture to a careful scrutiny. "I should say that the copy is well nigh perfect," was his verdict. "Of course, in its absence, I couldn't say exactly, but it is certainly a superb piece of work."

The curtains of a wide door almost in front of them were thrown aside suddenly, and Detective Mallory entered. He carried something in his hand, but at the sight of them, concealed it behind himself. Unrepressed triumph was in his face.

"Ah, professor, we meet often, don't we?" he said.

"This reporter here and his friend seem to be trying to drag de Lesseps into this affair somehow," Kale complained to the detective. "I don't want anything like that to happen. He is liable to go out and print anything. They always do."

The Thinking Machine glared at him unwaveringly straight in the eye for an instant, then extended his hand toward Mallory. "Where did you find it?" he asked.

"Sorry to disappoint you, professor," said the detective sarcastically, "but this is the time when you were a little late," and he produced the object which he held behind him. "Here is your picture, Mr. Kale."

Kale gasped a little in relief and astonishment, and held up the canvas with both hands to examine it. "Fine!" he told the detective. "I'll see that you don't lose anything by this. Why, that thing cost me fifty thousand dollars!" Kale didn't seem able to get over that.

The Thinking Machine leaned forward to squint at the upper right hand corner of the canvas. "Where did you find it?" he asked again.

"Rolled up tight and concealed in the bottom of a trunk in the room of one of the servants," explained Mallory. "The servant's name is Jennings. He is now under arrest."

"Jennings!" exclaimed Kale. "Why, he has been with me for years."

"Did he confess?" asked the scientist imperturbably.

"Of course not," said Mallory. "He says some of the other servants must have put it there."

The Thinking Machine nodded at Hatch. "I think perhaps that is all," he remarked. "I congratulate you, Mr. Mallory, upon bringing the matter to such a quick and satisfactory conclusion."

Ten minutes later they left the house and caught a car for the scientist's home. Hatch was a little chagrined at the unexpected termination of the affair, and was thoughtfully silent for a time.

"Mallory does occasionally show a gleam of human intelligence, doesn't he?" he said at last, quizzically.

"Not that I ever noticed," remarked the scientist.

"But he found the picture," Hatch insisted.

"Of course he found it. It was put there for him to find."

"Put there for him to find," repeated the reporter. "Didn't Jennings steal it?"

"If he did, he's a fool."

"Well, if he didn't steal it, who put it there?"

"De Lesseps."

"De Lesseps!" echoed Hatch. "Why the deuce did he steal a fifty-thousand dollar picture and put it in a servant's trunk to be found?"

The Thinking Machine twisted around in his seat and squinted at him oddly for a moment. "At times, Mr. Hatch, I am absolutely amazed at your stupidity," he said frankly. "I can understand it in a man like Mallory, but I have always given you credit for being an astute, quick-witted man."

Hatch smiled at the reproach. It was not the first time he had heard of it. But nothing bearing on the problem in hand was said until they reached The Thinking Machine's apartments.

"The only real question in my mind, Mr. Hatch," said the scientist then, "is whether or not I should take the trouble to restore Mr. Kale's picture at all. He is perfectly satisfied, and will probably never know the difference. So——"

Suddenly Hatch saw something. "Great Scott!" he exclaimed. "Do you mean that the picture that Mallory found was——"

"A copy of the original," finished The Thinking Machine. "Personally I know nothing whatever about art, therefore, I could not say from observation that it is a copy, but I know it from the logic of the thing. When the original was cut from the frame, the knife swerved a little at the upper right hand corner. The canvas remaining in the frame told me that. The picture that Mr. Mallory found did not correspond in this detail with the canvas in the frame The conclusion is obvious."

"And de Lesseps has the original?"

"De Lesseps has the original. How did he get it? In any one of a dozen ways. He might have rolled it up and stuck it under his coat. He might have had a confederate, but I don't think that any ordinary method of theft would have appealed to him. I am giving him credit for being clever, as I must when we review the whole case——

"For instance, he asked for permission to copy the Whistler, which you saw was the same size as the Rubens. It was granted. He copied it practically under guard, always with the chance that Mr. Kale himself would drop in. It took him three days to copy it,

so he says. He was alone in the room all that time. He knew that
Mr. Kale had not the faintest idea of art. Taking advantage of that,
what would have been simpler than to have copied the Rubens in
oil? He could have removed it from the frame immediately after he
canvassed it over, and kept it in a position near him where it could
be quickly covered if he was interrupted. Remember, the picture is
worth fifty thousand dollars, therefore was worth the trouble.

"De Lesseps is an artist—we know that—and dealing with a man
who knew nothing whatever of art, he had no fears. We may
suppose his idea all along was to use the copy of the Rubens as a
sort of decoy after he got away with the original. You saw that
Mallory didn't know the difference and it was safe for de Lesseps
to suppose that Mr. Kale wouldn't, either. His only danger until he
could get away gracefully was of some critic or connoisseur, perhaps,
seeing the copy. His boldness we see readily in the fact that he
permitted himself to discover the theft, that he discovered it after
he had volunteered to assist Mr. Kale in the general work of rehanging the pictures in the gallery. Just how he put the picture in
Jenning's trunk, I don't happen to know. We can imagine many
ways——" He lay back in his chair for a minute without speaking,
eyes steadily turned upward, fingers placed precisely tip to tip.

"The only thing remaining is to go get the picture. It is in de
Lesseps's room now—you told me that—and so we know it is safe.
I dare say he knows that if he tried to run away, it would inevitably
put him under suspicion."

"But how did he take the picture from the Kale home?" asked
Hatch.

"He took it with him probably under his arm the day he left the
house with Mr. Kale," was the astonishing reply.

Hatch stared at him in amazement. After a moment the scientist
rose and passed into the adjoining room, and the telephone bell
there jingled. When he joined Hatch again, he picked up his hat
and they went out together.

De Lesseps was in when their cards went up, and received them.
They conversed of the case generally for ten minutes, while the
scientist's eyes were turned inquiringly here and there about the
room. At last there came a knock on the door.

"It is Detective Mallory, Mr. Hatch," remarked The Thinking
Machine. "Open the door for him."

De Lesseps seemed startled for just one instant, then quickly recovered. Mallory's eyes were full of questions when he entered.

"I should like, Mr. Mallory," began The Thinking Machine quietly, "to call your attention to this copy of Mr. Kale's picture by Whistler—over the mantel here. Isn't it excellent? You have seen the original?"

Mallory grunted. De Lesseps's face, instead of expressing appreciation at the compliment, blanched suddenly, and his hands closed tightly. Again he recovered himself and smiled.

"The beauty of this picture lies not only in its faithfulness to the original," the scientist went on, "but also in the fact that it was painted under extraordinary circumstances. For instance, I don't know if you know, Mr. Mallory, that it is possible so to combine glue and putty and a few other commonplace things into a paste which would effectively blot out an oil painting and offer at the same time an excellent surface for water-color work."

There was a moment's pause, during which the three men stared at him silently—with singularly conflicting emotions depicted on their faces.

"This water color—this copy of Whistler," continued the scientist evenly, "is painted on such a paste as I have described. That paste in turn covers the original Rubens picture. It can be removed with water without damage to the picture, which is in oil, so that instead of a copy of the Whistler painting, we have an original by Rubens, worth fifty thousand dollars. That is true; isn't it, Mr. de Lesseps?"

There was no reply to the question—none was needed. It was an hour later, after de Lesseps was safely in his cell, that Hatch called up The Thinking Machine on the telephone and asked one question.

"How did you know that the water color was painted over the Rubens?"

"Because it was the only absolutely safe way in which the Rubens could be hopelessly lost to those who were looking for it, and at the same time perfectly preserved," was the answer. "I told you de Lesseps was a clever man, and a little logic did the rest. Two and two always makes four, Mr. Hatch, not sometimes, but all the time."

THE MISSING NECKLACE

I

Mr. Bradlee Cunnyngham Leighton was clever. His most ardent enemies admitted that. Scotland Yard, for instance, not only admitted it but insisted on it. It wasn't any half hearted insistence, either, for in the words of Herbert Conway, one of the Yard's chief operators, he was smooth—"so smooth that he made ice feel like sandpaper." Whether or not Mr. Leighton was aware of this delicate compliment does not appear. It was perfectly possible that he was, although he had never mentioned it. He was a well bred gentleman and was aware of many things that he never mentioned.

In his person Mr. Leighton had the distinguished honor of closely resembling the immaculate villain of melodrama. In his mental attainments, however, Scotland Yard gave him credit for being a genius—far beyond the cigarette smoking mummer of crime who is always transparent and is inevitably caught. Mr. Leighton had never been caught. Perhaps that was why Scotland Yard insisted on his cleverness and was prepared to argue the point.

Mr. Leighton went everywhere. At those functions where the highest in the social world met, there was Mr. Leighton. He was on every matron's selected list of guests, a charming addition to any gathering. Scotland Yard knew this. Of course it may have been only the merest chance that he was always present at those functions where valuable jewels had been "lost" or "mislaid." Yet Scotland Yard did not regard it as chance. That it did not was another compliment to Mr. Leighton.

From deep down in its innermost conscience Scotland Yard looked up to Mr. Leighton as the master mind, if not the actual vital instrument, in a long series of baffling jewel robberies. There was a finesse and delicacy—not to mention regularity—about these robberies that annoyed Scotland Yard. Yet believing all this Scotland Yard had never been so indiscreet as to mention the matter to

Mr. Leighton. As a matter of fact Scotland Yard had never seen its way clear to mentioning it to anyone.

Conway had some ideas of his own about Mr. Leighton whom he exalted to a position that would have surprised if not flattered him. Conway perhaps, more nearly expressed the opinion of Scotland Yard in a few brief remarks than I could at greater length.

"He's a crook and the cleverest in the world," he said of Mr. Leighton, almost enthusiastically. "He got the Hemingway jewels, the Cheltenham bracelet and the Quez shiners all right. I *know* he got them. But that doesn't do any good—merely knowing it. I can't put a finger on him because he's too blooming smooth. I think I've got him and then—I haven't."

This was before the Varron necklace affair. When that remarkable episode came to be known to Scotland Yard, Conway's admiration for Mr. Leighton increased immeasurably. He *knew* that Leighton was the responsible one—he knew it in his own head and heart—but that was all. He gnawed his scrubby mustache fiercely and set to work to prove it, feeling beforehand that it was a vain task.

The absolute simplicity of the thing—and in this it was like the others—was its most puzzling feature. Lady Varron had tendered a reception to the United States Ambassador at her London house. She had gathered about her a most distinguished company. There were representatives of England, France and Russia; there were some of the most beautiful women of the continent; there were two American Duchesses; there were a chosen few of the American colony—and Mr. Leighton. It may be well to repeat that he went everywhere.

Lady Varron on this occasion wore the famous Varron necklace. Its intrinsic value was said to be £40,000; associations made it priceless. She was dancing with the American Ambassador when she slipped on the smooth floor and fell, dragging him down with her. It was an undignified, unromantic thing, but it happened. Mr. Leighton chanced to be one of those nearest and rushed to her assistance. In an instant Lady Varron and the Ambassador were the center of a little group. It was Mr. Leighton who lifted Lady Varron to her feet.

"It's nothing," she assured him, smiling uncertainly. "I was a little awkward, that's all."

Mr. Leighton turned to assist the Ambassador but found him standing again and puffing inordinately, then turned back to Lady Varron.

"You dropped your necklace," he remarked blandly.

"My necklace?"

Lady Varron's white hand flew to her bare throat, and she paled a little as Mr. Leighton and others of the group stood back to look for the jewel. It was not to be seen. Lady Varron controlled herself admirably.

"It must have fallen somewhere," she said finally.

"Are you sure you had it on?" asked another guest solicitously.

"Oh, yes," she replied positively, "but I may have dropped it somewhere else."

"I noticed it just before you—we—fell," said the Ambassador. "It must be here."

But it wasn't. In that respect—that is visible non-existence—it resembled the Cheltenham bracelet. Mr. Leighton had, on that occasion, strolled out on the lawn at night with the Honorable Miss Cheltenham and she had dropped the bracelet. That was all. It was never found.

In this Varron affair it would be useless to go into details of what immediately followed the loss of the necklace. It is sufficient to say that it was not found; that men and women stared at each other in bewildered embarrassment and mutual suspicion, and that finally Mr. Leighton, who still stood beside Lady Varron, intimated courteously, tactfully, that a personal search of her guests would not be amiss. He did not say it in so many words but the others understood.

Mr. Leighton was seconded heartily by the American Ambassador, a democratic individual with honest ideas which were foremost when a question of personal integrity was involved. But the search was not made and the reception proceeded. Lady Varron bore her loss marvelously well.

"She's a brick," was the audible compliment of one of the American Duchesses whose father owned $20,000,000 worth of soap somewhere in vague America. "I'd have had a fit if I'd lost a necklace like that."

It was not until next day that Scotland Yard was notified of Lady Varron's loss.

"Leighton there?" was Conway's first question.

"Yes."

"Then he got it," Conway asserted positively. "I'll get him this time or know why."

Yet at the end of a month he neither had him, nor did he know why. He had intercepted messengers, he had opened letters, telegrams, cable dispatches; he had questioned servants; he had taken advantage of the absence of both Mr. Leighton and his valet to search his exquisite apartments. He had done all these things and more—all that a severely conscientious man of his profession could do, and had gnawed his scrubby mustache down to a disreputable ragged line. But of the necklace there was no clue, no trace, nothing.

Then Conway heard that Mr. Leighton was going to the United States for a few months.

"To take the necklace and dispose of it," he declared out of the vexation of his own heart. "If he ever gets aboard ship with it I've got him—either *I've* got him or the United States customs officials will have him."

Conway could not bring himself to believe that Mr. Leighton, with all his cleverness, would dare try to dispose of the pearls in England and he flattered himself that Leighton could not have sent them elsewhere—too close a watch had been kept.

It transpired naturally that when the Boston-bound liner Romanic, sailed from Liverpool four days later not only was Mr. Leighton aboard but Conway was there. He knew Leighton, but was secure in the thought that Leighton did not know him.

On the second day out he was disabused on this point. He was beginning to think that it might not be a bad idea to know Leighton casually so when he noticed that immaculate gentleman alone, leaning on the rail, smoking, he sauntered up and joined him in contemplation of the infinite ocean.

"Beautiful weather," Conway remarked after a long time.

"Yes," replied Leighton as he glanced around and smiled. "I should think you Scotland Yard men would enjoy a junket like this?"

Conway didn't do any such foolish thing as start or show astonishment, whatever he might have felt. Instead he smiled pleasantly.

"I've been working pretty hard on that Varron affair," he said frankly. "And now I'm taking a little vacation."

"Oh, that thing at Lady Varron's?" inquired Leighton lazily. "Indeed? I happened to be the one to notice that the necklace was gone."

"Yes, I know it," responded Conway, grimly.

The conversation drifted to other things. Conway found Leighton an agreeable companion, and a democratic one. They smoked together, walked together and played shuffle-board together. That evening Leighton took a hand at "bridge" in the smoking room. For hours Conway stared at the phosphorescent points in the sinister green waters, and smoked.

"If he did it," he remarked at last, "he's the cleverest scoundrel on earth, and if he did not I'm the biggest fool."

Six bells—eleven o'clock struck. The deck was deserted. Conway stumbled along through the dark toward the smoking room. Inside he saw Leighton still at play. As he paused at the open door he heard Leighton's voice.

"I'll play until two o'clock, not later," it said.

Conway made up his mind instantly. He turned, retraced his steps along the deck to Leighton's room where he stopped. He knew Leighton had not burdened himself with a valet and thought he knew why, so without hesitation he drew out several keys and fumbled at the lock. It yielded at last and he stepped inside the state room, closing the door. His purpose was instantly apparent. It was to search.

Now Conway had his own ideas of just how a search should be conducted. First he took Leighton's wearing apparel and patted and pinched it inch by inch; he squeezed up neckties, unrolled handkerchiefs, examined shirts and crumpled up silken hosiery. Then he took the shoes—half a dozen pairs. He had been suspicious of shoes since he once found a dozen diamonds concealed in false heels. But these heels weren't false.

Next, still without haste or apparent disappointment, he turned his attention to the handbag, the suit case and the steamer trunk, all of which he had emptied. Such things had been known to have false bottoms and secret compartments. These had none. He satisfied himself absolutely on this point by every method known to his art.

In due time his examination came down to the room itself. He unmade the bed and closely felt of and scrutinized the mattress, sheets, blankets, pillows, and coverlid. He took the three drawers from the dressing cabinet and looked behind them. He turned over several English newspapers and shook them one by one. He peered into the water pitcher and fumbled around the plumbing in the tiny bath room adjoining. He examined the carpet to see if anything had been hidden beneath it. Finally he climbed on a chair and from this elevated position looked for a crack or crevice where a necklace or unset pearls could be hidden.

"There are still three possibilities," he told himself at the end as he carefully restored the room to its previous condition. "He might have left them in a package in the ship's safe but that's improbable— too risky; he might have left them in a trunk in the hold, which is still more improbable, or he might have them on his person. That is more than likely."

So Conway went out, extinguishing the light and locking the door behind him. He stepped into his own state room a moment and took a mouthful of whiskey which he spat out again. But it must have had some deep, potent effect for a few minutes later when he appeared in the smoking room he was in a lamentable state of intoxication and exhaled whiskey noticeably. His was a maudlin, thick-tongued condition. Leighton glanced up at him with well-bred reproach.

It may have been only accident that Conway stumbled over Leighton's feet and noted that he wore flat-soled, loose slippers *without heels,* and also accident that he embraced him with exaggerated affection as he struggled to recover his equilibrium.

Be those things as they may, Leighton excused himself good-naturedly from the bridge party and urged Conway to bed. Conway would only agree on condition that Leighton would assist him. Leighton consented cheerfully and they left the smoking room together, Conway clinging to him as the vine to the oak.

Half way down the deck Conway stumbled and fell despite the friendly supporting arm, and in his effort to save himself his hands slid all the way down Leighton's shapely legs. Then he was deposited in his state room and Leighton returned to his cards smiling.

"And he hasn't got them on him," declared Conway enigmatically to the bare walls. He was not intoxicated now.

It was an easy matter next day for him to learn that Leighton had left nothing in the ship's safe and that his four trunks in the hold were inaccessible, being buried under hundreds of others. Whereupon Conway sat down to wait and learn what new and original ideas of searching Uncle Sam's Customs officers had invented.

At last came a morning when the wireless telegraph operator aboard picked up a signal from shore and announced that the Romanic was less than a hundred miles from Boston Light. Later Conway found Leighton leaning on the rail, smoking and gazing shoreward.

It was three hours or so after that that several passengers noticed a motor boat coming toward them. Leighton watched it with idle interest. Finally it circled widely and it became apparent that it was coming alongside the now slow moving liner. When it was only a hundred feet off and the liner was barely creeping along, Leighton grew suddenly interested.

"By Jove," he exclaimed, then shouted: "Hello, Harry!"

"Hello Leighton," came an answering shout. "Heard you were aboard and came out to meet you."

There was a rapid fire of uninteresting pleasantries as the motor boat slid in under the Romanic's lee and bobbed up and down in her wash. The man aboard stood up with a package of newspapers in his hand.

"Here are some American papers for you," he called.

He flung the bundle and Leighton caught it, left the rail and passed into his state room. He returned after a moment with a bundle of European papers—those Conway had previously seen.

"Catch," he called. "There's something in these that will interest you."

The man in the small boat caught the package and dropped it carelessly on a seat.

Then, suddenly, Conway awoke.

"There goes the necklace," he told himself with a start. A quick grasping movement of his hands attracted Leighton's attention and he smiled inscrutably, daringly into the blazing eyes of the Scotland Yard man. The motor boat with a parting shot of "I'll meet you on the wharf" sped away.

Thoughts began to flow rapidly through Conway's fertile brain. Five minutes later he burst in on the wireless operator and sent a long dispatch to officials ashore. Then from the bow rail he watched the motor boat speeding away in the direction of Boston. It drew off about two miles and remained relatively in that position for nearly all the forty miles into Boston Harbor. It spoke no other craft, passed near none in fact while in Conway's sight, which was until it disappeared in Boston Harbor.

An hour later the Romanic was warped in and tied up. Conway was the first man off. He went straight to a man who seemed to be waiting for him.

"Did you search the motor boat?" he demanded.

"Yes," was the reply. "We nearly tore it to pieces, even took it out of the water. We also searched the man on her, Harry Cheshire. You must have been mistaken."

"Are you sure she spoke no one or got rid of the jewels to another vessel?"

"She didn't go near another vessel," was the reply. "I met her at the Harbor mouth and came in with her."

For an instant Conway's face showed disappointment, then came animation again. He was just beginning to get really interested in the affair.

"Do you know the Customs officer in charge?" he asked.

"Yes."

"Introduce me."

There was an introduction and the three men spoke aside for several minutes. The result of it was that when Leighton sauntered down the gang plank he was invited into a private office. He went smilingly and submitted to a search of his person without anger or the slightest trace of uneasiness. As he came out Conway was standing at the door.

"Are you satisfied?" Leighton asked.

"No," blazed Conway, savagely.

"What? Not after searching me twice and my state room once?"

Conway didn't answer. He didn't dare to at the moment, but he stood by when Leighton's four trunks were taken from the hold, and he saw that they were searched with the same minute care that he had given to the state room. At the fruitless end of it he sat down on one of the trunks and stared at Leighton in a sort of admiration.

Leighton stared back for a moment, smiled, nodded pleasantly and strolled up the dock chatting carelessly with Harry Cheshire. Conway made no attempt to follow them. It wasn't worth while— nothing was worth while any more.

"But he *did* get them and he's got them now," he told himself savagely, "or he has disposed of them in some way that I can't find."

II

The Thinking Machine did not seem to regard the problem as at all difficult when it came to his attention a couple of days later. Hutchinson Hatch, reporter, brought it to him. Hatch had some good friends in the Customs office where Conway had told his story. He learned from them that that office had refused to have anything to do with the case, insisting that the Scotland Yard man must be mistaken.

Crushed in spirit, mangled in reputation and taunted by Leighton's final words Conway took a desolate view of life. Momentarily he lost even that bull-dog tenacity which had never before faltered—lost it all except in so far as he still believed that Leighton was *the* man. It was about this time Hatch met him. Would he talk? He was burning to talk; caution was a senseless thing anyway. Then Hatch took him gently by the hand and led him to The Thinking Machine.

Conway unburdened himself at length and with vitriolic emphasis. For an hour he went on while the scientist leaned back in his chair with his great yellow head pillowed on a cushion and squinted aggressively at the ceiling. At the end of the hour The Thinking Machine knew as much of the Varron problem as Conway knew and knew as much of Leighton as any man knew, except Leighton.

"How many stones were in the necklace," the scientist asked.

"One hundred and seventy-two," replied Conway.

"Was the man in the motor boat—Harry Cheshire you call him—an Englishman?"

"Yes, in speech, manner and appearance."

For a long time The Thinking Machine twiddled his fingers while Conway and the reporter sat staring at him impatiently. Hatch knew, from the past, that something tangible, something that led somewhere, would come from that wonderful analytical brain; Conway not knowing, was only hopefully curious. But like most men of his profession he wanted action; sitting down and thinking didn't seem to get anywhere.

"You see, Mr. Conway," said the scientist as last, "you haven't proven anything. Your investigations, as a matter of fact, indicate that Leighton did *not* take the pearls, therefore did not bring them with him. There is only one thing that indicates that he might have. That is the throwing of the newspapers into the motor boat. That one act seems to have been a senseless one, unless——"

"Unless the pearls were concealed in the bundle," interrupted the Scotland Yard man.

"Or unless he was amusing himself at your expense and is perfectly innocent," added The Thinking Machine. "It is perfectly possible that if he were an innocent man and discovered that you were on his track that he has merely made a fool of you. If we take any other view of it we must base it on an assumption which has no established fact to support it. We will have to dispose of every other person who *might* have stolen the necklace and pin it down to Leighton. Further, we will have to assume out of hand that he brought the jewels to this country."

The Scotland Yard man was getting interested.

"That is not good logic, yet when we assume all this for our present purposes the problem is a simple one. And by assuming it we prove that your search of the state room was not thorough. Did you, for instance, happen to look on the *under* side of the slats in the berth? Do you *know* that the necklace, or its unset pearls, did not hang down in the drain pipe from the water bowl?"

Conway snapped his fingers in annoyance. These were two things he had not done.

"There are other possibilities of course," resumed The Thinking Machine, "therefore the search for the necklace was useless. Now we must take for granted that, if they came to this country at all, they came in one of those places and you overlooked them. Obviously Mr. Leighton would not have left them in the trunks in the hold. Therefore we assume further that he hid them in his state room and threw them into the motor boat.

"In that event they were in the motor boat when it left the Romanic and we must believe they were not in it when it docked. Yet the motor boat neither spoke nor approached any other vessel. The jewels were *not* thrown into the water. The man Cheshire could not have swallowed one hundred and seventy-two pearls—or any great part of them—therefore, what have we?"

"Nothing," responded Conway promptly. "That's what's the matter. I've had to give it all up."

"Instead of nothing we have the answer," replied The Thinking Machine tartly. "Let's see. Perhaps I can give you the name and address of the man who has the jewels now, assuming of course that Leighton brought them."

He arose suddenly and passed into the adjoining room. Conway turned and stared at Hatch inquiringly with a queer expression on his face.

"Is he anything of a joker?" he asked.

"No, but he's a good deal of a wonder," replied Hatch.

"Do you mean to say that I have been working on this thing for months and months without learning anything about it and all he's got to do is to go in there and get the name and address of the man who has the necklace?" demanded Conway in bewilderment.

"If he went into that room and said he'd bring back the Pacific

Ocean in a tea cup I'd believe him," said the reporter. "I *know* him."

They were interrupted by the tinkling of the telephone bell in the next room, then for a long time the subdued hum of the scientist's irritable voice as he talked over the 'phone. It was twenty-five or thirty minutes before he appeared in the door again. He paused there and scribbled something on a card which he handed to Hatch. The reporter read this: "Henry C. H. Manderling, Scituate, Mass."

"There is the name and address of the man who has the jewels now," said The Thinking Machine quite as a matter of fact. "Mr. Hatch, you accompany Mr. Conway, let him see the surroundings and act as his judgment dictates. You must search this man's house. I don't think you'll have much trouble finding them because they cannot foresee their danger. The pearls will be unset and you will find them possibly in small oil-silk bags, no larger than your little finger. When you find them take steps to apprehend both this man and Leighton. Call Detective Mallory when you get them and bring them here."

"But—but—" stammered Conway.

"Come on," commented Hatch.

And Conway went.

The sleepy little old town of Scituate sprawls along two or three miles of Massachusetts coast, facing the sea boldly in a series of cliffs which rise up and sink away with the utmost suddenness. The town was settled two or three hundred years ago and nothing has ever happened there since. It was here, atop one of the cliffs, that Henry C. H. Manderling had lived alone for two or three months. He had gone there in the Spring with other city folks who dreamed their Summers away, and occupied a queer little shack through which the salt breezes wandered at will. A tiny barn was attached to the house.

Hutchinson Hatch and the Scotland Yard man found the house without difficulty and entered it without hesitation. There was no one at hand to stop them, or to interfere with the search they made. The simple lock on the door was no obstacle. In less than half an hour the skilful hands of the Scotland Yard man had turned out a score or more small oil-silk bags, no larger than his little finger. He ripped one open and six pearls dropped into his hand.

"They're the Varron pearls all right," he exclaimed triumphantly after an examination. He dropped them all into his pocket.

"Sh-h-h-h!" warned Hatch suddenly.

He had heard a step at the door, then two voices as some one inserted a key in the lock. After a moment the door opened and crouching back in the shadow they heard two men enter. It was just at that psychological moment that Conway stepped out and faced them.

"I want you, Leighton," he said calmly.

Hatch could not see beyond the Scotland Yard man but he heard a shot and a bullet whistled uncomfortably close to his head. Conway leaped forward; Hatch saw his arm swing and one of the men fell. Then came another shot. Conway staggered a little, took another step forward and again swung his great right arm. There was a scurrying of feet, the clatter of a revolver on the floor and the front door slammed.

"Tie up that chap there," commanded Conway.

He opened the door and Hatch heard him run along the veranda and leap off. He turned his attention to the senseless man on the floor. It was Harry Cheshire. A blow on the point of the chin had rendered him unconscious. Hatch bound him hand and foot where he lay and ran out.

Conway was racing down the cliff to where a motor boat lay. Hatch saw a man climb into the boat and an instant later it shot out into the water. Conway ran on to where it had been; it was now fifty yards out.

"Not *this* time, Mr. Conway," came Leighton's voice as the boat sped on.

The Scotland Yard man stared after it a minute or more then returned to Hatch. The reporter saw that he was pale, very pale.

"Did you bind him?" Conway asked.

"Yes," Hatch responded. "Are you wounded?"

"Sure," replied the Scotland Yard man. "He got me in the left arm. I never knew him to carry a revolver before. It's lucky those two shots were all he had."

The Thinking Machine put the finishing touches on the binding of Conway's wound—it was trivial—then turned to his other visitors. These were Harry Cheshire, or Manderling, and Detective Mallory to whom he had been delivered a prisoner on the arrival of Hatch and Conway in Boston. A general alarm had been sent out for Leighton.

Conway apparently didn't care anything about the wound but he had a frank curiosity as to just what The Thinking Machine had done and how those things which had happened had been brought to pass.

"It was all ridiculously simple," began the scientist at last in explanation. "It came down to this: How could one hundred and seventy-two pearls be transferred from a boat forty miles at sea to a safe place ashore? The motor boat did not speak or approach any other vessel; obviously one oculd not *throw* them ashore and I have never heard of such a thing as a trained fish which might have brought them in. Now what are the only other ways they *could* have reached shore with comparative safety?"

He looked from one to another inquiringly. Each in turn shook his head. Manderling, or Cheshire, was silent.

"There are only two possible answers," said the scientist at last. "One, a submarine boat, which is improbable, and the other, birds— homing pigeons."

"By Jove!" exclaimed Conway and he stared at Manderling. "And I did notice dozens of pigeons about the place at Scituate."

"The jewels *were* on the ship as you suspected," resumed the scientist, "unset and probably suspended in a long oil-silk bag in the drain pipe I mentioned. They *were* thrown into the motor boat, wrapped in the newspapers. Two miles away from the Romanic they were fastened to homing pigeons and one by one the pigeons were released. You, Mr. Conway, could see the boat clearly at that distance but you could not possibly see a bird rise from it. The birds went to their home, Mr. Manderling's place at Scituate. Homing pigeons are generally kept in automatically closing compartments and each pigeon was locked in as it arrived. Mr. Manderling here and Mr. Leighton removed the pearls at their leisure.

"Of course with homing pigeons as a clue we could get some-where," The Thinking Machine went on after a moment. "There are numerous homing pigeon associations and fanciers and it was possible that one of these would know of an Englishman who had, say, twenty-five or fifty birds, and presumably lived somewhere near Boston. One *did* know. He gave me the name of Henry C. H. Manderling. Harry is a corruption of Henry and—Henry C? Henry Cheshire, or Harry Cheshire—the name Mr. Manderling gave when he was searched at the wharf."

"Can you explain how Leighton was able to get the necklace in the first place?" asked Conway, curiously.

"Just as he got the other things," replied The Thinking Machine, "by boldness and cleverness. Suppose, when Lady Varron fell, Leighton had had a stout elastic fastened high up at the shoulder, say, inside his coat sleeve and the end of this elastic had a clamp of some sort, and was drawn down until the elastic was taut, and fastened to his cuff? Remember that this man was always waiting for an opportunity, and was always prepared to take advantage of it. Of course he did not plan the thing as it happened.

"Say that the necklace dropped off as he leaned over to help Lady Varron. In the momentary excitement he could, under their very noses, have fastened the clamp to the necklace. Instantly the jewels would have disappeared up his sleeve and he could have submitted to any sort of perfunctory search of his pockets as he suggested."

"That's a trick professional gamblers have to get rid of cards," remarked Detective Mallory.

"Oh, it isn't new then?" asked The Thinking Machine. "Immediately he left the ball-room he hid this necklace as he had hidden other jewels, and before you knew of the theft, wrote and mailed full directions to Mr. Manderling here what to do. You did not intercept any letters, of course, until after you knew of this theft. Leighton had perhaps had other dealings with Mr. Manderling in other parts of the world, when he was not so closely watched as in this particular instance. I daresay, however, he had them all planned carefully for fear the very thing that did happen in this case would happen."

Half an hour later Conway shook hands with The Thinking Machine, thanked him heartily and the little party dispersed.

"I had given it up," Conway confessed as he was going out.

"You see," remarked The Thinking Machine, "gentlemen of your profession use too little common sense. Remember that two and two always make four—not *some* times but *all* the time."

Leighton has not yet been caught.

THE PHANTOM MOTOR

I

Two dazzling white eyes bulged through the night as an automobile swept suddenly around a curve in the wide road and laid a smooth, glaring pathway ahead. Even at the distance the rhythmical crackling-chug informed Special Constable Baker that it was a gasoline car, and the headlong swoop of the unblinking lights toward him made him instantly aware of the fact that the speed ordinance of Yarborough County was being a little more than broken—it was being obliterated.

Now the County of Yarborough was a wide expanse of summer estates and superbly kept roads, level as a floor and offered distracting temptations to the dangerous pastime of speeding. But against this was the fact that the county was particular about its speed laws, so particular in fact that it had stationed half a hundred men upon its highways to abate the nuisance. Incidentally it had found that keeping record of the infractions of the law was an excellent source of income.

"Forty miles an hour if an inch," remarked Baker to himself.

He arose from a camp stool where he was wont to make himself comfortable from six o'clock until midnight on watch, picked up his lantern, turned up the light and stepped down to the edge of the road. He always remained on watch at the same place—at one end of a long stretch which autoists had unanimously dubbed The Trap. The Trap was singularly tempting—a perfectly macadamized road bed lying between two tall stone walls with only enough of a sinuous twist in it to make each end invisible from the other. Another man, Special Constable Bowman was stationed at the other end of The Trap and there was telephonic communication between the points, enabling the men to check each other and incidentally, if one failed to stop a car or get its number, the other would. That at least was the theory.

So now, with the utmost confidence, Baker waited beside the road. The approaching lights were only a couple of hundred yards away. At the proper instant he would raise his lantern, the car would stop, its occupants would protest and then the county would add a mite to its general fund for making the roads even better and tempting autoists still more. Or sometimes the cars didn't stop. In that event it was part of the Special Constables' duties to get the number as it flew past, and reference to the monthly automobile register would give the name of the owner. An extra fine was always imposed in such cases.

Without the slightest diminution of speed the car came hurtling on toward him and swung wide so as to take the straight path of The Trap at full speed. At the psychological instant Baker stepped out into the road and waved his lantern.

"Stop!" he commanded.

The crackling-chug came on, heedless of the cry. The auto was almost upon him before he leaped out of the road—a feat at which he was particularly expert—then it flashed by and plunged into The Trap. Baker was, at the instant, so busily engaged in getting out of the way that he couldn't read the number, but he was not disconcerted because he knew there was no escape from The Trap. On the one side a solid stone wall eight feet high marked the eastern boundary of the John Phelps Stocker country estate, and on the other side a stone fence nine feet high marked the western boundary of the Thomas Q. Rogers country estate. There was no turnout, no place, no possible way for an auto to get out of The Trap except at one of the two ends guarded by the special constables. So Baker, perfectly confident of results, seized the 'phone.

"Car coming through sixty miles an hour," he bawled. "It won't stop. I missed the number. Look out"

"All right," answered Special Constable Bowman.

For ten, fifteen, twenty minutes Baker waited expecting a call from Bowman at the other end. It didn't come and finally he picked up the 'phone again. No answer. He rang several times, battered the box and did some tricks with the receiver. Still no answer. Finally he began to feel worried. He remembered that at that same post one Special Constable had been badly hurt by a reckless chauffeur who refused to stop or turn his car when the officer stepped out into the road. In his mind's eye he saw Bowman now lying helpless, perhaps badly injured. If the car held the pace at which it passed him it would be certain death to whoever might be unlucky enough to get in its path.

With these thoughts running through his head and with genuine solicitude for Bowman, Baker at last walked on along the road of The Trap toward the other end. The feeble rays of the lantern showed the unbroken line of the cold, stone walls on each side. There was no shrubbery of any sort, only a narrow strip of grass close to the wall. The more Baker considered the matter the more anxious he became and he increased his pace a little. As he turned a gentle curve he saw a lantern in the distance coming slowly toward him. It was evidently being carried by some one who was looking carefully along each side of the road.

"Hello!" called Baker, when the lantern came within distance. "That you, Bowman?"

"Yes," came the hallooed response.

The lanterns moved on and met. Baker's solicitude for the other constable was quickly changed to curiosity.

"What're you looking for?" he asked.

"That auto," replied Bowman. "It didn't come through my end and I thought perhaps there had been an accident so I walked along looking for it. Haven't seen anything."

"Didn't come through your end?" repeated Baker in amazement. "Why it must have. It didn't come back my way and I haven't passed it so it must have gone through."

"Well, it didn't," declared Bowman conclusively. "I was on the lookout for it, too, standing beside the road. There hasn't been a car through my end in an hour."

Special Constable Baker raised his lantern until the rays fell full upon the face of Special Constable Bowman and for an instant they stared each at the other. Suspicion glowed from the keen, avaricious eyes of Baker.

"How much did they give you to let em' by?" he asked.

"Give me?" exclaimed Bowman, in righteous indignation. "Give me nothing. I haven't seen a car."

A slight sneer curled the lips of Special Constable Baker.

"Of course that's all right to report at headquarters," he said, "but I happened to know that the auto came in here, that it didn't go back my way, that it couldn't get out except at the ends, therefore it went your way." He was silent for a moment. "And whatever you got, Jim, seems to me I ought to get half."

Then the worm—i.e., Bowman—turned. A polite curl appeared

about his lips and was permitted to show through the grizzled mustache.

"I guess," he said deliberately, "you think because you do that, everybody else does. I haven't seen any autos."

"Don't I always give you half, Jim?" Baker demanded, almost pleadingly.

"Well I haven't seen any car and that's all there is to it. If it didn't go back your way there wasn't any car." There was a pause; Bowman was framing up something particularly unpleasant. "You're seeing things, that's what's the matter."

So was sown discord between two officers of the County of Yarborough. After awhile they separated with mutual sneers and open derision and went back to their respective posts. Each was thoughtful in his own way. At five minutes of midnight when they went off duty Baker called Bowman on the 'phone again.

"I've been thinking this thing over, Jim, and I guess it would be just as well if we didn't report it or say anything about it when we go in," said Baker slowly. "It seems foolish and if we did say anything about it it would give the boys the laugh on us."

"Just as you say," responded Bowman.

Relations between Special Constable Baker and Special Constable Bowman were strained on the morrow. But they walked along side by side to their respective posts. Baker stopped at his end of The Trap; Bowman didn't even look around.

"You'd better keep your eyes open tonight, Jim," Baker called as a last word.

"I had 'em open last night," was the disgusted retort.

Seven, eight, nine o'clock passed. Two or three cars had gone through The Trap at moderate speed and one had been warned by Baker. At a few minutes past nine he was staring down the road which led into The Trap when he saw something that brought him quickly to his feet. It was a pair of dazzling white eyes, far away. He recognized them—the mysterious car of the night before.

"I'll get it this time," he muttered grimly, between closed teeth.

Then when the onrushing car was a full two hundred yards away Baker planted himself in the middle of the road and began to swing the lantern. The auto seemed, if anything, to be traveling even faster than on the previous night. At a hundred yards Baker began to shout. Still the car didn't lessen speed, merely rushed on. Again at the psychological instant Baker jumped. The auto whisked by as the chauffeur gave it a dextrous twist to prevent running down the Special Constable.

Safely out of its way Baker turned and stared after it, trying to read the number. He could see there was a number because a white board swung from the tail axle, but he could not make out the figures. Dust and a swaying car conspired to defeat him. But he did see that there were four persons in the car dimly silhouetted against the light reflected from the road. It was useless, of course, to conjecture as to sex for even as he looked, the fast receding car swerved around the turn and was lost to sight.

Again he rushed to the telephone; Bowman responded promptly.

"That car's gone in again," Baker called. "Ninety miles an hour. Look out!"

"I'm looking," responded Bowman.

"Let me know what happens," Baker shouted.

With the receiver to his ear he stood for ten or fifteen minutes, then Bowman hallooed from the other end.

"Well?" Baker responded. "Get 'em?"

"No car passed through and there's none in sight," said Bowman.

"But it went in," insisted Baker.

"Well it didn't come out here," declared Bowman. "Walk along the road till I meet you and look out for it."

Then was repeated the search of the night before. When the two men met in the middle of The Trap their faces were blank—blank as the high stone walls which stared at them from each side.

"Nothing!" said Bowman.

"Nothing!" echoed Baker.

Special Constable Bowman perched his head on one side and scratched his grizzly chin.

"You're not trying to put up a job on me?" he inquired coldly. "You did see a car?"

"I certainly did," declared Baker, and a belligerent tone underlay his manner. "I certainly saw it, Jim, and if it didn't come out your end, why—why—"

He paused and glanced quickly behind him. The action inspired a sudden similar caution on Bowman's part.

"Maybe—maybe—" said Bowman after a minute, "maybe it's a —a spook auto?"

"Well it must be," mused Baker. "You know as well as I do that no car can get out of this trap except at the ends. That car came in here, it isn't here now and it didn't go out your end. Now where is it?"

Bowman stared at him a minute, picked up his lantern, shook his head solemnly and wandered along the road back to his post. On his way he glanced around quickly, apprehensively three times— Baker did the same thing four times.

On the third night the phantom car appeared and disappeared precisely as it had done previously. Again Baker and Bowman met half way between posts and talked it over.

"I'll tell you what, Baker," said Bowman in conclusion, "maybe you're just imagining that you see a car. Maybe if I was at your end I couldn't see it."

Special Constable Baker was distinctly hurt at the insinuation.

"All right, Jim," he said at last, "if you think that way about it we'll swap posts tomorrow night. We won't have to say anything about it when we report."

"Now that's the talk," exclaimed Bowman with an air approaching enthusiasm. "I'll bet I don't see it."

On the following night Special Constable Bowman made himself comfortable on Special Constable Baker's camp-stool. And *he* saw the phantom auto. It came upon him with a rush and a crackling-chug of engine and then sped on leaving him nerveless. He called Baker over the wire and Baker watched half an hour for the phantom. It didn't appear.

Ultimately all things reach the newspapers. So with the story of the phantom auto. Hutchinson Hatch, reporter, smiled incredulously when his City Editor laid aside an inevitable cigar and tersely stated the known facts. The known facts in this instance were meager almost to the disappearing point. They consisted merely of a corroborated statement that an automobile, solid and tangible enough to all appearances, rushed into The Trap each night and totally disappeared.

But there was enough of the bizarre about it to pique the curiosity, to make one wonder, so Hatch journeyed down to Yarborough County, an hour's ride from the city, met and talked to Baker and Bowman and then, in broad daylight strolled along The Trap twice. It was a leisurely, thorough investigation with the end in view of finding out how an automobile once inside might get out again without going out either end.

On the first trip through Hatch paid particular attention to the Thomas Q. Rogers side of the road. The wall, nine feet high, was an unbroken line of stone with not the slightest indication of a secret wagon-way through it anywhere. Secret wagon-way! Hatch smiled at the phrase. But when he reached the other end—Bowman's end—of The Trap he was perfectly convinced of one thing—that no automobile had left the hard, macadamized road to go over, under or through the Thomas Q. Rogers wall. Returning, still leisurely, he paid strict attention to the John Phelps Stocker side, and when he reached the other end—Baker's end—he was convinced of another thing—that no automobile had left the road to go over, under or through the John Phelps Stocker wall. The only opening of any sort was a narrow footpath, not more than 16 inches wide.

Hatch saw no shrubbery along the road, nothing but a strip of scrupulously cared for grass, therefore the phantom auto could not be hidden any time, night or day. Hatch failed, too, to find any holes in the road so the automobile didn't go down through the earth. At this point he involuntarily glanced up at the blue sky above. Perhaps, he thought whimsically, the automobile was a strange sort of bird, or—or—and he stopped suddenly.

"By George!" he exclaimed. "I wonder if—"

And the remainder of the afternoon he spent systematically making inquiries. He went from house to house, the Stocker house, the Rogers house, both of which were at the time unoccupied, then to cottage, cabin and hut in turn. But he didn't seem overladen with information when he joined Special Constable Baker at his end of The Trap that evening about seven o'clock.

Together they rehearsed the strange points of the mystery and as the shadows grew about them until finally the darkness was so dense that Baker's lantern was the only bright spot in sight. As the chill of the evening closed in a certain awed tone crept into their voices. Occasionally an auto bowled along and each time as it hove in sight Hatch glanced at Baker questioningly. And each time Baker shook his head. And each time, too, he called Bowman, in this manner accounting for every car that went into The Trap.

"It'll come all right," said Baker after a long silence, "and I'll know it the minute it rounds the curve coming toward us. I'd know its two lights in a thousand."

They sat still and smoked. After awhile two dazzling white lights burst into view far down the road and Baker, in excitement, dropped his pipe.

"That's her," he declared. "Look at her coming!"

And Hatch did look at her coming. The speed of the mysterious car was such as to make one look. Like the eyes of a giant the two lights came on toward them, and Baker perfunctorily went through the motions of attempting to stop it. The car fairly whizzed past them and the rush of air which tugged at their coats was convincing enough proof of its solidity. Hatch strained his eyes to read the number as the auto flashed past. But it was hopeless. The tail of the car was lost in an eddying whirl of dust.

"She certainly does travel," commented Baker, softly.

"She does," Hatch assented.

Then, for the benefit of the newspaper man, Baker called Bowman on the wire.

"Car's coming again," he shouted. "Look out and let me know!"

Bowman, at his end, waited twenty minutes, then made the usual report—the car had not passed. Hutchinson Hatch was a calm, cold, dispassionate young man but now a queer, creepy sensation stole along his spinal column. He lighted a cigarette and pulled himself together with a jerk.

"There's one way to find out where it goes," he declared at last, emphatically, "and that's to place a man in the middle just beyond the bend of The Trap and let him wait and see. If the car goes up, down, or evaporates he'll see and can tell us."

Baker looked at him curiously.

"I'd hate to be the man in the middle," he declared. There was something of uneasiness in his manner.

"I rather think I would, too," responded Hatch.

On the following evening, consequent upon the appearance of the story of the phantom auto in Hatch's paper, there were twelve other reporters on hand. Most of them were openly, flagrantly sceptical; they even insinuated that no one had seen an auto. Hatch smiled wisely.

"Wait!" he advised with deep conviction.

So when the darkness fell that evening the newspaper men of a great city had entered into a conspiracy to capture the phantom auto. Thirteen of them, making a total of fifteen men with Baker and Bowman, were on hand and they agreed to a suggestion for all to take positions along the road of The Trap from Baker's post to Bowman's, watch for the auto, see what happened to it and compare notes afterwards. So they scattered themselves along a few hundred feet apart and waited. That night the phantom auto didn't appear at all and twelve reporters jeered at Hutchinson Hatch and told him to light his pipe with the story. And next night when Hatch and Baker and Bowman alone were watching the phantom auto reappeared.

II

Like a child with a troublesome problem, Hatch took the entire matter and laid it before Professor Augustus S. F. X. Van Dusen, the master brain. The Thinking Machine, with squint eyes turned steadily upward and long, slender fingers pressed tip to tip listened to the end.

"Now I know of course that automobiles don't fly," Hatch burst out savagely in conclusion, "and if this one doesn't fly, there is no earthly way for it to get out of The Trap, as they call it. I went over the thing carefully—I even went so far as to examine the ground and the tops of the walls to see if a runway had been let down for the auto to go over."

The Thinking Machine squinted at him inquiringly.

"Are you sure you saw an automobile?" he demanded irritably.

"Certainly I saw it," blurted the reporter. "I not only saw it—I smelled it. Just to convince myself that it was real I tossed my cane in front of the thing and it smashed it to tooth-picks."

"Perhaps, then, if everything is as you say, the auto actually *does* fly," remarked the scientist.

The reporter stared into the calm, inscrutable face of The Thinking Machine, fearing first that he had not heard aright. Then he concluded that he had.

"You mean," he inquired eagerly, "that the phantom may be an auto-aeroplane affair, and that it actually does fly?"

"It's not at all impossible," commented the scientist.

"I had an idea something like that myself," Hatch explained, "and questioned every soul within a mile or so but I didn't get anything."

"The perfect stretch of road there might be the very place for some daring experimenter to get up sufficient speed to soar a short distance in a light machine," continued the scientist.

"Light machine?" Hatch repeated. "Did I tell you that this car had four people in it?"

"Four people!" exclaimed the scientist. "Dear me! Dear me!

That makes it very different. Of course four people would be too great a lift for an—"

For ten minutes he sat silent, and tiny, cobwebby lines appeared in his dome-like brow. Then he arose and passed into the adjoining room. After a moment Hatch heard the telephone bell jingle. Five minutes later The Thinking Machine appeared, and scowled upon him unpleasantly.

"I suppose what you really want to learn is if the car is a—a material one, and to whom it belongs?" he queried.

"That's it," agreed the reporter, "and of course, why it does what it does, and how it gets out of The Trap."

"Do you happen to know a fast, long-distance bicycle rider?" demanded the scientist abruptly.

"A dozen of them," replied the reporter promptly. "I think I see the idea, but—"

"You haven't the faintest inkling of the idea," declared The Thinking Machine positively. "If you can arrange with a fast rider who can go a distance—it might be thirty, forty, fifty miles—we may end this little affair without difficulty."

Under these circumstances Professor Augustus S. F. X. Van Dusen, Ph.D., LL.D., F.R.S., M.D., etc., etc., scientist and logician, met the famous Jimmie Thalhauer, the world's champion long distance bicyclist. He held every record from five miles up to and including six hours, had twice won the six-day race and was, altogether, a master in his field. He came in chewing a tooth-pick. There were introductions.

"You ride the bicycle?" inquired the crusty little scientist.

"Well, *some*," confessed the champion modestly with a wink at Hatch.

"Can you keep up with an automobile for a distance of, say, thirty or forty miles?"

"I can keep up with anything that ain't got wings," was the response.

"Well, to tell you the truth," volunteered The Thinking Machine, "there is a growing belief that this particular automobile has wings. However, if you can keep up with it—"

"Ah, quit your kiddin'," said the champion, easily. "I can ride rings around anything on wheels. I'll start behind it and beat it where it's going."

The Thinking Machine examined the champion, Jimmie Thalhauer as a curiosity. In the seclusion of his laboratory he had never had an opportunity of meeting just such another worldly young person.

"How fast *can* you ride, Mr. Thalhauer?" he asked at last.

"I'm ashamed to tell you," confided the champion in a hushed voice. "I can ride so fast that I scare myself." He paused a moment. "But it seems to me," he said, "if there's thirty or forty miles to do I ought to do it on a motor-cycle."

"Now that's just the point," explained The Thinking Machine. "A motor-cycle makes noise and if it could have been used we would have hired a fast automobile. This proposition briefly is: I want you to ride without lights behind an automobile which may also run without lights and find out where it goes. No occupant of the car must suspect that it is followed."

"Without lights?" repeated the champion. "Gee! Rubber shoe, eh?"

The Thinking Machine looked his bewilderment.

"Yes, that's it," Hatch answered for him.

"I guess it's good for a four column head? Hunh?" inquired the champion. "Special pictures posed by the champion? Hunh?"

"Yes," Hatch replied.

" 'Tracked on a Bicycle' sounds good to me. Hunh?"

Hatch nodded.

So arrangements were concluded and then and there The Thinking Machine gave definite and conclusive instructions to the champion. While these apparently bore broadly on the problem in hand they conveyed absolutely no inkling of his plan to the reporter. At the end the champion arose to go.

"You're a most extraordinary young man, Mr. Thalhauer," commented The Thinking Machine, not without admiration for the sturdy, powerful figure.

And as Hatch accompanied the champion out the door and down the steps Jimmie smiled with easy grace.

"Nutty old guy, ain't he? Hunh?"

Night! Utter blackness, relieved only by a white, ribbon like road which winds away mistily under a starless sky. Shadowy hedges line either side and occasionally a tree thrusts itself upward out of the sombreness. The murmur of human voices in the shadows, then the crackling-chug of an engine and an automobile moves slowly, without lights, into the road. There is the sudden clatter of an engine at high speed and the car rushes away.

From the hedge comes the faint rustle of leaves as of wind stirring, then a figure moves impalpably. A moment and it becomes a separate entity; a quick movement and the creak of a leather bicycle saddle. Silently the single figure, bent low over the handle bars, moves after the car with ever increasing momentum.

Then a long, desperate race. For mile after mile, mile after mile the auto goes on. The silent cyclist has crept up almost to the rear axle and hangs there doggedly as a racer to his pace. On and on they rush together through the darkness, the chauffeur moving with a perfect knowledge of his road, the single rider behind clinging on grimly with set teeth. The powerful, piston-like legs move up and down to the beat of the engine.

At last, with dust-dry throat and stinging, aching eyes the cyclist feels the pace slacken and instantly he drops back out of sight. It is only by sound that he follows now. The car stops; the cyclist is lost in the shadows.

For two or three hours the auto stands deserted and silent. At last the voices are heard again, the car stirs, moves away and the cyclist drops in behind. Another race which leads off in another direction. Finally, from a knoll, the lights of a city are seen. Ten minutes elapse, the auto stops, the head lights flare up and more leisurely it proceeds on its way.

On the following evening The Thinking Machine and Hutchinson Hatch called upon Fielding Stanwood, President of the Fordyce National Bank. Mr. Stanwood looked at them with interrogative eyes.

"We called to inform you, Mr. Stanwood," explained The Thinking Machine, "that a box of securities, probably United States bonds, is missing from your bank."

"What?" exclaimed Mr. Stanwood, and his face paled. "Robbery?"

"I only know the bonds were taken out of the vault tonight by Joseph Marsh, your assistant cashier," said the scientist, "and that he, together with three other men, left the bank with the box and are now at—a place I can name."

Mr. Stanwood was staring at him in amazement.

"You know where they are?" he demanded.

"I said I did," replied the scientist, shortly.

"Then we must inform the police at once, and—"

"I don't know that there has been an actual crime," interrupted the scientist. "I do know that every night for a week these bonds have been taken out through the connivance of your watchman and in each instance have been returned, intact, before morning. They will be returned tonight. Therefore I would advise, if you act, not to do so until the four men return with the bonds."

It was a singular party which met in the private office of President Stanwood at the bank just after midnight. Marsh and three companions, formally under arrest, were present as were President Stanwood, The Thinking Machine and Hatch, besides detectives. Marsh had the bonds under his arms when he was taken. He talked freely when questioned.

"I will admit," he said without hesitating, "that I have acted beyond my rights in removing the bonds from the vault here, but there is no ground for prosecution. I am a responsible officer of this bank and have violated no trust. Nothing is missing, nothing is stolen. Every bond that went out of the bank is here."

"But why—why did you take the bonds?" demanded Mr. Stanwood.

Marsh shrugged his shoulders.

"It's what has been called a get-rich-quick scheme," said The Thinking Machine. "Mr. Hatch and I made some investigations today. Mr. Marsh and these other three are interested in a business venture which is ethically dishonest but which is within the law. They have sought backing for the scheme amounting to about a million dollars. Those four or five men of means with whom they have discussed the matter have called each night for a week at Marsh's country place. It was necessary to make them believe that there was already a million or so in the scheme, so these bonds were borrowed and represented to be owned by themselves. They were taken to and fro between the bank and his home in a kind of an automobile. This is really what happened, based on knowledge which Mr. Hatch has gathered and what I myself developed by the use of a little logic."

And his statement of the affair proved to be correct. Marsh and the others admitted the statement to be true. It was while The Thinking Machine was homeward bound that he explained the phantom auto affair to Hatch.

"The phantom auto as you call it," he said, "is the vehicle in which the bonds were moved about. The phantom idea came merely by chance. On the night the vehicle was first noticed it was rushing along—we'll say to reach Marsh's house in time for an appointment. A road map will show you that the most direct line from the bank to Marsh's was through The Trap. If an automobile should go half way through there, then out across the Stocker estate to the other road, the distance would be lessened by a good five miles. This saving at first was of course valuable, so the car in which they rushed into The Trap was merely taken across the Stocker estate to the road in front."

"But how?" demanded Hatch. "There's no road there."

"I learned by 'phone from Mr. Stocker that there is a narrow walk from a very narrow foot-gate in Stocker's wall on The Trap leading through the grounds to the other road. The phantom auto wasn't really an auto at all—it was merely two motor cycles arranged with seats and a steering apparatus. The French Army has been experimenting with them. The motor cycles are, of course, separate machines and as such it was easy to trundle them through a narrow gate and across to the other road. The seats are light; they can be carried under the arm."

"Oh!" exclaimed Hatch suddenly, then after a minute: "But what did Jimmie Thalhauer do for you?"

"He waited in the road at the other end of the foot-path from The Trap," the scientist explained, "When the auto was brought through and put together he followed it to Marsh's home and from there to the bank. The rest of it you and I worked out today. It's merely logic, Mr. Hatch, logic."

There was a pause.

"That Mr. Thalhauer is really a marvelous young man, Mr. Hatch, don't you think?"

THE BROWN COAT

I

There was no mystery whatever about the identity of the man who, alone and unaided, robbed the Thirteenth National Bank of $109,437 in cash and $1.29 in postage stamps. It was "Mort" Dolan, an expert safe-cracker albeit a young one, and he had made a clean sweep. Nor yet was there any mystery as to his whereabouts. He was safely in a cell at Police Headquarters, having been captured within less than twelve hours after the robbery was discovered.

Dolan had offered no resistance to the officers when he was cornered, and had attempted no denial when questioned by Detective Mallory. He knew he had been caught fairly and squarely and no argument was possible, so he confessed with a glow of pride at a job well done. It was four or five days after his arrest that the matter came to the attention of The Thinking Machine. Then the problem was—

But perhaps it were better to begin at the beginning.

Despite the fact that he was considerably less than thirty years old, "Mort" Dolan was a man for whom the police had a wholesome respect. He had a record, for he had started early. This robbery of the Thirteenth National was his "big" job and was to have been his last. With the proceeds he had intended to take his wife and quietly disappear beneath a full beard and an alias in some place far removed from former haunts. But the mutability of human events is a matter of proverb. While the robbery as a robbery was a thoroughly artistic piece of work and in full accordance with plans which had been worked out to the minutest details months before, he had made one mistake. This was leaving behind him in the bank the can in which the nitro-glycerine had been bought. Through this carelessness he had been traced.

Dolan and his wife occupied three poor rooms in a poor tenement house. From the moment the police got a description of the person who bought the explosive they were confident for they knew their men. Therefore four clever men were on watch about the poor tenement. Neither Dolan nor his wife was there then, but from the condition of things in the rooms the police believed that they intended to return so took up positions to watch.

Unsuspecting enough, for his one mistake in the robbery had not recurred to him, Dolan came along just about dusk and started up the five steps to the front door of the tenement. It just happened that he glanced back and saw a head drawn suddenly behind a projecting stoop. But the electric light glared strongly there and Dolan recognized Detective Downey, one of many men who revolved around Detective Mallory within a limited orbit. Dolan paused on the stoop a moment and rolled a cigarette while he thought it over. Perhaps instead of entering, it would be best to stroll on down the street, turn a corner and make a dash for it. But just at that moment he spied another head in the direction of contemplated flight. That was Detective Blanton.

Deeply thoughtful Dolan smoked half the cigarette and stared blankly in front of him. He knew of a back door opening on an alley. Perhaps the detectives had not thought to guard that! He tossed his cigarette away, entered the house with affected unconcern and closed the door. Running lightly through the long, unclean hall which extended the full length of the building he flung open the back door. He turned back instantly—just outside he had seen and recognized Detective Cunningham.

Then he had an inspiration! The roof! The building was four stories. He ran up the four flights lightly but rapidly and was half way up the short flight which led to the opening in the roof when he stopped. From above he caught the whiff of a bad cigar, then the measured tread of heavy boots. Another detective! With a sickening depression at his heart Dolan came softly down the stairs again, opened the door of his flat with a latch-key and entered.

Then and there he sat down to figure it all out. There seemed no escape for him. Every way out was blocked, and it was only a question escape for him. Every way out was blocked, and it was only a question of time before they would close in on him. He imagined now they were only waiting for his wife's return. He could fight for his freedom of course—even kill one, perhaps two, of the detectives who were waiting for him. But that would only mean his own death.

If he tried to run for it past either of the detectives he would get a shot in the back. And besides, murder was repugnant to Dolan's artistic soul. It didn't do any good. But could he warn Isabel, his wife? He feared she would walk into the trap as he had done, and she had had no connection of any sort with the affair.

Then, from a fear that his wife would return, there swiftly came a fear that she would not. He suddenly remembered that it was necessary for him to see her. The police could not connect her with the robbery in any way; they could only hold her for a time and then would be compelled to free her for her innocence of this particular crime was beyond question. And if he were taken before she returned she would be left penniless; and that was a thing which Dolan dreaded to contemplate. There was a spark of human tenderness in his heart and in prison it would be comforting to know that she was well cared for. If she would only come now he would tell her where the money—!

For ten minutes Dolan considered the question in all possible lights. A letter telling her where the money was? No. It would inevitably fall into the hands of the police. A cipher? She would never get it. How? How? How? Every moment he expected a clamor at the door which would mean that the police had come for him. They knew he was cornered. Whatever he did must be done quickly. Dolan took a long breath and started to roll another cigarette. With the thin white paper held in his left hand and tobacco bag raised in the other he had an inspiration.

For a little more than an hour after that he was left alone. Finally his quick ear caught the shuffle of stealthy feet in the hall, then came an imperative rap on the door. The police had evidently feared to wait longer. Dolan was leaning over a sewing machine when the summons came. Instinctively his hand closed on his revolver, then he tossed it aside and walked to the door.

"Well?" he demanded.

"Let us in, Dolan," came the reply.

"That you, Downey?" Dolan inquired.

"Yes. Now don't make any mistakes, Mort. There are three of us here and Cunningham is in the alley watching your windows. There's no way out."

For one instant—only an instant—Dolan hesitated. It was not that he was repentant; it was not that he feared prison—it was regret at being caught. He had planned it all so differently, and the little woman would be heart-broken. Finally, with a quick backward glance at the sewing machine, he opened the door. Three revolvers were thrust into his face with unanimity that spoke well for the police opinion of the man. Dolan promptly raised his hands over his head.

"Oh, put down your guns," he expostulated. "I'm not crazy. My gun is over on the couch there."

Detective Downey, by a personal search, corroborated this statement then the revolvers were lowered.

"The chief wants you," he said. "It's about that Thirteenth National Bank robbery."

"All right," said Dolan, calmly and he held out his hands for the steel nippers.

"Now, Mort," said Downey, ingratiatingly, "you can save us a lot of trouble by telling us where the money is."

"Doubtless I could," was the ambiguous response.

Detective Downey looked at him and understood. Cunningham was called in from the alley. He and Downey remained in the apartment and the other two men led Dolan away. In the natural course of events the prisoner appeared before Detective Mallory at Police Headquarters. They were well acquainted, professionally.

Dolan told everything frankly from the inception of the plan to the actual completion of the crime. The detective sat with his feet on his desk listening. At the end he leaned forward toward the prisoner.

"And where is the money?" he asked.

Dolan paused long enough to roll a cigarette.

"That's my business," he responded, pleasantly.

"You might just as well tell us," insisted Detective Mallory. "We will find it, of course, and it will save us trouble."

"I'll just bet you a hat you don't find it," replied Dolan, and there was a glitter of triumph in his eyes. "On the level, between man and man now I will bet you a hat that you never find that money."

"You're on," replied Detective Mallory. He looked keenly at his prisoner and his prisoner stared back without a quiver. "Did your wife get away with it?"

From the question Dolan surmised that she had not been arrested.

"No," he answered.

"Is it in your flat?"

"Downey and Cunningham are searching now," was the rejoinder. "They will report what they find."

There was silence for several minutes as the two men—officer and prisoner—stared each at the other. When a thief takes refuge in a refusal to answer questions he becomes a difficult subject to handle. There was the "third degree" of course, but Dolan was the kind of man who would only laugh at that; the kind of man from whom anything less than physical torture could not bring a statement if he didn't choose to make it. Detective Mallory was perfectly aware of this dogged trait in his character.

"It's this way, chief," explained Dolan at last. "I robbed the bank, I got the money, and it's now where you will never find it. I did it by myself, and am willing to take my medicine. Nobody helped me. My wife—I know your men waited for her before they took me— my wife knows nothing on earth about it. She had no connection with the thing at all and she can prove it. That's all I'm going to say. You might just as well make up your mind to it."

Detective Mallory's eyes snapped.

"You will tell where that money is," he blustered, "or—or I'll see that you get—"

"Twenty years is the absolute limit," interrupted Dolan quietly. "I expect to get twenty years—that's the worst you can do for me."

The Detective stared at him hard.

"And besides," Dolan went on, "I won't be lonesome when I get where you're going to send me. I've got lots of friends there— been there before. One of the jailers is the best pinochle player I ever met."

Like most men who find themselves balked at the outset Detective Mallory sought to appease his indignation by heaping invective upon the prisoner, by threats, by promises, by wheedling, by bluster. It was all the same, Dolan remained silent. Finally he was led away and locked up.

A few minutes later Downey and Cunningham appeared. One glance told their chief that they could not enlighten him as to the whereabouts of the stolen money.

"Do you have any idea where it is?" he demanded.

"No, but I have a very definite idea where it isn't," replied Downey grimly. "It isn't in that flat. There's not one square inch of it that we didn't go over—not one object there that we didn't tear to pieces looking. It simply isn't there. He hid it somewhere before we got him."

"Well take all the men you want and keep at it," instructed Detective Mallory. "One of you, by the way, had better bring in Dolan's wife. I am fairly certain that she had nothing to do with it but she might know something and I can bluff a woman." Detective Mallory announced that accomplishment as if it were a thing to be proud of. "There's nothing to do now but get the money. Meanwhile I'll see that Dolan isn't permitted to communicate with anybody."

"There is always the chance," suggested Downey, "that a man as clever as Dolan could in a cipher letter, or by a chance remark, inform her where the money is if we assume she doesn't know, and that should be guarded against."

"It will be guarded against," declared Detective Mallory emphatically. "Dolan will not be permitted to see or talk to anyone for the present—not even an attorney. He may weaken later on."

But day succeeded day and Dolan showed no signs of weakening. His wife, meanwhile, had been apprehended and subjected to the "third degree." When this ordeal was over, the net result was that Detective Mallory was convinced that she had had nothing whatever to do with the robbery, and had not the faintest idea where the money was. Half a dozen times Dolan asked permission to see her or to write to her. Each time the request was curtly refused.

Newspaper men, with and without inspiration, had sought the money vainly; and the police were now seeking to trace the movements of "Mort" Dolan from the moment of the robbery until the moment of his appearance on the steps of the house where he lived. In this way they hoped to get an inkling of where the money had been hidden, for the idea of the money being in the flat had been abandoned. Dolan simply wouldn't say anything. Finally, one day, Hutchinson Hatch, reporter, made an exhaustive search of Dolan's flat, for the fourth time, then went over to Police Headquarters to talk it over with Mallory. While there President Ashe and two directors of the victimized bank appeared. They were worried.

"Is there any trace of the money?" asked Mr. Ashe.

"Not yet," responded Detective Mallory.

"Well, could we talk to Dolan a few minutes?"

"If we didn't get anything out of him you won't," said the detective. "But it won't do any harm. Come along."

Dolan didn't seem particularly glad to see them. He came to the bars of his cell and peered through. It was only when Mr. Ashe was introduced to him as the President of the Thirteenth National that he seemed to take any interest in his visitors. This interest took the form of a grin. Mr. Ashe evidently had something of importance on his mind and was seeking the happiest method of expression. Once or twice he spoke aside to his companions, and Dolan watched them curiously. At last he turned to the prisoner.

"You admit that you robbed the bank?" he asked.

"There's no need of denying it," replied Dolan.

"Well," and Mr. Ashe hesitated a moment, "the Board of Directors held a meeting this morning, and speaking on their behalf I want to say something. If you will inform us of the whereabouts of the money we will, upon its recovery, exert every effort within our power to have your sentence cut in half. In other words, as I understand it, you have given the police no trouble, you have confessed the crime and this, with the return of the money, would weigh for you when sentence is pronounced. Say the maximum is twenty years, we might be able to get you off with ten if we get the money."

Detective Mallory looked doubtful. He realized, perhaps, the futility of such a promise yet he was silent. The proposition might draw out something on which to proceed.

"Can't see it," said Dolan at last. "It's this way. I'm twenty-seven years old. I'll get twenty years. About two of that'll come off for good behavior, so I'll really get eighteen years. At the end of that time I'll come out with one hundred and nine thousand dollars odd—rich for life and able to retire at forty-five years. In other words while in prison I'll be working for a good, stiff salary—something really worth while. Very few men are able to retire at forty-five."

Mr. Ashe readily realized the trust of this statement. It was the point of view of a man to whom mere prison has few terrors—a man content to remain immured for twenty years for a consideration. He turned and spoke aside to the two directors again.

"But I'll tell you what I *will* do," said Dolan, after a pause. "If you'll fix it so I get only two years, say, I'll give you half the money."

There was silence. Detective Mallory strolled along the corridor beyond the view of the prisoner and summoned President Ashe to his side by a jerk of his head.

"Agree to that," he said. "Perhaps he'll really give up."

"But it wouldn't be possible to arrange it, would it?" asked Mr. Ashe.

"Certainly not," said the detective, "but agree to it. Get your money and then we'll nail him anyhow."

Mr. Ashe stared at him a moment vaguely indignant at the treachery of the thing, then greed triumphed. He walked back to the cell.

"We'll agree to that, Mr. Dolan," he said briskly. "Fix a two years sentence for you in return for half the money."

Dolan smiled a little.

"All right, go ahead," he said. "When sentence of two years is pronounced and a first class lawyer arranges it for me so that the matter can never be reopened I'll tell you where you can get your half."

"But of course you must tell us that now," said Mr. Ashe.

Dolan smiled cheerfully. It was a taunting, insinuating, accusing sort of smile and it informed the bank president that the duplicity contemplated was discovered. Mr. Ashe was silent for a moment, then blushed.

"Nothing doing," said Dolan, and he retired into a recess of his cell as if his interest in the matter were at an end.

"But—but we need the money now," stammered Mr. Ashe. "It was a large sum and the theft has crippled us considerably."

"All right," said Dolan carelessly. "The sooner I get two years the sooner you get it."

"How could it be—be fixed?"

"I'll leave that to you."

That was all. The bank president and the two directors went out fuming impotently. Mr. Ashe paused in Detective Mallory's office long enough for a final word.

"Of course it was brilliant work on the part of the police to capture Dolan," he said caustically, "but it isn't doing us a particle of good. All I see now is that we lose a hundred and nine thousand dollars."

"It looks very much like it," assented the detective, "unless we find it."

"Well, why *don't* you find it?"

Detective Mallory had to give it up.

II

"What did Dolan do with the money?" Hutchinson Hatch was asking of Professor Augustus S. F. X. Van Dusen—The Thinking Machine. "It isn't in the flat. Everything indicates that it was hidden somewhere else."

"And Dolan's wife?" inquired The Thinking Machine in his perpetually irritated voice. "It seems conclusive that she had no idea where it is?"

"She has been put through the 'third degree,' " explained the reporter, "and if she had known she would probably have told."

"Is she living in the flat now?"

"No. She is stopping with her sister. The flat is under lock and key. Mallory has the key. He has shown the utmost care in everything he has done. Dolan has not been permitted to write to or see his wife for fear he would let her know some way where the money is; he has not been permitted to communicate with anybody at all, not even a lawyer. He did see President Ashe and two directors of the bank but naturally he wouldn't give them a message for his wife."

The Thinking Machine was silent. For five, ten, twenty minutes he sat with long, slender fingers pressed tip to tip, squinting unblinkingly at the ceiling. Hatch waited patiently.

"Of course," said the scientist at last, "one hundred and nine thousand dollars, even in large bills would make a considerable bundle and would be extremely difficult to hide in a place that has been gone over so often. We may suppose, therefore, that it isn't in the flat. What have the detectives learned as to Dolan's whereabouts after the robbery and before he was taken?"

"Nothing," replied Hatch, "nothing, absolutely. He seemed to disappear off the earth for a time. That time, I suppose, was when he was disposing of the money. His plans were evidently well laid."

"It would be possible of course, by the simple rules of logic, to sit still here and ultimately locate the money," remarked The Thinking Machine musingly, "but it would take a long time. We might begin, for instance, with the idea that he contemplated flight. When? By rail or steamer? The answers to those questions would, in a way, enlighten us as to the probable location of the money, because, remember, it would have to be placed where it was readily accessible in case of flight. But the process would be a long one. Perhaps it would be best to make Dolan tell us where he hid it."

"It would if he would tell," agreed the reporter, "but he is reticent to a degree that is maddening when the money is mentioned."

"Naturally," remarked the scientist. "That really doesn't matter. I have no doubt he will inform me."

So Hatch and The Thinking Machine called upon Detective Mallory. They found him in deep abstraction. He glanced up at the intrusion with an appearance, almost, of relief. He knew intuitively what it was.

"If you can find out where that money is, Professor," he declared emphatically, "I'll—I'll—well you can't."

The Thinking Machine squinted into the official eyes thoughtfully and the corners of his straight mouth were drawn down disapprovingly.

"I think perhaps there has been a little too much caution here, Mr. Mallory," he said. "I have no doubt Dolan will inform me as to where the money is. As I understand it his wife is practically without means?"

"Yes," was the reply. "She is living with her sister."

"And he has asked several times to be permitted to write to or see her?"

"Yes, dozens of times."

"Well, now suppose you do let him see her," suggested The Thinking Machine.

"Lord, that's just what he wants," blurted the detective. "If he ever sees her I know he will, in some way, by something he says, by a gesture, or a look inform her where the money is. As it is now I know she doesn't know where it is."

"Well, if he informs her won't he also inform us?" demanded The Thinking Machine tartly. "If Dolan wants to convey knowledge of the whereabouts of the money to his wife let him talk to her—let him give her the information. I daresay if she is clever enough to interpret a word as a clue to where the money is I am too."

The detective thought that over. He knew this crabbed little scientist with the enormous head of old; and he knew, too, some of the amazing results he had achieved by methods wholly unlike those of the police. But in this case he was frankly in doubt.

"This way," The Thinking Machine continued. "Get the wife here, let her pass Dolan's cell and speak to him so that he will know that it is her, then let her carry on a conversation with him while she is beyond his sight. Have a stenographer, without the knowledge of either, take down just what is said, word for word. Give me a transcript of the conversation, and hold the wife on some pretext until I can study it a little. If he gives her a clue I'll get the money."

There was not the slightest trace of egotism in the irritable tone. It seemed merely a statement of fact. Detective Mallory, looking at the wizened face of the logician, was doubtfully hopeful and at last he consented to the experiment. The wife was sent for and came eagerly, a stenographer was placed in the cell adjoining Dolan, and the wife was led along the corridor. As she paused in front of Dolan's cell he started toward her with an exclamation. Then she was led on a little way out of his sight.

With face pressed close against the bars Dolan glowered out upon Detective Mallory and Hatch. An expression of awful ferocity leapt into his eyes.

"What're you doing with her?" he demanded.

"Mort, Mort," she called.

"Belle, is it you?" he asked in turn.

"They told me you wanted to talk to me," explained the wife. She was panting fiercely as she struggled to shake off the hands which held her beyond his reach.

"What sort of a game is this, Mallory?" demanded the prisoner.

"You've wanted to talk to her," Mallory replied, "now go ahead. You may talk, but you must not see her."

"Oh, that's it, eh?" snarled Dolan. "What did you bring her here for then? Is she under arrest?"

"Mort, Mort," came his wife's voice again. "They won't let me come where I can see you."

There was utter silence for a moment. Hatch was overpowered by a feeling that he was intruding upon a family tragedy, and tiptoed beyond reach of Dolan's roving eyes to where The Thinking Machine was sitting on a stool, twiddling his fingers. After a moment the detective joined them.

"Belle?" called Dolan again. It was almost a whisper.

"Don't say anything, Mort," she panted. "Cunningham and Blanton are holding me—the others are listening."

"I don't want to say anything," said Dolan easily. "I did want to see you. I wanted to know if you are getting along all right. Are you still at the flat?"

"No, at my sister's," was the reply. "I have no money—I can't stay at the flat."

"You know they're going to send me away?"

"Yes," and there was almost a sob in the voice. "I—I know it."

"That I'll get the limit—twenty years?"

"Yes."

"Can you—get along?" asked Dolan solicitously. "Is there anything you can do for yourself?"

"I will do something," was the reply. "Oh, Mort, Mort, why—"

"Oh never mind that," he interrupted impatiently. "It doesn't do any good to regret things. It isn't what I planned for, little girl, but it's here so—so I'll meet it. I'll get the good behavior allowance—that'll save two years, and then—"

There was a menace in the tone which was not lost upon the listeners.

"Eighteen years," he heard her moan.

For one instant Dolan's lips were pressed tightly together and in that instant he had a regret—regret that he had not killed Blanton and Cunningham rather than submit to capture. He shook off his anger with an effort.

"I don't know if they'll permit me ever to see you," he said, desperately, "as long as I refuse to tell where the money is hidden, and I know they'll never permit me to write to you for fear I'll tell you where it is. So I suppose the good-bye'll be like this. I'm sorry, little girl."

He heard her weeping and hurled himself against the bars in a passion; it passed after a moment. He must not forget that she was penniless, and the money—that vast fortune—!

"There's one thing you must do for me, Belle," he said after a moment, more calmly. "This sort of thing doesn't do any good. Brace up, little girl, and wait—wait for me. Eighteen years is not forever, we're both young, and—but never mind that. I wish you would please go up to the flat and—do you remember my heavy, brown coat?"

"Yes, the old one?" she asked.

"That's it," he answered. "It's cold here in this cell. Will you please go up to the flat when they let you loose and sew up that tear under the right arm and send it to me here? It's probably the last favor I'll ask of you for a long time so will you do it this afternoon?"

"Yes," she answered, tearfully.

"The rip is under the right arm, and be certain to sew it up," said Dolan again. "Perhaps, when I am tried, I shall have a chance to see you and—"

The Thinking Machine arose and stretched himself a little.

"That's all that's necessary, Mr. Mallory," he said. "Have her held until I tell you to release her."

Mallory made a motion to Cunningham and Blanton and the woman was led away, screaming. Hatch shuddered a little, and Dolan, not understanding, flung himself against the bars of his cell like a caged animal.

"Clever, aren't you?" he snarled as he caught sight of Detective Mallory. "Thought I'd try to tell her where it was, but I didn't and you never will know where it is—not in a thousand years."

Accompanied by The Thinking Machine and Hatch the detective went back to his private office. All were silent but the detective glanced from time to time into the eyes of the scientist.

"Now, Mr. Hatch, we have the whereabouts of the money settled," said The Thinking Machine, quietly. "Please go at once to the flat and bring the brown coat Dolan mentioned. I daresay the secret of the hidden money is somewhere in that coat."

"But two of my men have already searched that coat," protested the detective.

"That doesn't make the least difference," snapped the scientist.

The reporter went without a word. Half an hour later he returned with the brown coat. It was a commonplace looking garment, badly worn and in sad need of repair not only in the rip under the arm but in other places. When he saw it The Thinking Machine nodded his head abruptly as if it were just what he had expected.

"The money can't be in that and I'll bet my head on it," declared Detective Mallory, flatly. "There isn't room for it."

The Thinking Machine gave him a glance in which there was a touch of pity.

"We know," he said, "that the money isn't in this coat. But can't you see that it is perfectly possible that a slip of paper on which Dolan has written down the hiding place of the money can be hidden in it somewhere? Can't you see that he asked for this coat—which is not as good a one as the one he is wearing now—in order to attract his wife's attention to it? Can't you see it is the one definite thing that he mentioned when he knew that in all probability he would not be permitted to see his wife again, at least for a long time?"

Then, seam by seam, the brown coat was ripped to pieces. Each piece in turn was submitted to the sharpest scrutiny. Nothing resulted. Detective Mallory frankly regarded it all as wasted effort and when there remained nothing of the coat save strips of cloth and lining he was inclined to be triumphant. The Thinking Machine was merely thoughtful.

"It went further back than that," the scientist mused, and tiny wrinkles appeared in the dome-like brow. "Ah! Mr. Hatch please go back to the flat, look in the machine drawers, or work basket and you will find a spool of brown thread. Bring it to me."

"Spool of brown thread?" repeated the detective in amazement. "Have you been through the place?"

"No."

"How do you know there's a spool of brown thread there, then?"

"I know it because Mr. Hatch will bring it back to me," snapped The Thinking Machine. "I know it by the simplest, most rudimentary rules of logic."

Hatch went out again. In half an hour he returned with a spool of brown thread. The Thinking Machine's white fingers seized upon it eagerly, and his watery, squint eyes examined it. A portion of it had been used—the spool was only halfgone. But he noted—and as he did his eyes reflected a glitter of triumph—he noted that the paper cap on each end was still in place.

"Now, Mr. Mallory," he said, "I'll demonstrate to you that in Dolan the police are dealing with a man far beyond the ordinary bank thief. In his way he is a genius. Look here!"

With a pen-knife he ripped off the paper caps and looked through the hole of the spool. For an instant his face showed blank amazement. Then he put the spool down on the table and squinted at it for a moment in absolute silence.

"It must be here," he said at last. "It must be, else why did he— of course!"

With quick fingers he began to unwind the thread. Yard after yard it rolled off in his hand, and finally in the mass of brown on the spool appeared a white strip. In another instant The Thinking Machine held in his hand a tiny, thin sheet of paper—a cigarette paper. It had been wound around the spool and the thread wound over it so smoothly that it was impossible to see that it had ever been removed.

The detective and Hatch were leaning over his shoulder watching him curiously. The tiny paper unfolded—something was written on it. Slowly The Thinking Machine deciphered it.

"47 Causeway street, basement, tenth flagstone from northeast corner."

And there the money was found—$109,000. The house was unoccupied and within easy reach of a wharf from which a European bound steamer sailed. Within half an hour of sailing time it would have been an easy matter for Dolan to have recovered it all and that without in the least exciting the suspicion of those who might be watching him. For a saloon next door opened into an alley behind, and a broken window in the basement gave quick access to the treasure.

"Dolan reasoned," The Thinking Machine explained, "that even if he was never permitted to see his wife she would probably use that thread and in time find the directions for recovering the money. Further he argued that the police would never suspect that a spool contained the secret for which they sought so long. His conversation with his wife, today, was merely to draw her attention to something which would require her to use the spool of brown thread. The brown coat was all that he could think of. And that's all I think."

Dolan was a sadly surprised man when news of the recovery of the money was broken to him. But a certain quaint philosophy didn't desert him. He gazed at Detective Mallory incredulously as the story was told and at the end went over and sat down on his cell cot.

"Well, chief," he said, "I didn't think it was in you. That makes me owe you a hat."

HIS PERFECT ALIBI

I

Skulking along through the dense gloom, impalpably a part of the murky mist which pressed down between the tall board fences on each side, moved the figure of a man. Occasionally he shot a glance behind him but the general direction of his gaze was to his left, where a fence cut off the small back-yards of an imposing row of brown-stone residences. At last he stopped and tried a gate. It opened noiselessly and he disappeared inside. A pause. A man came out of the gate, closed it carefully and walked on through the alley toward an arc-light which spread a generous glare at the intersection of a street.

Patrolman Gillis was standing idly on a corner, within the light-radius of a street lamp debating some purely personal questions when he heard the steady clack, clack, clack of foot-steps a block or more away. He glanced up and dimly he saw a man approaching. As he came nearer the policeman noticed that the man's right hand was pressed to his face.

"Good evening, officer," said the stranger nervously. "Can you tell me where I can find a dentist?"

"Toothache?" inquired the policeman.

"Yes, and it's nearly killing me," was the reply. "If I don't get it pulled I'll—I'll go crazy."

The policeman grinned sympathetically.

"Had it myself—I know what it is," he said. "You passed one dentist down in the other block, but there's another just across the street here," and he indicated a row of brown-stone residences. "Dr. Paul Sitgreaves. He'll charge you good and plenty."

"Thank you," said the other.

He crossed the street and the policeman gazed after him until he mounted the steps and pulled the bell. After a few minutes the door opened, the stranger entered the house and Patrolman Gillis walked on.

"Dr. Sitgreaves here?" inquired the stranger of a servant who answered the bell.

"Yes."

"Please ask him if he can draw a tooth for me. I'm in a perfect agony, and—"

"The doctor rarely gets up to attend so such cases," interrupted the servant.

"Here," said the stranger and he pressed a bill in the servant's hand. "Wake him for me, won't you? Tell him it's urgent."

The servant looked at the bill, then opened the door and led the patient into the reception room.

Five minutes later, Dr. Sitgreaves, gaping ostentatiously, entered and nodded to his caller.

"I hated to trouble you, Doctor," explained the stranger, "but I haven't slept a wink all night."

He glanced around the room until his eye fell upon a clock. Dr. Sitgreaves glanced in that direction. The hands of the clock pointed to 1:53.

"Phew!" said Dr. Sitgreaves. "Nearly two o'clock. I must have slept hard. I didn't think I'd been asleep more than an hour." He paused to gape again and stretch himself. "Which tooth is it?" he asked.

"A molar, here," said the stranger, and he opened his mouth.

Dr. Sitgreaves gazed officially into his innermost depths and fingered the hideous instruments of torture.

"That tooth's too good to lose," he said after an examination. "There's only a small cavity in it."

"I don't know what's the matter with it," replied the other impatiently, "except that it hurts. My nerves are fairly jumping."

Dr. Sitgreaves was professionally serious as he noted the drawn face, the nervous twitching of hands and the unusual pallor of his client.

"They are," he said finally. "There's no doubt of that. But it isn't the tooth. It's neuralgia."

"Well, pull it anyway," pleaded the stranger. "It always comes in that tooth, and I've got to get rid of it some time."

"It wouldn't be wise," remonstrated the dentist. "A filling will save it. Here," and he turned and stirred an effervescent powder in a glass. "Take this and see if it doesn't straighten you out."

The stranger took the glass and gulped down the foaming liquid.

"Now sit right there for five minutes or so," instructed the dentist. "If it doesn't quiet you and you insist on having the tooth pulled, of course—"

He sat down and glanced again at the clock after which he looked at his watch and replaced it in a pocket of his pajamas. His visitor was sitting, too, controlling himself only with an obvious effort.

"This is real neuralgia weather," observed the dentist at last, idly. "Misty and damp."

"I suppose so," was the reply. "This began to hurt about twelve o'clock, just as I went to bed, and finally it got so bad that I couldn't stand it. Then I got up and dressed and came out for a walk. I kept on, thinking that it would get better but it didn't and a policeman sent me here."

There was a pause of several minutes.

"Feel any better?" inquired the dentist, at last.

"No," was the reply. "I think you'd better take it out."

"Just as you say!"

The offending tooth was drawn, the stranger paid him with a sigh of relief, and after a minute or so started out. At the door he turned back.

"What time is it now, please?" he asked.

"Seventeen minutes past two," replied the dentist.

"Thanks," said the stranger. "I'll just have time to catch a car back home."

"Good night," said the dentist.

"Good night."

Skulking along through the dense gloom, impalpably a part of the murky mist which pressed down between tall board fences on each side, moved the figure of a man. Occasionally he shot a glance behind him, but the general direction of his gaze was to his left, where a fence cut off the small back-yards of an imposing row of brown-stone residences. At last he stopped and tried a gate. It opened noiselessly and he disappeared inside. A pause. A man came out of the gate, closed it carefully and walked on through the alley toward an arc-light which spread a generous glare at the intersection of a street.

Next morning at eight o'clock, Paul Randolph De Forrest, a

young man of some social prominence, was found murdered in the sitting room of his suite in the big Avon apartment house. He had been dead for several hours. He sat beside his desk, and death left him sprawled upon it face downward. The weapon was one of several curious daggers which had been used ornamentally on the walls of his apartments. The blade missed the heart only a quarter of an inch or so; death must have come within a couple of minutes.

Detective Mallory went to the apartments, accompanied by the Medical Examiner. Together they lifted the dead man. Beneath his body, on the desk, lay a sheet of paper on which were scrawled a few words; a pencil was clutched tightly in his right hand. The detective glanced then stared at the paper; it startled him. In the scrawly, trembling, incoherent handwriting of the dying man were these disjointed sentences and words:

"Murdered * * * * Franklin Chase * * * * quarrel * * * * stabbed me * * * * am dying * * * * God help me * * * * clock striking 2 * * * * good-bye."

The detective's jaws snapped as he read. Here was crime, motive and time. After a sharp scrutiny of the apartments, he went down the single flight of stairs to the office floor to make some inquiries. An elevator man, Moran, was the first person questioned. He had been on duty the night before. Did he know Mr. Franklin Chase? Yes. Had Mr. Franklin Chase called to see Mr. De Forrest on the night before? Yes.

"What time was he here?"

"About half past eleven, I should say. He and Mr. De Forrest came in together from the theater."

"When did Mr. Chase go away?"

"I don't know, sir. I didn't see him."

"It might have been somewhere near two o'clock?"

"I don't know, sir," replied Moran again, "I'll—I'll tell you all I know about it. I was on duty all night. Just before two o'clock a telegram was 'phoned for a Mr. Thomas on the third floor. I took it and wrote on it the time that I received it. It was then just six minutes before two o'clock. I walked up from this floor to the third— two flights to give the message to Mr. Thomas. As I passed Mr. De Forrest's door, I heard loud voices, two people evidently quarreling. I paid no attention then but went on. I was at Mr. Thomas's door possibly five or six minutes. When I came down I heard nothing further and thought no more of it."

"You fix the time of passing Mr. De Forrest's door first at, say, five minutes of two?" asked the detective.

"Within a minute of that time, yes, sir."

"And again about two or a minute or so after?"

"Yes."

"Ah," exclaimed the detective. "That fits in exactly with the other and establishes beyond question the moment of the murder." He was thinking of the words "clock striking 2" written by the dying man. "Did you recognize the voices?"

"No sir, I could not. They were not very clear."

That was the substance of Moran's story. Detective Mallory then called at the telegraph office and indisputable records there showed that they had telephoned a message for Mr. Thomas at precisely six minutes of two. Detective Mallory was satisfied.

Within an hour Franklin Chase was under arrest. Detective Mallory found him sound asleep in his room in a boarding house less than a block away from the Avon. He seemed somewhat astonished when informed of his arrest for murder, but was quite calm.

"It's some sort of a mistake," he protested.

"I don't make mistakes," said the detective. He had a short memory.

Further police investigation piled up the evidence against the prisoner. For instance, minute blood stains were found on his hands, and a drop or so on the clothing he had worn the night before; and it was established by three fellow lodgers—young men who had come in late and stopped at his room—that he was not in his boarding house at two o'clock the night before.

That afternoon Chase was arraigned for a preliminary hearing. Detective Mallory stated the case and his statement was corroborated by necessary witnesses. First he established the authenticity of the dying man's writing. Then he proved that Chase had been with De Forrest at half past eleven o'clock; that there had been a quarrel—or argument—in De Forrest's room just before two o'clock; and finally, with a dramatic flourish, he swore to the blood stains on the prisoner's hands and clothing.

The august Court stared at the prisoner and took up his pen to sign the necessary commitment.

"May I say something before we go any further?" asked Mr. Chase.

The Court mumbled some warning about anything the prisoner might say being used against him.

"I understand," said the accused, and he nodded, "but I will show that there has been a mistake—a serious mistake. I admit that the writing was Mr. De Forrest's; that I was with him at half past eleven o'clock and that the stains on my hands and clothing were blood stains."

The Court stared.

"I've known Mr. De Forrest for several years," the prisoner went on quietly. "I met him at the theater last night and walked home with him. We reached the Avon about half past eleven o'clock and I went to his room but I remained only ten or fifteen minutes. Then I went home. It was about five minutes of twelve when I reached my room. I went to bed and remained in bed until one o'clock, when for a reason which will appear, I arose, dressed and went out, say about ten minutes past one. I returned to my room a few minutes past three."

Detective Mallory smiled sardonically.

"When I was arrested this morning I sent notes to three persons," the prisoner went on steadily. "Two of these happen to be city officials, one the City Engineer. Will he please come forward."

There was a little stir in the room and the Court scratched one ear gravely. City Engineer Malcolm appeared inquiringly.

"This is Mr. Malcolm?" asked the prisoner. "Yes? Here is a map of the city issued by your office. I would like to ask please the approximate distance between this point—" and he indicated on the map the location of the Avon— "and this." He touched another point far removed.

The City Engineer studied the map carefully.

"At least two and a half miles," he explained.

"You would make that statement on oath?"

"Yes, I've surveyed it myself."

"Thank you," said the prisoner, courteously, and he turned to face the crowd in the rear. "Is Policeman No. 1122 in Court?—I don't know his name?"

Again there was a stir, and Policeman Gillis came forward.

"Do you remember me?" inquired the prisoner.

"Sure," was the reply.

"Where did you see me last night?"

"At this corner," and Gillis put his finger down on the map at the second point the prisoner had indicated.

The Court leaned forward eagerly to peer at the map: Detective Mallory tugged violently at his mustache. Into the prisoner's manner there came tense anxiety.

"Do you know what time you saw me there?" he asked.

Policeman Gillis was thoughtful a moment.

"No," he replied at last. "I heard a clock strike just after I saw you but I didn't notice."

The prisoner's face went deathly white for an instant, then he recovered himself with an effort.

"You didn't count the strokes?" he asked.

"No, I wasn't paying any attention to it."

The color rushed back into Chase's face and he was silent a moment. Then:

"It was two o'clock you heard strike?" It was hardly a question, rather a statement.

"I don't know," said Gillis. "It might have been. Probably was."

"What did I say to you?"

"You asked me where you could find a dentist, and I directed you to Dr. Sitgreaves across the street."

"You saw me enter Dr. Sitgreaves' house?"

"Yes."

The accused glanced up at the Court and that eminent jurist proceeded to look solemn.

"Dr. Sitgreaves, please?" called the prisoner.

The dentist appeared, exchanging nods with the prisoner.

"You remember me, doctor?"

"Yes."

"May I ask you to tell the court where you live? Show us on this map please."

Dr. Sitgreaves put his finger down at the spot which had been pointed out by the prisoner and by Policeman Gillis, two and a half miles from the Avon.

"I live three doors from this corner," explained the dentist.

"You pulled a tooth for me last night?" went on the prisoner.

"Yes."

"Here?" and the prisoner opened his mouth.

The dentist gazed down him.

"Yes," he replied.

"You may remember, doctor," went on the prisoner, quietly, "that you had occasion to notice the clock just after I called at your house. Do you remember what time it was?"

"A few minutes before two—seven or eight minutes, I think."

Detective Mallory and the Court exchanged bewildered glances.

"You looked at your watch, too. Was that exactly with the clock?"

"Yes, within a minute."

"And what time did I leave your office?" the prisoner asked.

"Seventeen minutes past two—I happen to remember," was the reply.

The prisoner glanced dreamily around the room twice, his eyes met Detective Mallory's. He stared straight into that official for an instant then turned back to the dentist.

"When you drew the tooth there was blood of course. It is possible that I got the stains on my fingers and clothing?"

"Yes, certainly."

The prisoner turned to the Court and surprised a puzzled expression on that official countenance.

"Is anything else necessary?" he inquired courteously. "It has been established that the moment of the crime was two o'clock; I have shown by three witnesses—two of them city officials—that I was two and a half miles away in less than half an hour; I couldn't have gone on a car in less than fifteen minutes—hardly that."

There was a long silence as the Court considered the matter. Finally he delivered himself, briefly.

"It resolves itself into a question of the accuracy of the clocks," he said. "The accuracy of the clock in the Avon is attested by the known accuracy of the clock in the telegraph office, while it seems established that Dr. Sitgreaves' clock was also accurate, because it was with his watch. Of course there is no question of varacity of witnesses—it is merely a question of the clock in Dr. Sitgreaves' office. If that is shown to be absolutely correct we must accept the alibi."

The prisoner turned to the elevator man from the Avon.

"What sort of a clock was that you mentioned?"

"An electric clock, regulated from Washington Observatory," was the reply.

"And the clock at the telegraph office, Mr. Mallory?"

"An electric clock, regulated from Washington Observatory."

"And yours, Dr. Sitgreaves?"

"An electric clock, regulated from Washington Observatory."

The prisoner remained in his cell until seven o'clock that evening while experts tested the three clocks. They were accurate to the second; and it was explained that there could have been no variation of either without this variation showing in the delicate testing apparatus. Therefore it came to pass that Franklin Chase was released on his own recognizance, while Detective Mallory wandered off into the sacred precincts of his private office to hold his head in his hands and think.

II

Hutchinson Hatch, reporter, had followed the intricacies of the mystery from the discovery of De Forrest's body, through the preliminary hearing, up to and including the expert examination of the clocks, which immediately preceded the release of Franklin Chase. When this point was reached his mental condition was not unlike that of Detective Mallory—he was groping hopelessly, blindly in the mazes of the problem.

It was then that he called to see Professor Augustus S. F. X. Van Dusen—The Thinking Machine. That distinguished gentleman listened to a recital of the known facts with petulant, drooping mouth and the everlasting squint in his blue eyes. As the reporter talked on, corrugations appeared in the logician's expansive brow, and these gave way in turn to a net-work of wrinkles. At the end The Thinking Machine sat twiddling his long fingers and staring upward.

"This is one of the most remarkable cases that has come to my attention," he said at last, "because it possesses the unusual quality of being perfect in each way—that is the evidence against Mr. Chase is perfect and the alibi he offers is perfect. But we know instantly that if Mr. Chase killed Mr. De Forrest there *was* something the matter with the clocks despite expert opinion.

"We *know* that as certainly as we know that two and two make four, not *some* times but *all* the time, because our reason tells us that Mr. Chase was not in two places at once at two o'clock. Therefore we must assume either one or two things—that something was the matter with the clocks—and if there was we must assume that Mr. Chase was responsible for it—or that Mr. Chase had nothing whatever to do with Mr. De Forrest's death, at least personally."

The last word aroused Mr. Hatch to a new and sudden interest. It suggested a line of thought which had not yet occurred to him.

"Now," continued the scientist, "if we can find one flaw in Mr. Chase's story we will have achieved the privilege of temporarily setting aside his defense and starting over. If, on the contrary, he told the full and exact truth and our investigation proves that he did, it instantly clears him. Now just what have you done, please?"

"I talked to Dr. Sitgreaves," replied Hatch. "He did not know Chase—never saw him until he pulled the tooth, and then didn't know his name. But he told me really more than appeared in court, for instance, that his watch had been regulated only a few days ago, that it had been accurate since, and that he knew it was accurate next day because he kept an important engagement. That being accurate the clock must be accurate, because they were together almost to the second.

"I also talked to every other person whose name appears in the case. I questioned them as to all sort of possibilities, and the result was that I was compelled to accept the alibi—not that I'm unwilling to of course, but it seems peculiar that De Forrest should have written the name as he was dying."

"You talked to the young men who went into Mr. Chase's room at two o'clock?" inquired The Thinking Machine casually.

"Yes."

"Did you ask either of them the condition of Mr. Chase's bed when they went in?"

"Yes," replied the reporter. "I see what you mean. They agreed that it was tumbled as if someone had been in it."

The Thinking Machine raised his eyebrows slightly.

"Suppose, Mr. Hatch, that you had a violent toothache," he asked after a moment, still casually, "and were looking for relief, would you stop to notice the number of a policeman who told you where there was a dentist's office?"

Hatch considered it calmly, as he stared into the inscrutable face of the scientist.

"Oh, I see," he said at last. "No, I hardly think so, and yet I might."

Later Hatch and The Thinking Machine by permission of Detective Mallory, made an exhaustive search of De Forrest's apartments in the Avon, seeking some clue. When The Thinking Machine went down the single flight of stairs to the office he seemed perplexed.

"Where is your clock?" he inquired of the elevator man.

"In the inside office, opposite the telephone booth," was the reply.

The scientist went in and taking a stool, clambered up and squinted fiercely into the very face of the time-piece. He said "Ah!" once, non-commitally, then clambered down.

"It would not be possible for any one here to see a person pass through the hall," he mused. "Now," and he picked up a telephone book, "just a word with Dr. Sitgreaves."

He asked the dentist only two questions and their nature caused Hatch to smile. The first was:

"You have a pocket in the shirt of your pajamas?"

"Yes," came the wondering reply.

"And when you are called at night you pick up your watch and put it in that pocket?"

"Yes."

"Thanks. Good-bye."

Then The Thinking Machine turned to Hatch.

"We are safe in believing," he said, "that Mr. De Forrest was not killed by a thief, because his valuables were undisturbed, therefore we must believe that the person who killed him was an acquaintance. It would be unfair to act hastily, so I shall ask you to devote three or four days to getting this man's history in detail; see his friends and enemies, find out all about him, his life, his circumstances, his love affairs—all those things."

Hatch nodded; he was accustomed to receiving large orders from The Thinking Machine.

"If you uncover nothing in that line to suggest another line of investigation I will give you the name of the person who killed him and an arrest will follow. The murderer will not run away. The solution of the affair is quite clear, unless—" he emphasised the word—"unless some unknown fact gives it another turn."

Hatch was forced to be content with that and for the specified four days labored arduously and vainly. Then he returned to The Thinking Machine and summed up results briefly in one word: "Nothing."

The Thinking Machine went out and was gone two hours. When he returned he went straight to the 'phone and called Detective Mallory. The Detective appeared after a few minutes.

"Have one of your men go at once and arrest Mr. Chase," The Thinking Machine instructed. "You might explain to him that there is new evidence—an eye witness if you like. But don't mention my name or this place to him. Anyway bring him here and I'll show you the flaw in the perfect alibi he set up!"

Detective Mallory started to ask questions.

"It comes down simply to this," interrupted The Thinking Machine impatiently. "Somebody killed Mr. De Forrest and that being true it must be that that somebody can be found. Please, when Mr. Chase comes here do not interrupt me, and introduce me to him as an important new witness."

An hour later Franklin Chase entered with Detective Mallory. He was somewhat pale and nervous and in his eyes lay a shadow of apprehension. Over it all was the gloss of ostentatious nonchalance and self control. There were introductions. Chase started visibly at actual reference to the "important new witness."

"An eye witness," added The Thinking Machine.

Positive fright came into Chase's manner and he quailed under the steady scrutiny of the narrow blue eyes. The Thinking Machine dropped back into his chair and pressed his long, white fingers tip to tip.

"If you'll just follow me a moment, Mr. Chase," he suggested at last. "You know Dr. Sitgreaves of course? Yes. Well, it just happens that I have a room a block or so away from his house around the corner. These are Mr. Hatch's apartments." He stated it so convincingly that there was no possibility of doubt. "Now my room faces straight up an alley which runs directly back of Dr. Sitgreaves's house. There is an electric light at the corner."

Chase started to say something, gulped, then was silent.

"I was in my room the night of Mr. De Forrest's murder," went on the scientist, "and was up moving about because I, too, had a toothache. It just happened that I glanced out my front window." His tone had been courteous in the extreme; now it hardened perceptibly. "I saw you, Mr. Chase, come along the street, stop at the alley, glance around and then go into the alley. *I saw your face clearly* under the electric light, and that was *at twenty minutes to three o'clock*. Detective Mallory has just learned of this fact and I have signified my willingness to go on the witness stand and swear to it."

The accused man was deathly white now; his face was working strangely, but still he was silent. It was only by a supreme effort that he restrained himself.

"I saw you open a gate and go into the back yard of Dr. Sitgreaves's house," resumed The Thinking Machine. "Five minutes or so later you came out and walked on to the cross street, where you disappeared. Naturally I wondered what it meant. It was still in my mind about half past three o'clock, possibly later, when I saw you enter the alley again, disappear in the same yard, then come out and go away."

"I—I was not—not there," said Chase weakly. "You were—were mistaken."

"When we know," continued The Thinking Machine steadily, "that you entered that house *before* you entered by the front door, we *know* that you tampered with Dr. Sitgreaves's watch and clock, and when we know that you tampered with those we know that you murdered Mr. De Forrest as his dying note stated. Do you see it?"

Chase arose suddenly and paced feverishly back and forth across the room; Detective Mallory discreetly moved his chair in front of the door. Chase saw and understood.

"I know how you tampered with the clock so as not to interfere with its action or cause any vibration at the testing apparatus. You were too superbly clever to stop it, or interfere with the circuit. Therefore I see that you simply took out the pin which held on the hands and moved them backward one hour. It was then actually a quarter of three—you made it a quarter of two. You showed your daring by invading the dentist's sleeping room. You found his watch on a table beside his bed, set that with the clock, then went out, spoke to Policeman Gillis whose number you noted and rang the front door bell. After you left by the front door you allowed time for the household to get quiet again, then re-entered from the rear and reset the watch and clock. Thus your alibi was perfect. You took desperate chances and you knew it, but it was necessary."

The Thinking Machine stopped and squinted up into the pallid face. Chase made a hopeless gesture with his hands and sat down, burying his face.

"It was clever, Mr. Chase," said the scientist finally. "It is the only murder case I know where the criminal made no mistake. You probably killed Mr. De Forrest in a fit of anger, left there while the elevator boy was upstairs, then saw the necessity of protecting yourself and devised this alibi at the cost of one tooth. Your only real danger was when you made Patrolman Gillis your witness, taking the desperate chance that he did not know or would not remember just when you spoke to him."

Again there was silence. Finally Chase looked up with haggard face.

"How did you know all this?" he asked.

"Because under the circumstances, nothing else *could* have happened," replied the scientist. "The simplest rules of logic proved conclusively that this did happen." He straightened up in the chair. "By the way," he asked, "what was the motive of the murder?"

"Don't you know?" asked Chase, quickly.

"No."

"Then you never will," declared Chase, grimly.

When Chase had gone with the detective, Hatch lingered with The Thinking Machine.

"It's perfectly astonishing," he said. "How did you get at it anyway?"

"I visited the neighborhood, saw how it could have been done, learned through your investigation that no one else appeared in the case, then, knowing that this must have happened, tricked Mr. Chase into believing I was an eye witness to the incidents in the alley. That was the only way to make him confess. Of course there was no one else in it."

One of the singular points in the Chase murder trial was that while the prisoner was convicted of murder on his own statement no inkling of a motive ever appeared.

THE LOST RADIUM

I

One ounce of radium! Within his open palm Professor Dexter held practically the world's entire supply of that singular and seemingly inexhaustible force which was, and is, one of the greatest of all scientific riddles. So far as known there were only a few more grains in existence—four in the Curie laboratory in Paris, two in Berlin, two in St. Petersburg, one at Leland Stanford and one in London. All the remainder was here—here in the Yarvard laboratory, a tiny mass lumped on a small piece of steel.

Gazing at this vast concentrated power Professor Dexter was a little awed and a little appalled at the responsibility which had suddenly devolved upon him, naturally enough with this culmination of a project which he had cherished for months. Briefly this had been to gather into one cohesive whole the many particles of the precious substance scattered over the world for the purpose of elaborate experiments as to its motive power practicability. Now here it was.

Its value, based on scarcity of supply, was incalculable. Millions of dollars would not replace it. Minute portions had come from the four quarters of the globe, in each case by special messenger, and each separate grain had been heavily insured by Lloyd's at a staggering premium. It was only after months of labor, backed by the influence at the great university of Yarvard in which he held the chair of physics, that Professor Dexter had been able to accomplish his purpose.

At least one famous name had been loaned to the proposed experiments, that of the distinguished scientist and logician, Professor Augustus S. F. X. Van Dusen—so called The Thinking Machine. The interest of this master mind in the work was a triumph for Professor Dexter, who was young and comparatively unknown. The elder scientist—The Thinking Machine—was a court of last appeal in the sciences and from the moment his connection with Professor Dexter's plans was announced his fellows all over the world had been anxiously awaiting a first word.

Naturally the task of gathering so great a quantity of radium had not been accomplished without extensive, and sometimes sensational, newspaper comment all over the United States and Europe, therefore that news of the receipt of the final portion of the radium at Yarvard had been known in the daily press and with it a statement that Professors Van Dusen and Dexter would immediately begin their experiments.

The work was to be done in the immense laboratory at Yarvard, a high-ceilinged room with roof partially of glass, and with windows set high in the walls far above the reach of curious eyes. Full preparations had been made;—the two men were to work together, and a guard was to be stationed at the single door. This door led into a smaller room, a sort of reception hall, which in turn connected with the main hallway of the building.

Now Professor Dexter was alone in the laboratory, waiting impatiently for The Thinking Machine and turning over in his mind the preliminary steps in the labor he had undertaken. Every instrument was in place, all else was put aside, for these experiments, which were either to revolutionize the motive power of the world or else demonstrate the utter uselessness of radium as a practical force.

Professor Dexter's line of thought was interrupted by the appearance of Mr. Bowen, one of the instructors of the University.

"A lady to see you, Professor," he said as he handed him a card. "She said it was a matter of great importance to you."

Professor Dexter glanced at the card as Mr. Bowen turned and went out through the small room into the main hallway. The name, Mme. Therese du Chastaigny, was wholly unfamiliar. Puzzled a little and perhaps impatient too, he carefully laid the steel with its burden of radium on the long table, and started out into the reception room. Almost in the door he stumbled against something, recovered his equilibrium with an effort and brought up with an undignified jerk.

The color mounted to his modest ears as he heard a woman laugh —a pleasant, musical, throaty sort of ripple that under other circumstances would have been agreeable. Now, being directed at his own discomfiture, it was irritating, and the Professor's face tingled a little as a tall woman arose and came towards him.

"Please pardon me," she said contritely, but there was still a flicker of a smile upon her red lips. "It was my carelessness. I should not have placed my suit case in the door." She lifted it easily and replaced it in that identical position. "Or perhaps," she suggested, inquiringly, "someone else coming might stumble as you did?"

"No," replied the Professor, and he smiled a little through his blushes. "There is no one else in there."

As Mme. du Chastaigny straightened up, with a rustle of skirts, to greet him Professor Dexter was somewhat surprised at her height and at the splendid lines of her figure. She was apparently of thirty years and seemed from a casual glance, to be five feet nine or ten inches tall. In addition to a certain striking indefinable beauty she was of remarkable physical power if one might judge from her poise and manner. Professor Dexter glanced at her and then at the card inquiringly.

"I have a letter of introduction to you from Mme. Curie of France," she explained as she produced it from a tiny chatelaine bag. "Shall we go over here where the light is better?"

She handed the letter to him and together they seated themselves under one of the windows near the door into the outer hallway. Professor Dexter pulled up a light chair facing her and opened the letter. He glanced through it and then looked up with a newly kindled interest in his eyes.

"I should not have disturbed you," Mme. du Chastaigny explained pleasantly, "had I not known it was a matter of the greatest possible interest to you."

"Yes?" Professor Dexter nodded.

"It's radium," she continued. "It just happens that I have in my possession practically an ounce of radium of which the world of science has never heard."

"An ounce of radium!" repeated Professor Dexter, incredulously. "Why, Madame, you astonish, amaze me. An ounce of radium?"

He leaned further forward in his chair and waited expectantly while Mme. du Chastaigny coughed violently. The paroxysm passed after a moment.

"That is my punishment for laughing," she explained, smilingly. "I trust you will pardon me. I have a bad throat—and it was quick retribution."

"Yes, yes," said the other courteously, "but this other—it's most interesting. Please tell me about it."

Mme. du Chastaigny made herself comfortable in the chair, cleared her throat, and began.

"It's rather an unusual story," she said apologetically, "but the radium came into my possession in quite a natural manner. I am English, so I speak the language, but my husband was French as my name indicates, and, he, like you, was a scientist. He was little known to the world at large, however, as he was not connected with any institution. His experiments were undertaken for amusement and gradually led to a complete absorption of his interest. We were not wealthy as Americans count it, but we were comfortably well off.

"That much for my affairs. The letter I gave you from Mme. Curie will tell you the rest as to who I am, Now when the discovery of radium was made by M. and Mme. Curie, my husband began some investigations along the same line and they proved to be remarkably successful. His efforts were first directed towards producing radium, with what object, I was not aware at that time. In the course of months he made grain after grain by some process unlike that of the Curies', and incidentally he spent practically all our little fortune. Finally he had nearly an ounce."

"Most interesting!" commented Professor Dexter. "Please go on."

"It happened that during the production of the last quarter of an ounce, my husband contracted an illness which later proved fatal," Mme. du Chastaigny resumed after a slight pause, and her voice dropped. "I did not know the purpose of his experiments; I only knew what they had been and their comparative cost. On his death bed he revealed this purpose to me. Strangely enough it was identical with yours as the newspapers have announced it—that is, the practicability of radium as a motive power. He was at work on plans looking to the utilization of its power when he died but these plans were not perfected and unfortunately were in such shape as to be unintelligible to another."

She paused and sat silent for a moment. Professor Dexter watching her face, traced a shadow of grief and sorrow there and his own big heart prompted a ready sympathy.

"And what," he asked, "was your purpose in coming to me now?"

"I know of the efforts you have made and the difficulties you have encountered in gathering enough radium for the experiments you have in mind," Mme. du Chastaigny continued, "and it occurred to me that what I have, which is of no possible use to me, might be sold to you or to the university. As I said, there is nearly an ounce of it.

It is where I can put my hands on it, and you of course are to make the tests to prove it is what it should be."

"Sell it?" gasped Professor Dexter. "Why, Madame, it's impossible. The funds of the college are not so plentiful that the vast fortune necessary to purchase such a quantity would be forth-coming."

A certain hopeful light in the face of the young woman passed and there was a quick gesture of her hands which indicated disappointment.

"You speak of a vast fortune," she said at last. "I could not hope, of course, to realize anything like the actual value of the substance— a million perhaps? Only a few hundred thousands? Something to convert into available funds for me the fortune which has been sunk."

There was almost an appeal in her limpid voice and Professor Dexter considered the matter deeply for several minutes as he stared out the window.

"Or perhaps," the woman hurried on after a moment, "it might be that you need more radium for the experiments you have in hand now, and there might be some sum paid me for the use of what I have? A sort of royalty? I am willing to do anything within reason."

Again there was a long pause. Ahead of him, with this hitherto unheard of quantity of radium available, Professor Dexter saw rosy possibilities in his chosen work. The thought gripped him more firmly as he considered it. He could see little chance of a purchase— but the use of the substance during his experiments! That might be arranged.

"Madame," he said at last, "I want to thank you deeply for coming to me. While I can promise nothing definite I can promise that I will take up the matter with certain persons who may be able to do something for you. It's perfectly astounding. Yes, I may say that I *will* do something, but I shall perhaps, require several days to bring it about. Will you grant me that time?"

Mme. du Chastaigny smiled.

"I must of course," she said, and again she went off into a paroxysm of coughing, a distressing, hacking outburst which seemed to shake her whole body. "Of course," she added, when the spasm passed, "I can only hope that you can do something either in purchasing or using it."

"Could you fix a definite price for the quantity you have—that is a sale price—and another price merely for its use?" asked Professor Dexter.

"I can't do that offhand of course, but here is my address on this card—Hotel Teutonic. I expect to remain there for a few days and you may reach me any time. Please, now please," and again there was a pleading note in her voice, and she laid one hand on his arm, "don't hesitate to make any offer to me. I shall be only too glad to accept it if I can."

She arose and Professor Dexter stood beside her.

"For your information," she went on, "I will explain that I only arrived in this country yesterday by steamer from Liverpool and my need is such that within another six months I shall be absolutely dependent upon what I may realize from the radium."

She crossed the room, picked up the suit case and again she smiled, evidently at the recollection of Professor Dexter's awkward stumble. Then with her burden she turned to go.

"Permit me, Madame," suggested Professor Dexter, quickly as he reached for the bag.

"Oh no, it is quite light," she responded easily.

There were a few commonplaces and then she went out. Gazing through the window after her Professor Dexter noted, with certain admiration in his eyes the graceful strong lines of her figure as she entered a carriage and was driven away. He stood deeply thoughtful for a minute considering the possibilities arising from her casual announcement of the existence of this unknown radium.

"If I only had that too," he muttered as he turned and re-entered his work room.

An instant later, a cry—a wild amazed shriek—came from the laboratory and Professor Dexter, with pallid face, rushed out through the reception room and flung open the door into the main hallway. Half a dozen students gathered about him and from across the hall Mr. Bowen, the instructor, appeared with startled eyes.

"The radium is gone—stolen!" gasped Professor Dexter.

The members of the little group stared at one another blankly while Professor Dexter raved impotently and ran his fingers through his hair. There were questions and conjectures; a babble was raging about him when a new figure loomed up in the picture. It was that of a small man with an enormous yellow head and an eternal petulant droop to the corners of his mouth. He had just turned a corner in the hall.

"Ah, Professor Van Dusen," exclaimed Professor Dexter, and he seized the long, slender hand of The Thinking Machine in a frenzied grip.

"Dear me! Dear me!" complained The Thinking Machine as he sought to extract his fingers from the vise. "Don't do that. What's the matter?"

"The radium is gone—stolen!" Professor Dexter explained.

The Thinking Machine drew back a little and squinted aggressively into the distended eyes of his fellow scientist.

"Why that's perfectly silly," he said at last. "Come in, please, and tell me what happened."

With perspiration dripping from his brow and hands atremble, Professor Dexter followed him into the reception room, whereupon The Thinking Machine turned, closed the door into the hallway and snapped the lock. Outside Mr. Bowen and the students heard the click and turned away to send the astonishing news hurtling through the great university. Inside Professor Dexter sank down on a chair with staring eyes and nervously twitching lips.

"Dear me, Dexter, are you crazy?" demanded The Thinking Machine irritably. "Compose yourself. What happened? What were the circumstances of the disappearance?"

"Come—come in here—the laboratory and see," suggested Professor Dexter.

"Oh, never mind that now," said the other impatiently. "Tell me what happened?"

Professor Dexter paced the length of the small room twice then sat down again, controlling himself with a perceptible effort. Then, ramblingly but completely, he told the story of Mme. du Chastaigny's call, covering every circumstance from the time he placed the radium on the table in the laboratory until he saw her drive away in the carriage. The Thinking Machine leaned back in his chair with squint eyes upturned and slender white fingers pressed tip to tip.

"How long was she here?" he asked at the end.

"Ten minutes, I should say," was the reply.

"Where did she sit?"

"Right where you are, facing the laboratory door."

The Thinking Machine glanced back at the window behind him.

"And you?" he asked.

"I sat here facing her."

"You know that she did not enter the laboratory?"

"I know it, yes" replied Professor Dexter promptly. "No one save me has entered that laboratory today. I have taken particular pains to see that no one did. When Mr. Bowen spoke to me I had the radium in my hand. He merely opened the door, handed me her card and went right out. Of course it's impossible that—"

"Nothing is impossible, Mr. Dexter," blazed The Thinking Machine suddenly. "Did you at any time leave Mme. du Chastaigny in this room alone?"

"No, no," declared Dexter emphatically. "I was looking at her every moment she was here; I did not put the radium out of my hand until Mr. Bowen was out of this room and in the hallway there. I then came into this room and met her."

For several minutes The Thinking Machine sat perfectly silent, squinting upward while Professor Dexter gazed into the inscrutable face anxiously.

"I hope," ventured the Professor at last, "that you do not believe it was any fault of mine?"

The Thinking Machine did not say.

"What sort of a voice has Mme. du Chastaigny?" he asked instead.

The Professor blinked a little in bewilderment.

"An ordinary voice—the low voice of a woman of education and refinement," he replied.

"Did she raise it at any time while talking?"

"No."

"Perhaps she sneezed or coughed while talking to you?"

Unadulterated astonishment was written on Professor Dexter's face.

"She coughed, yes, violently," he replied.

"Ah!" exclaimed The Thinking Machine and there was a flash of comprehension in the narrow blue eyes. "Twice, I suppose?"

Professor Dexter was staring at the scientist blankly.

"Yes, twice," he responded.

"Anything else?"

"Well, she laughed I think."

"What was the occasion of her laughter?"

"I stumbled over a suitcase she had set down by the laboratory door there."

The Thinking Machine absorbed that without evidence of emotion, then reached for the letter of introduction which Mme. du Chastaigny had given to Professor Dexter and which he still carried crumpled up in his hand. It was a short note, just a few lines in French, explaining that Mme. du Chastaigny desired to see Professor Dexter on a matter of importance.

"Do you happen to know Mme. Curie's hand-writing?" asked The Thinking Machine after a cursory examination. "Of course you had some correspondence with her about this work?"

"I know her writing, yes," was the reply. "I think that is genuine, if that's what you mean."

"We'll see after a while," commented The Thinking Machine.

He arose and led the way into the laboratory. There Professor Dexter indicated to him the exact spot on the work table where the radium had been placed. Standing beside it he made some mental calculation as he squinted about the room, at the highly placed windows, the glass roof above, the single door. Then wrinkles grew in his tall brow.

"I presume all the wall windows are kept fastened?"

"Yes, always."

"And those in the glass roof?"

"Yes."

"Then bring me a tall step-ladder please!"

It was produced after a few minutes. Professor Dexter looked on curiously and with a glimmer of understanding as The Thinking Machine examined each catch on every window, and tapped the panes over with a pen-knife. When he had examined the last and found all locked he came down the ladder.

"Dear me!" he exclaimed petulantly. "It's perfectly extraordinary—most extraordinary. If the radium was not stolen through the reception room, then—then—" He glanced around the room again.

Professor Dexter shook his head. He had recovered his self-possession somewhat, but bewilderment left his helpless.

"Are you sure, Professor Dexter," asked The Thinking Machine at last coldly, "*are you sure* you placed the radium where you have indicated?"

There was almost an accusation in the tone and Professor Dexter flushed hotly.

"I am positive, yes," he replied.

"And you are absolutely certain that neither Mr. Bowen nor Mme. du Chastaigny entered this room?"

"I am absolutely positive."

The Thinking Machine wandered up and down the long table apparently without any interest, handling the familiar instruments and glittering appliances as a master.

"Did Mme. du Chastaigny happen to mention any children?" he at last asked, irrelevantly.

Professor Dexter blinked again.

"No," he replied.

"Adopted or otherwise?"

"No."

"Just what sort of a suit case was that she carried?"

"Oh, I don't know," replied Professor Dexter. "I didn't particularly notice. It seemed to be about the usual kind of a suit case—sole leather I imagine."

"She arrived in this country yesterday you said?"

"Yes."

"It's perfectly extraordinary," The Thinking Machine grunted. Then he scribbled a line or two on a scrap of paper and handed it to Professor Dexter.

"Please have this sent by cable at once."

Professor Dexter glanced at it. It was:

"*Mme. Curie, Paris:*

"Did you give Mme. du Chastaigny letter of introduction for Professor Dexter? Answer quick.

"Augustus S. F. X. Van Dusen."

As Professor Dexter glanced at the dispatch his eyes opened a little.

"You don't believe that Mme. du Chastaigny could have—" he began.

"I daresay I know what Mme. Curie's answer will be," interrupted the other abruptly.

"What?"

"It will be no," was the positive reply. "And then—" He paused.

"Then—?"

"Your veracity may be brought into question."

With flaming face and tightly clenched teeth but without a word, Professor Dexter saw The Thinking Machine unlock the door and pass out. Then he dropped into a chair and buried his face in his hands. There Mr. Bowen found him a few minutes later.

"Ah, Mr. Bowen," he said, as he glanced up, "please have this cable sent immediately."

II

Once in his apartments The Thinking Machine telephoned to Hutchinson Hatch, reporter, at the office of his newspaper. That long, lean, hungry looking young man was fairly bubbling with suppressed emotion when he rushed into the booth to answer and the exhilaration of pure enthusiasm made his voice vibrant when he spoke. The Thinking Machine readily understood.

"It's about the radium theft at Yarvard that I wanted to speak to you," he said.

"Yes," Hatch replied. "Just heard of it this minute—a bulletin from Police Headquarters. I was about to go out on it."

"Please do something for me first," requested The Thinking Machine. "Go at once to the Hotel Teutonic and ascertain indisputably for me whether or not Mme. du Chastaigny, who is stopping there, is accompanied by a child."

"Certainly, of course," said Hatch, "but the story—"

"This *is* the story," interrupted The Thinking Machine, tartly. "If you can learn nothing of any child at the hotel go to the steamer on which she arrived yesterday from Liverpool and inquire there. I must have definite, absolute, indisputable evidence."

"I'm off," Hatch responded.

He hung up the receiver and rushed out. He happened to be professionally acquainted with the chief clerk of the Teutonic, a monosyllabic, rotund gentleman who was an occasional source of private information and who spent his life adding up a column of figures.

"Hello, Charlie," Hatch greeted him. "Mme. du Chastaigny stopping here?"

"Yep," said Charlie.

"Husband with her?"

"Nope."

"By herself when she came?"

"Yep."

"Hasn't a child with her?"

"Nope."

"What does she look like?"

"A corker!" said Charlie.

This last loquacious outburst seemed to appease the reporter's burning thirst for information and he rushed away to the dock where the steamship, Granada from Liverpool, still lay. Aboard he sought out the purser and questioned him along the same lines with the same result. There was no trace of a child. Then Hatch made his way to the home of The Thinking Machine.

"Well?" demanded the scientist.

The reporter shook his head.

"She hasn't seen or spoken to a child since she left Liverpool so far as I can ascertain," he declared.

It was not quite surprise, it was rather perturbation in the manner of The Thinking Machine now. It showed in a quick gesture of one hand, in the wrinkles on his brow, in the narrowing down of his eyes. He dropped back into a chair and remained there silent, thoughtful for a long time.

"It couldn't have been, it couldn't have been, it couldn't have been," the scientist broke out finally.

Having no personal knowledge on the subject, whatever it was, Hatch discreetly remained silent. After a while The Thinking Machine aroused himself with a jerk and related to the reporter the story of the lost radium so far as it was known.

"The letter of introduction from Mme. Curie opened the way for Mme. du Chastaigny," he explained. "Frankly I believe that letter to be a forgery. I cabled asking Mme. Curie. A 'No' from her will mean that my conjecture is correct; a 'Yes' will mean—but that is hardly worth considering. The question now is: What method was employed to cause the disappearance of the radium from that room?"

The door opened and Martha appeared. She handed a cablegram to The Thinking Machine and he ripped it open with hurried fingers. He glanced at the sheet once, then arose suddenly after which he sat down again, just as suddenly.

"What is it?" ventured Hatch.

"It's 'Yes'," was the reply.

In the seclusion of his own small laboratory The Thinking Machine was making some sort of chemical experiment about eight o'clock that night. He was just hoisting a graduated glass, containing a purplish, hazy fluid, to get the lamp light through it, when an idea flashed into his mind. He permitted the glass to fall and smash on the floor.

"Perfectly stupid of me," he grumbled and turning he walked into an adjoining room without so much as a glance at the wrecked glass. A minute later he had Hutchinson Hatch on the telephone.

"Come right up," he instructed.

There was that in his voice which caused Hatch to jump. He seized his hat and rushed out of his office. When he reached The Thinking Machine's apartments that gentleman was just emerging from the room where the telephone was.

"I have it," the scientist told the reporter, forestalling a question. "It's ridiculously simple. I can't imagine how I missed it except through stupidity."

Hatch smiled behind his hand. Certainly stupidity was not to be charged against The Thinking Machine.

"Come in a cab?" asked the scientist.

"Yes, it's waiting."

"Come on then."

They went out together. The scientist gave some instruction to the cabby and they clattered off.

"You're going to meet a very remarkable person," The Thinking Machine explained. "He may cause trouble and he may not—any way look out for him. He's tricky."

That was all. The cab drew up in front of a large building, evidently a boarding house of the middle class. The Thinking Machine jumped out, Hatch following, and together they ascended the steps. A maid answered the bell.

"Is Mr.—Mr.—oh, what's his name?" and The Thinking Machine snapped his fingers as if trying to remember. "Mr.——, the small gentleman who arrived from Liverpool yesterday—"

"Oh," and the maid smiled broadly, "you mean Mr. Berkerstrom?"

"Yes, that's the name," exclaimed the scientist, "Is he in, please?"

"I think so, sir," said the maid, still smiling. "Shall I take your card?"

"No, it isn't necessary," replied The Thinking Machine. "We are from the theater. He is expecting us."

"Second floor, rear," said the maid.

They ascended the stairs and paused in front of a door. The Thinking Machine tried it softly. It was unlocked and he pushed it open. A bright light blazed from a gas jet but no person was in sight. As they stood silent, they heard a newspaper rattle and both looked in the direction whence came the sound.

Still no one appeared. The Thinking Machine raised a finger and tiptoed to a large upholstered chair which faced the other way. One slender hand disappeared on the other side to be lifted immediately. Wriggling in his grasp was a man—a toy man—a midget miniature in smoking jacket and slippers who swore fluently in German. Hatch burst out laughing, an uncontrollable fit which left him breathless.

"Mr. Berkerstrom, Mr. Hatch," said The Thinking Machine gravely. "This is the gentleman, Mr. Hatch, who stole the radium. Before you begin to talk, Mr. Berkerstrom, I will say that Mme. du Chastaigny has been arrested and has confessed."

"*Ach, Gott!*" raged the little German. "Let me down, der chair in, ef you blease."

The Thinking Machine lowered the tiny wriggling figure into the chair while Hatch closed and locked the door. When the reporter came back and looked, laughter was gone. The drawn wrinkled face of the midget, the babyish body, the toy clothing, added to the pitiful helplessness of the little figure. His age might have been fifteen or fifty, his weight was certainly not more than twenty-five pounds, his height barely thirty inches.

"It iss as we did him in der theater, und—" Mr. Berkerstrom started to explain limpingly.

"Oh, that was it?" inquired The Thinking Machine curiously as if some question in his own mind had been settled. "What is Mme. du Chastaigny's correct name?"

"She iss der famous Mlle. Fanchon, und I am der marvelous midget, Count von Fritz," proclaimed Mr. Berkerstrom proudly in play-bill fashion.

Then a glimmer of what had actually happened flashed through Hatch's mind; he was staggered by the sublime audacity which made it possible. The Thinking Machine arose and opened a closet door at which he had been staring. From a dark recess he dragged out a suit case and from this in turn a small steel box.

"Ah, here is the radium," he remarked as he opened the box. "Think of it, Mr. Hatch. An actual value of millions in that small box."

Hatch *was* thinking of it, thinking all sorts of things as he mentally framed an opening paragraph for this whooping big yarn. He was still thinking of it as he and The Thinking Machine accompanied willingly enough by the midget, entered the cab and were driven back to the scientist's house.

An hour later Mme. du Chastaigny called by request. She imagined her visit had something to do with the purchase of an ounce of radium; Detective Mallory, watching her out a corner of his official eye, imagined she imagined that. The next caller was Professor Dexter. Dumb anger gnawed at his heart, but he had heeded a telephone request. The Thinking Machine and Hatch completed the party.

"Now, Mme. du Chastaigny, please," The Thinking Machine began quietly, "will you please inform me if you have *another* ounce of radium in addition to that you stole from the Yarvard laboratory?"

Mme. du Chastaigny leaped to her feet. The Thinking Machine was staring upward with squint eyes and finger tips pressed together. He didn't alter his position in the slightest at her sudden move—but Detective Mallory did.

"Stole?" exclaimed Mme. du Chastaigny. "Stole?"

"That's the word I used," said The Thinking Machine almost pleasantly.

Into the woman's eyes there leapt a blaze of tigerish ferocity. Her face flushed, then the color fled and she sat down again, perfectly pallid.

"Count von Fritz has recounted his part in the affair to me," went on The Thinking Machine. He leaned forward and took a package from the table. "Here is the radium. Now have you any radium in addition to this?"

"The radium!" gasped the Professor incredulously.

"If there is no denial Count von Fritz might as well come in, Mr. Hatch," remarked The Thinking Machine.

Hatch opened the door. The midget bounded into the room true theatric style.

"Is it enough, Mlle. Fanchon?" inquired the scientist. There was an ironic touch in his voice.

Mme. du Chastaigny nodded, dumbly.

"It would interest you, of course, to know how it came out," went on The Thinking Machine. "I daresay your inspiration for the theft came from a newspaper article, therefore you probably know that I was directly interested in the experiments planned. I visited the laboratory immediately after you left with the radium. Professor Dexter told me your story. It was clever, clever, but there was too much radium, therefore unbelievable. If not true, then why had you been there? The answer is obvious.

"Neither you or anyone else save Mr. Dexter entered that laboratory. Yet the radium was gone. How? My first impression was that your part in the theft had been to detain Mr. Dexter while someone entered the laboratory or else fished out the radium through a window in the glass roof by some ingenious contrivance. I questioned Mr. Dexter as to your precise acts, and ventured the opinion that you had either sneezed or coughed. You had coughed twice— obviously a signal—thus that view was strengthened.

"Next, I examined window and roof fastenings—all were locked. I tapped over the glass to see if they had been tampered with. They had not. Apparently the radium had not gone through the reception room; certainly it had not gone any other way—yet it was gone. It was a nice problem until I recalled that Mr. Dexter had mentioned a suit case. Why did a woman, on business, go out carrying a suit case. Or why, granting that she had a good reason for it, should she take the trouble to drag it into the reception room instead of leaving it in the carriage?

"Now I didn't believe you had any radium; I knew you had signaled to the real thief by coughing. Therefore I was prepared to believe that the suit case was the solution of the theft. How? Obviously, something concealed in it. What? A monkey? I dismissed that because the thief must have had the reasoning instinct. If not a monkey then what? A child? That seemed more probable, yet it was improbable. I proceeded, however, on the hypothesis that a child carefully instructed had been the actual thief."

Open eyes were opened wider. Mme. du Chastaigny, being chiefly concerned, followed the plain, cold reasoning as if fascinated. Count von Fritz straightened his necktie and smiled.

"I sent a cable to Mme. Curie asking if the letter of introduction were genuine; and sent Mr. Hatch to get a trace of a child. He informed me that there was no child just about the time I heard from Mme. Curie that the letter was genuine. The problem immediately went back to the starting point. Time after time I reasoned it out, always the same way—finally the solution came. If not a monkey or a child then what? A midget. Of course it was stupid of me not to have seen that possibility at first.

"Then there remained only the task of finding him. He probably came on the same boat with the woman, and I saw a plan to find him. It was through the driver of the carriage which Mme. du Chastaigny used. I got his number by 'phone at the Hotel Teutonic. Where had

Mme. du Chastaigny left a suit case? He gave me an address. I went there.

"I won't attempt to explain how this woman obtained the letter from Mme. Curie. I will only say that a woman who undertakes to sell an ounce of radium to a man from whom she intends to steal it is clever enough to do anything. I may add that she and the midget are theatrical people and that the idea of a person in a suit case came from some part of their stage performance. Of course the suit case is so built that the midget could open and close it from inside."

"Und it always gets der laugh," interposed the midget, complacently.

After awhile the prisoners were led away. Count von Fritz escaped three times the first day by the simple method of wriggling between the bars of his cell.

KIDNAPPED BABY BLAKE, MILLIONAIRE

Douglas Blake, millionaire, sat flat on the floor and gazed with delighted eyes at the unutterable beauties of a highly colored picture book. He was only fourteen months old, and the picture book was quite the most beautiful thing he had ever beheld. Evelyn Barton, a lovely girl of twenty-two or -three years, sat on the floor opposite, and listened with a slightly amused smile as Baby Blake in his infinite wisdom discoursed learnedly on the astonishing things he found in the book.

The floor whereon Baby Blake sat was that of the library of the Blake home, in the outskirts of Lynn. This home, handsomely but modestly furnished, had been built by Baby Blake's father, Langdon Blake, who had died four months previously, leaving Baby Blake's beautiful mother, Elizabeth Blake, heartbroken and crushed by the blow, and removing her from the social world of which she had been the leader.

Here, quietly, with but three servants and Miss Barton, the nurse, who could hardly be classed as a servant—rather a companion—Mrs. Blake had lived on for the present.

The great house was gloomy, but it had been the scene of all her happiness, and she had clung to it. The building occupied relatively a central position in a plot of land facing the street for 200 feet or so, and stretching back about 300 feet. A stone wall enclosed it.

In summer this plot was a great velvety lawn; now the first snow of the winter had left an inch deep blanket over all, unbroken save the cement-paved walk which extended windingly from the gap in the street wall to the main entrance of the house. This path had been cleaned of snow and was now a black thread through the whiteness.

Near the front stoop this path branched off and led on around the building toward the back. This, too, had been cleared of snow, but beyond the back door entrance the white blanket covered everything back to the rear wall of the property. There, against the rear wall, to the right as one stood behind the house, was a roomy barn and stable; in the extreme left hand corner of the property was a cluster of tall trees, with limbs outstretched fantastically.

The driveway from the front was covered with snow. It had been several weeks since Mrs. Blake had had occasion to use either of her vehicles or horses, so she had closed the barn and stabled the horses outside. Now the barn was wholly deserted. From one of the great trees a swing, which had been placed there for the delight of Baby Blake, swung idly.

In the summer Baby Blake had been wont to toddle the hundred or more feet from the house to the swing; but now that pleasure was forbidden. He was confined to the house by the extreme cold.

When the snow began to fall that day, about two o'clock, Baby Blake had shown enthusiasm. It was the first snow he remembered. He stood at a window of the warm library and, pointing out with a chubby finger, told Miss Barton:

"Me want doe."

Miss Barton interpreted this as a request to be taken out or permitted to go out in the snow.

"No, no," she said firmly. "Cold. Baby must not go. Cold. Cold."

Baby Blake had raised his voice in lusty protestation at this unkindness of his nurse, and finally Mrs. Blake had had to pacify him. "We can go to the mailbox if the snow stops." Since then a hundred things had been used to divert Baby Blake's mind from the outside.

This snow had fallen for an hour, then stopped, and the clouds passed. Now, at fifteen minutes of six o'clock in the evening, the moon glittered coldly and clearly over the unbroken surface of the snow. Star points spangled the sky; the wind had gone, and extreme quiet lay over the place. Even the sound from the street, where an occasional vehicle passed, was muffled by the snow. Baby Blake heard a jingling sleigh bell somewhere in the distance and raised his head inquiringly.

"Pretty horse," said Miss Barton, quickly indicating a splash of color in the open book.

"Pitty horsie," said Baby Blake.

"Horse," said Miss Barton. "Four legs. One, two, three, four," she counted.

"Pitty horsie," said Baby Blake again.

He turned another page with a ruthless disregard of what might happen to it.

"Pitty kitty," he went on, wisely.

"Yes, pretty kitty," the nurse agreed.

"Pitty doggie, 'n' pitty ev'fing, ooo-ah," Baby Blake was gravely enthusiastic. "Efnit," he added as his eye caught a full-page picture.

"Elephant, yes," said Miss Barton.

Then Baby Blake arose from his seat on the floor and toddled over to where Miss Barton sat, plumping down heavily, directly in front of her.

"We shall go out for a short walk to the mailbox in a few minutes," said Miss Barton, and she helped Baby Blake into his warm coat.

Just at that moment Mrs. Blake appeared at the door.

"Miss Barton," she said. "Could you help me for a moment?"

The girl arose and went into the adjoining room with Mrs. Blake, leaving the boy alone in the library, where he turned again to the picture book outspread on the floor.

The two women returned to the library after about ten minutes, to where Baby Blake had been looking at the picture book. The baby was not there. Miss Barton looked puzzled for a moment, but the mother paid no attention. The nurse passed into another room, thinking Douglas had gone there.

Within ten minutes the household was in an uproar. Baby Blake had disappeared. Miss Barton, the servant and the distracted mother raced through the roomy building, searching every nook and corner, calling for Douglas. No answer. At last Miss Barton and Mrs. Blake met face to face in the library over the picture book the baby had been admiring.

"He isn't outside, either," said Miss Barton. Her face was pale as she looked at Mrs. Blake.

"Could it be—kidnapping?" half whispered the mother.

"I—I don't know," faltered the nurse. "I hope not."

"Oh," exclaimed Mrs. Blake, and with waxen, white face she sank back on the couch. "The police!"

Evelyn Barton ran to the telephone and notified the police. They responded promptly, three detectives and two uniformed officers. One of them explained the situation to his chief by 'phone, and an alarm was sent out.

While the uniformed men searched the house again from attic to cellar, the others, plainclothes men, searched outside. Together the three men went over the ground, but the surface of the snow was unbroken save for their own footprints and the paved path. From the front wall, which faced the street, the detectives walked slowly back, one on each side of the house, searching in the snow for some trace of a footprint. There was nothing to reward their search, and they met behind the house. Each shook his head. Then one stopped suddenly and pointed to the snow which lay at their feet, spreading away over the immense back yard. The other detective looked intently, then stopped.

What he saw was the footprint of a child, a baby. The tracks led straight away through the snow toward the back walk, and without a word the two men followed them, one by one: the regular toddling steps of a baby who is only fairly certain on his feet. Ten, twenty, thirty feet they went on in a straight line, and already the detectives saw a possible solution. It was that Baby Blake had wandered away of his own free will.

Then, as they were following the tracks, they stopped suddenly confounded. Each dropped on his knees in the snow and sought vainly for something, sought over a space of many feet, then turned back to the tracks again.

"Well, if that——" one began.

The footprints, going steadily forward across the yard, had stopped. There was the last, made as if Baby Blake had intended to go forward, but there were no more tracks, no more traces of tracks—nothing. Baby Blake had walked to this point, and then——

"Why he must have gone straight up in the air," gasped one of the detectives. He sank down on a small wooden box three or four feet from where the tracks ended, and wiped the perspiration from his face.

"All problems may be reduced to an arithmetical basis by a simple mental process," declared Professor Augustus S. F. X. Van Dusen, emphatically. "Once a problem is so reduced, no matter what it is, it may be solved. If you play chess, Mr. Hatch, you will readily grasp what I mean. Our great chess masters are really our greatest logicians and mathematicians, yet their efforts are directed in a way which can be of no use save to demonstrate, theatrically, I may say, the unlimited possibilities of the human mind."

Hutchinson Hatch, reporter, leaned back in his chair and watched the great scientist and logician as he pottered around the long work-bench beside the big window of his tiny laboratory. It was here that Professor Van Dusen had achieved some of those marvels which had attracted the attention of the world at large and had won for him a long list of honorary initials.

Hatch doubted if the Professor himself could recall these—that is beyond the more common ones of Ph.D., LL.D., M.D., and M.A. There were strange combinations of letters bestowed by French, Italian, German and English educational and scientific institutions, which were delighted to honor so eminent a scientist as Professor Van Dusen, so called The Thinking Machine.

The slender body of the scientist, bowed from close study and minute microscopic observation, gave the impression of physical weakness—an impression which was wholly correct—and made the enormous head which topped the figure seem abnormal. Added to this was the long yellow hair of the scientist, which sometimes as he worked fell over his face and almost obscured the keen blue eyes perpetually squinting through unusually thick glasses.

"By the reduction of a problem to an arithmetical basis," The Thinking Machine went on, "I mean the finding of the cause of an effect. For instance, a man is dead. We know only that. Reason tells us that he died naturally or was killed.

"If killed, it may have been an accident, design or suicide. There are no alternatives. The average mind grasps those possibilities instantly as facts because the average mind has to do with death and understands. We may call this primary reasoning instinct.

"In the higher reasoning which can only come from long study and experiment, imagination is necessary to supply temporarily gaps caused by absence of facts. Imagination is the backbone of the scientific mind. Marconi had to imagine wireless telegraphy before he accomplished it. It is the same with the telephone, the telegraph, the steam engine and those scores of commonplace marvels which are a part of our everyday life.

"The higher scientific mind is, perforce, the mind of a logician. It must possess imagination to a remarkable extent. For instance, science proved that all matter is composed of atoms—the molecular theory. Having proven this, scientific imagination saw that it was possible that atoms were themselves composed of more minute atoms, and sought to prove this. It did so.

"Therefore, we know atoms make atoms and that more minute

atoms make those atoms, and so on down to the point of absolute indivisibility. This is logic.

"Applied in the other direction, this imagination—really logic—leads to amazing possibilities. It would grade upward something like this: Man is made of atoms; man and his works as other atoms make cities; cities and nature as atoms make countries; countries and oceans as atoms make worlds.

"Then comes the supreme imaginative leap which would make worlds merely atoms, pinpoint parts of a vast solar system itself merely an atom in some greater scheme of creation which the imagination refuses to grasp, which staggers the mind. It is all logic, logic, logic."

The irritated voice stopped as the scientist lifted a graded measuring glass to the light and squinted for an instant at its contents, which, under the amazed eyes of Hutchinson Hatch, swiftly changed from a brilliant scarlet to a pure white.

"You have heard me say frequently, Mr. Hatch," The Thinking Machine resumed, "that two and two make four, not sometimes, but all the time—atoms make atoms, therefore atoms make creations." He paused. "That change of color in this chemical is merely a change of atoms; it has in no way affected the consistency or weight of the liquid. Yet the red atoms have disappeared, eliminated by the white."

"The logic being that the white atoms are the stronger?" asked Hatch, almost timidly.

"Precisely," said The Thinking Machine, "and also constant and victorious enemies of the red atoms. In other words that was a war between red and white atoms you just witnessed. Who shall say that a war on this earth is not as puny to the observer of this earth as an atom in the greater creation, as was that little war to us?"

Hatch blinked a little at the question. It opened up something bigger than his mind had ever struggled with before, and he was a newspaper reporter, too. Professor Van Dusen turned away and stirred up more chemicals in another glass, then poured the contents of one glass into another.

Hatch heard the telephone bell ring in the next room, and after a moment, Martha, the aged woman who was the household staff of the scientist's modest home, appeared at the door.

"Someone to speak to Mr. Hatch at the 'phone," she said.

Hatch went to the 'phone. At the other end was his city editor bursting with impatience.

"A disappearance, probably a kidnapping," the city editor said. "I've been looking for you everywhere. Happened tonight about 6 o'clock—It's now 8:30. Jump up to Lynn quick and get it."

Then the city editor went on to detail the known points of the mystery, as the police of Lynn had learned them: the child left alone for a few minutes, the footsteps in the snow, which led to—nothing.

Thoroughly alive with the instinct of the reporter, Hatch returned to the laboratory where The Thinking Machine was at work.

"Another mystery," he said persuasively.

"What is it?" asked The Thinking Machine without turning.

Hatch repeated what information he had and The Thinking Machine listened without comment, down to the discovery of the tracks in the snow, and the abrupt ending of these.

"Babies don't have wings, Mr. Hatch," said The Thinking Machine severely.

"I know," said Hatch. "Would you like to go out with me and look it over?"

"It's silly to say the tracks end there," declared The Thinking Machine aggressively. "They must go somewhere. If they don't, they are not the boy's tracks."

"If you'd like to go," said Hatch coaxingly, "we could get there by half-past nine. It's half-past eight now."

"I'll go," said the other suddenly.

An hour later, they were at the front gate of the Blake home in Lynn. The Thinking Machine talked for a long time to the mother, to the nurse, Evelyn Barton, to the servants, then went out into the back yard where the tiny tracks were found.

Here, seeing perfectly by the brilliant light of the moon, The Thinking Machine remained for an hour. He saw the last of the tiny footprints which led nowhere, and he sat on the box where the detective had sat. Then he arose suddenly and examined the box. It was, he found, of wood, approximately two feet square, raised only four or five inches above the ground. It was built to cover and protect the main water connection with the house. The Thinking Machine satisfied himself on this point by looking inside.

From this box he sought in every direction for footprints, tracks which were not obviously those of the detectives or his own or Hatch's. No one else had been permitted to go over the ground, the detectives objecting to this until they had completed their investigations.

No other tracks or footprints appeared; there was nothing to indicate that there had been tracks which had been skillfully covered up by whoever made them.

Again The Thinking Machine sat down on the box and studied his surroundings. Hatch watched him curiously. First he looked away toward the stone wall, nearly a hundred feet in front of him. There was positively no mark in the snow of any kind so far as Hatch could see. Then the scientist looked back toward the house— one of the detectives had told him it was just forty-eight feet from the box—but there were no tracks there save those the detectives and Hatch and himself had made.

Then The Thinking Machine looked toward the back of the lot. Here in the bright moonlight he could see the barn and the clump of trees, several inside the enclosure made by the stone wall and others outside, extending away indefinitely, snow-laden and grotesque in the moonlight. From the view in this direction, The Thinking Machine turned to the other stone wall, a hundred feet or so. Here, too, he vainly sought footprints in the snow.

Finally he arose and walked in this direction with an expression as near bewilderment on his face as Hatch had ever seen. A small dark spot in the snow had attracted his attention. It was eight or ten feet from the box. He stopped and looked at it; it was a stone of flat surface, perhaps a foot square and devoid of snow.

"Why hasn't this any snow on it?" he asked Hatch.

Hatch stared and shook his head. The Thinking Machine, bowed almost to the ground, continued to stare at the stone for a moment, then straightened up and continued walking toward the wall. A few feet further on a rope, evidently a clothes line, barred his way. Without stopping, he ducked his head beneath it and walked on toward the wall, still staring at the ground.

From the wall he retraced his steps to the clothes line, then walked along under that, still staring at the snow, to its end, sixty or seventy feet toward the back of the enclosure. Two or three supports placed at regular intervals beneath the line were closely examined.

"Find anything?" asked Hatch finally.

The Thinking Machine shook his head impatiently.

"It's amazing," he exclaimed petulantly, like a disappointed child.

"It is," Hatch agreed.

The Thinking Machine turned and walked back toward the house as he had come, Hatch following.

"I think we'd better go back to Boston," he said tartly.

Hatch silently acquiesced. Neither spoke until they were in the train, and The Thinking Machine turned suddenly to the wondering reporter.

"Did it seem possible to you that those are not the footprints of the baby at all, only the prints of his shoes?" he demanded suddenly.

"How did they get there?" asked Hatch in turn.

The Thinking Machine shook his head.

On the afternoon of the next day, when the newspapers were full of the mystery, Mrs. Blake received this letter:

> We hav kiddnaped yore baby. It wont do no good to tel the polece we hav the baby ann will bring him bak for twenny fiv thousan dolers. will you give it. Advertis YES or NOA ann sine yore name in a *Boston Amurikan*. Then we wull tel you wat to doe. (sined) Three. (3)

When Hutchinson Hatch went late in the afternoon to inform The Thinking Machine of the appearance of this letter, he found the scientist sitting in his little laboratory, fingertips pressed together, staring steadily at the ceiling. There was a little puzzled line on the high brow, a line Hatch never saw there before, and frank perplexity was in the blue eyes.

The Thinking Machine listened without changing his position as Hatch told him of the letter and its contents.

"What do you make of it all, professor?" asked the reporter.

"I don't know," was the reply—one which was a little startling to Hatch. "It's most perplexing."

"The only known facts seem to be that Baby Blake was kidnapped, and is now in the possession of the kidnappers," said Hatch.

"Those tracks—the footprints in the snow, I mean—furnish the real problem in this case," said the other after a moment. "Presumably they were made by the baby, yet they might not have been. They might have been put there merely to mislead anyone who began a search. If the baby made them—how and why do they stop as they do? If they were made merely with the baby's shoes to mislead investigation the same question remains—how?

"Let's consider a moment. We will dismiss the seeming fact that the baby walked off into the air and disappeared, granting that those tracks were made by the baby. We will also dismiss the possibility that the baby was with anyone when it made the tracks, if it did make them. There were certainly no other footprints but those. There were no footprints leading from or to that point where the baby tracks stopped.

"What are the possibilities? What remains? A balloon? If we accept the balloon as a possibility we must at the same time relinquish the theory of a preconceived plan of abduction. Why? Because any successful plan would have to be arranged so that the baby, of its own will, would have been in that particular spot at that particular moment. Therefore a balloon might have been floated over the place a thousand times without success, and balloons are large—they attract attention, therefore are to be avoided.

"There is a possibility—a bare one—that a balloon with a trailing anchor or hook did pass over the place, and that this hook caught up the baby by its clothing, lifting it clear of the ground. But in that event it was not kidnapping—it was accident. But here against the theory of accident we have the kidnappers' letter.

"If not a balloon, then an eagle? Hardly possible. It would take a bird of exceptional strength to have lifted a fourteen-month child, and besides, there are a thousand things against such a possibility. Certainly the winged man is not known to science, yet there is every evidence of his handiwork here. Briefly, the problem is—granting that the baby itself made the tracks—how was a baby lifted out of the relative centre of a large yard?

"Consider for a moment that the baby did not make the tracks—that they were placed there by someone else. Then we are confronted by the same question—how? A person might have fastened shoes to a long pole and rigged up some arrangement of the sort, and made the tracks for a distance say of twenty feet out into the snow, but remember the tracks run out forty-eight feet to the box, you say.

"If it would have been possible for a person to stand on that box without leaving a track to it or from it, he might have finished the tracks with the shoes on a pole, but nobody went to that box."

The Thinking Machine was silent for several minutes. Hatch had nothing to say. The Thinking Machine seemed to have covered the possibilities thoroughly.

"Of course it might have been possible for a person in a balloon to have put the tracks there, but it would have been a senseless proceeding," the scientist went on. "Certainly there could have been no motive in it to make a person risk discovery by sailing about the

house in a balloon, even at night. We face a stone wall, Mr. Hatch—
a stone wall. It is possible for the mind to follow it only to a certain
point as it now stands."

He arose and disappeared into an adjoining room, returning in
a few minutes with his hat and overcoat.

"Of course," he said to Hatch, "if the baby is alive and in the
possession of the kidnappers, it is possible to recover it, and we'll
do that, but the real problem remains."

"If it is alive?" Hatch repeated.

"Yes, if," said the other shortly. "There are in my mind grave
doubts on that point."

"But the kidnappers' letter?" said Hatch.

"Let's go find out who wrote it," said the other enigmatically.

Together the two ment went to Lynn, and there for half an hour
The Thinking Machine talked to Mrs. Blake. He came out finally
with a package in his hand.

Miss Barton, with eyes red, apparently from weeping, and evident
sorrow imprinted on her pretty face, entered the room almost at the
same moment.

"Miss Barton," the scientist asked, "could you tell me how much
the baby Douglas weighed—roughly, I mean?"

The girl gazed at him a moment, as if startled. "About thirty
pounds, I should say," she answered.

"Thanks," said The Thinking Machine, and turned to Hatch. "I
have twenty-five thousand dollars in this package," he said.

Miss Barton turned and glanced quickly toward him, then passed
out of the room.

"What are you going to do with it?" asked Hatch.

"It's for the kidnappers," was the reply. "The police advised Mrs.
Blake not to try to make terms. I advised her the other way, and
she gave me this."

"What's the next step?" Hatch asked.

"To put the advertisement 'Yes' signed by Mrs. Blake in the
newspaper," said The Thinking Machine. "That's in accordance
with the stipulations of the letter."

An hour later the two men were in Boston. The advertisement
was inserted in the *Boston American* as directed. The next day Mrs.
Blake received a second letter.

"Rapp the munny in a ole nuspaipr ann thow it onn the trash-heeps
at the adres of the vakant lott one blok down the street frum wear

you liv," it directed. "Putt it on top. We wil gett it ann yore baby wil be in yore armms two ours latter. Three (3)."

This letter was immediately placed in the hands of The Thinking Machine. Mrs. Blake's face flushed with hope, and believing that the child would be restored to her, she waited in a fever of impatience.

"Now, Mr. Hatch," instructed The Thinking Machine. "Do with this package as directed. A man will come for it some time. I shall leave the task of finding out who he is, where he goes, and all about him to you. He is probably a man of low mentality, though not so low as the misspelled words of his letter would have you believe. He should be easily trapped. Don't interfere with him, merely report to me when you find out these things."

Alone, The Thinking Machine returned to Boston. Thirty-six hours later, in the early morning, a telegram came for him. It was as follows:

> HAVE MAN LOCATED IN LYNN AND TRACE OF BABY. COME QUICK, IF
> POSSIBLE, TO————HOTEL. HATCH.

The Thinking Machine answered the telegraphic summons immediately, but instead of elation on his face there was another expression, possibly surprise. On the train he read and reread the telegram.

"Have trace of baby," he mused. "Why, it's perfectly astonishing."

White-faced from exhaustion, and with eyes drooping from lack of sleep, Hutchinson Hatch met The Thinking Machine in the hotel lobby, and they immediately went to a room, which the reporter had engaged on the third floor.

The Thinking Machine listened without comment as Hatch told the story of what he had done. He had placed the bundle, then hired a room overlooking the vacant lot, and had remained there at the window for hours. At last night came, but there were clouds which effectively hid the moon. Then Hatch had gone out and secreted himself near the trash pile.

Here from six o'clock in the evening until four in the morning he had remained, numbed with cold and not daring to move. At last his long vigil was rewarded. A man suddenly appeared near the trash heap, glanced around furtively, and then picked up the newspaper package, felt of it to assure himself that it contained something, and then started away quickly.

The work of following him Hatch had not found difficult. He had gone straight to a tenement in the eastern end of Lynn and disappeared inside. Later in the morning, after the occupants in the house were about, Hatch made enquiries which established the identity of the man without question.

His name was Charles Gates and he lived with his wife on the fourth floor of the tenement. His reputation was not wholly savory, and he drank a great deal. He was a man of some education, not of such ignorance as the letters he had written would seem to indicate.

"After learning all these facts," Hatch went on, "my idea was to see the man and talk to him or to his wife. I went there this morning about nine o'clock, as a book agent." The reporter smiled a little. "His wife, Mrs. Gates, didn't want any books, but I nearly sold her a sewing machine.

"Anyway, I got into the apartment and remained there for fifteen or twenty minutes. There was only one room which I didn't enter of the four there. In that room, she explained, her husband was asleep. He had been out late the night before. Of course I knew that.

"I asked if she had any babies and received a negative. From other people in the house I learned that this was true so far as they knew. There was not and has not been a baby in the apartment so far as anyone could tell me. And in spite of that fact I found this."

Hatch drew something from his pocket and spread it on his open hand. It was a baby stocking of fine texture. The Thinking Machine took it and looked at it closely.

"Baby Blake's?" he asked.

"Yes," replied the reporter. "Both Mrs. Blake and the nurse, Miss Barton, identify it."

"Dear me! Dear me!" exclaimed the scientist, thoughtfully. Again the puzzled expression came into his face.

"Of course, the baby hasn't been returned?" went on the scientist.

"Of course, no!" said Hatch.

"Did Mrs. Gates behave like a woman who had suddenly received a share of twenty-five thousand dollars?" asked The Thinking Machine.

"No," Hatch replied. "She looked as if she had attended a mixed ale party. Her lip was cut and bruised, and one eye was black."

"That's what her husband did when he found out what was in the newspaper," commented The Thinking Machine.

"It wasn't money, at all, then?" asked Hatch.

"Certainly not."

Neither said anything for several minutes. The Thinking Machine sat idly twisting the tiny stocking between his long slender fingers, with the little puzzled line in his brow.

"How do you account for that stocking in Gates's possession?" asked the reporter at last.

"Let's go talk to Mrs. Blake," was the reply. "You didn't tell her anything about this man Gates getting the package?"

"No," said the reporter.

"It would only worry her," explained the scientist. "Better let her hope, because——"

Hatch looked at The Thinking Machine quickly, startled.

"Because, what?" he asked.

"There seems to be a very strong probability that Baby Blake is dead," the other responded.

Pondering that, yet conceiving no motive which would cause the baby's death, Hatch was silent as he and the scientist together went to the house of Mrs. Blake. Miss Barton, the nurse, answered the door.

"Miss Barton," said The Thinking Machine testily as they entered, "just when did you give this stocking," and he produced it, "to Charles Gates?"

The girl flushed quickly, and she stammered a little.

"I—I don't know what you mean," she said. "Who is this Charles Gates?"

"May we see Mrs. Blake?" asked the scientist. He squinted steadily into the girl's eyes.

"Yes, of course, that is, I suppose so," she stammered.

She disappeared, and in a few minutes Mrs. Blake appeared. There was an eager, expectant look in her face. It was hope. It faded when she saw the solemn face of The Thinking Machine.

"What recommendations did Miss Barton have when you engaged her?" he began pointedly.

"The best I could ask," was the reply. "She was formerly a governess in the family of the Governor General of Canada. She is well-educated, and came to me from that position."

"Is she well acquainted in Lynn?" asked the scientist.

"That I couldn't say," replied Mrs. Blake. "If you are thinking that she might have some connection with this affair——"

"Ever go out much?" interrupted her questioner.

"Rarely, and then usually with me. She is more of a companion than servant."

"How long have you had her?"

"Since a week or so after my baby—" and the mother's lips trembled a little—"was born. She has been devoted to me since the death of my husband. I would trust her with my life."

"This is your baby's stocking?"

"Beyond any doubt," she replied as she examined it.

"I suppose he had several pairs like this?"

"I really don't know. I should think so."

"Will you please have Miss Barton, or someone else, find those stockings and see if all the pairs like this are complete," instructed The Thinking Machine.

Wonderingly, Mrs. Blake gave the order to Miss Barton, who as wonderingly received it and went out of the room with a quick, resentful look at the bowed figure of the scientist.

"Did you ever happen to notice, Mrs. Blake, whether or not your baby could open a door? For instance, the front door?"

"I believe he could," she replied. "The handles are low, as you see," and she indicated the knob on the front door, which was visible through the reception hall room where they stood.

The Thinking Machine turned suddenly and strode to the window of the library, looking out on the back yard. He was debating something in his own mind. It was whether or not he should tell this mother his fear of her son's death, or should hide it from her until such time as it would appear itself. For some reason known only to himself he considered the child's death not only a possibility, but a probability.

Whatever might have resulted from this mental debate was not to be known then, for suddenly, as he stood staring out the rear window overlooking the spot where the baby's tracks had been seen in the snow—now melted, he started a little and peered eagerly out. It was the first sight he had had of the yard since the night he had examined it by moonlight.

"Dear me, dear me," he exclaimed, suddenly.

Turning abruptly he left the room, and a moment later Hatch saw him in the back yard. Mrs. Blake at the window watched curiously. Outside The Thinking Machine walked straight out to the spot where the baby's tracks had been, and from there Hatch saw him stop and stare at the slightly raised box which covered the water connections.

From this box the scientist took five steps toward a flat-topped stone, the one he had noticed previously, and Hatch saw that it was about ten feet. Then from this he saw The Thinking Machine take four steps to where the sagging clothesline hung. It was probably eight feet. Then the bowed figure of The Thinking Machine walked on out toward the rear wall of the back yard, under the clothesline.

When he stopped at the end of the line he was within fifteen feet of the dangling swing which had been Baby Blake's. This swing was attached to a limb twenty feet above—a stout limb which jutted straight out from the tree trunk for fifteen feet. The Thinking Machine studied this for a moment, then passed on beyond the tree, still looking up, until he disappeared.

Fifteen minutes later he returned to the library where Mrs. Blake awaited him. There was a question in Hatch's eyes.

"I've got it," snapped The Thinking Machine, much as if there had been a denial. "I've got it!"

On the following day, by direction of The Thinking Machine, Mrs. Blake ordered the following advertisement inserted in all Boston and Lynn newspapers, to occupy one-quarter of a page.

TO THE PERSONS WHO NOW HOLD DOUGLAS BLAKE: Your names, residence and place of concealment of Douglas Blake, fourteen months old, and the manner in which he came into your possession are now known.

Mrs. Blake, the mother, does not desire to prosecute for reasons you know, and will give you twenty-four hours in which to return the baby safely to its home in Lynn.

Any attempt to escape of either person concerned will be followed instantly by arrest. Meanwhile, you are closely watched, and will be for twenty-four hours, at which time arrest and prosecution will follow.

No questions will be asked when the child is returned and your names will be fully protected. There will also be a reward of $1,000 for the person who returns the baby.

Hutchinson Hatch read this when The Thinking Machine had completed it and had stared at the scientist in wonderment.

"Is it true?" he asked.

"I am afraid the child is dead," repeated The Thinking Machine evasively. "I am very much afraid of it."

"What gives you that impression?" Hatch asked.

"I know now how the child was taken from that back yard, if we grant that the child itself made the tracks," was the rejoinder. "And knowing how it was taken away makes me more fearful than I have been that it is not alive; in fact, that it may never be seen again."

"How did the child leave the yard?"

"If the child does not appear within twenty-four hours," was the reply, "I shall tell you. It is a hideous story."

Hatch had to be content with that statement of the case for the moment. None knew better than he how useless it would be to question The Thinking Machine.

"Did you happen to know, Mr. Hatch," The Thinking Machine asked, "that in the event of the death of Douglas Blake, his fortune of nearly three million dollars left in trust by his father, would be divided among four relatives of Mrs. Blake?"

"What?" asked Hatch, a little startled.

"Suppose for instance, Baby Blake was never found, as seems possible," went on the other. "After a certain number of years, there is an assumption of death and property passes to heirs. You see then, there could be a motive, and a strong one, underlying this entire affair."

"But, surely there wouldn't be murder?"

"Not murder," responded The Thinking Machine tartly. "I haven't even suggested murder. I said I believe the child is dead. If it is not dead, who would benefit from his disappearance? The four whom I named. Well, suppose Baby Blake fell into the hands of those people. It would be a comparatively easy matter for them to hide it in some way, not necessarily kill it; have it adopted in some orphan asylum, place it anywhere to hide its identity. That's the main thing."

Hatch began to see light faintly, he thought.

"Then this advertisement is to the people who may be holding the child now?" he asked.

"It is so addressed," was the other's reply.

"But, but——" Hatch began.

"Once upon a time a hated wit, who was of necessity a student of human nature," The Thinking Machine began, "declared there was one thing carefully hidden in every man's life which would ruin him, should it be known, or land him in prison. He volunteered to prove this, taking any man whose name was suggested. An eminent minister of the gospel was named as the victim. The wit sent a telegram to the minister, who was attending a banquet. 'All is discovered. Flee while there is opportunity,' signed 'Friend.' The minister read it, arose and left the room, and from that day to this he has never been seen again."

Hatch laughed, and The Thinking Machine glanced at him with an annoyed expression on his face.

"I had no intention of arousing your laughter," he said sharply. "I merely intended to illustrate the possible effect of a guilty conscience."

When the flaming advertisement in the newspapers was called to the attention of the police, they were first surprised, then amused. Then they grew serious. After a while an officer went to Mrs. Blake and asked what it meant. She informed him that she had acted at the suggestion of Professor Van Dusen. Then the police were amused again; they are wont to feign an amusement which they never feel in the presence of a superior mind.

That afternoon, Hatch, who by direction of The Thinking Machine was on watch again near the Blake home, received a strange request from the scientist by telephone. It was:

"Go to the Blake home immediately, see the picture book which Baby Blake was looking at just before his disappearance, and report to me by phone what is in it."

"The picture book?" Hatch repeated.

"Certainly, the picture book," said the scientist irritably. "Also find out for me from the nurse and Mrs. Blake if the baby cried easily, that is from a slight hurt, or anything of that kind."

With these things in his mind, Hatch went to the Blake house, had a look at the picture book, asked the questions as to Baby Blake's propensity to weep on slight provocation, and returned to the 'phone. Feeling singularly foolish, he enumerated to The Thinking Machine the things he had seen in the picture book.

"There's a horse, and a cat with three kittens," he explained. "Also a pale purple rhinoceros, and a dog, an elephant, a deer, an alligator, a monkey, three chicks, and a whole lot of birds."

"Any eagle?" queried the other.

"Yes, an eagle among them, with a rabbit in his claws."

"And the monkey, what is it doing?"

"Hanging by its tail to a palm tree with a coconut in its hands," replied the reporter. The humor of the situation was beginning to appeal to him.

"And about the baby crying?" the scientist asked.

"He does not cry readily, both the mother and nurse say," replied the reporter. "They both describe him as a brave little chap who cries sometimes when he can't have his own way, but never from fright or a minor hurt."

"Good," he heard The Thinking Machine say. "Watch in front of the Blake house tonight until half-past eight. If the child returns it will probably be earlier than that. Speak to the person who brings him, as he leaves the house, and he will tell you his story I think, if you can make him understand that he is in no danger. Immediately after that come to my home in Boston."

Hatch was treading on air; when The Thinking Machine gave positive directions of that sort it usually meant that the final curtain was to be drawn aside. He so construed this.

Thus it came to pass that Hutchinson Hatch planted himself, carefully hidden so he might command a view of the front of the Blake home, and waited there for many hours.

Mrs. Blake had just finished her dinner and had retired to a small parlor off the library, where she reclined on a couch. It was ten minutes of seven o'clock in the evening. After a moment Miss Barton entered the room.

The girl heard a sob from the couch and impulsively ran to Mrs. Blake, who was weeping softly—she was always weeping now. A few comforting words, a little consolation such as one woman is able to give another, and the girl arose from her knees and started into the library, where a dim light burned.

As she was entering that room again, she paused, screamed, and without a word sank down on the floor, fainting. Mrs. Blake rose from the couch and rushed toward the door. She screamed too, but that scream was of a different tone from that of the girl—it was a fierce scream of mother-love satisfied.

For there on the floor of the library sat Baby Blake, millionaire, gazing with enraptured eyes at his brilliantly colored picture book.

"Pitty hossie," he said to his mother. "See! See!"

It was an affecting scene that Hutchinson Hatch witnessed in the Blake home about half-past seven o'clock. It was that of a mother, clasping a baby to her breast, while tears of joy and hysteria streamed from her eyes. Baby Blake struggled manfully to free himself, but his mother clung to him.

"My boy, my boy," she sobbed, again and again.

Miss Barton sat on the floor beside the mother and wept too. Hatch saw it, and received some thanks, heartfelt, but broken with a little sobbing laughter. Then he had to dry his eye, too, and Hutchinson Hatch was not a sentimental man.

"There will be no prosecution, Mrs. Blake, I suppose?" he asked.

"No, no, no," was the half laughing, half tearful reply. "I am content."

"I would like to ask a favor, if you don't mind," he suggested.

"Anything—anything for you and Professor Van Dusen," was the reply.

"Will you lend me the baby's picture book until tomorrow," he asked.

"Certainly," and in her happiness the mother forgot to note the strangeness of the request.

Hatch's purpose in borrowing the book was not clear, even to himself. In his mind had grown the idea that some way The Thinking Machine connected this book with the disappearance of the child, and he was burning with curiosity to get the book, and return to Boston, where The Thinking Machine might throw some light on the mystery. For it was still a mystery—a perplexing, baffling mystery that he could in no way grasp, even now that the baby was safe at home again.

In Boston the reporter went straight to the home of The Thinking Machine. The scientist was pottering about the little laboratory, and only turned to look at Hatch when he entered.

"Baby back home?" he asked shortly.

"Yes," said the reporter.

"Good," said the other, and he rubbed his slender hands together briskly. "Sit down, Mr. Hatch. It was a little better after all than I hoped for. Now your story first. What happened when the baby was brought back home?"

"I waited as you directed from afternoon until a few minutes before seven," Hatch explained. "I could plainly see anyone who approached the front gate of the Blake place, although I could not be seen well, remaining in the shadow of the building opposite.

"I saw two or three people go up to the gate and enter the yard, but they were trades people. I spoke to them as they came out and ascertained this for myself. At last I saw a man approaching, carrying something closely wrapped in his arms. He stopped at the gate, stared at the path a moment, glanced around several times and entered the yard. He was carrying Baby Blake.

"He went to the front door of the house and there I lost him in the shadow for a moment. Subsequent developments showed that he opened this front door, which was not locked, put the baby down and closed the door softly. Then he came rapidly down the path toward the gate. An instant later I heard two screams from the house. I knew then that the baby was there, dead or alive, probably alive.

"The man who had brought it also heard the screams and accelerated his pace somewhat, so that I had to run. He heard me coming, and ran, too. It was a two-block chase before I caught him, and when I did, he turned on me. I thought it was to fight.

" 'There was a promise of no arrest or prosecution,' he said.

"I assured him hurriedly, and then walked down the street beside him. He told me a queer story. It might be true, or it might not, but I believe it. This was that the baby had been in his and his wife's care from about half-past six o'clock of the evening it disappeared until a few minutes before, when he had returned it to its home.

"The man's name is Sheldon—Michael Sheldon—and he is an ex-convict. He served four terms for burglary, and at one time had a pretty nasty record. He told me of it in explanation of his reasons for not turning the baby over to the police. Now he has reformed and is leading a new life. He is a clerk in a store here in Lynn, and despite his previous record, is, I ascertained, a trusted and reliable man.

"Now here come the queer part of the story. It seems that Sheldon and his wife live on the third floor of a tenement in northern Lynn. Their dining room has one window, which leads to a fire escape. He and his wife were at supper at half-past six—in other words, a little more than a half hour from the time the baby disappeared from the Blake home.

"After a while they heard a noise, they didn't know what, on the fire escape. They paid no attention. Finally they heard another noise from the fire escape—that of a baby crying. Then Sheldon went to the window and opened it. There on the fire escape was Baby Blake. How he got there no human being knows."

"I know now," said The Thinking Machine. "Go on".

"Puzzled and bewildered they took the child off the iron structure, where only the merest chance had prevented it from falling and being killed on the pavement below. The baby was apparently uninjured, save for a few bruises, but his clothing was soiled and rumpled, and he was terribly cold. The wife, mother-like, set out to warm the little fellow and make him comfortable with hot milk and a steaming bath. The husband, Sheldon, he says, went out to find how it was possible for the baby to have reached the fire escape. He knew no baby lived in the building.

"He looked long and carefully. There was no possible way by which a man could have climbed the fire escape to the third floor, and there was certainly no way by which a fourteen-month-old baby could have. There is a fence there that is pretty high, about six feet, but even standing on this, someone would have had to leap straight up in the air for five feet. And no one, I know, could have done it with a baby in his arms, especially when the snow was there, and everything was so slippery a person could hardly stand.

"Then Sheldon made inquiries of some of his neighbors, occupants of the house, but no one could throw any light on the subject. He did not tell them then of the baby, indeed, never told them. First, from the fine quality of the clothing, there had been an idea in his mind that the baby was one of a well-to-do family, and he remained quiet that night hoping that next day he might be able to learn something and possibly get a reward for the return of the child. He had given up the problem of how it got where he found it."

Hatch paused a moment and lighted a cigar.

"Well, next day," he went on, "Sheldon and his wife both saw the newspaper account of the mysterious disappearance of Baby Blake. The photographs of the missing child convinced them that Baby Blake was the child they had—the child they had really saved from death. Then came the question of returning the child to its home or turning it over to the police.

"Instantly the fact that a demand for ransom had been made was borne in on Sheldon he became frightened. Remember he had a bad record. He was afraid of the police. He did not believe that he—however innocent he might be—could go to the police, turn the child over and make them believe the strange story. I readily see how some wooden-headed department officials would have made his life a burden. I know the police. It is ninety-nine dollars to a cent they would have made him a prisoner and perhaps railroaded him for the kidnapping."

"Yes, I see," interrupted The Thinking Machine.

"So then he and his wife tried to devise a method of getting the baby back home. They thought of all sorts of things, but none satisfied them entirely. And they were still debating this point and considering it when your advertisement promised immunity. As a matter of fact it scared Sheldon. He imagined that you knew, and knew if he were even remotely connected with the matter it would get him in trouble. Then he resolved to take the baby back home on the promise of immunity."

There was a little pause. The Thinking Machine sat staring steadily at the ceiling.

"Is that all?" he asked at last.

"I think so," replied Hatch. "And now how—how in the name of all that's good or evil did that baby disappear from the middle of its own backyard and then suddenly appear on a fire escape three blocks away, to be taken in by strangers?"

"It's quite the most remarkable thing I have ever come across," The Thinking Machine said. "A balloon anchor, which picked up the child by its clothing, through accident, and then dropped it safely on the fire escape might answer the question in a way. But it does not fully answer it. The baby was carried there.

"Frankly, I will say that I could see no possible explanation of the affair until the day you and I were talking to Mrs. Blake and I stood looking out of the library window. Then it all flashed on me instantly. I went out and satisfied myself. When I returned to the library I was satisfied in all reason that Baby Blake was dead. I had had such an idea before. I was firmly convinced the child was dead when I put those advertisements in the newspapers. But there was still a chance that he was not.

"Several seemingly unanswerable questions faced me when I found the end of the baby's footprints in the snow. I instantly saw that if the baby had made those tracks it had been lifted suddenly from the ground, but by what? From where? How had it been taken away? The balloon I could not consider seriously, although as I say it offered a possible solution. An eagle? I could not consider that seriously. Eagles are rare; eagles powerful enough to lift a baby weighing thirty pounds are extremely rare, practically unknown except in the Far West; certainly I never heard of one doing such a thing as this. Therefore I passed the eagle by as an improbability.

"I satisfied myself that there were no other footsteps save the baby's in the yard. Then—what? It occurred to me that someone standing on the little box might have reached out and lifted the child out of its tracks. But it was too far away, I thought, and if someone did stand there and lift the child that someone could not have leaped from that box over the stone wall, which was approximately a hundred feet away in all directions.

"I saw the stone ten feet away. Could a man stand on the box and leap to the stone? Generally, no. And from the stone, where could he have gone? Obviously, nowhere. I considered this matter not minutes but hours and days, and no light came to me. I was convinced, though, that the box was the starting point if the baby had made the tracks. I was now fairly certain that the baby did make the tracks. He wanted to get out in the snow, was left alone, opened the front door and wandered out.

"Then it all occurred to me in a new light. What living animal could have stood on the box and lifted the child clear four feet away, then leaped from there to the stone, and from the stone where? The clothes line is eight feet or so from the stone. It is a pretty sturdy rope and capable of bearing a considerable weight, supported as it is."

He stopped and turned his eyes toward Hatch, who listened eagerly.

"Do you see it now?" he asked.

The reporter shook his head, bewildered.

"The thing that lifted Baby Blake from the snow stood on the box, leaped from there to the stone, from there to the clothes line, along which it climbed to the end. From the wooden support at the end it is a clear distance of fifteen feet to the nearest thing—the swing. This thing made that leap, climbed the swing rope, disappeared into the trees, moving through the branches freely from one tree to another, and dropped to the ground nearly a block away."

"A monkey?" suggested Hatch.

"An orang-outan," nodded The Thinking Machine.

"An orang-outan?" gasped Hatch, and he shuddered a little. "I see now why you were positive the child was dead."

"An orang-outan is the only living thing in the knowledge of man which could have done all these things—therefore an orang-outan did them," said the other emphatically. "Remember a full-sized orang-outan is nearly as tall as a man, has a reach relatively a third longer than a very tall man would have, and a strength which is enormous. It could have made the leaps and probably would have made them rather than step in the snow. They despise snow, being from the tropics themselves, and will not step in it unless they are compelled to. The leap of fifteen feet to the swing rope from the clothes line would have been comparatively easy, even with a child in its arms.

"Where could it have come from? I don't know. Possibly it escaped from a ship; sailors have strange pets. Or it might have gotten away from a menagerie somewhere, or a circus. I only know that an orang-outan was the actual abductor. The difficulties a man would have climbing that fire escape would have been nothing to an orang-outan, merely an upward leap of five feet."

The Thinking Machine stopped as if he had finished. Hatch respected this silence for a moment, but he had questions yet to be answered.

"Who wrote the kidnapping letters demanding money?" was the first.

"You found him—Charles Gates," was the reply. "The letter demanding twenty-five thousand dollars was a bluff, of course. This poor, deluded fool imagined that someone would actually go out and toss $25,000 on a trash-heap where he could find it, and then he could escape. There have been several kidnappings lately, and he was counting on hysteria. He knew nothing of the whereabouts of the baby. He beat his wife when he found that instead of money I had put some good advice in the newspaper bundle for him."

"But the stocking in his room, and your question to Miss Barton?"

"It is perfectly possible that after the kidnapping he stole the little stocking and two or three other things from the laundry, for Miss Barton noticed they were missing. Or he got someone to do so for him. And, the baby being gone, he intended to send these to the mother, one at a time, I imagine, to make her believe he had the child. That is transparent. I asked Miss Barton the question about giving them to Gates to see if she did—her manner would have told me. I instantly saw she did not—had never even heard of him, as a matter of fact. I also dropped that remark about there being $25,000 in the package to see what effect it would have on her."

"And the facts you had about the baby's fortune going to relatives of Mrs. Blake in the event of the baby's death?"

"I got from her, by a casual question as to the succession of the estate. There was still a possibility that the baby was in their hands, despite the manner of the disappearance. As it transpired, they had nothing whatever to do with it. The advertisement I put in the paper was a palpable trick—but it had the desired effect. It touched a guilty conscience. The guilty conscience feared it was trapped and acted accordingly."

"It seems perfectly incomprehensible that the baby should have come out of it alive," mused Hatch. "I had always imagined orang-outans to be extremely ferocious."

"Read up on them a bit, Mr. Hatch," said The Thinking Machine. "You will find they are of strangely contradictory and mischievous natures. Where this child was permitted to escape safely, others might have been torn limb from limb."

There was silence for a time. Hatch considered the matter all explained, until suddenly the picture book occurred to him.

"You phoned me to see the picture book and tell you what's in it," he said. "Why?"

"Suppose there was a picture of a monkey in it," rejoined the other. "I merely wanted to know if the baby would know a monkey, in other words an orang-outan, if it saw one. Why? Because if the baby knew one, it would not necessarily be afraid of one in the flesh, and would not of necessity cry out when the orang-outan picked it up. As a matter of fact no one heard it scream when taken away."

"Oh, I see," said Hatch. "There was a picture of a monkey in the book. I told you." He took out the book and looked at it. "Here," and he extended it to the scientist, who glanced at it casually, and nodded.

"If you want to prove this just as I have told it," said The Thinking Machine, "go to the Blake home tomorrow, put your finger on that picture and show it to Baby Blake. He will prove it."

It came to pass that Hatch did this very thing.

"Pitty monkey," said Baby Blake. "Doe, doe."

"He means he wants to go," Miss Barton explained to Hatch. Hatch was satisfied.

Two days later the *Boston American* carried a dispatch from a village near Lynn stating that a semi-tame orang-outan had been killed by a policeman. It had belonged to a sailor, from whose vessel it had escaped more than two weeks before.

THE FATAL CIPHER

For the third time Professor Augustus S. F. X. Van Dusen—so-called The Thinking Machine—read the letter. It was spread out in front of him on the table, and his blue eyes were narrowed to mere slits as he studied it through his heavy eyeglasses. The young woman who had placed the letter in his hands, Miss Elizabeth Devan, sat waiting patiently in the sofa in the little reception room of The Thinking Machine's house. Her blue eyes were opened wide and she stared as if fascinated at this man who had become so potent a factor in the solution of intangible mysteries.

Here is the letter:

To THOSE CONCERNED:

Tired of it all I seek the end, and am content. Ambition is now dead; the grave yawns greedily at my feet, and with the labor of my own hands lost I greet death of my own will, by my own act.

To my son I leave all, and you who maligned me, you who discouraged me, you may read this and know I punish you thus. It's for him, my son, to forgive.

I dared in life and dare dead your everlasting anger, not alone that you didn't speak but that you cherished secret, and my ears are locked forever against you. My vault is my resting place. On the brightest and dearest page of life I wrote (7) my love for him. Family ties, binding as the Bible itself, bade me give all to my son. Good-bye. I die

POMEROY STOCKTON

"Under just what circumstances did this letter come into your possession, Miss Devan?" The Thinking Machine asked. "Tell me the full story; omit nothing."

The scientist sank back into his chair with his enormous yellow head pillowed comfortably against the cushion and his long, steady fingers pressed tip to tip. He didn't even look at his pretty visitor.

She had come to ask for information; he was willing to give it, because it offered another of those abstract problems which he always found interesting. In his own field—the sciences—his fame was world wide. This concentration of a brain which had achieved so much on more material things was perhaps a sort of relaxation.

Miss Devan had a soft, soothing voice, and as she talked it was broken at times by what seemed to be a sob. Her face was flushed a little, and she emphasized her points by a quick clasping and un-clasping of her dainty gloved hands.

"My father, or rather, my adopted father, Pomeroy Stockton, was an inventor," she began. "We lived in a great old-fashioned house in Dorchester. We have lived there since I was a child. When I was only five or six years old, I was left an orphan and was adopted by Mr. Stockton, who always treated me as a daughter. His death, therefore, was a great blow to me.

"Mr. Stockton was a widower with only one child of his own, a son, John Stockton, who is now about thirty-one years old. He is a man of irreproachable character, and has always, since I first knew him, been religiously inclined. He is the junior partner in a great commercial company, Dutton and Stockton, leather men. I suppose he has an immense fortune, for he gives largely to charity, and is, too, the active head of a large sunday School.

"Pomeroy Stockton, my adopted father, almost idolized this son, although there was in his manner toward him something akin to fear. Close work had made my father querulous and irritable. Yet I don't believe a better-hearted man ever lived. He worked most of the time in a little shop, which he had installed in a large back room on the ground floor of the house. He always worked with the door locked. There were furnaces, moulds, and many things that I didn't know the use of.

"I know who he was," said The Thinking Machine. "He was working to rediscover the secret of hardened copper—a secret which was lost in ancient Egypt. I knew Mr. Stockton very well by reputa-tion. Go on."

Miss Devan resumed: "Whatever it was he worked on, he guarded it very carefully. He would permit no one at all to enter the room. I have never seen more than a glimpse of what was in it. His son, particularly, I have seen barred out of the shop a dozen times and every time there was a quarrel to follow.

"Those were the conditions at the time Mr. Stockton first became ill, six or seven months ago. At that time he double-locked the doors of his shop, retired to his rooms on the second floor, and remained there in practical seclusion for two weeks or more. These rooms adjoined mine, and twice during that time I heard the son and the father talking loudly, as if quarreling. At the end of the two weeks, Mr. Stockton returned to work in the shop and shortly afterward the son, who had also lived in the house, took apartments in Beacon Street and removed his belongings from the house.

"From that time up to last Monday—this is Thursday—I never saw the son in the house. On Monday the father was at work as usual in the shop. He had previously told me that the work he was engaged in was practically ended and he expected a great fortune to result from it. About 5 o'clock in the afternoon on Monday the son came to the house. No one knows when he went out. It is a fact, however, that Father did not have dinner at the usual time, 6.30. I presumed he was at work, and did not take time for his dinner. I have known him to do this many times."

For a moment the girl was silent and seemed to be struggling with some deep grief which she could not control.

"And next morning?" asked The Thinking Machine gently.

"Next morning," the girl went on, "Father was found dead in the workshop. There were no marks on his body, nothing to indicate at first the manner of death. It was as if he had sat in his chair beside one of the furnaces and had taken poison and died at once. A small bottle of what I presume to be prussic acid was smashed on the floor, almost beside his chair. We discovered him dead after we had rapped on the door several times and got no answer. Then Montgomery, our butler, smashed in the door, at my request. There we found Father.

"I immediately telephoned to the son, John Stockton, and he came to the house. The letter you now have was found in my father's pocket. It was just as you see it. Mr. Stockton seemed greatly agitated and started to destroy the letter. I induced him to give it to me, because instantly it occurred to me that there was something wrong about all of it. My father had talked too often to me about the future, what he intended to do and his plans for me. There may not be anything wrong. The letter may be just what it purports to be. I hope it is—oh—I hope it is. Yet everything considered——"

"Was there an autopsy?" asked The Thinking Machine.

"No. John Stockton's actions seemed to be directed against any investigation. He told me he thought he could do certain things which would prevent the matter coming to the attention of the police. My father was buried on a death certificate issued by a Dr. Benton, who has been a friend of John Stockton since their college days. In that way the appearance of suicide or anything else was covered up completely.

"Both before and after the funeral John Stockton made me promise to keep this letter hidden or else destroy it. In order to put an end to this I told him I had destroyed the letter. This attitude on his part, the more I thought of it, seemed to confirm my original idea that it had not been suicide. Night after night I thought of this, and finally decided to come to you rather than to the police. I feel that there is some dark mystery behind it all. If you can help me now——"

"Yes, yes," broke in The Thinking Machine. "Where was the key to the workshop? In Pomeroy's pocket? In his room? In the door?"

"Really, I don't know," said Miss Devan. "It hadn't occurred to me."

"Did Mr. Stockton leave a will?"

"Yes, it is with his lawyer, a Mr. Sloane."

"Has it been read? Do you know what is in it?"

"It is to be read in a day or so. Judging from the second paragraph of the letter, I presume he left everything to his son."

For the fourth time The Thinking Machine read the letter. At its end he again looked up at Miss Devan.

"Just what is your interpretation of this letter from one end to the other," he asked.

"Speaking from my knowledge of Mr. Stockton and the circumstances surrounding him," the girl explained, "I should say the letter means just what it says. I should imagine from the first paragraph that something he invented had been taken away from him, stolen perhaps. The second paragraph and the third, I should say, were intended as a rebuke to certain relatives—a brother and two distant cousins—who had always regarded him as a crank and took frequent occasion to tell him so. I don't know a great deal of the history of that other branch of the family. The last two paragraphs explain themselves except——"

"Except the figure seven," interrupted the scientist. "Do you have any idea whatever as to the meaning of that?"

The girl took the letter and studied it closely for a moment.

"Not the slightest," she said. "It does not seem to be connected with anything else in the letter."

"Do you think it possible, Miss Devan, that this letter was written under coercion?"

"I do," said the girl quickly, and her face flamed. "That's just what I do think. From the first I have imagined some ghastly, horrible mystery back of it all."

"Or, perhaps Pomeroy Stockton never saw this letter at all," mused The Thinking Machine. "It may be a forgery?"

"Forgery!" gasped the girl. "Then John Stockton . . ."

"Whatever it is, forged or genuine," The Thinking Machine went on quietly, "it is a most extraordinary document. It might have been written by a poet: it states things in such a roundabout way. It is not directly to the point, as a practical man would have written."

There was silence for several minutes. The girl sat leaning forward on the table, staring into the inscrutable eyes of the scientist.

"Perhaps, perhaps," she said, "there is a cipher of some sort in it?"

"That is probably correct," said The Thinking Machine emphatically. "There is a cipher in it, and a very ingenious one."

It was twenty-four hours later that The Thinking Machine sent for Hutchinson Hatch, reporter, and talked over the matter with him. He had always found Hatch a discreet, resourceful individual, who was willing to aid in any way in his power.

Hatch read the letter, which The Thinking Machine had said contained a cipher, and then the circumstances as related by Miss Devan were retold to the reporter.

"Do you think it is a cipher?" asked Hatch in conclusion.

"It is a cipher," replied The Thinking Machine. "If what Miss Devan has said is correct, John Stockton cannot have said anything about the affair. I want you to go and talk to him, find out all about him and what division of the property is made by the will. Does this will give everything to the son?

"Also find out what personal enmity there is between John Stockton and Miss Devan, and what was the cause of it. Was there a man in it? If so, who? When you have done all this, go to the house in Dorchester and bring me the family Bible, if there is one there. It's probably a big book. If it is not there, let me know immediately by phone. Miss Devan will, I suppose, give it to you, if she has it."

With these instructions Hatch went away. Half an hour later he was in the private office of John Stockton at the latter's place of business. Mr. Stockton was a man of long visage, rather angular and clerical in appearance. There was a smug satisfaction about the man that Hatch didn't quite approve of, and yet it was a trait which found expression only in a soft voice and small acts of needless courtesy.

A deprecatory look passed over Stockton's face when Hatch asked the first question, which bore on his relationship with Pomeroy Stockton.

"I had hoped that this matter would not come to the attention of the press," said Stockton in an oily, gentle tone. "It is something which can only bring disgrace upon my poor father's memory, and his has been a name associated with distinct achievements in the progress of the world. However, if necessary, I will state my knowledge of the affair, and invite the investigation which, frankly, I will say, I tried to stop."

"How much was your father's estate?" asked Hatch.

"Something more than a million," was the reply. "He made most of it through a device for coupling cars. This is now in use on practically all the railroads."

"And the division of this property by will?" asked Hatch.

"I haven't seen the will, but I understand that he left practically everything to me, settling an annuity and the home in Dorchester on Miss Devan, whom he had always regarded as a daughter."

"That would give you then, say, two-thirds or three-quarters of the estate."

"Something like that, possibly $800,000."

"Where is this will now?"

"I understand in the hands of my father's attorney, Mr. Sloane."

"When is it to be read?"

"It was to have been read today, but there has been some delay about it. The attorney postponed it for a few days."

"What, Mr. Stockton, was the purpose in making it appear that your father died naturally, when obviously he committed suicide and there is even a suggestion of something else?" demanded Hatch.

John Stockton sat up straight in his chair with a startled expression in his eyes. He had been rubbing his hands together complacently; now he stopped and stared at the reporter.

"Something else?" he asked. "Pray what else?"

Hatch shrugged his shoulders, but in his eyes there lay almost an accusation.

"Did any motive ever appear for your father's suicide?"

"I know of none," Stockton replied. "Yet, admitting that this is suicide, without a motive, it seems that the only fault I have committed is that I had a friend report it otherwise and avoided a police inquiry."

"It's just that. Why did you do it?"

"Naturally to save the family name from disgrace. But this something else you spoke of? Do you mean that anyone else thinks that anything other than suicide or natural death is possible?"

As he asked the question there came some subtle change over his face. He leaned forward toward the reporter. All trace of the sanctimonious smirk about the thin-lipped mouth had gone now.

"Miss Devan has produced the letter found on your father at death and has said——" began the reporter.

"Elizabeth! Miss Devan!" exclaimed John Stockton. He arose suddenly, paced several times across the room, then stopped in front of the reporter. "She gave me her word of honor that she would not make the existence of that letter known."

"But she has made it public," said Hatch. "And further she intimates that your father's death was not even what it appeared to be, suicide."

"She's crazy, man, crazy," said Stockton in deep agitation. "Who could have killed my father? What motive could there have been?"

There was a grim twitching of Hatch's lips.

"Was Miss Devan legally adopted by your father?" he asked, irrelevantly.

"Yes."

"In that event, disregarding other relatives, doesn't it seem strange even to you that he gives three-quarters of the estate to you—you have a fortune already—and only a small part to Miss Devan, who has nothing?"

"That's my father's business."

There was a pause. Stockton was still pacing back and forth. Finally he sank down in his chair at the desk, and sat for a moment looking at the reporter.

"Is that all?" he asked.

"I should like to know, if you don't mind telling me, what direct cause there is for ill feeling between Miss Devan and you?"

"There is no ill feeling. We merely never got along well together. My father and I have had several arguments about her for reasons which it is not necessary to go into."

"Did you have such an argument on the night before your father was found dead?"

"I believe there was something said about her."

"What time did you leave the shop that night?"

"About 10 o'clock."

"And you had been in the room with your father since afternoon, had you not?"

"Yes."

"No dinner?"

"No."

"How did you come to neglect that?"

"My father was explaining a recent invention he had perfected, which I was to put on the market."

"I suppose the possibility of suicide or his death in any way had not occurred to you?"

"No, not at all. We were making elaborate plans for the future."

Possibly it was some prejudice against the man's appearance which made Hatch so dissatisfied with the result of the interview. He felt that he had gained nothing, yet Stockton had been absolutely frank, as it seemed. There was one last question.

"Have you any recollection of a large family Bible in your father's house?" he asked.

"I have seen it several times," Stockton said.

"Is it still there?"

"So far as I know, yes."

That was the end of the interview, and Hatch went straight to the house in Dorchester to see Miss Devan. There, in accordance with instructions from The Thinking Machine, he asked for the family Bible.

"There was one here the other day," said Miss Devan, "but it has disappeared."

"Since your father's death?" asked Hatch.

"Yes, the next day."

"Have you any idea who took it?"

"Not unless—unless——"

"John Stockton! Why did he take it?" blurted Hatch.

There was a little resigned movement of the girl's hands, a movement which said, "I don't know."

"He told me, too," said Hatch indignantly, "that he thought the Bible was still here."

The girl drew close to the reporter and laid one white hand on his sleeve. She looked up into his eyes and tears stood in her own. Her lips trembled.

"John Stockton has that book," she said. "He took it away from here the day after my father died, and he did it for a purpose. What, I don't know,"

"Are you absolutely positive he has it?" asked Hatch.

"I saw it in his room, where he had hidden it," replied the girl.

Hatch laid the results of the interviews before the scientist at the Beacon Hill home. The Thinking Machine listened without comment up to that point where Miss Devan had said she knew the family Bible to be in the son's possession.

"If Miss Devan and Stockton do not get along well together, why should she visit Stockton's place at all?" demanded The Thinking Machine.

"I don't know," Hatch replied, "except that she thinks he must have had some connection with her father's death, and is investigating on her own account. What has this Bible to do with it anyway?"

"It may have a great deal to do with it," said The Thinking Machine enigmatically. "Now the thing to do is to find out if the girl told the truth and if the Bible is in Stockton's apartment. Now, Mr. Hatch, I leave that to you. I would like to see that Bible. If you can bring it to me, well and good. If you can't bring it, look at and study the seventh page for any pencil marks in the text, anything whatever. It might even be advisable, if you have the opportunity, to tear out that page and bring it to me. No harm will be done, and it can be returned in proper time."

Perplexed wrinkles were gathering on Hatch's forehead as he listened. What had page 7 of a Bible to do with what seemed to be a murder mystery? Who had said anything about a Bible, anyway? The letter left by Stockton mentioned a Bible, but that didn't seem to mean anything. Then Hatch remembered that the same letter carried a figure seven in parentheses, which had apparently nothing to do and no connection with any other part of the letter. Hatch's introspective study of the affair was interrupted by The Thinking Machine.

"I shall await your report here, Mr. Hatch. If it is what I expect, we shall go out late tonight on a little voyage of discovery. Meanwhile, see that Bible and tell me what you find."

Hatch found the apartments of John Stockton on Beacon Street without any difficulty. In a manner best known to himself, he entered and searched the place. When he came out, there was a look of chagrin on his face as he hurried to the house of The Thinking Machine nearby.

"Well?" asked the scientist.

"I saw the Bible," said Hatch.

"And page 7?"

"Was torn out, missing, gone," replied the reporter.

"Ah," exclaimed the scientist. "I thought so. Tonight we shall make the little trip I spoke of. By the way, did you happen to notice if John Stockton had or used a fountain pen?"

"I didn't see one," said Hatch.

"Well, please see for me if any of his employees have ever noticed one. Then meet me here tonight at 10 o'clock."

Thus Hatch was dismissed. A little later he called casually on Stockton again. There, by inquiries, he established to his own satisfaction that Stockton did not own a fountain pen. Then with Stockton himself he took up the matter of the Bible again.

"I understand you to say, Mr. Stockton," he began in his smoothest tone, "that you knew of the existence of a family Bible, but you did not know if it was still at the Dorchester place."

"That's correct," said Stockton.

"How is it then," Hatch resumed, "that that identical Bible is now at your apartments, carefully hidden in a box under a sofa?"

Mr. Stockton seemed to be amazed. He arose suddenly and leaned over toward the reporter with hands clenched. There was glitter of what might have been anger in his eyes.

"What do you know about this? What are you talking about?" he demanded.

"I mean you had said you did not know where this book was and meanwhile have it hidden. Why?"

"Have you seen the Bible in my rooms?" asked Stockton.

"I have," said the reporter coolly.

Now a new determination came over the face of the merchant. The oiliness of his manner was gone, the sanctimonious smirk had been obliterated, the thin lips closed into a straight rigid line.

"I shall have nothing further to say," he declared almost fiercely.

"Will you tell me why you tore out the seventh page of the Bible?" asked Hatch.

Stockton stared at him dully, as if dazed for a moment. All the color left his face. There came a startling pallor instead. When next he spoke, his voice was tense and strained.

"Is—is—the seventh page missing?"

"Yes," Hatch replied. "Where is it?"

"I'll have nothing further to say under any circumstances. That's all."

With not the slightest idea of what it might mean or what bearing it had on the matter, Hatch had brought out statements which were wholly at variance with facts. Why was Stockton so affected by the statement that page 7 was gone? Why had the Bible been taken from the Dorchester home? Why had it been so carefully hidden? How did Miss Devan know it was there?

These were only a few of the questions that were racing through the reporter's mind. He did not seem to be able to grasp anything tangible. If there were a cipher hidden in the letter, what was it? What bearing did it have on the case?

Seeking a possible answer to some of these questions, Hatch took a cab and was soon back at the Dorchester house. He was somewhat surprised to see The Thinking Machine standing on the stoop waiting to be admitted. The scientist took his presence as a matter of course.

"What did you find out about Stockton's fountain pen?" he asked.

"I satisfied myself that he had not owned a fountain pen, at least recently enough for the pen to have been used in writing that letter. I presume that's what inquiries in that direction mean."

The two men were admitted to the house and after a few minutes Miss Devan entered. She understood when The Thinking Machine explained that they merely wished to see the shop in which Mr. Stockton had been found dead.

"And also if you have a sample of Mr. Stockton's handwriting," asked the scientist.

"It's rather peculiar," Miss Devan explained, "but I doubt if there is an authentic example in existence, large enough, that is, to be compared with the letter. He had a certain amount of corres- pondence, but this I did for him on the typewriter. Occasionally he would prepare an article for a scientific journal, but these were also dictated to me. He has been in the habit of doing so for years."

"This letter seems to be all there is?"

"Of course the signature appears on checks and in other places. I can produce some of those for you. I don't think, however, that there is the slightest doubt that he wrote this letter. It is his handwriting."

"I suppose he never used a fountain pen?" asked The Thinking Machine.

"Not that I know of."

"Do you own one?"

"Yes," the girl replied, and she took a pen out of a little gold fascinator she wore at her bosom.

The scientist pressed the point of the pen against his thumbnail, and a tiny drop of blue ink appeared. The letter was written in black. The Thinking Machine seemed satisfied.

"And now the shop," he suggested.

Miss Devan led the way through the long wide hall to the back of the building. There she opened a door, which showed signs of having been battered in, and admitted them. Then at the request of The Thinking Machine she rehearsed the story in full, showed him where Stockton had been found, where the bottle of prussic acid had been broken, where the servant, Montgomery, had broken in the door at her request.

"Did you ever find the key to the door?"

"No. I can't imagine what became of it."

"Is this room precisely as it was when the body was found? That is, has anything been removed from it?"

"Nothing," replied the girl.

"Have the servants taken anything out? Did they have access to this room?"

"They have not been permitted to enter it at all. The body was removed, and the fragments of the acid bottle were taken away, but nothing else."

"Have you ever known of pen and ink being in this room?"

"I hadn't thought of it."

"You haven't taken them out since the body was found, have you?"

"I—I—have not," the girl stammered.

Miss Devan left the room and for an hour Hatch and The Thinking Machine conducted their search.

"Find a pen and ink," The Thinking Machine instructed.

They were not found.

At midnight, which was six hours later, The Thinking Machine and Hutchinson Hatch were groping through the cellar of the Dorchester house with the aid of a small electric lamp which shot a straight beam aggressively through the murky, damp air. Finally the ray fell on a tiny door set in the solid wall of the cellar.

There was a slight exclamation from The Thinking Machine, and this was followed by the sharp, unmistakable click of a revolver somewhere behind them in the dark.

"Down, quick," gasped Hatch, and with a sudden blow he dashed aside the electric light, extinguishing it. Simultaneously with this came a revolver shot, and a bullet struck the wall behind Hatch's head.

The reverberation of the pistol shot was still ringing in Hatch's ears when he felt the hand of The Thinking Machine on his arm, and then through the utter blackness of the cellar came the irritable voice of the scientist:

"To your right, to your right," it said sharply.

Then, contrary to this advice Hatch felt the scientist drawing him to the left. In another moment there came a second shot, and by the flash Hatch could see that it was aimed at a point a dozen feet to the right of the point they had been when the first shot was fired. The person with the revolver had heard the scientist and had been duped.

Firmly the scientist drew Hatch on until they were almost to the cellar steps. There, outlined against a dim light which came down the stairs, they could see a tall figure peering through the darkness toward a spot opposite where they stood. Hatch saw only one thing to do and did it. He leaped forward and landed on the back of the figure, bearing the man to the ground. An instant later his hand closed on the revolver, and he wrested it away.

"All right," he sang out, "I've got it."

The electric light which he had dashed from the hand of The Thinking Machine gleamed again through the cellar and fell upon the face of John Stockton, still helpless and gasping in the hands of the reporter.

"Well?" asked Stockton calmly. "Are you burglars or what?"

"Let's go upstairs, to the light," suggested The Thinking Machine.

It was under these peculiar circumstances that the scientist came

face to face for the first time with John Stockton. Hatch introduced
the two men in a most matter-of-fact tone and restored to Stockton
his revolver. This was suggested by a nod of the scientist's head.
Stockton laid the revolver on a table.

"Why did you try to kill us?" asked The Thinking Machine.

"I presumed you were burglars," was the reply. "I heard the
noise down stairs and came down to investigate."

"I thought you lived on Beacon Street," said the scientist.

"I do, but I came here tonight on a little business which is all my
own, and happened to hear you. What were you doing in the cellar?"

"How long have you been here?"

"Five or ten minutes."

"Have you a key to this house?"

"I have had one for many years. What is all this, anyway? How
did you get in this house? What right had you here?"

"Is Miss Devan in the house tonight?" asked The Thinking
Machine, entirely disregarding the other's questions.

"I don't know. I suppose so."

"You haven't seen her, of course?"

"Certainly not."

"And you came here secretly without her knowledge?"

Stockton shrugged his shoulders and was silent. The Thinking
Machine raised himself on the chair on which he had been sitting
and squinted steadily into Stockton's eyes. When he spoke it was to
Hatch, but his gaze did not waver.

"Arouse the servants, find where Miss Devan's room is, and see
if anything has happened to her," he directed.

"I think that will be unwise," broke in Stockton quickly.

"Why?"

"If I may put it on personal grounds," said Stockton. "I would
ask as a favor that you do not make known my visit here, or your
own, for that matter, to Miss Devan."

There was a certain uneasiness in the man's attitude, a certain
eagerness to keep things away from Miss Devan that spurred Hatch
to instant action. He went out of the room hurriedly and ten minutes
later Miss Devan, who had dressed quickly, came into the room
with him. The servants stood outside in the hall, all curiosity. The
closed door barred them from knowledge of what was happening.

There was a little dramatic pause as Miss Devan entered and
Stockton arose from his seat. The Thinking Machine glanced from

one to the other. He noted the pallor of the girl's face and the frank embarrassment of Stockton.

"What is it?" asked Miss Devan, and her voice trembled a little. "Why are you all here? What has happened?"

"Mr. Stockton came here tonight," The Thinking Machine began quietly, "to remove the contents from the locked vault in the cellar. He came without your knowledge and found us ahead of him. Mr. Hatch and myself are here in the course of our inquiry into the matter which you placed in my hands. We also came without your knowledge. I considered this best. Mr. Stockton was very anxious that his visit should be kept from you. Have you anything to say now?"

The girl turned on Stockton with magnificent scorn. Accusation was in her very attitude. Her small hand was pointed directly at Stockton and into his face came a strange emotion, which he struggled to repress.

"Murderer! Thief!" the girl almost hissed.

"Do you know why he came?" asked The Thinking Machine.

"He came to rob the vault, as you said," said the girl fiercely. "It was because my father would not give him the secret of his last invention that this man killed him. How he compelled him to write that letter I don't know."

"Elizabeth, for God's sake what are you saying," asked Stockton with ashen face.

"His greed is so great that he wanted all of my father's estate," the girl went on impetuously. "He was not content that I should get even a small part of it."

"Elizabeth, Elizabeth!" said Stockton, as he leaned forward with his head in his hands.

"What do you know about this secret vault?" asked the scientist.

"I—I—have always thought there was a secret vault in the cellar," the girl explained. "I may say I know there was one because those things my father took the greatest care of were always disposed of by him somewhere in the house. I can imagine no other place than the cellar."

There was a long pause. The girl stood rigid, staring down at the bowed figure of Stockton with not a gleam of pity in her face. Hatch caught the expression and it occurred to him for the first time that Miss Devan was vindictive. He was more convinced than ever that there had been some long-standing feud between these two. The Thinking Machine broke the long silence.

Do you happen to know, Miss Devan, that page 7 of the Bible which you found hidden in Mr. Stockton's place is missing?"

"I didn't notice," said the girl.

Stockton had arisen with the words and now stood with white face listening intently.

"Did you ever happen to see a page 7 in that Bible?" the scientist asked.

"I don't recall."

"What were you doing in my rooms?" demanded Stockton of the girl.

"Why did you tear out page 7?" asked The Thinking Machine.

Stockton thought the question was addressed to him and turned to answer. Then he saw it unmistakably a question to Miss Devan and turned again to her.

"I didn't tear it out," exclaimed Miss Devan. "I never saw it. I don't know what you mean."

The Thinking Machine made an impatient gesture with his hands; his next question was to Stockton.

"Have you a sample of your father's handwriting?"

"Several," said Stockton. "Here are three or four letters from him."

Miss Devan gasped a little as if startled and Stockton produced the letters and handed them to The Thinking Machine. The latter glanced over two of them.

"I thought, Miss Devan, you said your father always dictated his letters to you?"

"I did say so," said the girl. "I didn't know of the existence of these."

"May I have these?" asked The Thinking Machine.

"Yes. They are of no consequence."

"Now let's see what is in the secret vault," the scientist went on.

He arose and led the way again into the cellar, lighting his path with the electric bulb. Stockton followed immediately behind, then came Miss Devan, her white dressing gown trailing mystically in the dim light and last came Hatch. The Thinking Machine went straight to that spot where he and Hatch had been when Stockton had fired at them. Again the rays of the light revealed the tiny door set into the walls of the cellar. The door opened readily enough at his touch; the small vault was empty.

Intent on his examination of this, The Thinking Machine was oblivious for a moment to what was happening. Suddenly there came again a pistol shot, followed instantly by a woman's scream.

"My God, he's killed himself! He's killed himself!"

It was Miss Devan's voice.

When The Thinking Machine flashed his light back into the gloom of the cellar, he saw Miss Devan and Hatch leaning over the prostrate figure of John Stockton. The latter's face was perfectly white save just at the edge of his hair, where there was a trickle of red. In his right hand he clasped a revolver.

"Dear me! Dear me!" exclaimed the scientist. "What is it?"

"Stockton shot himself," said Hatch, and there was excitement in his tone.

On his knees the scientist made a hurried examination of the wounded man, then suddenly—it may have been inadvertently—he flashed the light in the face of Miss Devan.

"Where were you?" he demanded quickly.

"Just behind him," said the girl. "Will he die? Is it fatal?"

"Hopeless," said the scientist, "Let us carry him upstairs."

The unconscious man was lifted and with Hatch leading was again taken to the room which they had left only a few minutes before. Hatch stood by helplessly while The Thinking Machine, in his capacity of physician, made a more minute examination of the wound. The bullet mark just above the right temple was almost bloodless; around it there were the unmistakeable marks of burned powder.

"Help me just a moment, Miss Devan," requested The Thinking Machine, as he bound an improvised handkerchief bandage about the head. Miss Devan tied the final knots of the bandage and The Thinking Machine studied her hands closely as she did so. When the work was completed, he turned to her in a most matter of fact way.

"Why did you shoot him?" he asked.

"I—I——" stammered the girl. "I didn't shoot him. He shot himself."

"How came those powder marks on your right hand?"

Miss Devan glanced down at her right hand, and the color which had been in her face faded as if by magic. There was fear, now, in her manner.

"I—I don't know," she stammered. "Surely you don't think that I——"

"Mr. Hatch, phone at once for an ambulance and then see if it is

possible to get Detective Mallory here immediately. I shall give Miss
Devan into custody on the charge of shooting this man."

The girl stared at him dully for a moment and then dropped back
into a chair with dead white face and fear-distended eyes. Hatch
went out, seeking a telephone, and for a time Miss Devan sat silent,
as if dazed. Finally, with an effort, she aroused herself and facing
The Thinking Machine defiantly burst out:

"I didn't shoot him. I didn't. I didn't. He did it himself."

The long slender fingers of The Thinking Machine closed on the
revolver and gently removed it from the hand of the wounded man.

"Ah, I was mistaken," he said suddenly. "he is not as badly
wounded as I thought. See! he is reviving."

"Reviving!" exclaimed Miss Devan. "Won't he die, then?"

"Why?" asked The Thinking Machine sharply.

"It seems so pitiful, almost a confession of guilt," she hurriedly
exclaimed. "Won't he die?"

Gradually the color was coming back into Stockton's face. The
Thinking Machine bending over him, with one hand on the heart, saw
the eyelids quiver, and then slowly the eyes opened. Almost immediately the strength of the heartbeat grew perceptibly stronger. Stockton
stared at him a moment, then wearily his eyelids drooped again.

"Why did Miss Devan shoot you?" The Thinking Machine
demanded.

There was a pause and the eyes opened for the second time. Miss
Devan stood within range of the glance, her hands outstretched
entreatingly toward Stockton.

"Why did she shoot you?" repeated The Thinking Machine.

"She—did—not," said Stockton slowly. "I—did—it—myself."

For an instant there was a little wrinkle of perplexity on the brow
of The Thinking Machine and then it passed.

"Purposely?" he asked.

"I did it myself."

Again the eyes closed and Stockton seemed to be passing into
unconsciousness. The Thinking Machine glanced up to find an
infinite expression of relief on Miss Devan's face. His own manner
changed; he became almost abject, in fact, as he turned to her again.

"I beg your pardon," he said. "I made a mistake."

"Will he die?"

"No, that was another mistake. He will recover."

Within a few minutes a City Hospital ambulance rattled up to the door and John Stockton was removed. It was with a feeling of pity that Hatch assisted Miss Devan, now almost in fainting condition, to her room. The Thinking Machine had previously given her a slight stimulant. Detective Mallory had not answered the call by phone.

The Thinking Machine and Hatch returned to Boston. At the Park Street subway they separated, after The Thinking Machine had given certain instructions. Hatch spent most of the following day carrying out these instructions. First he went to see Dr. Benton, the physician who had issued the death certificate on which Pomeroy Stockton had been buried. Dr. Benton was considerably alarmed when the reporter broached the subject of his visit. After a time he talked freely of the case.

"I have known John Stockton since we were in college together," he said, "and I believe him to be one of the few really good men I know. I can't believe otherwise. Singularly enough, he is also one of the few good men who have made their own fortunes. There is nothing hypocritical about him.

"Immediately after his father was found dead, he phoned to me and I went out to the house in Dorchester. He explained then that it was apparent that Pomeroy Stockton had committed suicide. He dreaded the disgrace that public knowledge would bring on an honored name, and asked me what could be done. I suggested the only thing I knew—that was the issuance of a death certificate specifying natural causes—heart disease, I said. This act was due entirely to my friendship for him.

"I examined the body and found a trace of prussic acid on Pomeroy's tongue. Beside the chair on which he sat a bottle of prussic acid had been broken. I made no autopsy. Of course, ethically I may have sinned, but I feel that no real harm has been done. Of course, now that you know the real facts, my entire career is at stake."

"There is no question in your mind but that it was suicide?" asked Hatch.

"Not the slightest. Then, too, there was the letter, which was found in Pomeroy's pocket. I saw that and if there had been any doubt then it was removed. This letter, I think, was then in Miss Devan's possession. I presume it is still."

"Do you know anything about Miss Devan?"

"Nothing, except that she is an adopted daughter who for some reason retained her own family name. Three or four years ago she had a little love affair, to which John Stockton objected. I believe he was the cause of it being broken off. As a matter of fact, I think at one time he was himself in love with her and she refused to accept him as a suitor. Since that time there has been some slight friction, but I know nothing of this except in a general way, from what he has said to me."

Then Hatch proceeded to carry out the other part of The Thinking Machine's instructions. This was to see the attorney in whose possession Pomeroy Stockton's will was supposed to be and to ask him why there had been a delay in the reading of the will.

Hatch found the attorney, Frederick Sloane, without difficulty. Without reservation Hatch laid all the circumstances as he knew them before Mr. Sloane. Then came the question of why the will had not been read. Mr. Sloane, too, was frank.

"It's because the will is not now in my possession," he said. "It has either been mislaid, lost, or possibly stolen. I did not care for the family to know this just now, and delayed the reading of the will while I made a search for it. Thus far I have found not a trace. I haven't even the remotest idea where it is."

"What does the will provide?" asked Hatch.

"It leaves the bulk of the estate to John Stockton, settles an annuity of $5,000 a year on Miss Devan, gives her the Dorchester house, and specifically cuts off other relatives whom Pomeroy Stockton once accused of stealing an invention he made. The letter, found after Mr. Stockton's death——"

"You knew of that letter, too?" Hatch interrupted.

"Oh, yes, this letter confirms the will, except, in general terms, it also cuts off Miss Devan."

"Would it not be to the interest of the other immediate relatives of Stockton, those who were specifically cut off, to get possession of that will and destroy it?"

"Of course, it might be, but there has been no communication between the two branches of the family for several years. That branch lives in the Far West and I have taken particular pains to ascertain that they could not have had anything to do with the disappearance of the will."

With these new facts in his possession, Hatch started to report to The Thinking Machine. He had to wait half an hour or so. At last the scientist came in.

"I've been attending an autopsy," he said.

"An autopsy? Whose?"

"On the body of Pomeroy Stockton."

"Why, I had thought he had been buried."

"No, only placed in a receiving vault. I had to call the attention of the Medical Examiner to the case in order to get permission to make an autopsy. We did it together."

"What did you find?" asked Hatch.

"What did *you* find?" asked The Thinking Machine, in turn.

Briefly Hatch told him of the interview with Dr. Benton and Mr. Sloane. The scientist listened without comment and at the end sat back in his big chair squinting at the ceiling.

"That seems to finish it," he said. "These are the questions which were presented: First, in what manner did Pomeroy Stockton die? Second, if not suicide, as appeared, what motive was there for anything else? Third, if there was a motive, to whom does it lead? Fourth, what was in the cipher letter? Now, Mr. Hatch, I think I may make all of it clear. There was a cipher in the letter—what may be described as a cipher in five, the figure five being the key to it.

"First, Mr. Hatch," The Thinking Machine resumed, as he drew out and spread on a table the letter which had been originally placed in his hands by Miss Devan, "the question of whether there was a cipher in this letter was to be definitely decided.

"There are a thousand different kinds of ciphers. One of them, which we will call the cipher, is excellently illustrated in Poe's story, 'The Gold Bug.' In that cipher, a figure or symbol is made to represent each letter of the alphabet.

"Then, there are book ciphers, which are perhaps the safest of all ciphers, because without a clue to the book from which words may be chosen and designated by numbers, no one can solve it.

"It would be useless for me to go into the matter at any length, so let us consider this particular letter as a cipher possibility. A careful study of the letter develops three possible starting points. The first of these is the general tone of the letter. It is not a direct, straight-away statement such as a man about to commit suicide would write unless he had a purpose—that is, a purpose beyond the mere apparent meaning of the surface text itself. Therefore we will suppose there was another purpose hidden behind a cipher.

"The second starting point is that offered by the absence of one word. You will see that the word 'in' should appear between the word 'cherished' and 'secret.' This, of course, may have been an oversight in writing, the sort of thing anyone might do. But further down we find the third starting point.

"This is the figure 7 in parentheses. It apparently has no connection whatever with what precedes or follows. It could not have been an accident. Therefore what did it mean? Was it a crude outward indication of a hurriedly constructed cipher?

"I took the figure 7 at first to be a sort of key to the entire letter, always presuming there was a cipher. I counted seven words down from that figure and found the word 'binding.' Seven words from that down made the next word 'give.' Together the two words seemed to mean something.

"I stopped there and started back. The seventh word up is 'and'. The seventh word from 'and,' still counting backwards seemed meaningless. I pursued that theory of seven all the way through the letter and found only a jumble of words. It was the same way counting seven letters. These letters meant nothing unless each letter was arbitrarily taken to represent another letter. This immediately led to intracacies. I always believe in exhausting simple possibilities first, so I started over again.

"Now what word nearest to the seven meant anything when taken together with it? Not 'family,' not 'Bible,' not 'son,' as the vital words appear from the seven down. Going up from the seven, I did find a word which applied to it and meant something. That was the word 'page.' 'Page' was the fifth word up from the seven.

"What was the next fifth word, still going up? This was 'on'; Then I had 'on page 7'—connected words appearing in order, each being the fifth from the other. The fifth word down from seven I found was 'family'; the next fifth word was 'Bible.' Thus I had 'on page 7 family Bible.'

"It is unnecessary to go further into the study I made of the cipher. I worked upward from the seven, taking each fifth word, until I had all the cipher words. I have underscored them here. Read the words underscored and you have the cipher."

Hatch took the letter marked as follows:

To those concerned:
Tired of it all I seek the end, and AM content. Ambition is DEAD; the grave yawns greedily AT my feet, and with THE labor of my own HANDS lost I greet death OF my own will, by MY own act.

To my SON I leave all, and YOU who maligned me, you WHO discouraged me, you may READ this and know I PUNISH you thus. It's for HIM, my son, to forgive.

I dared in life and DARE dead your everlasting anger, NOT alone that you didn't SPEAK, but that you cherished SECRET, and my ears are LOCKED forever against you. My VAULT is my resting place.

ON the brightest and dearest PAGE of life I wrote (7) my love for him. FAMILY ties, binding as the BIBLE itself, bade me GIVE all to my son.

Good-bye. I die.

POMEROY STOCKTON

Slowly Hatch read this: "I am dead at the hands of my son. You who read punish him. I dare not speak. Secret locked vault on page 7 family Bible."

"Well, by George!" exclaimed the reporter. It was a tribute to The Thinking Machine, as well as an expression of amazement at what he read.

"You see," explained The Thinking Machine. "If the word 'in' had appeared between 'cherished' and 'secret,' as it would naturally have done, it would have lost the order of the cipher, therefore it was purposely left out."

"It's enough to send Stockton to the electric chair," said Hatch.

"It would be if it were not a forgery," said the scientist testily.

"A forgery," gasped Hatch. "Didn't Pomeroy Stockton write it?"

"No."

"Surely not John Stockton?"

"Well, who then?"

"Miss Devan."

"Miss Devan!" Hatch repeated in amazement. "Then, Miss Devan killed Pomeroy Stockton?"

"No, he died a natural death."

Hatch's head was whirling. A thousand questions demanded an immediate answer. He stared mouth agape at The Thinking Machine. All his ideas of the case were tumbling about him. Nothing remained.

"Briefly, here is what happened," said The Thinking Machine. "Pomeroy Stockton died a natural death of heart disease. Miss Devan found him dead, wrote this letter, put it in his pocket, put a drop of prussic acid on his tongue, smashed the bottle of acid, left the room, locked the door, and next day had it broken down.

"It was she who shot John Stockton. It was she who tore out page 7 of that family Bible, and then hid the book in Stockton's room. It was she who in some way got hold of the will. She either has it or has destroyed it. It was she who took advantage of her aged bene- factor's sudden death to further as weird and inhuman a plot against another as a woman can devise. There is nothing on God's earth as bad as a bad woman. I think that has been said before."

"But as to this case," Hatch interrupted, "How? What? Why?"

"I read the cipher within a few hours after I got the letter," replied The Thinking Machine. "Naturally I wanted to find out then who and what this son was.

"I had Miss Devan's story, of course—a short story of dis- agreement between father and son, quarreling and all that. It was also a story which showed a certain underlying animosity despite Miss Devan's cleverness. She had so mingled fact with fiction that it was not altogether easy to weed out the truth, therefore I believed what I chose.

"Miss Devan's idea, as expressed to me, was that the letter was written under coercion. Men who are being murdered don't write cipher letters as intricate as that; and men who are committing suicide have no obvious reasons for writing such letters. The line 'I dare not speak' was silly. Pomeroy Stockton was not a prisoner. If he had feared a conspiracy to kill him, why shouldn't he speak?

"All these things were in my mind when I asked you to see John Stockton. I was particularly anxious to hear what he had to say as to the family Bible. And yet I may say I knew that page 7 had been torn out of the book and was then in Miss Devan's possession.

"I may say, too, that I knew that the secret vault was empty. Whatever these two things contained, supposing she wrote the cipher, had been removed or she would not have called attention to them in the cipher. I had an idea that she might have written it from the mere fact that it was she who first called my attention to the pos- sibility of a cipher.

"Assuming then that the cipher was a forgery, that she wrote it, that it directly accused John Stockton, that she brought it to me, I had fairly conclusive proof that if Pomeroy Stockton had been murdered, she had had a hand in it. John Stockton's motive in trying to suppress the fact of a suicide, as he thought it, was perfectly clear. It was, as he said, to avoid disgrace. Such things are done frequently.

"From the moment you told him of the possibility of murder, he suspected Miss Devan. Why? Because, above all, she had the opportunity, because there was some animosity against John Stockton.

"This now proves to have been a broken-off love affair. John Stockton broke it off. He himself had loved Miss Devan. She had refused him. Later, when he broke off the love affair, she hated him.

"Her plan for revenge was almost diabolical. It was intended to give her full revenge and the estate at the same time. She hoped, she knew, that I would read that cipher. She planned that it would send John Stockton to the electric chair."

"Horrible," commented Hatch with a little shudder.

"It was a fear that this plan might go wrong that induced her to try to kill Stockton by shooting him. The cellar was dark, but she forgot that ninety-nine revolvers out of a hundred leave slight powder stains on the hand of the person who fires them. Stockton said that she did not shoot him, because of that inexplicable loyalty which some men show to a woman they love or have loved.

"Stockton made his secret visit to the house that night to get what was in that vault without her knowledge. He knew of its existence. His father had probably told him. The thing that appeared on page 7 of the family Bible was in all probability the copper hardening process he was perfecting. I should think it had been written there in invisible ink. John Stockton knew this was there. His father told him. If his father told it, Miss Devan probably overheard it. She knew it, too.

"Now the actual circumstances of the death. The girl must have had and used a key to the workroom. After John Stockton left the house that Monday night she entered that room. She found his father dead of heart disease. The autopsy proved this.

"Then the whole scheme was clear to her. She forged that cipher letter—as Pomeroy Stockton's secretary she probably knew the handwriting better than anyone else in the world—placed it in his pocket, and the rest of it you know."

"But the Bible in John Stockton's room?" asked Hatch.

"Was placed there by Miss Devan," replied The Thinking Machine. "It was a part of the general scheme to hopelessly implicate Stockton. She is a clever woman. She showed that when she produced the fountain pen, having carefully filled it with blue instead of black ink."

"What was in the locked vault?"

"That I can only conjecture. It is not impossible that the inventor had only part of the formula he so closely guarded written on the Bible leaf, and the other part of it in that vault, together with other valuable documents.

"I may add that the letters which John Stockton had were not forged. They were written without Miss Devan's knowledge. There was a vast difference in the handwriting of the cipher letter which she wrote and those others which the father wrote.

"Of course it is obvious that the missing will is now, or was, in Miss Devan's possession. How she got it, I don't know. With that out of the way and this cipher unravelled apparently proving the son's guilt, at least half, possibly all, of the estate would have gone to her."

Hatch lighted a cigarette thoughtfully and was silent for a moment.

"What will be the end of it all?" he asked. "Of course, I understand that John Stockton will recover."

"The result will be that the world will lose a great scientific achievement—the secret of hardening copper, which Pomeroy Stockton had rediscovered. I think it safe to say that Miss Devan has burned every scrap of this."

"But what will become of her?"

"She know nothing of this. I believe she will disappear before Stockton recovers. He wouldn't prosecute anyway. Remember he loved her once."

John Stockton was convalescent two weeks later, when a nurse in the City Hospital placed an envelope in his hands. He opened it and a little cloud of ashes filtered through his fingers onto the bed clothing. He sank back on his pillow, weeping.

POSTSCRIPT

If you have enjoyed this collection of the adventures of The Thinking Machine and would like to read more, drop a note to the publisher. We have enough material for another collection of excellent stories, none of which has ever appeared in book form. We will issue a second volume about Professor Augustus S. F. X. Van Dusen if there is sufficient demand.

A CATALOGUE OF SELECTED DOVER BOOKS
IN ALL FIELDS OF INTEREST

A CATALOGUE OF SELECTED DOVER BOOKS
IN ALL FIELDS OF INTEREST

AMERICA'S OLD MASTERS, James T. Flexner. Four men emerged unexpectedly from provincial 18th century America to leadership in European art: Benjamin West, J. S. Copley, C. R. Peale, Gilbert Stuart. Brilliant coverage of lives and contributions. Revised, 1967 edition. 69 plates. 365pp. of text.
21806-6 Paperbound $3.00

FIRST FLOWERS OF OUR WILDERNESS: AMERICAN PAINTING, THE COLONIAL PERIOD, James T. Flexner. Painters, and regional painting traditions from earliest Colonial times up to the emergence of Copley, West and Peale Sr., Foster, Gustavus Hesselius, Feke, John Smibert and many anonymous painters in the primitive manner. Engaging presentation, with 162 illustrations. xxii + 368pp.
22180-6 Paperbound $3.50

THE LIGHT OF DISTANT SKIES: AMERICAN PAINTING, 1760-1835, James T. Flexner. The great generation of early American painters goes to Europe to learn and to teach: West, Copley, Gilbert Stuart and others. Allston, Trumbull, Morse; also contemporary American painters—primitives, derivatives, academics—who remained in America. 102 illustrations. xiii + 306pp.
22179-2 Paperbound $3.50

A HISTORY OF THE RISE AND PROGRESS OF THE ARTS OF DESIGN IN THE UNITED STATES, William Dunlap. Much the richest mine of information on early American painters, sculptors, architects, engravers, miniaturists, etc. The only source of information for scores of artists, the major primary source for many others. Unabridged reprint of rare original 1834 edition, with new introduction by James T. Flexner, and 394 new illustrations. Edited by Rita Weiss. 6⅝ x 9⅝.
21695-0, 21696-9, 21697-7 Three volumes, Paperbound $15.00

EPOCHS OF CHINESE AND JAPANESE ART, Ernest F. Fenollosa. From primitive Chinese art to the 20th century, thorough history, explanation of every important art period and form, including Japanese woodcuts; main stress on China and Japan, but Tibet, Korea also included. Still unexcelled for its detailed, rich coverage of cultural background, aesthetic elements, diffusion studies, particularly of the historical period. 2nd, 1913 edition. 242 illustrations. lii + 439pp. of text.
20364-6, 20365-4 Two volumes, Paperbound $6.00

THE GENTLE ART OF MAKING ENEMIES, James A. M. Whistler. Greatest wit of his day deflates Oscar Wilde, Ruskin, Swinburne; strikes back at inane critics, exhibitions, art journalism; aesthetics of impressionist revolution in most striking form. Highly readable classic by great painter. Reproduction of edition designed by Whistler. Introduction by Alfred Werner. xxxvi + 334pp.
21875-9 Paperbound $3.00

VISUAL ILLUSIONS: THEIR CAUSES, CHARACTERISTICS, AND APPLICATIONS, Matthew Luckiesh. Thorough description and discussion of optical illusion, geometric and perspective, particularly; size and shape distortions, illusions of color, of motion; natural illusions; use of illusion in art and magic, industry, etc. Most useful today with op art, also for classical art. Scores of effects illustrated. Introduction by William H. Ittleson. 100 illustrations. xxi + 252pp.

21530-X Paperbound $2.00

A HANDBOOK OF ANATOMY FOR ART STUDENTS, Arthur Thomson. Thorough, virtually exhaustive coverage of skeletal structure, musculature, etc. Full text, supplemented by anatomical diagrams and drawings and by photographs of undraped figures. Unique in its comparison of male and female forms, pointing out differences of contour, texture, form. 211 figures, 40 drawings, 86 photographs. xx + 459pp. 5⅜ x 8⅜.

21163-0 Paperbound $3.50

150 MASTERPIECES OF DRAWING, Selected by Anthony Toney. Full page reproductions of drawings from the early 16th to the end of the 18th century, all beautifully reproduced: Rembrandt, Michelangelo, Dürer, Fragonard, Urs, Graf, Wouwerman, many others. First-rate browsing book, model book for artists. xviii + 150pp. 8⅜ x 11¼.

21032-4 Paperbound $2.50

THE LATER WORK OF AUBREY BEARDSLEY, Aubrey Beardsley. Exotic, erotic, ironic masterpieces in full maturity: Comedy Ballet, Venus and Tannhauser, Pierrot, Lysistrata, Rape of the Lock, Savoy material, Ali Baba, Volpone, etc. This material revolutionized the art world, and is still powerful, fresh, brilliant. With *The Early Work,* all Beardsley's finest work. 174 plates, 2 in color. xiv + 176pp. 8⅛ x 11.

21817-1 Paperbound $3.00

DRAWINGS OF REMBRANDT, Rembrandt van Rijn. Complete reproduction of fabulously rare edition by Lippmann and Hofstede de Groot, completely reedited, updated, improved by Prof. Seymour Slive, Fogg Museum. Portraits, Biblical sketches, landscapes, Oriental types, nudes, episodes from classical mythology—All Rembrandt's fertile genius. Also selection of drawings by his pupils and followers. "Stunning volumes," *Saturday Review.* 550 illustrations. lxxviii + 552pp. 9⅛ x 12¼.

21485-0, 21486-9 Two volumes, Paperbound $10.00

THE DISASTERS OF WAR, Francisco Goya. One of the masterpieces of Western civilization—83 etchings that record Goya's shattering, bitter reaction to the Napoleonic war that swept through Spain after the insurrection of 1808 and to war in general. Reprint of the first edition, with three additional plates from Boston's Museum of Fine Arts. All plates facsimile size. Introduction by Philip Hofer, Fogg Museum. v + 97pp. 9⅜ x 8¼.

21872-4 Paperbound $2.00

GRAPHIC WORKS OF ODILON REDON. Largest collection of Redon's graphic works ever assembled: 172 lithographs, 28 etchings and engravings, 9 drawings. These include some of his most famous works. All the plates from *Odilon Redon: oeuvre graphique complet,* plus additional plates. New introduction and caption translations by Alfred Werner. 209 illustrations. xxvii + 209pp. 9⅛ x 12¼.

21966-8 Paperbound $4.50

DESIGN BY ACCIDENT; A BOOK OF "ACCIDENTAL EFFECTS" FOR ARTISTS AND DESIGNERS, James F. O'Brien. Create your own unique, striking, imaginative effects by "controlled accident" interaction of materials: paints and lacquers, oil and water based paints, splatter, crackling materials, shatter, similar items. Everything you do will be different; first book on this limitless art, so useful to both fine artist and commercial artist. Full instructions. 192 plates showing "accidents," 8 in color. viii + 215pp. 8⅜ x 11¼. 21942-9 Paperbound $3.75

THE BOOK OF SIGNS, Rudolf Koch. Famed German type designer draws 493 beautiful symbols: religious, mystical, alchemical, imperial, property marks, runes, etc. Remarkable fusion of traditional and modern. Good for suggestions of timelessness, smartness, modernity. Text. vi + 104pp. 6⅛ x 9¼. 20162-7 Paperbound $1.25

HISTORY OF INDIAN AND INDONESIAN ART, Ananda K. Coomaraswamy. An unabridged republication of one of the finest books by a great scholar in Eastern art. Rich in descriptive material, history, social backgrounds; Sunga reliefs, Rajput paintings, Gupta temples, Burmese frescoes, textiles, jewelry, sculpture, etc. 400 photos. viii + 423pp. 6⅜ x 9¾. 21436-2 Paperbound $5.00

PRIMITIVE ART, Franz Boas. America's foremost anthropologist surveys textiles, ceramics, woodcarving, basketry, metalwork, etc.; patterns, technology, creation of symbols, style origins. All areas of world, but very full on Northwest Coast Indians. More than 350 illustrations of baskets, boxes, totem poles, weapons, etc. 378 pp. 20025-6 Paperbound $3.00

THE GENTLEMAN AND CABINET MAKER'S DIRECTOR, Thomas Chippendale. Full reprint (third edition, 1762) of most influential furniture book of all time, by master cabinetmaker. 200 plates, illustrating chairs, sofas, mirrors, tables, cabinets, plus 24 photographs of surviving pieces. Biographical introduction by N. Bienenstock. vi + 249pp. 9⅞ x 12¾. 21601-2 Paperbound $4.00

AMERICAN ANTIQUE FURNITURE, Edgar G. Miller, Jr. The basic coverage of all American furniture before 1840. Individual chapters cover type of furniture—clocks, tables, sideboards, etc.—chronologically, with inexhaustible wealth of data. More than 2100 photographs, all identified, commented on. Essential to all early American collectors. Introduction by H. E. Keyes. vi + 1106pp. 7⅞ x 10¾. 21599-7, 21600-4 Two volumes, Paperbound $11.00

PENNSYLVANIA DUTCH AMERICAN FOLK ART, Henry J. Kauffman. 279 photos, 28 drawings of tulipware, Fraktur script, painted tinware, toys, flowered furniture, quilts, samplers, hex signs, house interiors, etc. Full descriptive text. Excellent for tourist, rewarding for designer, collector. Map. 146pp. 7⅞ x 10¾. 21205-X Paperbound $2.50

EARLY NEW ENGLAND GRAVESTONE RUBBINGS, Edmund V. Gillon, Jr. 43 photographs, 226 carefully reproduced rubbings show heavily symbolic, sometimes macabre early gravestones, up to early 19th century. Remarkable early American primitive art, occasionally strikingly beautiful; always powerful. Text. xxvi + 207pp. 8⅜ x 11¼. 21380-3 Paperbound $3.50

ALPHABETS AND ORNAMENTS, Ernst Lehner. Well-known pictorial source for decorative alphabets, script examples, cartouches, frames, decorative title pages, calligraphic initials, borders, similar material. 14th to 19th century, mostly European. Useful in almost any graphic arts designing, varied styles. 750 illustrations. 256pp. 7 x 10. 21905-4 Paperbound $4.00

PAINTING: A CREATIVE APPROACH, Norman Colquhoun. For the beginner simple guide provides an instructive approach to painting: major stumbling blocks for beginner; overcoming them, technical points; paints and pigments; oil painting; watercolor and other media and color. New section on "plastic" paints. Glossary. Formerly *Paint Your Own Pictures*. 221pp. 22000-1 Paperbound $1.75

THE ENJOYMENT AND USE OF COLOR, Walter Sargent. Explanation of the relations between colors themselves and between colors in nature and art, including hundreds of little-known facts about color values, intensities, effects of high and low illumination, complementary colors. Many practical hints for painters, references to great masters. 7 color plates, 29 illustrations. x + 274pp. 20944-X Paperbound $2.75

THE NOTEBOOKS OF LEONARDO DA VINCI, compiled and edited by Jean Paul Richter. 1566 extracts from original manuscripts reveal the full range of Leonardo's versatile genius: all his writings on painting, sculpture, architecture, anatomy, astronomy, geography, topography, physiology, mining, music, etc., in both Italian and English, with 186 plates of manuscript pages and more than 500 additional drawings. Includes studies for the Last Supper, the lost Sforza monument, and other works. Total of xlvii + 866pp. $7\frac{7}{8}$ x $10\frac{3}{4}$. 22572-0, 22573-9 Two volumes, Paperbound $11.00

MONTGOMERY WARD CATALOGUE OF 1895. Tea gowns, yards of flannel and pillow-case lace, stereoscopes, books of gospel hymns, the New Improved Singer Sewing Machine, side saddles, milk skimmers, straight-edged razors, high-button shoes, spittoons, and on and on . . . listing some 25,000 items, practically all illustrated. Essential to the shoppers of the 1890's, it is our truest record of the spirit of the period. Unaltered reprint of Issue No. 57, Spring and Summer 1895. Introduction by Boris Emmet. Innumerable illustrations. xiii + 624pp. $8\frac{1}{2}$ x $11\frac{5}{8}$. 22377-9 Paperbound $6.95

THE CRYSTAL PALACE EXHIBITION ILLUSTRATED CATALOGUE (LONDON, 1851). One of the wonders of the modern world—the Crystal Palace Exhibition in which all the nations of the civilized world exhibited their achievements in the arts and sciences—presented in an equally important illustrated catalogue. More than 1700 items pictured with accompanying text—ceramics, textiles, cast-iron work, carpets, pianos, sleds, razors, wall-papers, billiard tables, beehives, silverware and hundreds of other artifacts—represent the focal point of Victorian culture in the Western World. Probably the largest collection of Victorian decorative art ever assembled—indispensable for antiquarians and designers. Unabridged republication of the Art-Journal Catalogue of the Great Exhibition of 1851, with all terminal essays. New introduction by John Gloag, F.S.A. xxxiv + 426pp. 9 x 12. 22503-8 Paperbound $5.00

A History of Costume, Carl Köhler. Definitive history, based on surviving pieces of clothing primarily, and paintings, statues, etc. secondarily. Highly readable text, supplemented by 594 illustrations of costumes of the ancient Mediterranean peoples, Greece and Rome, the Teutonic prehistoric period; costumes of the Middle Ages, Renaissance, Baroque, 18th and 19th centuries. Clear, measured patterns are provided for many clothing articles. Approach is practical throughout. Enlarged by Emma von Sichart. 464pp.   21030-8 Paperbound $3.50.

Oriental Rugs, Antique and Modern, Walter A. Hawley. A complete and authoritative treatise on the Oriental rug—where they are made, by whom and how, designs and symbols, characteristics in detail of the six major groups, how to distinguish them and how to buy them. Detailed technical data is provided on periods, weaves, warps, wefts, textures, sides, ends and knots, although no technical background is required for an understanding. 11 color plates, 80 halftones, 4 maps. vi + 320pp. 6⅛ x 9⅛.   22366-3 Paperbound $5.00

Ten Books on Architecture, Vitruvius. By any standards the most important book on architecture ever written. Early Roman discussion of aesthetics of building, construction methods, orders, sites, and every other aspect of architecture has inspired, instructed architecture for about 2,000 years. Stands behind Palladio, Michelangelo, Bramante, Wren, countless others. Definitive Morris H. Morgan translation. 68 illustrations. xii + 331pp.   20645-9 Paperbound $3.00

The Four Books of Architecture, Andrea Palladio. Translated into every major Western European language in the two centuries following its publication in 1570, this has been one of the most influential books in the history of architecture. Complete reprint of the 1738 Isaac Ware edition. New introduction by Adolf Placzek, Columbia Univ. 216 plates. xxii + 110pp. of text. 9½ x 12¾.   21308-0 Clothbound $12.50

Sticks and Stones: A Study of American Architecture and Civilization, Lewis Mumford.One of the great classics of American cultural history. American architecture from the medieval-inspired earliest forms to the early 20th century; evolution of structure and style, and reciprocal influences on environment. 21 photographic illustrations. 238pp.   20202-X Paperbound $2.00

The American Builder's Companion, Asher Benjamin. The most widely used early 19th century architectural style and source book, for colonial up into Greek Revival periods. Extensive development of geometry of carpentering, construction of sashes, frames, doors, stairs; plans and elevations of domestic and other buildings. Hundreds of thousands of houses were built according to this book, now invaluable to historians, architects, restorers, etc. 1827 edition. 59 plates. 114pp. 7⅞ x 10¾.   22236-5 Paperbound $3.50

Dutch Houses in the Hudson Valley Before 1776, Helen Wilkinson Reynolds. The standard survey of the Dutch colonial house and outbuildings, with constructional features, decoration, and local history associated with individual homesteads. Introduction by Franklin D. Roosevelt. Map. 150 illustrations. 469pp. 6⅝ x 9¼.   21469-9 Paperbound $5.00

THE ARCHITECTURE OF COUNTRY HOUSES, Andrew J. Downing. Together with Vaux's *Villas and Cottages* this is the basic book for Hudson River Gothic architecture of the middle Victorian period. Full, sound discussions of general aspects of housing, architecture, style, decoration, furnishing, together with scores of detailed house plans, illustrations of specific buildings, accompanied by full text. Perhaps the most influential single American architectural book. 1850 edition. Introduction by J. Stewart Johnson. 321 figures, 34 architectural designs. xvi + 560pp.
22003-6 Paperbound $4.00

LOST EXAMPLES OF COLONIAL ARCHITECTURE, John Mead Howells. Full-page photographs of buildings that have disappeared or been so altered as to be denatured, including many designed by major early American architects. 245 plates. xvii + 248pp. 7⅞ x 10¾. 21143-6 Paperbound $3.50

DOMESTIC ARCHITECTURE OF THE AMERICAN COLONIES AND OF THE EARLY REPUBLIC, Fiske Kimball. Foremost architect and restorer of Williamsburg and Monticello covers nearly 200 homes between 1620-1825. Architectural details, construction, style features, special fixtures, floor plans, etc. Generally considered finest work in its area. 219 illustrations of houses, doorways, windows, capital mantels. xx + 314pp. 7⅞ x 10¾. 21743-4 Paperbound $4.00

EARLY AMERICAN ROOMS: 1650-1858, edited by Russell Hawes Kettell. Tour of 12 rooms, each representative of a different era in American history and each furnished, decorated, designed and occupied in the style of the era. 72 plans and elevations, 8-page color section, etc., show fabrics, wall papers, arrangements, etc. Full descriptive text. xvii + 200pp. of text. 8⅜ x 11¼.
21633-0 Paperbound $5.00

THE FITZWILLIAM VIRGINAL BOOK, edited by J. Fuller Maitland and W. B. Squire. Full modern printing of famous early 17th-century ms. volume of 300 works by Morley, Byrd, Bull, Gibbons, etc. For piano or other modern keyboard instrument; easy to read format. xxxvi + 938pp. 8⅜ x 11.
21068-5, 21069-3 Two volumes, Paperbound $10.00

KEYBOARD MUSIC, Johann Sebastian Bach. Bach Gesellschaft edition. A rich selection of Bach's masterpieces for the harpsichord: the six English Suites, six French Suites, the six Partitas (Clavierübung part I), the Goldberg Variations (Clavierübung part IV), the fifteen Two-Part Inventions and the fifteen Three-Part Sinfonias. Clearly reproduced on large sheets with ample margins; eminently playable. vi + 312pp. 8⅛ x 11. 22360-4 Paperbound $5.00

THE MUSIC OF BACH: AN INTRODUCTION, Charles Sanford Terry. A fine, nontechnical introduction to Bach's music, both instrumental and vocal. Covers organ music, chamber music, passion music, other types. Analyzes themes, developments, innovations. x + 114pp. 21075-8 Paperbound $1.50

BEETHOVEN AND HIS NINE SYMPHONIES, Sir George Grove. Noted British musicologist provides best history, analysis, commentary on symphonies. Very thorough, rigorously accurate; necessary to both advanced student and amateur music lover. 436 musical passages. vii + 407 pp. 20334-4 Paperbound $2.75

JOHANN SEBASTIAN BACH, Philipp Spitta. One of the great classics of musicology, this definitive analysis of Bach's music (and life) has never been surpassed. Lucid, nontechnical analyses of hundreds of pieces (30 pages devoted to St. Matthew Passion, 26 to B Minor Mass). Also includes major analysis of 18th-century music. 450 musical examples. 40-page musical supplement. Total of xx + 1799pp.
(EUK) 22278-0, 22279-9 Two volumes, Clothbound $17.50

MOZART AND HIS PIANO CONCERTOS, Cuthbert Girdlestone. The only full-length study of an important area of Mozart's creativity. Provides detailed analyses of all 23 concertos, traces inspirational sources. 417 musical examples. Second edition. 509pp.
21271-8 Paperbound $3.50

THE PERFECT WAGNERITE: A COMMENTARY ON THE NIBLUNG'S RING, George Bernard Shaw. Brilliant and still relevant criticism in remarkable essays on Wagner's Ring cycle, Shaw's ideas on political and social ideology behind the plots, role of Leitmotifs, vocal requisites, etc. Prefaces. xxi + 136pp.
(USO) 21707-8 Paperbound $1.75

DON GIOVANNI, W. A. Mozart. Complete libretto, modern English translation; biographies of composer and librettist; accounts of early performances and critical reaction. Lavishly illustrated. All the material you need to understand and appreciate this great work. Dover Opera Guide and Libretto Series; translated and introduced by Ellen Bleiler. 92 illustrations. 209pp.
21134-7 Paperbound $2.00

BASIC ELECTRICITY, U. S. Bureau of Naval Personel. Originally a training course, best non-technical coverage of basic theory of electricity and its applications. Fundamental concepts, batteries, circuits, conductors and wiring techniques, AC and DC, inductance and capacitance, generators, motors, transformers, magnetic amplifiers, synchros, servomechanisms, etc. Also covers blue-prints, electrical diagrams, etc. Many questions, with answers. 349 illustrations. x + 448pp. 6½ x 9¼.
20973-3 Paperbound $3.50

REPRODUCTION OF SOUND, Edgar Villchur. Thorough coverage for laymen of high fidelity systems, reproducing systems in general, needles, amplifiers, preamps, loudspeakers, feedback, explaining physical background. "A rare talent for making technicalities vividly comprehensible," R. Darrell, *High Fidelity.* 69 figures. iv + 92pp.
21515-6 Paperbound $1.35

HEAR ME TALKIN' TO YA: THE STORY OF JAZZ AS TOLD BY THE MEN WHO MADE IT, Nat Shapiro and Nat Hentoff. Louis Armstrong, Fats Waller, Jo Jones, Clarence Williams, Billy Holiday, Duke Ellington, Jelly Roll Morton and dozens of other jazz greats tell how it was in Chicago's South Side, New Orleans, depression Harlem and the modern West Coast as jazz was born and grew. xvi + 429pp.
21726-4 Paperbound $3.00

FABLES OF AESOP, translated by Sir Roger L'Estrange. A reproduction of the very rare 1931 Paris edition; a selection of the most interesting fables, together with 50 imaginative drawings by Alexander Calder. v + 128pp. 6½x9¼.
21780-9 Paperbound $1.50

AGAINST THE GRAIN (A REBOURS), Joris K. Huysmans. Filled with weird images, evidences of a bizarre imagination, exotic experiments with hallucinatory drugs, rich tastes and smells and the diversions of its sybarite hero Duc Jean des Esseintes, this classic novel pushed 19th-century literary decadence to its limits. Full unabridged edition. Do not confuse this with abridged editions generally sold. Introduction by Havelock Ellis. xlix + 206pp.   22190-3 Paperbound $2.50

VARIORUM SHAKESPEARE: HAMLET. Edited by Horace H. Furness; a landmark of American scholarship. Exhaustive footnotes and appendices treat all doubtful words and phrases, as well as suggested critical emendations throughout the play's history. First volume contains editor's own text, collated with all Quartos and Folios. Second volume contains full first Quarto, translations of Shakespeare's sources (Belleforest, and Saxo Grammaticus), Der Bestrafte Brudermord, and many essays on critical and historical points of interest by major authorities of past and present. Includes details of staging and costuming over the years. By far the best edition available for serious students of Shakespeare. Total of xx + 905pp.
21004-9, 21005-7, 2 volumes, Paperbound $7.00

A LIFE OF WILLIAM SHAKESPEARE, Sir Sidney Lee. This is the standard life of Shakespeare, summarizing everything known about Shakespeare and his plays. Incredibly rich in material, broad in coverage, clear and judicious, it has served thousands as the best introduction to Shakespeare. 1931 edition. 9 plates. xxix + 792pp.   21967-4 Paperbound $3.75

MASTERS OF THE DRAMA, John Gassner. Most comprehensive history of the drama in print, covering every tradition from Greeks to modern Europe and America, including India, Far East, etc. Covers more than 800 dramatists, 2000 plays, with biographical material, plot summaries, theatre history, criticism, etc. "Best of its kind in English," New Republic. 77 illustrations. xxii + 890pp.
20100-7 Clothbound $10.00

THE EVOLUTION OF THE ENGLISH LANGUAGE, George McKnight. The growth of English, from the 14th century to the present. Unusual, non-technical account presents basic information in very interesting form: sound shifts, change in grammar and syntax, vocabulary growth, similar topics. Abundantly illustrated with quotations. Formerly Modern English in the Making. xii + 590pp.
21932-1 Paperbound $3.50

AN ETYMOLOGICAL DICTIONARY OF MODERN ENGLISH, Ernest Weekley. Fullest, richest work of its sort, by foremost British lexicographer. Detailed word histories, including many colloquial and archaic words; extensive quotations. Do not confuse this with the Concise Etymological Dictionary, which is much abridged. Total of xxvii + 830pp. 6½ x 9¼.
21873-2, 21874-0 Two volumes, Paperbound $7.90

FLATLAND: A ROMANCE OF MANY DIMENSIONS, E. A. Abbott. Classic of science-fiction explores ramifications of life in a two-dimensional world, and what happens when a three-dimensional being intrudes. Amusing reading, but also useful as introduction to thought about hyperspace. Introduction by Banesh Hoffmann. 16 illustrations. xx + 103pp.   20001-9 Paperbound $1.00

POEMS OF ANNE BRADSTREET, edited with an introduction by Robert Hutchinson. A new selection of poems by America's first poet and perhaps the first significant woman poet in the English language. 48 poems display her development in works of considerable variety—love poems, domestic poems, religious meditations, formal elegies, "quaternions," etc. Notes, bibliography. viii + 222pp.

22160-1 Paperbound $2.50

THREE GOTHIC NOVELS: THE CASTLE OF OTRANTO BY HORACE WALPOLE; VATHEK BY WILLIAM BECKFORD; THE VAMPYRE BY JOHN POLIDORI, WITH FRAGMENT OF A NOVEL BY LORD BYRON, edited by E. F. Bleiler. The first Gothic novel, by Walpole; the finest Oriental tale in English, by Beckford; powerful Romantic supernatural story in versions by Polidori and Byron. All extremely important in history of literature; all still exciting, packed with supernatural thrills, ghosts, haunted castles, magic, etc. xl + 291pp.

21232-7 Paperbound $2.50

THE BEST TALES OF HOFFMANN, E. T. A. Hoffmann. 10 of Hoffmann's most important stories, in modern re-editings of standard translations: Nutcracker and the King of Mice, Signor Formica, Automata, The Sandman, Rath Krespel, The Golden Flowerpot, Master Martin the Cooper, The Mines of Falun, The King's Betrothed, A New Year's Eve Adventure. 7 illustrations by Hoffmann. Edited by E. F. Bleiler. xxxix + 419pp. 21793-0 Paperbound $3.00

GHOST AND HORROR STORIES OF AMBROSE BIERCE, Ambrose Bierce. 23 strikingly modern stories of the horrors latent in the human mind: The Eyes of the Panther, The Damned Thing, An Occurrence at Owl Creek Bridge, An Inhabitant of Carcosa, etc., plus the dream-essay, Visions of the Night. Edited by E. F. Bleiler. xxii + 199pp. 20767-6 Paperbound $1.50

BEST GHOST STORIES OF J. S. LEFANU, J. Sheridan LeFanu. Finest stories by Victorian master often considered greatest supernatural writer of all. Carmilla, Green Tea, The Haunted Baronet, The Familiar, and 12 others. Most never before available in the U. S. A. Edited by E. F. Bleiler. 8 illustrations from Victorian publications. xvii + 467pp. 20415-4 Paperbound $3.00

MATHEMATICAL FOUNDATIONS OF INFORMATION THEORY, A. I. Khinchin. Comprehensive introduction to work of Shannon, McMillan, Feinstein and Khinchin, placing these investigations on a rigorous mathematical basis. Covers entropy concept in probability theory, uniqueness theorem, Shannon's inequality, ergodic sources, the E property, martingale concept, noise, Feinstein's fundamental lemma, Shanon's first and second theorems. Translated by R. A. Silverman and M. D. Friedman. iii + 120pp. 60434-9 Paperbound $2.00

SEVEN SCIENCE FICTION NOVELS, H. G. Wells. The standard collection of the great novels. Complete, unabridged. *First Men in the Moon, Island of Dr. Moreau, War of the Worlds, Food of the Gods, Invisible Man, Time Machine, In the Days of the Comet.* Not only science fiction fans, but every educated person owes it to himself to read these novels. 1015pp. (USO) 20264-X Clothbound $6.00

LAST AND FIRST MEN AND STAR MAKER, TWO SCIENCE FICTION NOVELS, Olaf Stapledon. Greatest future histories in science fiction. In the first, human intelligence is the "hero," through strange paths of evolution, interplanetary invasions, incredible technologies, near extinctions and reemergences. Star Maker describes the quest of a band of star rovers for intelligence itself, through time and space: weird inhuman civilizations, crustacean minds, symbiotic worlds, etc. Complete, unabridged. v + 438pp. (USO) 21962-3 Paperbound $2.50

THREE PROPHETIC NOVELS, H. G. WELLS. Stages of a consistently planned future for mankind. *When the Sleeper Wakes,* and *A Story of the Days to Come,* anticipate *Brave New World* and *1984,* in the 21st Century; *The Time Machine,* only complete version in print, shows farther future and the end of mankind. All show Wells's greatest gifts as storyteller and novelist. Edited by E. F. Bleiler. x + 335pp. (USO) 20605-X Paperbound $2.50

THE DEVIL'S DICTIONARY, Ambrose Bierce. America's own Oscar Wilde—Ambrose Bierce—offers his barbed iconoclastic wisdom in over 1,000 definitions hailed by H. L. Mencken as "some of the most gorgeous witticisms in the English language." 145pp. 20487-1 Paperbound $1.25

MAX AND MORITZ, Wilhelm Busch. Great children's classic, father of comic strip, of two bad boys, Max and Moritz. Also Ker and Plunk (Plisch und Plumm), Cat and Mouse, Deceitful Henry, Ice-Peter, The Boy and the Pipe, and five other pieces. Original German, with English translation. Edited by H. Arthur Klein; translations by various hands and H. Arthur Klein. vi + 216pp. 20181-3 Paperbound $2.00

PIGS IS PIGS AND OTHER FAVORITES, Ellis Parker Butler. The title story is one of the best humor short stories, as Mike Flannery obfuscates biology and English. Also included, That Pup of Murchison's, The Great American Pie Company, and Perkins of Portland. 14 illustrations. v + 109pp. 21532-6 Paperbound $1.25

THE PETERKIN PAPERS, Lucretia P. Hale. It takes genius to be as stupidly mad as the Peterkins, as they decide to become wise, celebrate the "Fourth," keep a cow, and otherwise strain the resources of the Lady from Philadelphia. Basic book of American humor. 153 illustrations. 219pp. 20794-3 Paperbound $2.00

PERRAULT'S FAIRY TALES, translated by A. E. Johnson and S. R. Littlewood, with 34 full-page illustrations by Gustave Doré. All the original Perrault stories—Cinderella, Sleeping Beauty, Bluebeard, Little Red Riding Hood, Puss in Boots, Tom Thumb, etc.—with their witty verse morals and the magnificent illustrations of Doré. One of the five or six great books of European fairy tales. viii + 117pp. 8⅛ x 11. 22311-6 Paperbound $2.00

OLD HUNGARIAN FAIRY TALES, Baroness Orczy. Favorites translated and adapted by author of the *Scarlet Pimpernel.* Eight fairy tales include "The Suitors of Princess Fire-Fly," "The Twin Hunchbacks," "Mr. Cuttlefish's Love Story," and "The Enchanted Cat." This little volume of magic and adventure will captivate children as it has for generations. 90 drawings by Montagu Barstow. 96pp. (USO) 22293-4 Paperbound $1.95

THE RED FAIRY BOOK, Andrew Lang. Lang's color fairy books have long been children's favorites. This volume includes Rapunzel, Jack and the Bean-stalk and 35 other stories, familiar and unfamiliar. 4 plates, 93 illustrations x + 367pp.
21673-X Paperbound $2.50

THE BLUE FAIRY BOOK, Andrew Lang. Lang's tales come from all countries and all times. Here are 37 tales from Grimm, the Arabian Nights, Greek Mythology, and other fascinating sources. 8 plates, 130 illustrations. xi + 390pp.
21437-0 Paperbound $2.50

HOUSEHOLD STORIES BY THE BROTHERS GRIMM. Classic English-language edition of the well-known tales — Rumpelstiltskin, Snow White, Hansel and Gretel, The Twelve Brothers, Faithful John, Rapunzel, Tom Thumb (52 stories in all). Translated into simple, straightforward English by Lucy Crane. Ornamented with headpieces, vignettes, elaborate decorative initials and a dozen full-page illustrations by Walter Crane. x + 269pp.
21080-4 Paperbound **$2.00**

THE MERRY ADVENTURES OF ROBIN HOOD, Howard Pyle. The finest modern versions of the traditional ballads and tales about the great English outlaw. Howard Pyle's complete prose version, with every word, every illustration of the first edition. Do not confuse this facsimile of the original (1883) with modern editions that change text or illustrations. 23 plates plus many page decorations. xxii + 296pp.
22043-5 Paperbound $2.50

THE STORY OF KING ARTHUR AND HIS KNIGHTS, Howard Pyle. The finest children's version of the life of King Arthur; brilliantly retold by Pyle, with 48 of his most imaginative illustrations. xviii + 313pp. 6⅛ x 9¼.
21445-1 Paperbound $2.50

THE WONDERFUL WIZARD OF OZ, L. Frank Baum. America's finest children's book in facsimile of first edition with all Denslow illustrations in full color. The edition a child should have. Introduction by Martin Gardner. 23 color plates, scores of drawings. iv + 267pp.
20691-2 Paperbound $2.50

THE MARVELOUS LAND OF OZ, L. Frank Baum. The second Oz book, every bit as imaginative as the Wizard. The hero is a boy named Tip, but the Scarecrow and the Tin Woodman are back, as is the Oz magic. 16 color plates, 120 drawings by John R. Neill. 287pp.
20692-0 Paperbound $2.50

THE MAGICAL MONARCH OF MO, L. Frank Baum. Remarkable adventures in a land even stranger than Oz. The best of Baum's books not in the Oz series. 15 color plates and dozens of drawings by Frank Verbeck. xviii + 237pp.
21892-9 Paperbound $2.25

THE BAD CHILD'S BOOK OF BEASTS, MORE BEASTS FOR WORSE CHILDREN, A MORAL ALPHABET, Hilaire Belloc. Three complete humor classics in one volume. Be kind to the frog, and do not call him names . . . and 28 other whimsical animals. Familiar favorites and some not so well known. Illustrated by Basil Blackwell. 156pp.
(USO) 20749-8 Paperbound $1.50

EAST O' THE SUN AND WEST O' THE MOON, George W. Dasent. Considered the best of all translations of these Norwegian folk tales, this collection has been enjoyed by generations of children (and folklorists too). Includes True and Untrue, Why the Sea is Salt, East O' the Sun and West O' the Moon, Why the Bear is Stumpy-Tailed, Boots and the Troll, The Cock and the Hen, Rich Peter the Pedlar, and 52 more. The only edition with all 59 tales. 77 illustrations by Erik Werenskiold and Theodor Kittelsen. xv + 418pp. 22521-6 Paperbound $3.50

GOOPS AND HOW TO BE THEM, Gelett Burgess. Classic of tongue-in-cheek humor, masquerading as etiquette book. 87 verses, twice as many cartoons, show mischievous Goops as they demonstrate to children virtues of table manners, neatness, courtesy, etc. Favorite for generations. viii + 88pp. 6½ x 9¼. 22233-0 Paperbound $1.25

ALICE'S ADVENTURES UNDER GROUND, Lewis Carroll. The first version, quite different from the final *Alice in Wonderland,* printed out by Carroll himself with his own illustrations. Complete facsimile of the "million dollar" manuscript Carroll gave to Alice Liddell in 1864. Introduction by Martin Gardner. viii + 96pp. Title and dedication pages in color. 21482-6 Paperbound $1.25

THE BROWNIES, THEIR BOOK, Palmer Cox. Small as mice, cunning as foxes, exuberant and full of mischief, the Brownies go to the zoo, toy shop, seashore, circus, etc., in 24 verse adventures and 266 illustrations. Long a favorite, since their first appearance in St. Nicholas Magazine. xi + 144pp. 6⅝ x 9¼. 21265-3 Paperbound $1.75

SONGS OF CHILDHOOD, Walter De La Mare. Published (under the pseudonym Walter Ramal) when De La Mare was only 29, this charming collection has long been a favorite children's book. A facsimile of the first edition in paper, the 47 poems capture the simplicity of the nursery rhyme and the ballad, including such lyrics as I Met Eve, Tartary, The Silver Penny. vii + 106pp. (USO) 21972-0 Paperbound $1.25

THE COMPLETE NONSENSE OF EDWARD LEAR, Edward Lear. The finest 19th-century humorist-cartoonist in full: all nonsense limericks, zany alphabets, Owl and Pussycat, songs, nonsense botany, and more than 500 illustrations by Lear himself. Edited by Holbrook Jackson. xxix + 287pp. (USO) 20167-8 Paperbound $2.00

BILLY WHISKERS: THE AUTOBIOGRAPHY OF A GOAT, Frances Trego Montgomery. A favorite of children since the early 20th century, here are the escapades of that rambunctious, irresistible and mischievous goat—Billy Whiskers. Much in the spirit of *Peck's Bad Boy,* this is a book that children never tire of reading or hearing. All the original familiar illustrations by W. H. Fry are included: 6 color plates, 18 black and white drawings. 159pp. 22345-0 Paperbound $2.00

MOTHER GOOSE MELODIES. Faithful republication of the fabulously rare Munroe and Francis "copyright 1833" Boston edition—the most important Mother Goose collection, usually referred to as the "original." Familiar rhymes plus many rare ones, with wonderful old woodcut illustrations. Edited by E. F. Bleiler. 128pp. 4½ x 6⅜. 22577-1 Paperbound $1.00

TWO LITTLE SAVAGES; BEING THE ADVENTURES OF TWO BOYS WHO LIVED AS INDIANS AND WHAT THEY LEARNED, Ernest Thompson Seton. Great classic of nature and boyhood provides a vast range of woodlore in most palatable form, a genuinely entertaining story. Two farm boys build a teepee in woods and live in it for a month, working out Indian solutions to living problems, star lore, birds and animals, plants, etc. 293 illustrations. vii + 286pp.

20985-7 Paperbound $2.50

PETER PIPER'S PRACTICAL PRINCIPLES OF PLAIN & PERFECT PRONUNCIATION. Alliterative jingles and tongue-twisters of surprising charm, that made their first appearance in America about 1830. Republished in full with the spirited woodcut illustrations from this earliest American edition. 32pp. 4½ x 6⅜.

22560-7 Paperbound $1.00

SCIENCE EXPERIMENTS AND AMUSEMENTS FOR CHILDREN, Charles Vivian. 73 easy experiments, requiring only materials found at home or easily available, such as candles, coins, steel wool, etc.; illustrate basic phenomena like vacuum, simple chemical reaction, etc. All safe. Modern, well-planned. Formerly *Science Games for Children.* 102 photos, numerous drawings. 96pp. 6⅛ x 9¼.

21856-2 Paperbound $1.25

AN INTRODUCTION TO CHESS MOVES AND TACTICS SIMPLY EXPLAINED, Leonard Barden. Informal intermediate introduction, quite strong in explaining reasons for moves. Covers basic material, tactics, important openings, traps, positional play in middle game, end game. Attempts to isolate patterns and recurrent configurations. Formerly *Chess.* 58 figures. 102pp.   (USO) 21210-6 Paperbound $1.25

LASKER'S MANUAL OF CHESS, Dr. Emanuel Lasker. Lasker was not only one of the five great World Champions, he was also one of the ablest expositors, theorists, and analysts. In many ways, his Manual, permeated with his philosophy of battle, filled with keen insights, is one of the greatest works ever written on chess. Filled with analyzed games by the great players. A single-volume library that will profit almost any chess player, beginner or master. 308 diagrams. xli x 349pp.

20640-8 Paperbound $2.75

THE MASTER BOOK OF MATHEMATICAL RECREATIONS, Fred Schuh. In opinion of many the finest work ever prepared on mathematical puzzles, stunts, recreations; exhaustively thorough explanations of mathematics involved, analysis of effects, citation of puzzles and games. Mathematics involved is elementary. Translated bv F. Göbel. 194 figures. xxiv + 430pp.   22134-2 Paperbound $3.50

MATHEMATICS, MAGIC AND MYSTERY, Martin Gardner. Puzzle editor for Scientific American explains mathematics behind various mystifying tricks: card tricks, stage "mind reading," coin and match tricks, counting out games, geometric dissections, etc. Probability sets, theory of numbers clearly explained. Also provides more than 400 tricks, guaranteed to work, that you can do. 135 illustrations. xii + 176pp.

20335-2 Paperbound $1.75

MATHEMATICAL PUZZLES FOR BEGINNERS AND ENTHUSIASTS, Geoffrey Mott-Smith. 189 puzzles from easy to difficult—involving arithmetic, logic, algebra, properties of digits, probability, etc.—for enjoyment and mental stimulus. Explanation of mathematical principles behind the puzzles. 135 illustrations. viii + 248pp.
20198-8 Paperbound $1.75

PAPER FOLDING FOR BEGINNERS, William D. Murray and Francis J. Rigney. Easiest book on the market, clearest instructions on making interesting, beautiful origami. Sail boats, cups, roosters, frogs that move legs, bonbon boxes, standing birds, etc. 40 projects; more than 275 diagrams and photographs. 94pp.
20713-7 Paperbound $1.00

TRICKS AND GAMES ON THE POOL TABLE, Fred Herrmann. 79 tricks and games—some solitaires, some for two or more players, some competitive games—to entertain you between formal games. Mystifying shots and throws, unusual caroms, tricks involving such props as cork, coins, a hat, etc. Formerly *Fun on the Pool Table*. 77 figures. 95pp.
21814-7 Paperbound $1.25

HAND SHADOWS TO BE THROWN UPON THE WALL: A SERIES OF NOVEL AND AMUSING FIGURES FORMED BY THE HAND, Henry Bursill. Delightful picturebook from great-grandfather's day shows how to make 18 different hand shadows: a bird that flies, duck that quacks, dog that wags his tail, camel, goose, deer, boy, turtle, etc. Only book of its sort. vi + 33pp. 6½ x 9¼. 21779-5 Paperbound $1.00

WHITTLING AND WOODCARVING, E. J. Tangerman. 18th printing of best book on market. "If you can cut a potato you can carve" toys and puzzles, chains, chessmen, caricatures, masks, frames, woodcut blocks, surface patterns, much more. Information on tools, woods, techniques. Also goes into serious wood sculpture from Middle Ages to present, East and West. 464 photos, figures. x + 293pp.
20965-2 Paperbound $2.00

HISTORY OF PHILOSOPHY, Julián Marias. Possibly the clearest, most easily followed, best planned, most useful one-volume history of philosophy on the market; neither skimpy nor overfull. Full details on system of every major philosopher and dozens of less important thinkers from pre-Socratics up to Existentialism and later. Strong on many European figures usually omitted. Has gone through dozens of editions in Europe. 1966 edition, translated by Stanley Appelbaum and Clarence Strowbridge. xviii + 505pp. 21739-6 Paperbound $3.50

YOGA: A SCIENTIFIC EVALUATION, Kovoor T. Behanan. Scientific but non-technical study of physiological results of yoga exercises; done under auspices of Yale U. Relations to Indian thought, to psychoanalysis, etc. 16 photos. xxiii + 270pp.
20505-3 Paperbound $2.50

Prices subject to change without notice.
Available at your book dealer or write for free catalogue to Dept. GI, Dover Publications, Inc., 180 Varick St., N. Y., N. Y. 10014. Dover publishes more than 150 books each year on science, elementary and advanced mathematics, biology, music, art, literary history, social sciences and other areas.